C000060495

Itinerant

Apocalypsis Immortuos, Volume 3

Marco de Hoogh

Published by Marco de Hoogh, 2021.

Disclaimer

This is a work of fiction. Names, characters, businesses, places, events and incidents are either the products of the author's imagination or used in a fictitious manner. Any resemblance to actual persons, living or dead, or actual events is purely coincidental

This book contains language, violence, gore, and adult situations.

Copyright

© 2021 By Marco de Hoogh
    Cover design by Rebecacovers (seriously, how awesome does this cover look?!)

    All rights reserved. No part of this book may be reproduced or used in any manner without the express written permission of the publisher except for the use of brief quotations in a book review.

    This ebook is licensed for your personal enjoyment only. This ebook may not be re-sold or given away to other people. If you would like to share this book with another person, please purchase an additional copy for each recipient. If you are reading this book and did not purchase it, or it was not purchased for your use only, then please return to your favorite ebook retailer and purchase your own copy. Thank you for respecting the hard work of this author.

Dedications

It's been a journey. Yeah, I know... But I'm a cheezy and cliché kind of guy!

The characters have taken me by the hand and led me to events that I had not planned for. They grew as people, on the pages and in my imagination. Hopefully in yours, also.

I do have to admit that it got out of hand. The book got far too large the time I had the story arcs done. There was nothing for it, but to hack, slash, and move content to book 4. Hopefully you will stick around with me! ☺

I want to thank several people for making this journey excellent. They all influenced me and made me a better writer – which is really all I want to be anyway.

Thank you to my dedicated alpha reader and wife, Carmen. You truly are amazing. Thank you to my excellent beta readers. Anita, Inge, Dorothy – you gave me the feeling that I was on the right path. A huge thank you to my amazing editor, C.B. Moore. You've once again stepped beyond expectations.

Finally, thank you to the reader. Thank you for giving my series a chance. Thank you for your support and comments – be they positive or critical. I love to hear from you so don't hesitate to drop me a note.

Marco

"I hope we once again have reminded people that man is not free unless government is limited. There's a clear cause and effect here that is as neat and predictable as a law of physics: as government expands, liberty contracts."

Ronald Reagan.

Chapter 1

Theodore

October 25, 10:25 A.M., The Oval Office

B *ANG.*
The sound reverberated through the room. Nobody dared to say a word. Theodore hung out near the back of the crowded room and likewise kept his mouth shut.

"Ow."

The pregnant pause ended abruptly as President David Clarkston rubbed his hand. He wasn't the first president to pound a fist into the Resolute Desk. He also wasn't the first one to discover how solid the oaken desk remained to this day.

"Somebody give me some good news," Clarkston told nobody in particular. He tapped the desk with his fingers. It was made up from the timber of an old exploration ship, which might have tweaked the president's thoughts.

"The Navy. What news from the Navy?"

He looked up at his remaining advisors and chiefs of staff. Fleet Admiral Alfredsson was missing. Nobody had heard from the top Navy man for several days now. Admiral Rodriguez was the most senior man left. The elderly man cleared his throat loudly.

"Mister President." The short man took a step forward. Theodore could tell with one glance that the man wasn't doing well.

He's sick, too...

"We've ordered all of our vessels to return to their ports of call immediately." Rodriguez looked around him uncertainly.

"What is it, man?" Dave wasn't known for his patience.

"Well, Mister President, I have a theory." Theodore spotted the deepening frown on Dave's face and didn't blame Rodriguez for rushing ahead. "One of our subs surfaced two days ago. None of the crew had any symptoms. However, some of the crew has started showing symptoms as of an hour ago. I contacted one of our other subs. This one is still submerged. Their crew has no symptoms either."

"Okay," Dave leaned forward slightly. "So, what you're telling me is that the crews of the submerged subs do not get sick, as long as they don't surface?"

Rodriguez nodded sharply.

"Order all of our subs to submerge. Report back on this ASAP." Dave was not a man to hesitate. Theodore nodded in agreement, although he wondered what the next move would be.

Can't leave the bubbleheads down there indefinitely.

"Yes, sir." Rodriguez turned on his heel and quickly cut through the crowd on his way out of the room. Another advisor had already taken a step forward to speak.

Theodore got another look at the man as Rodriguez approached on his way to the exit.

He's really not doing well.

"You all right?" Rodriguez asked him in passing.

"Uh? Yeah, I'm fine," Theodore answered. The admiral wasn't listening, though, and had already stepped out the door.

Guess I'm not looking too good, either.

Theodore let it go and turned his attention back to the president. General Andersen was still trying to convince him that China was behind all this.

"Sir, I urge you to let us strike now. I have it from reliable sources that they are preparing for something."

"Preparing for what, exactly, General?"

Andersen stammered. "Well, we haven't ascertained exactly what — but my advisors are convinced that it is something nefarious."

The president chuckled. "Nefarious. Nice word." He lifted his hand to forestall any further comment. "I will take it under consideration, General." He turned to the young aide at his side with a knowing look. "Winnie..."

With a quick nod, the young man stepped forward. His curly dark hair seemed to have a life of its own as he moved, much to the envy of the many bald or balding men in the room — Theodore included.

Huh. Vanity strikes again, he thought as he adjusted his cap.

"Gentlemen, it is time to adjourn. The president has meetings booked for the remainder of the day. Please get in touch with Betty or me if you require an audience tomorrow morning. Otherwise, we will see you here tomorrow at the same time for this general council meeting. Thank you."

He pushed his heavy rimmed glasses over the bridge of his nose and spread his arms, as if to herd the senior officials out. It looked rather comical to Theodore — this kid, herding men and women two to three times his age and many times his pay grade toward the exit.

Theodore was already in the hallway when he heard the president call out. "Davies! Hang back for a minute."

Surprised, Theodore stepped to the side. Several of the other council members stared at Theodore as they passed by him. The ones who didn't know him stared with suspicion, the ones who did gave him sad smiles and emphatic glares. Theodore stiffened under the attention. It was the latter type of looks that distressed him the most.

He re-entered the president's quarters after the last dignitary had exited. A stern-looking special agent stepped out, while an equally hard-nosed agent shut the door and stood off to the side.

The only other people left in the room were a couple more special agents and the aide. The young man quickly left through a side door, leaving Theodore alone with a group of grim-faced individuals.

Well, this ought to be fun.

"Davies."

Theodore stood uncomfortably as his old friend scrutinized him.

"You look like hell." The president's frown deepened. "You got this 'syndrome' thing, too?"

The question caught Theodore slightly off-guard. "Um." He patted his torso as if looking for some lost keys. "My stomach feels okay."

That was a lie. He'd puked his guts out that very morning.

"I mean, I don't feel great. But I don't think that I've got the syndrome, Mister President."

President Clarkston's first response was to glare at Theodore. "What the hell did I tell you, Davies? You call me Dave, unless there's a bunch of shitbirds around." Shitbirds used to mean ranking military officials to the two friends. Now, congressmen, senators, and pretty much any senior civil servant fell into that category as well.

"Sorry, Dave."

The president shrugged, already over it;

Theodore shrugged as well. Dave Clarkston was known for his overblown reactions. It kept those around him on their toes. He'd been doing that since well before he ever became the commander-in-chief.

Dave sighed and sorted through some notes on his desk while Theodore stood in place, waiting for his old friend. He figured that something was brewing in his thick head but knew better than to give voice to that thought.

After a moment, Dave had found what he was looking for and looked up at Theodore.

"Pull up a chair, Davies."

Theodore complied.

"I know you're still upset about my decision on Liberation." *Dave* hadn't even bothered to meet Theodore's eyes yet as he scrutinized the report in his hands. Theodore knew that it wasn't a question, so he didn't reply.

Dave noted the silence and looked up from his report. He locked eyes with Theodore. President Clarkston was an intimidating figure at the best of times. At the worst of times, he was a terrifying bully of a man. Theodore had known him for many years, though, so that steely gaze had lost its effect on him.

Besides, his give-a-fuck meter was running low.

Dave softened his gaze and nodded. "Heh." He chuckled to himself.

"Operation Liberation was the popular decision, Theodore. Sometimes a leader has to listen to his advisors." Dave seemed to be considering something. "Do you ever listen to your advisors, Theo?"

Theodore sat forward in his chair. It was a rare thing for Dave to call him by his first name. "What's going on, Dave?"

"It's this goddamn syndrome. I'm glad to hear that you're okay — but I'm not doing too well, Davies ... Time for me to start thinking about succession."

Theodore frowned at this admittance.

"You wouldn't be interested in the job, would you?" Dave said with a grin, breaking the tension.

"Hell, no." Theodore grinned back at his friend.

"All right. Who *do* I appoint?"

"Probably one of them." He waved his hand over his shoulder, toward the door that all the dignitaries had used. "You'd know better than me, Dave."

"Yeah. I suppose you're right." Dave dropped the subject and held up the report.

"This is the latest report on Liberation. Some good gains."

Theodore shrugged noncommittally.

"The report tells me that we're dropping zombies by the thousands. Maybe even hundreds of thousands." The president looked down at the sheet. "Says here that our forces have cleared our top fifteen infrastructure objectives. They're working through the second-level targets right now."

He looked up from the report. Theodore showed no emotion.

Dave grunted, then chuckled. "Ah, Davies. You're so goddamn stubborn." He put the report down.

Theodore had a comeback. Something along the lines of pots calling kettles black. But he wisely kept his mouth shut.

"At any rate, Liberation is a success." Theodore could see Dave reading him for a reaction. He continued, when none was forthcoming, "But we're going to change our strategy. I've instructed Andersen and some of our intelligence folks to come up with a new plan. I want you on the task force as well. Winston will fill you in."

Theodore nodded. He was about to ask a question, but Dave beat him to it.

"We're learning that some of the safe zones may not be as safe as we first thought..." Dave looked down and off to the side for a second. He sighed, deeply.

He was quiet for a long time. Theodore patiently waited.

"You've had a rough go." Theodore started as his old friend studied him a strange look. "Agatha was a wonderful woman. She left us too early."

The comment flustered Theodore. Agatha had been his everything.

"She was our little group's glue ..." Dave continued. He was right. Dave's ex-wife and Agatha had been close. Theodore started thinking of his beloved wife but was interrupted when Dave chuckled. "You disappeared with that dog of yours."

"Russel," Theodore supplied.

Dave grunted and nodded, his face pensive. He met Theodore's eyes once more.

The president's thoughts had already traveled elsewhere. Theodore could tell that the big man was conflicted.

"I thought that I'd be proud of what I've done as a president." He broke eye contact with Theodore and looked down, as if in shame. "Truth is, I've committed atrocities... I've protected criminals and prosecuted the innocent. I've destroyed careers." He stopped abruptly and shook his head.

"I'm sure you've done these things for the greater good." Theodore waited for Dave to look up, but he did not. It almost seemed that the president couldn't bear to meet his eyes anymore.

"Heh. Now you sound like one of the shitbirds. No, Theo. I look back at some of the things that I've done and can't see any good, much less any 'greater good.'"

He shook his head once more and finally looked up. It shocked Theodore to see such a pained expression on his face. "You would not have let them convince *you*, I think."

Theodore shrugged. He knew that politics was a dirty business. That was why he never so much as dipped a toe in that pond. Besides, the military had its share of politics, and that was more than enough for him.

"Did you know that I've had people assassinated? Assassinated — killed, Davies. Some of them even made the news." He scoffed. "The people were fine with it. That was a shocker to me. We just made up something about plots and terrorists, or sometimes we wouldn't even say anything! But the people, they just blindly agreed."

Theodore sat in silence. He didn't know how to respond, and he knew that his old friend had more to say.

"We fucking murdered people. Just because they knew too much or got in the way."

Dave lifted the palm of his hand and looked at it. Theodore followed his gaze. He could see an age spot on the back of the president's hand.

"I killed them." Theodore switched his eyes away from the hand to find Dave looking right at him again.

"Hey, Dave—"

"No, Theo. Don't try to lay some bullshit on me about doing the right things, and for the greater good, and all that other malarkey. We've done things, simply to extend our power and influence. We've done things for profits. Yeah, that's right, Theo. Money."

Theodore could feel the color drain from his face.

Dave just snorted and shrugged. "Do you know why I'm telling you this?"

"Because I don't have enough on my conscience?"

The president laughed then. A sharp barking laugh that rang through the Oval Office.

"No, my friend," he said when the laughter had died. "I've got two reasons. First of all, I don't give a fuck anymore." He hit the Resolute Desk with the palm of his hand this time.

"You see, these people that I answer to? Most of them are dead or dying anyway." He waved in one direction. "All those things that they asked me to do — that I did willingly enough! — didn't account for jack shit."

Theodore shook his head, unwilling to believe what he was hearing.

Dave just shrugged. "It's nothing new. The guy before me did it too. He even answered to mostly the same guys, even though he was a fucking Democrat. Same goes for the guy before that. ... It's been going on for a long time." He shook his head. "Anyway, I'm not here to throw the administration under the bus. I got offered the job because they knew I wasn't afraid to pull the trigger. ... And I did!"

Dave had started breathing rapidly. Theodore watched as he forced himself to calm down, his eyes on the papers on the desk.

"It's late in the game for us." Dave regained his composure. He picked up the report he had been staring at and held it out for Theodore to take, but didn't release it right away. "Too late, for most of us."

The moment passed, and the president let go of the papers. "Maybe we still have some cards to play," he said cryptically.

Dave nodded, once. Theodore got the hint and stood up. He turned away and stepped toward the door, pausing a few feet away.

"Mister President," Theodore said, then turned around to face his friend. "Dave," he added when he saw the anguish in his leader's face. "You said there were two reasons for telling me this stuff. What was your second reason?"

It took the president a long time to answer. He gradually lifted his face, looking more like the proud man he had been.

"Power corrupts, Davies. It's true. The world will go on, and so will you."

Theodore nodded. Despite all the shit he'd gone through, he somehow knew that he would survive.

The president stared at his friend with a fierce expression, bordering on rage. "Somebody has to make sure that this doesn't happen again."

Chapter 2

Charles

November 10, 2:30 P.M., Premiere Apartment Complex, Apartment 602

K*nock, knock, knock.*

Charles ignored the sound. He sat on his couch and luxuriated in the afternoon sunlight shining through his west-facing living room window.

Not now, Evelyn, he wanted to call. Or, *Just a minute, dear.* As he so often had in the past.

But that would do no good now. In fact, it would only spur his wife of thirty-eight years into a frenzied assault on the bedroom door.

Not that she would be able to get through. Evelyn had weighed all of a hundred and ten pounds. When she was soaking wet.

And now, decidedly less, Charles figured, although he had not looked upon his wife for over two weeks.

Oh, my poor Evelyn.

She'd been the one constant thing in Charles' life. Their house, the career, the children: Those things all came and went. But Evelyn had always been there, from the moment he'd first met her. That ended on a fateful night. When she succumbed to the syndrome. Charles had run to the telephone, anxious to call for help even though deep down he knew there would be no help.

There wasn't even an answer.

He did not expect to see her standing beside the very bed she had died in when he returned several minutes later. The look on her face and the way she moved freaked him out, but this was his wife, so he went to her. She'd attacked him, of course. He'd seen enough footage on TV and the internet to know what was truly going on. Still, he refused to believe it. This was his Evelyn. He had held her down and tried to talk to her.

It took him nearly a half hour, until exhaustion threatened to give her the upper hand, for Charles to finally give in to the facts. Evelyn had died. Then she rose from the dead and attacked him. Charles wrapped her in blankets to keep her immobile for a minute. He quickly pulled three entire drawers out of their chest and tossed them out of the door. Charles had even had the foresight to run to their en-suite bathroom and grab his glasses, teeth, and toothbrush. He drew the door shut just as Evelyn wormed most of her body free of the blankets.

He still thought that he could get some help, so he ran out of his apartment and knocked on all the doors on his floor, begging for assistance. Nobody opened. The only response he got was somebody yelling from inside their home for him to go away.

Actually, that's not true. There was another response. Charles shuddered as he remembered somebody pounding on the door without uttering a single word. He backed away from it as if it had caught on fire. He ran into his own apartment and locked his door.

Evelyn started pounding on the bedroom door once he got back into the apartment. She had sensed that he had returned. Charles had dragged the drawers away from the bedroom door and now lived out of them, like some tourist living out of luggage.

Forgot your pants though, didn't you ... Charles looked down at his knobby knees. He'd been walking around in boxer shorts since that night. So far, it had not been a problem. Nobody complained, anyway. At least he got his t-shirts. Today he sported the deep purple shirt of his favorite college team. The shirt was too large for him and hung down nearly past his boxers. It almost looked ridiculous, like he was wearing a purple dress.

Forgetting his pants was not the worst thing, however. Those same knobby knees were a testament to that, as they complained whenever he got up. He could almost picture the little orange bottle of arthritis medicine, sitting there on the counter of their bathroom.

They were right beside your teeth, in fact. Why didn't you grab them, you fool!

He berated himself every time his joints complained. Going back to get the medicine was out of the question, though. Charles did not want to see Evelyn in her current state. Instead, he bore the discomfort and spent his days on the couch.

Charles had spent the first couple of days glued to the television. There wasn't much on. Just some shaky footage of cities burning and acts of violence, on a repeating cycle. The local channel was off the air. Had been for about a week now.

Maybe we should have called. His mind slid back, to the days before Evelyn got sick and died.

He remembered watching the local channel produce some reports from the safe zone just outside of downtown. They had been sitting on the couch, watching the end of the world unfold on their television.

"That's us, dear," Evelyn confirmed on the second go-round of the news ticker as it crawled from right to left beneath the speaking head of Tammy Jensen. "Do you think we should call?"

Charles had grumbled a non-committal reply. He was comfortable here, in their luxurious apartment. They had everything they needed, right here, which was exactly what he had strived to accomplish for their retirement years. The kitchen was state of the art, with the latest in appliance technology. The fridge practically stocked itself, creating a shopping list for them that they submitted to the local grocery store. By the next day, the groceries would be hand-delivered right to their front door.

They really did have all the luxuries they needed, without ever leaving the apartment. Although, to be honest, they had bought the apartment mostly for the view. Charles liked the view of downtown — although he hardly ever ventured out there anymore. He had little use of going out, and the excuses to stay at home just got bigger as the years passed by.

His response was no different this time. "No. I think we ought to stay here and ride this thing out."

Evelyn had argued some, but not much. She had also come to find comfort in their hermitized existence.

They were proven right when, not more than two days later, the president appeared on TV to tell people about the safe zones failing. It wasn't much comfort to the couple, though, as Evelyn had started showing symptoms of illness. She had caught the syndrome.

Two nights later, she was dead.

Knock, knock, knock.

Dead, but not gone.

There had been no day when Charles had not thought about rushing into that bedroom and silencing the thing that used to be his wife. He'd lost count of how many days that made. A week. He guessed.

The simple truth was that he was scared. The incessant knocking on his bedroom door scared him. The fragments of news on TV and the internet scared him. The flashes of explosions and burning fires he spotted from his window scared him. Even the deadly silence scared him.

But what scared him the most were the unexplained noises. The sounds of violence he heard at all hours. He would jump at every bump in the night and hold his breath at every scream.

Then there was that tense moment when somebody had knocked on his front door the other day.

Tap, tap, tap, taptaptaptap. The urgency in the tapping made it quite clear that somebody was in distress. He knew that it was a living person when he heard a sob.

Knock, knock, knock. Evelyn reminded Charles of her presence.

Charles sat up straight on his couch, trying to block out his dead wife and waiting to hear the tapping again. When it did sound, he got up and cautiously moved over to the front door. He never got closer than six feet to the portal.

The tapping sounded one more time. Charles could almost sense the desperation of the person in the hallway. Still, he made no move to open the door. The hair on his neck rose as he sensed the person standing just on the other side, probably listening as intently as he was. The door rattled slightly as somebody tried the handle. Charles feared that a more violent attempt would follow.

Thankfully, he heard the person move on down the hall. Charles breathed a sigh of relief and returned to his couch.

He felt guilty about it later. Charles figured that he probably knew the person knocking. There were only six apartments on the floor, after all. A bit later, he even opened his door and had a quick peek down the hallway. Somewhat to Charles' relief, it was deserted. He closed and locked his door, reminding himself that his neighbors had refused to assist him as well. He went to sleep on the couch that night contemplating karma.

This morning was different. Evelyn still knocked — Charles had conditioned himself to ignore that — but then there was the sound of a door opening out in the hallway. He was lucky to catch it as he was in the proximity of his own entrance. He crept up to his door and placed his ear against it. Sure enough, he could clearly hear something moving out there now.

It's moving this way, he realized to his horror. Charles felt an urgent need to urinate and rushed to the toilet. He focused on peeing on the ceramic bowl and not directly into the water, for fear of making too much noise. He focused so hard on controlling the stream that he cut it off well before his bladder was empty.

By the time he got back, he thought he had heard yet another door open.

Maybe he or she is gone? Charles could only hope.

He eased himself against the wood and looked through the spyhole. Charles breathed a sigh of relief; there was nothing to see.

That sigh turned into a gasp as somebody stepped right up to his door. It was a naked man.

Surprise turned into recognition. *It's that dickhead from upstairs!*

Desmond or something.

Dermott, he corrected. Dermott's eyes were open wide, as was his mouth. His head hung at a slight angle, like he was listening.

Why did he come here? I've been quiet as a mouse... Charles continued to watch Dermott, but the zombie remained motionless.

Dermott lived in the penthouse apartment upstairs. The guy was arrogant and barely civil to the other residents of the building. He also had quite the reputation. There was always some different floozy up there with him. The worst part for Evelyn and Charles had been the noise.

They had complained several times to management about him. He played his awful music incredibly loud, and at times it sounded like he was playing basketball up there. Things got even worse after those complaints.

Dermott had somehow figured out that they had complained about him and adopted an elephant walk out of spite.

Maybe they have some memory. Why else did dickhead come here, to my door?

Evelyn didn't like that term, but Charles had started referring to him as 'dickhead' every time they heard him move around upstairs.

They used to complain about it to each other endlessly. It was one of the daily topics for the reclusive couple. He missed those talks.

That reminded him of Evelyn.

The knocking! It's stopped! Charles frowned in confusion. A disturbing noise had been replaced by a sinister silence.

Charles backed away from the front door to investigate. He was about ten feet from his bedroom when he gasped in surprise.

The handle was turning!

Charles lunged, catching the handle just as it had turned sufficiently to draw the door open. His momentum carried him into the door, slamming him into the person on the other side. Charles heard a small crash as he sent Evelyn tumbling down. He did not dare to look, and quickly pulled the door closed.

She's learned to open the door! There was no lock on the door from this side. There was no way he could stop her from turning that handle again.

Charles ran into his living room, looking for something to block the door. It was at that moment that Dermott started his assault on their home. Charles looked from right to left, hoping to spot any item that he could use as a barricade.

It seemed that Charles' eyes worked faster than his mind, as they came to rest on an object. It was a small lamp on their fireplace mantle. The lamp was a retirement gift. It was very old, and very heavy. The base was made of wrought iron. Evelyn always used to joke that it would be their weapon of self-defense if a burglar broke into their place.

"Mind the bloody lamp," She used to say anytime I came close to that mantle. *"That thing will crush your little toe!"*

Evelyn had always thought that was so funny. Always going on about that little toe. Charles was lost in memories for a moment, until the pounding at his door brought him back to the present.

He rushed to the mantle and grabbed the lamp up high, close to the bulb. He almost dropped the item as he lifted it.

Damn, it's heavy!

He got a better grip on it, using both hands. The base was a solid block of iron.

Good for more than little toes. He took a practice swing. The heft of it felt good, although it almost unbalanced him. It did fill him with confidence for what he was about to do.

Charles rushed to the bedroom, getting to the door just as the handle started to turn again. He froze for a moment.

She's using the door handle. Maybe she is feeling better? It tasted like false hope. Nevertheless, Charles couldn't resist calling out to his wife.

"Evelyn? Are you okay?"

Evelyn responded by twisting the handle more. Watching that handle twist filled Charles with dread. He heard the latch pull free past the lip and the door started swinging inwards.

Charles knew he had no more time. He pushed hard against the door and sent Evelyn flying. This time, he followed into the room. He paused as he saw his wife lying beside the bed. Her back was turned to him as she attempted to pick herself up.

"Oh, Evelyn! I've missed you so." His voice was heavy with emotion. He lowered his hand and the heavy lamp base bumped into his own leg. He hardly felt it as he watched his best friend struggle to her feet, her hands on the bed and her back still to him.

She's so skinny.

Then: *Please. Please don't turn around...*

But she did.

Before he knew it, Charles had raised his weapon once more.

He brought it down on her hand as she reached for him, registering the small crunching noise it made. Tears started to blind him as he stepped forward and pushed Evelyn. She lost her balance and bounced off the side of the bed, catching the dresser on her way down and landing in a heap.

Charles stepped up so that he stood over her.

That thing
CRACK
Will crush
CRACK
Your little
CRUNCH
Toe
SPLAT

Charles wiped the tears and blood from his face. The first thing he noticed was that the remainder of his bladder had emptied sometime during the assault. Then he looked down at his handiwork. Evelyn's face and skull were crushed, but he recognized the hair. He recognized the clothes and the ring on her finger.

He released his grip on the lamp and it fell to the carpeted floor with a hollow sound.

"Oh, Evelyn." He slowly sank to his knees before the remains of his wife.

"I'm so sorry," Charles whimpered as he collapsed onto the floor next to her. "I'm so sorry," he repeated, oblivious to the cracking sounds coming from the front door.

Chapter 3

Jack

November 12, 7:40 A.M., The Renaissance School for Gifted
Children (The Ren)

J ack was asleep. He was in that place halfway between a dream
and wakefulness, where the sounds in the conscious world are
transferred into the dream. In this case it was tinkling. The tinkling
sounds that he made as he ran through a field of bells. This was a
real problem for dream-Jack, as he was running away from something. In true dream fashion, he didn't really know what he was
running from, only that he had to be swift and silent. The field of
bells was unfortunate for the noise it made when what he really
needed was stealth. The last thing he remembered was coming to a
stop, the bells still ringing in his wake, and turning to face that
which was chasing him.

Jack opened his eyes. The pockmarked off-white tiles hanging
above reminded Jack of a scarred moonscape. He was considering
what material the ceiling tiles were made from when ringing entered his consciousness once more.

Ding—ding—ding—ding.

"Huh?"

Jack sat up in his cot, finally recognizing the alarm bell.

"Mom! It's the alarm." She moaned and started to stir. Jack
quickly got up and put on his trousers, t-shirt and socks. He threw
on his shoes at the door before rushing out to see what was going
on.

He was still groggy when he trooped down the stairs. He wasn't the only one, as several folks moved as slowly and looked as confused as he did. By the time he got to the bell, next to the cafeteria entrance, he had missed the announcement.

He moved next to Ethan and poked him in the side.

"What happened?" he whispered.

"Nancy took off sometime during the night. She left the front door wide open." Ethan had to raise his voice higher than a whisper, as several people were speaking up.

"We have to go find her," Claire pleaded to the group in general. Several people voiced their agreement.

"What about this, though?" Nat held up a letter. She saw the confused looks on the late arrivals' faces and quickly read the letter out loud. Especially the last line stuck with Jack:

I've gone home. Please don't follow me. I don't want to be rescued.

"She's obviously not herself," Claire stated as soon as the young woman was done.

"I think Claire is right." Rosa had taken a position beside the older woman. "We should at least go and make sure that Nancy is doing okay." Her voice could barely be heard above the din of conversations that had started.

"Right," Joe said. The slight nasal tinge to his voice drew attention to the bandaging on his nose, held in place by strips of tape over his cheeks. The bruising was just starting to show as black shading in the corners of his eyes. Shelley had done an excellent job setting that nose, from what Jack could see.

"Right," Joe repeated as the last mumblings died down.

It surprised Jack. *He's our leader now.*

"John, Mike." John looked at each man in turn. "Get a crew ready. Count me in too. Let's take the vehicles, and we'll see if we can find her. I don't think she will have made it to the wall, so let's limit our search to the immediate area."

"Emily," Joe had to look over some people to see the short woman. "You stay by the radio so we can stay in touch. Ethan..." He turned to his son. "You and Q are on lookout duty. I don't want any surprises while we're out looking for Nancy."

Joe indicated that he was done with a nod. People started moving.

"Hold on!" Romy took a few steps to the front of the group.

"Nancy specifically wrote that she didn't want anybody to go after her. And still you're going? Just like that?"

"Yes. Just like that." Jack was surprised when his mom spoke up. She had said little since her husband died.

"Why?" Romy's question was more out of curiosity than argument.

"Because life is precious." Sarah reached out to put her hand on her son's shoulder. "Because Nancy is part of our family, and she is important to us."

"Losing Ern was a big blow to Nancy." She looked around her. "Believe me, I know what that's like." Tears rolled down her cheeks, unchecked and unheeded.

Joe walked over and stood next to Sarah. He did not place a comforting hand on the woman or touch her in any way, instead letting his presence provide support.

"We owe it to her," Joe stated. "No, we owe it to *ourselves* to go look for her. If she is adamant about going to her house, then I will take her there personally. But not until after we have made sure that she is okay." He received a lot of nods at that.

"Now, we've wasted enough time talking about it. Let's get going."

1:45 P.M.

Jack was in the middle of a takedown move when the alarm bell rang. It was the slow ring, indicating it was nothing serious. Keith interrupted the aikido session, and they all made their way out of the gym. The small group included Q and Ethan, who had managed to trade off their duties as lookouts to attend.

"You boys are learning quickly," Keith said as they walked up the stairs. Jack felt himself swell with pride. One look at Ethan and Q confirmed that Keith's words had the same effect on the other boys.

Jack wondered what the alarm meant. He figured that the teams had returned from their search for Nancy.

Sure enough, he overheard Maria say that John and Mike had returned when he got to the top of the stairs. Jack immediately walked toward the front doors along with everybody else that had made it down. He noted a nervousness around him, as people speculated whether Nancy had been found, and if so, whether she was still alive. One look around impressed upon him how much Nancy meant to the people at the Ren. Practically everybody was there.

The doors were already open, and Jack followed the crowd out. They walked into an overcast afternoon. It felt like it could rain at any time. He brought his eyes down from the skies to catch the Humvees pulling into the school grounds. He nodded at Ethan, who had walked up to stand beside him, then swung his gaze back to the vehicles. The crowd buzzed as they pulled past them and into the parking lot. Finally, the Humvees parked and people started getting out.

Jack could tell that their search had proven in vain. He could tell by the way the search party walked. Their heads hung, and the frustration on their faces when they did look up was obvious.

"Hmm. Not a good sign." Ethan gave voice to the same thought.

Several minutes later, everybody had congregated in the cafeteria. John quickly reported their lack of findings.

"We drove to both gates, and a bunch of places in between," he summed up. "We destroyed at least another thirty zombies inside the community. We made enough noise to draw her out... if she wanted to be found."

"Maybe she was hiding in a house?" Claire suggested.

John nodded. His face was unreadable.

"What do we do now?" Claire continued.

"I know this may sound harsh," John said. "But we have other things that need doing."

This was followed by sounds of discontent. John waited for the crowd to quiet down somewhat before continuing. "There are still zombies inside our community. Lots of them, probably. I think we need to spend our energy, and the remainder of the day, clearing out the area immediately around our school."

Mike nodded in agreement. "I know that I'd feel a lot better if we did that. They seem to be drawn by sound, so maybe they won't bother us if we clear a large enough area."

Jack didn't totally agree with that hypothesis.

They're drawn to us, somehow. I think it's more than sound...

He did agree that it was a good plan, though, and he stuck up his hand when the time came to volunteer. To her credit, his mom did not put up a fuss. She merely placed her hand on his shoulder and smiled. "Just be safe."

John also seemed pleased with his willingness to help. "Thanks, Jack. Glad to have you on board for this." He clapped the young man on the back.

Jack wasn't the only one to volunteer, though. John had twelve people to work with. The first thing he did was divide them up into teams of four. Romy, Emily, Abi, and Michelle would stay near the front gate of the school, while the other two teams would start at the houses immediately across the street and work outward. Jack was paired up with John, Bill, and Keith. Mike would lead the other team, which included BB, Nat, and Ben.

Jack was disappointed not to be paired up with Nat. He had hardly spoken to her since their moment together.

It was so intense!

But then, that noise outside. The separation, that had felt so abrupt — as if she'd opened her eyes, seen him, and leapt away. The mumbled apology as she put her clothes back on.

And that had been the end of it.

He'd tried to talk to her once. That attempt had ended with him not being able to find the words and her bounding away like a cornered antelope.

A hand on his shoulder brought Jack back to the present. Keith stood beside him. His eyes showed concern.

"I—I'm okay." Jack stammered.

Keith regarded him for a moment, then nodded. "Okay, Kemosabe. Let's go get geared up."

They were told to wait in the hallway, while John and Mike took stock of the weapons in the armory. Jack was close enough to the door to hear the mumblings of a conversation. Mike walked out after a couple of minutes, followed by John. Both men had their arms full.

"Guys." Mike called, indicating that he wanted everybody to come closer. Curious, Jack and Keith approached.

"Mike and I were discussing our strategy. We're going to add one person to each breach team and leave two people at the gate. The reason is that we are going to try to avoid using firearms for this mission."

That was a surprise. Jack and Keith exchanged a look. The Asian man seemed pleased with the decision. Mike and John dumped the items they were carrying on the floor.

It was a collection of protective equipment and melee weapons.

"Choose your weapon, as they say," Mike told them with a grin. "There are entrenchment tools, hatchets, and enough Ka-Bar knives for everybody."

"Along with that, we've got some tactical knee and elbow pads and some other armor. We can thank Tammy and her team for that stuff," John added, indicating the pile he had in front of him.

"We also have a couple of axes in with the camping equipment," Bill said. John immediately nodded and asked him to gather them.

A minute later, all combatants had grabbed their weapons. Keith had run upstairs to put on his carpentry belt, including his hammers.

Donning the armor was a bit of a challenge. People ended up helping each other strap on the armor, knee, and elbow pads. Keith had stuck with Jack and was helping him with the tactical knee pads.

"I look like Rambo," Jack said jokingly.

Keith's eyes lit up at the comment. "No, man. Commando! 'I eat green berets for breakfast.'" He mimicked the Austrian accent. Poorly. Jack laughed.

A minute later, John came striding out of the armory. He'd also gotten geared up.

"Whoa," Keith said under his breath. Jack had to agree. If anybody looked like Commando, it was John.

"Urban combat is a bitch," John said, slapping an elbow pad with his prosthetic and making a loud clack for effect. "Each one of you will also have a handgun in case things get hairy. This won't make it any less stressful. But as long as we got each other's backs, then we should be fine."

Keith raised his hand and John invited him to speak. "You're one of our most effective fighters, Keith. Any suggestions?"

"We're going to need to bust skulls. Literally. We should be using blunt force instruments. Those knives might do the job, but you'd have to get really close..."

He eyed the two axes Bill had brought back from the gym. "Those might be good. Especially the one with the spike on the other end." He pointed at the axe. "Just make sure that you have enough room to swing the weapon."

"Thanks, Keith. Good points." John nodded and addressed the rest of the group. "We'll give this a shot, and if it works, then we'll try to get some better melee weapons for the next mission. Anyway, I've figured out our tactics. Gather around."

The group gathered in tight as John spoke about breaching, clearing, and close-quarter battle, or CQB. He obviously spoke from experience. Jack could see the memories play across the man's face as he spoke. John went on to assign roles so that each in the five-person team knew what his or her job was.

Jack was slightly dismayed when he got assigned the 'doorman' role. That just meant that he would stay at the front door and prevent any surprises.

The real surprise happened when they started the mission.

Everybody approached the fence with nervous energy, along with a dose of trepidation. Emily and Abi stayed behind at the gate and Jack followed his team to the first house. To his left, the second team arrived at their first house.

Less than five minutes later, they all gathered outside, doing some serious head-scratching. It seemed that these houses had already been cleared. There was some good loot, including foodstuffs in the houses. John ran over and asked Emily to relay that info to the folks at the Ren.

The fact that these houses were cleared made sense, though. "It must have been Matheson and his men," John concluded. They had discovered that the bodies of the former occupants had been dragged into the back yards. The entire row of houses was devoid of the living or dead.

The disconcerting thing was when they discovered signs of obvious violence. It looked like there had been a gunfight in one house. "Do you think Matheson's men killed civvies?" Jack overheard Bill asking John.

"Honestly ... I'm not sure." The look that crossed John's face told Jack that he suspected the worst. Some of the corpses in those back yards had not been zombies.

Jack had to put those thoughts out of his head as the next set of houses had not been cleared. There was something utterly horrifying about walking up to a house and seeing a face in the window staring back at you.

5:00 P.M.

Three hours later, a tired crew returned to the Ren. They had cleared a total of forty houses to add to the twenty that had already been secured. Only a dozen of those contained zombies, and most were decrepit seniors or weak children. Jack never got into the action, but he wasn't terribly upset about that. It was bad enough to have to drag the corpses into the back yards.

One incident in particular had given him all the excitement he needed. He had dragged a corpse into a back yard and laid it against the far fence, then returned to the house to collect the second corpse. He was dragging it when he glanced up and saw the first body move. Jack dropped the corpse and drew his gun, only to find a rodent had crawled onto the first body. That rodent had just about given Jack a heart attack. He literally felt the pain in his chest.

Thankfully, nobody had witnessed what happened.

The only injuries suffered were a couple of bruises as people bumped into counters or door frames. Other than that, Mike got a splinter. It was the only blood lost in the mission.

Mike's team met John's, and ten fighters walked back toward the Ren. "We did some good work today, guys." John squinted at his troops in the late afternoon sun. Jack felt enormous pride in that comment and glance — and looking around him, he wasn't the only one.

After all, they *had* done some good work. The area was a bit safer, and they did that without making much noise.

The best thing that happened to him was when he felt a hand in his own. He looked beside him to see Nat there. She smiled up at Jack and everything felt okay.

They were greeted by a warm meal when they got back into the school. The twenty-pound bag of potatoes and box of frozen pork chops found in one of the houses across the street earlier had been put to good use. As a matter of fact, the haul of edible food from the empty houses was huge. Joe had promptly petitioned several of the younger members to act as pack mules, and they had been running back and forth for hours.

Jack could thank his mom and Claire for the feast. The two women had been the driving force in providing a quality meal to everybody. Jack figured that this was their way of comforting the group as they dealt with losing yet another member.

Jack observed several people eating their pork chops with gusto at supper. He wasn't crazy about the meal, though. He picked at it and complimented his mom as a good son should, but his appetite was lacking after having seen and smelled rotten meat all day.

Besides, he was anxious to meet up with Nat right after the meal. He had hoped that she would eat with him but was dismayed when Tammy approached Nat as she was dishing out her meal. The two women talked for a few seconds and ended up sitting a couple of tables over.

All through supper he stole glances at them. They got into quite the conversation. Jack wanted to move to their table to find out what all the excitement was about, but he didn't want to abandon his mother. He decided to wait until the end of the meal, figuring that he could steal her away then.

However, he was to be disappointed. Jack felt rather crestfallen as the two women stood and moved to the exit of the cafeteria together.

What's that all about? he wondered as he watched them leave, continuing their animated conversation.

Chapter 4

Nancy

November 13, 4:30 P.M.

*C*louds *are coming in.*

They rolled in over the foothills far to the north, like an inexorable, unstoppable titan. Nancy could see the impossibly high, towering white clouds, their bottoms various hues of gray and blue.

They promised violence.

Nancy looked at those distant hills, their surfaces swallowed by darkness as the oncoming storm blocked out the sun. It was a sharp contrast to Nancy's current location, which was still basking in late afternoon sunlight. The skies were clear and blue directly overhead. For now.

She had taken a break in an attached townhouse, only a block away and still within sight of a wall. It was that very wall that protected her friends along with the home she had known for a couple of weeks. She hadn't gotten far, and the going had been slow.

Nancy had to admit that traveling by foot was a tiring endeavor.

Especially getting over that wall.

She remembered staring at the wall from the other side, and almost turning around on the spot. As usual, her stubbornness and the imagined words of Ern had won out. She had found a ladder in the shed of a nearby house. This helped her get to the top of the wall. Nancy perched on that wall and pulled the ladder up after her. She was just about to place it on the ground on the other side when a gust of wind nearly upended her. She dropped the ladder, making a very unladylike sound at the same time.

Getting off that wall was not quite as graceful. She had no choice. She jumped. She hit the ground hard and one of her feet twisted on the very ladder that was supposed to get her safely down. Then she rolled on the ground like an injured soccer player.

Nancy had definitely hurt her ankle but had no time to feel sorry for herself, having to scurry away before any zombie saw her. The first house that had looked promising became her destination.

She was still in that same house now.

It wasn't much to look at, but at least it was empty and secure. That first night she'd slept in an abandoned bed, the sheets and blanket still askew as evidence of the person who had rolled out of that very bed not too long ago.

It felt wrong. Almost invasive. So she added an apology to the previous homeowner to her prayer that evening. She had hoped it would put her mind at ease. Help her sleep.

It didn't help at all.

Her ankle was quite swollen when she woke up the next morning. She was also barely able to put any weight on it when she got out of bed. Nancy was forced to spend a second day in the same abode. An unwelcome intruder.

Ern's words of guidance might have been: *Get used to it, Nancy. You'll be breaking and entering for many days to come before you get home.*

She spent the day exploring the previous homeowner's extensive collection of trash romance novels. Nancy had been an avid reader before the syndrome hit and realized that this was her first opportunity to read again.

She finished four of them over the course of the day. The rest of her activities consisted of bathroom and kitchen runs. It amazed Nancy how people had stocked up when the syndrome had struck, and this place was no different. All the kitchen cupboards were jam-packed full of stuff. She had even found a box of her favorite cookies. Sadly, she found no tea to go with it.

Spending a day reading and munching on cookies. Could be worse.

But then, just before nightfall, it did get worse.

Without electricity, things got dark quickly. It got so dark that it became impossible to read, so Nancy figured that she might as well get some more rest. She was almost asleep when she heard a noise. It had come from outside. Down the street.

She hopped out of bed, ignoring the pain that lanced up her calf, and made her way to the children's bedroom. Nancy knew from her earlier explorations that there was a good view of the street from there.

She made it to the window just in time to hear another noise. It was a yell followed by a commotion, which sounded like a garbage can being upended. She looked up one side of the street and down the other side.

Where did it come from? The darkness outside made it hard to see anything.

She got her answer a moment later when she heard a man scream.

Nancy put her face against the window, trying to see as far up the street as possible. Her eyes grew wide when she spotted movement.

A man was struggling with a zombie about half a block away. He tripped and fell even as a second zombie lurched into view. It got close to the struggling forms and lunged into the fray. To Nancy's dismay, a third zombie was close behind.

He's doomed.

Miraculously, the man had rolled out from under his attackers. He got to his feet and unsteadily advanced down the road.

He's coming this way!

The man was obviously hurt as he stumbled and nearly fell. He managed to stumble about twenty yards from where he'd first got taken down before a zombie got close enough to lunge at him once more. He almost got away as he twisted at the right moment, but the zombie managed to snag the man's foot, sending him tumbling to the ground.

Nancy knew there was nothing she could do. She knew it was too late as the second and third zombie jumped on the man a few seconds later. Nancy stayed hidden and watched in horror as the man stopped screaming while arms flailed down upon him. All she could see of the victim was his legs. He kicked out his feet, hitting the pavement with his heels.

Pat—pat—pat.

She could just make out the sound of it.

Pat—pat—pat.

It continued as the zombies devastated the man. A spurt of blood geysered up between the bobbing bodies.

Pat—pat—pat.

Yet the legs just kept pumping. Much longer than they should have. Nancy wanted nothing more than to turn away, or to run out there and destroy those monstrosities. But she didn't. Nancy stayed frozen in place, watching.

Then the legs stopped.

Abruptly. Thankfully.

Nancy dropped her gaze and backed away from the window. She sat on a bed, briefly noticing the children's cartoon characters on the bedspread.

Another lost soul.

She had done her best to ignore them, but the silent ghosts were all around her. They pressed in on her from every angle. Mothers and fathers — and yes, children. Many children. They wailed in dismay.

They wanted answers, they demanded apologies, and begged desperately for assurances.

Nancy had none to give. The normal life of only a few weeks ago was gone. Even the semblance of community she had felt just a few days before was shattered. She had abandoned the last living people in the world that she cared about.

The ghosts pressed in closer. Now she could imagine the strained and sad face of Claire, the anguished Maria, her expression far too ancient for her age. The hurt puppy-dog eyes of Shelley...

She couldn't bear to look at them and dropped her eyes to the duvet. The smiling face of some character beamed up at her until her hand contracted into a fist, pulling the duvet cover out of shape and distorting that smile.

Nancy felt sad but had no tears left. Guilt battled with despair, as she considered what she and the world had come to. Despair triumphed.

"We're doomed," she whispered.

November 14, 7:30 A.M.

Nancy awoke. She opened her eyes and looked around the room without moving. It was fully light outside, so she knew she had slept well. Everything came back to her, and she remembered where she was and what she was doing. She stayed in bed with false hopes of falling back asleep, wanting to deny the truth of the world by fading out of consciousness.

She did finally get up, spurred on by the thought of what Ern would say and the need to urinate. Nancy had slept in her clothes, something which she thought was a smart thing in this world.

You never know when you've got to run.

Her ankle was slightly better than it had been the day before. Still, Nancy had to be careful as she limped to the bathroom. She washed up, then caught sight of her smudged clothing in the mirror.

Should I look for some clean clothes that fit?

She shook her head, deciding against it. Stealing clothes from the dead just seemed wrong. After all, she still had some clean clothes in her bag.

Her belly rumbled. *I will have some of their food, though. Surely, they wouldn't mind that.*

She gingerly walked back into the bedroom and had a look out of the window. A corpse was lying in the street. It was the man from last night.

No sign of zombies, thankfully.

Nancy decided that it was time for breakfast. She left the bedroom and started down the stairs. Her ankle did feel better. That cheered her up some. She got to the bottom of the stairs and was about to turn toward the kitchen when she thought she heard something.

What was that? She froze and listened intently. Silence greeted her.

Did I imagine it?

Just to be sure, Nancy turned away from the kitchen and toward the front hallway.

I'll have a look through the peephole. She decided as she approached the portal.

Nancy stood a step away from the door and stopped there. For some reason, she dreaded looking through that little peephole. She was convinced she would see a zombie standing there.

Don't be silly, Nancy. There's probably nothing out there. She still hesitated for another moment. Finally, she steeled herself. She took the last step and peered through the hole.

The eyeless face of a zombie stood mere inches from the other side of the door.

It took all of Nancy's self-control not to cry out. Instead she stood transfixed, watching the zombie's face. Both eyes seemed to have fallen out or rotted away, and the sockets contained nothing more than a black-green mass at the back. It still appeared to be watching her, though. It tilted its head slightly, like a dog.

Nancy wanted nothing more than to scream in terror, but she knew to do so would mean the end for her. Besides, her throat was constricted by fear. She watched as the zombie tilted its head the other way. Unconsciously, she had been holding her breath.

Oh my god, it knows I'm here!

She knew that she could not make a sound now. She took a step back, then another. She finally let out her breath as she turned and stepped into the living room.

What do I do? I need to get out of here.

She stared at the back door, but something kept Nancy rooted to the spot. Then she remembered that her pack lay in the bedroom upstairs.

Nancy knew that she needed it, so she carefully ascended the treads, placing her feet with infinite care.

How much noise did I make coming down the stairs?

She got to the bedroom and grabbed her pack. Nancy returned to the stairs but stopped at the top. Morbid curiosity took over. She silently crept back to the children's room, from where she had watched last night's massacre. Stepping to the window carefully, she caught sight of the broken corpse lying in the street. There was no sign of any zombies. She stepped closer to the glass, to look down upon the front lawn.

Oh my God... She could see at least half a dozen zombies at the waist-high fence, and several in the yard.

That's more than there were last night! How did they find me? Fear crawled up her spine like icy tendrils. Nancy squeezed her eyes shut and forced it down.

She quietly crept to the stairs and secured her backpack. She got downstairs without so much as a creak and had a good look at the backyard. It was a small, grassy yard, surrounded by high wooden fencing. To her relief, it was clear of zombies and there was a gate. There was a way out.

But what's behind that fence? She could see the second story of another set of attached townhouses and imagined an alleyway ran between the back yards.

What are you lollygagging for? You can't go out the front way. That gate there — that's your only option, Ern's disembodied voice reprimanded her.

With a small nod, she strode to the back door. She flipped the locks as quietly as possible, then opened the back door with a patience she did not feel. The outside air was cold and stank like rot. It felt like a physical slap, and instantly brought back her fear.

This time Nancy was ready for it, though. She grimaced in determination and opened the door further. Enough to step out onto the small concrete deck. She stepped across the grass and to the gate, then hesitated once more. The wooden fencing did not allow her to see beyond. She was about to put her face to the edge of the gate so that she could have a look through the small gap between it and the fence when she heard a noise toward the front of the house.

Go. Now!

She grabbed the handle and pulled down. The mechanism squeaked and the noises at the front of the house intensified. She pushed the gate outward violently and shot through the portal into a single-lane alleyway. The hair on her neck rose as she stepped out, expecting undead shapes to lurch toward her from everywhere, but the alley was clear.

Nancy let her breath out in an explosive gasp. She winced as a stab of pain shot up her ankle.

Okay. No more lunging. She agreed with the complaining joint.

Nancy closed the gate behind her, eliciting another squeak from the handle. She could hear multiple zombies moving around the front of the house now.

They're tracking me. She looked down at the handle on the gate. *They can open that.*

Nancy backed up from the handle as if it were on fire. She looked up and down the alley once more, convinced that hordes of zombies were heading her way. Then she looked across the alley. Another fence and another gate.

Nancy quickly shuffled to the other side. She hesitated at the gate, her hand on its handle. Just then, she heard the tinkling of glass breaking behind her. It was accompanied by yet more noises of movement.

I'd hear them if they were here. She pulled down on the handle before she could change her mind. As luck would have it, this gate was unlocked. Nancy stepped through and into the back yard. The gate had a lock, which Nancy quickly engaged.

That will hold them. She looked at the sturdy fence with a satisfied grin. Then she remembered hearing young Nat say that some zombies could climb.

Nancy wasn't sure about that, but hastened away nonetheless.

The undead slowly lost their sense of Nancy, like a flickering flame of a candle as it runs out of consumable wax. The sounds she had made in her exodus briefly stimulated the chasing zombies. However, obstacles stood in the way in the form of buildings and fences. The zombies railed against these obstacles. It was not rage, though. The undead knew no rage. All they knew was their objective. That tiny glow just at the edge of their sense. It must be extinguished.

A single person emitted a tiny glow, barely perceptible by the undead unless it was accompanied by sound. A group of people, however...

The zombies stopped their assault at a silent signal. As one, they turned away and marched toward the greater consciousness. For that mass consciousness had become cognizant of a brighter glow altogether...

Chapter 5

Jack

November 14, 4:30 P.M., The Ren.

Jack stood on the roof of the Ren. He had come up here to be alone.

The roof ledge was missing chunks of concrete and plaster here and there — a reminder of an earlier assault. He caught sight of the destroyed solar panel, useless now but luckily bypassed, so the school still had power.

Yeah, I guess that's changed. Jack reflected. The power had finally gone out for their part of town. The residents of the Ren hardly noticed it, however, as they were hooked up to their own source.

Of course, that source was only delivering limited power today. Jack looked out over the horizon. The sky was overcast and gray. Off to the west, he saw the sign of rain approaching, as dark-gray tufts of cloud reached down, almost looking like they were trying to caress the ground. Jack imagined a sheet of rain, moving slowly toward him.

Like a giant broom, sweeping the world clean. Yeah, you wish. Jack sighed and stood on the edge of the roof. A few weeks ago, standing like that would have unsettled him. Now he found it comforting.

"Hey, Dad…" he began. "I met a girl." Jack shifted uncomfortably on his feet, still not used to the idea.

"I love her, Dad. … Is it too early to say that?" He sighed. "Well, maybe we don't have time to take it slow." Jack stopped speaking for a second, realizing the truth in the words he'd just blurted out.

"Anyway, Dad, it's Nat." A smile slowly crept onto his face. "Tracksuit girl. I'm going to take care of her, like you took care of Mom and me. No. No, that's not right. Nat is strong, Dad. And Mom is getting stronger too. I can see it."

Jack watched the shades of gray and blue and purple in the approaching clouds for a moment.

"We're going to take care of each other," he finished.

"Anyway, I love you, Dad. ... I miss you." Jack swallowed hard.

He let his gaze drop from the threatening sky. Down to the threatening ground. A solitary shape lurked at the fence. Not enough to cause a panic, although two weeks ago a single zombie at the fence would have accomplished that.

Still, something that needed to be taken care of. He'd go tell John about it as soon as he got back downstairs. John would want to destroy the zombie before the weather got bad.

Jack heard the rumble of thunder, rolling along in a continuous growl. And there. Lightning.

There is a storm coming.

Chapter 6

John

November 14, 5:00 P.M.

John's fingers traced over the scabs, feeling the rough surface through his fingertips.

"I can't believe how fast you're healing."

Mel placed her hand on top of John's. Then, with gentle but persistent pressure, guided his hand between her legs. Their eyes met and they grinned at each other, feeling like teenagers.

His fingers found what they had been searching for. Mel closed her eyes, tilted her head, and started that low moan that never failed to light John's fire.

A few minutes later, John was washing at the sink in their room. Mel watched him from the bed.

"Thanks," she said once he turned off the tap.

He dried his hands on a towel and cast a mischievous grin toward his wife. "My pleasure."

"Oh, I'm sure I can think of something which *will* be your pleasure!" she replied with a laugh. Mel sat up gingerly, a small spasm of pain crossing her face as she swung her legs off the cot.

"Need an Advil?" John was already reaching to the small shelf which held the painkillers.

Mel nodded, then grimaced. "I think I used the last one this morning..."

John shook the small pill bottle to reveal that, indeed, the container was empty. "Darn. Okay, why don't you hang out here for a few minutes while I run down and get you some more?" He was already halfway to the door when he finished speaking.

"Thanks, babe."

John was in luck. Shelley was just walking out of the clinic as he approached.

"Hey, Shelley. I was wondering if I could get some more Advil for Mel?" He held up the empty container to the nurse.

"Of course." She smiled as she reached for the pill bottle and led the way into the clinic. John followed the nurse toward the cupboards that lined one wall.

"Got some right here," she said as she opened one of the cupboards.

She dug around for a few seconds. John heard her give a surprised grunt.

"Everything all right?" John stepped closer.

Shelley turned, and her large eyes, which so often betrayed her emotions, now showed concern. "I think some of the medications have gone missing." She turned back to the cupboard. "I—I'm not sure, but I swear we had more..." She quickly opened a drawer and reached in, pulling out a clipboard.

She scanned the clipboard, flipping pages and following the lines with her finger. She shook her head, once, as she scanned one page. Then shook her head again as she scanned another. "Hmm." She grunted. "This looks right." She placed the clipboard on the counter and stared back into the cupboard. "I could have sworn..."

John stepped up beside Shelley. He'd never had a look inside the cupboard, so could not judge on the situation. He did, however, know people. "Go with your first instinct, Shelley. It's usually correct."

Shelley nodded, her expression severe. "Then I think somebody has been taking some of the pharmaceuticals." She turned to face John and waved at the clipboard. "And whoever this person is knew to change the inventory listing." She frowned, clearly frustrated. "Why did we use a pencil for that?"

"Hey, it's all right." John reassured her. "I'll bring it up with Joe and Christine. See if either of them noticed anything strange."

Finding the Advil, Shelley quickly counted out twenty of the little red painkillers. She still looked concerned as she handed the pill bottle back to him. The fact that somebody was stealing medications clearly upset the nurse.

It's her faith in people that has been shaken. He put a hand on her shoulder.

"It will be okay. We'll get to the bottom of this and make it right. We've got a lot of good people here. Don't let one rotten apple spoil that for you."

"Wow. You've just read my mind." Shelley looked surprised.

John just grinned. "You're not the hardest person to read." With that, he said goodbye and left the clinic.

His face changed the moment he started up the stairs.

There is a thief among us. Maybe a drug addict...

He was going to find the rotten apple, and he had a good idea about what he would do to that person once he got his hands on him.

Chapter 7

Joe

November 14, 6:30 P.M.

J oe looked at himself in the mirror. The bruising had really shown up over the last couple of days, leaving him with a definite raccoon-like face. He gingerly felt his nose and was pleased to note that it didn't hurt to touch anymore. Instead, there was the dull ache of healing bone.

He turned his head one way then the other, pleased to see how straight it was healing.

You almost can't tell that it was broken.

He caught sight of the slight bump near the top.

Well... Almost.

"Shelley did a hell of a job setting this thing," he commented.

"What's that, dear?" Rachel said from her chair by the window.

"Oh, nothing." Joe had no desire to let the event of three nights ago resurface.

She seemed satisfied with that and continued to gaze out the window. Joe watched her reflection carefully through the mirror. He'd kept her heavily dosed since that night, but without the right medications, it was more like trying to dam a river with ice cubes.

Like giving Ritalin to someone with dementia. Then realized that he wasn't far from doing just that.

Adderall for schizophrenia.

"I'm sorry, Rach," he whispered to the image in the mirror. The one at the window couldn't hear him.

50

He checked his watch. Realizing that he was going to be late for his own meeting if he didn't hurry, he quickly walked over to his wife, kissed the top of her head, and left the room.

Joe had initiated a daily council meeting. It wasn't very formal and allowed people to voice their concerns once a day, right after supper. Actions for the next day were discussed and planned out. They had one strict rule: The meeting was never to last more than half an hour. Joe appreciated that.

The council consisted of anybody who showed interest, really. Joe was the only regular as the whole thing had been his idea. Actually, it had been Craig's idea. Joe just carried it out.

The council meetings were usually well-attended. Today was no different, as a baker's dozen sat around three tables. Several latecomers rushed to join in.

Just about everybody is here. Joe realized. It reminded him of something Craig had told him in private. *"Get everybody involved. We need people to take on a sense of ownership. The only way we're going to have success as a tribe is with members that are bought in."* Joe remembered the grin on Craig's face as he said the word "tribe." It was a brand-new concept and had sounded funny then.

We are becoming a tribe, Craig. Just like you hoped. The time for retrospection was done, however, as the meeting got started.

The first and most pressing topic was sobering. It concerned their missing matriarch, Nancy.

Sarah and Claire both complained that not enough was done to find the elderly lady. John and Mike took turns trying to explain that they had found no trace of her after many attempts.

"Look, guys," John started. "We've crisscrossed the entire community for two days straight now. There is no sign of her."

"Just the mornings," Claire said with a hint of accusation.

"Well, yes. We've been clearing houses every afternoon. ... Look, we have to make decisions that are for the best of this entire group. Zombies are a threat to us all. Clearing them is a priority."

"Ladies." Mike stepped into the breach. "It's easy for her to hide from us if she doesn't want to be found. The only good news I can give you is that we haven't found her body either..." Mike's words trailed off. They weren't the best choice.

Joe had heard enough. He lifted both hands in a calming gesture. "Claire... please," he said, noting that the latter was about to respond to Mike — and from the expression on her face, it wasn't going to be in a congenial way. "We're doing the best we can. Yes, we are only spending the mornings on looking for Nancy. But there are a lot of things to do. Surely you don't think that us clearing the community is a waste of time?"

Claire shrugged noncommittally. Sarah and Tammy nodded ever so slightly, while Michelle and Breanne nodded vigorously.

Okay, good. Some of them agree.

"We really are doing our best to find Nancy." Abi spoke up, the long-faced BB never far from her side. "I'm sorry that we haven't found her..." Her expression grew sad. It was the catalyst needed to prompt a few supportive murmurs from the crowd.

Joe decided to press the advantage. "I'll tell you what: John, Mike and their teams will continue to look for Nancy every morning, but maybe we can organize another search party for the afternoons between the rest of us?"

Sarah and Claire blanched at the proposal, obviously not comfortable with the prospect of leaving the safety of the school. The rest of the group perked up at the idea, though.

Joe turned to John. "Maybe we could use one of the Humvees, and you guys switch to the minivan?" He looked over at John anxiously. He had not discussed this option with their unofficial military leader.

John nodded in agreement, though. "Yeah. We can make that work."

"It's a good idea, Joe." Michelle looked around her. "I'm sure we can find four or five people willing to come along."

"Count me in, yeah," Emily piped up. Tammy also volunteered on the spot.

"I'll come along," Breanne offered. Her badly bruised and swollen face made it hard to read her emotion. "Could use some fresh air."

"You know what?" Joe added. "I'll come, too." This was met with raised eyebrows. "It's time I start pulling my own weight," he continued. "Besides, I want to find Nancy just as badly as the rest of you."

With that, the topic was closed. Joe noticed that the mood had lightened considerably.

Everybody wins.

"Do we have any more issues to discuss?" he asked the group.

"I have something to bring up." John stood up. He quickly relayed Shelley's findings about the missing medications.

"No!" Claire couldn't believe it. "Who would do such a thing?"

"I think it's that Q kid. Something isn't right about him," Michelle said with a look of suspicion.

"Now, hang on," Joe interjected. "Let's not blindly start accusing people."

"Yeah, Joe is right." Tammy said. "The truth always comes out."

Joe's eyes flicked toward the former reporter at that. He cleared his throat to hide his discomfort. "John. What do you suggest we do?"

John had the answer ready. "For starters, we put the medications under lock and key. Anybody can break into the clinic. I found a safe in the main office, with the key still in it."

Several people mumbled their agreement. "Joe, why don't you take custody of the one key? Always have it on you. That way we know who to go to if we need something," John said.

Joe nodded, not trusting himself to speak. The rest of the group quickly agreed.

The next order of business was security. Once again, John was the spokesman.

"Along with our searches for Nancy, we accomplished some good recon. As you know from yesterday, it looks like the armed forces, possibly Matheson and his men, had been clearing houses prior to our arrival here."

"We found an additional forty houses that had been cleared, directly to the south and north of the school property. They obviously wanted to clear a cordon around this location. We've been able to enlarge this cordon, clearing about an additional sixty houses. In fact, I'd say that there aren't any zombies present in an area of several blocks around us."

He was about to continue but was interrupted by some surprised noises. When he looked up, he was met with more raised eyebrows.

"Yeah. It surprised me too. The truth is that most of the houses we checked were already empty. It seems to me that this neighborhood was cleared by the army several days before the syndrome really took hold." He looked at his audience, letting that sink in. John reached into his pocket and pulled out a map, which he promptly opened and held up to the group. "This is a map of our community. I've marked the houses we've cleared already. When I first looked at this map, I figured that there could be up to five thousand zombies within the confines of the walls. However, based on what we've seen and found so far, my guess is that we're looking at less than a tenth of that."

He placed the map on the table in front of him.

"I've been driving around the inside of our gated community for the last two days now, and only ran into half a dozen zombies on the street. Our community is practically empty," he said.

"If by 'empty' you mean we are still outnumbered ten to one," Breanne said.

John treated her to a dead-pan stare.

"Well... Just saying." Breanne mostly held her ground.

"Anyway..." John's body language clearly showed that he wanted to drop the subject. "We made some discoveries. Basically, what I was saying before — that the army cleared the community as best as they could."

"That's a good thing," Joe looked from the group to John. The ex-soldier's expression gave cause for concern, though. "Right?!"

"Yeah. For the most part." John looked troubled.

"I'm confused," Joe pressed. "What part of this isn't good news?"

John grimaced. There was no easy way to say this. "We've found evidence that some of the houses had residents. Living residents. It seems to me like some of these folks took exception to the army coming into their houses. There were signs of violence. I'm pretty sure that some of these people ended up getting shot..."

"No..." Claire's shocked expression matched the disbelief in her voice.

"That's what it looks like." He nodded and sighed. "I've seen things like this before, albeit not here in America."

He paused for a second, then looked up to find all eyes on him.

"I don't want to make excuses for the army, but we *were* under martial law. I've been in other places where martial law meant that any transgression of the rules was punishable by death." He glanced around him. "It happened a lot more than you'd think."

"But this is America! These kinds of things don't happen here. Right?" Michelle was as shocked and uncertain as the rest of the group. For some reason most of them turned to Tammy then. They waited for her to speak.

"It's not something I hear about," Tammy said uncertainly. "There were always rumors. That dictator in Kazakhstan. The revolution in Cameroon. And then there were those military coups in Malaysia and Eritrea just last year..." She let her words trail off, realizing the truth of it. After a moment, she nodded with conviction. "I do believe that it could happen here, too."

"Look."

Everybody looked at John, who had called their attention. "I'm not going to defend these guys, but they were probably under strict orders and stressed to the tee. When so much shit goes down..." He hesitated again. "You don't fuck with the guys with the guns."

The crowd murmured. Joe heard the sounds of disapproval and consternation. He realized that he needed to move the meeting on.

"Maybe we can park that topic for now?" he suggested to the group, then turned to Mike. "I believe Mike has done some scouting and also has some information to share?"

The veteran radioman cleared his throat. "Hrrm. Yeah."

The crowd quieted down to listen.

"So, we've managed to follow along the entire length of the wall today. I'm pleased to report that there are no other gaps or weak spots. I've even got BB to take a look over the wall in a few spots, and he hardly saw any zombies out there. For now, that means there are no more large groups hanging out on the other side. That's a good thing."

"Thank you, Mike." Joe smiled half-heartedly. "Did you have anything else to report?"

"Yeah, just one more thing. You see, the Ren is a good location for our folks, but it's not the optimum position for a radio. We're kind of sitting in a low spot, and can only hope to bounce our signal off a radio tower or some other antenna..." He stopped, noticing that he seemed to have lost a large portion of his audience.

"We've located a good location for a radio setup," he continued when he had their attention again. "It's a house that's located no more than fifty feet from a radio tower. You might have seen it when you entered this community — it's about a mile away from one of the gates, on a hill that overlooks the area." Nobody seemed to remember a place like that, so Mike went on, "I suggest that we secure that house — I mean really shore it up so that no zombies can get in — and then set up our radio in there instead. It will also serve well as a lookout post because it has a commanding view of the area. I think you can even see this place from over there."

The reaction was mixed: lots of nodding heads, but also several concerned looks.

"Does that mean we'd have to be driving back and forth all the time?" Michelle asked. "Or are we talking about getting some permanent residents over there?"

More questions followed, and Mike was forced to raise his hands for silence.

"Whoa, people. I haven't figured any of that stuff out. All I'm saying is that we'll have a much better chance of establishing contact with other survivors if we set up out there."

Joe raised his hand. He was pleasantly surprised that all eyes turned to him immediately. "Thanks." He inexplicably felt emotional at the show of respect. "Can we agree to at least check out this place? Maybe clear it and secure it? The way I see it, we should be able to make a better, more informed decision after that. We have nothing to lose."

"That makes sense," Michelle agreed.

"Okay, let's hold a quick vote. Those in favor of checking it out, maybe securing the place, raise your hand."

The result was a unanimous yes.

"Great!" Joe beamed at his audience. "Glad to see that we can all agree on something."

With that, the meeting ended. Joe was about to head back to his room when he felt a touch on his elbow.

It was John. "Need to talk to you for a minute." The expression on John's face showed that this was about something serious.

Joe followed John out of the cafeteria. John turned toward the front doors, stopping on the rough carpet there. Joe looked down and pictured the hundreds of kids that must have shuffled their way through the rough bristles, inadvertently cleaning their shoes as they entered the school.

I wonder if any of those kids are still alive... He frowned.

John misread Joe's expression. "You're doing a great job. Really showing good leadership qualities."

"Oh. Ah, thanks." Joe felt even more embarrassed.

"Anyway, I'll get to the point. We haven't done anything with our Rosae Crucis intel. I think it's time we acted." John bit his lip for a moment before continuing. "I'm too curious to let it go. I want to travel to those coordinates in Georgia and see for my-self—"

"Now?" Joe interrupted. "Don't you think we've got too many issues closer to home?"

"Yeah, we do." John nodded as if he had expected this. "That's why I want to go alone."

Joe shook his head. "That's not a good idea, John." He took a deep breath in and could feel the numb pain of his healing nose as he exhaled, accompanied by the tiniest whistle. It reminded him of his own issues — of his own need to undertake an expedition of sorts. He licked his lips as he thought of a response.

John beat him to it, though. "There is more to all of this than we know." He waved his hand around him. "We need more information. Besides"—John's expression grew even more serious—"I don't think the danger is over."

Joe nodded as he thought about it. He met John's eyes. "I think you're right about that. But we have more immediate concerns, right here. There are still zombies inside the walls. We have to destroy those. Then we have to ... clear them."

They had already discussed the need to get rid of the corpses. The best solution they had come up with was to burn them. "We need everybody to help out. It won't do us any good if another Shaw shows up."

John wouldn't let it go, and Joe could see that there was no changing the man's mind. He lifted his hands in surrender.

"Fine. You want to go on this expedition — I won't stop you." The relief on John's face was plain to see. "But!" Joe continued, "I still don't think that it's a good idea to let you go out there on your own. At least put it out to the group to see if anybody wants to come with you. Mind you, I don't want too many people joining. Maybe just a couple..."

Both men grinned, having come to an agreement. Joe's grin dropped, however, when another thought occurred to him.

"How long do you figure it will take you? When are you thinking of setting off?"

John was ready for this. "I've mapped out the route — well, roughly, anyways. Before all this, I would have been able to make the trip there and back in less than twenty-four hours. But even so, it should take no more than a day or so to get there. I figured that the whole trip would take four days, max."

"Okay." It sounded reasonable.

"I was thinking of leaving here early in the morning on Sunday." John said.

"Sunday..." Joe repeated. "Sorry, I've kind of lost track of the days. What day is it now?"

"Thursday." John replied, his expression unreadable. "Guess it *is* getting hard to keep track."

"Yeah." Joe gave a small shake of the head. "Life isn't what it used to be... I know that it's November."

"It's the fourteenth today." John supplied, then shrugged when Joe frowned at him. "Sorry, old habits."

"Right. So, you're leaving three days from now."

"Yeah. I figure that we will be calling off the search for Nancy by then."

Joe nodded. "Poor woman. Hope she comes to her senses and returns to us. She is more important than she thinks."

"I know that we can get a fair bit done over the next three days." John started ticking off his prosthetic fingers as he spoke. They made an artificial sound. *Tick.* "We can clear a bunch more houses." *Tick.* "We can get that new radio location secured. I think that's a great idea, by the way." *Tick.* "We can get all of the walls surveyed and shored up where needed." *Tick.* "And to your point, we can start burning bodies."

"Right." Joe grimaced. The air out there had really started to smell, despite the near-freezing temperatures.

"All right. Thanks." John smiled.

"Good man." Joe responded with a smile of his own. He winced as the tape on his cheeks pulled at his nose.

John noticed. "How's the nose?" Joe could tell that John wanted to hear more about the circumstances around his injury than the injury itself.

"Oh, it's going to be fine. Two to three weeks and it will be as good as new." He caught the searching look in John's eyes and quickly added, "Maybe even better! But you've got to warn me if

I start looking like Michael Jackson." He grinned again, wincing once more as the tape pulled at his nose.

After another moment, John let it go and joined the big man in a grin. "You'll never be as good-looking as Michael Jackson, Joe." Both men chuckled.

John turned and started walking away. There was a definite spring in his step.

He's looking forward to this. Like it's a mission.

An hour later, John already had several volunteers. BB and Abi were natural additions as driver and communications experts. He was surprised with some of the other volunteers, though.

Tammy seemed very keen to come along, as did Nat and Q. John had to turn these volunteers away. "I only want to take a couple of people with me. One vehicle."

Tammy was one person who did not want to let it rest. She followed John all the way up to his room, finally challenging the man before he could retreat inside.

"I want to come along. There's room for at least one more." She continued quickly when John frowned, "Look, I want to record the facts for posterity. People out there need to learn the truth about what happened, how, and why."

"Yeah, but—"

"Let me finish. Please," she added, hoping not to antagonize the man. John shut his mouth. "I also think that I can contribute to the mission. First of all, I've been doing investigative reporting for years. I know how to get to the bottom of things. I think out of the box, too. You might need that." He didn't look convinced, so she quickly went on, "Also, I am good at speaking with people. Maybe I can help if we run into other survivors — or even the order."

John could tell that she was desperate to come along.

"Tell me, Tammy: What's your biggest reason for wanting to come along? Be honest."

She shrugged. "I just want to know what's going on. What happened. How. And why."

He looked at her. She defiantly returned his gaze, meeting his eyes. There was a pregnant pause as the two stared off, one desperately hoping she had convinced the other.

"Okay," John said simply. He shook his head slightly at Tammy. "I think you're nuts for wanting to come along, but I understand your motivation. Just make sure you pack light and don't get in the way."

Tammy smiled, relieved. "You got it, John. Thank you." She quickly retreated before he could change his mind.

Chapter 8

Kevin

November 16, 3:00 P.M., Rosae Crucis Primary Domicile

K evin was in a good mood.

For once, things were going his way. He'd received word this morning that not one, but two satellite locations had re-established contact. He'd feared those people lost, but as it turns out they were more resourceful than he'd given them credit for. One of the groups had even found a better and safer location.

Even the defection of a small group could not dampen his spirit.

Besides, I'm sure they will come around.

Kevin dropped the thought, continuing to focus on the positives.

Over the course of the last couple of days he'd received word from several captains and a handful of optios. He put them to work right away. Two captains, along with their teams, were to make their way to the bunker housing the remnants of the former administration.

Pretentious bastards. Who has the gall to call their center of operations "Olympus"?

Kevin considered that for a moment. The answer came to him easily.

That's the government for you. They think they're gods, and people are their playthings. Cruel and miserable beings... We're about to pull your mountain down.

Kevin figured that they would have plenty of firepower to take over the bunker between those two teams. Just to be sure, a third captain had been ordered to join the fight. He brought a considerable number of soldiers with him. He'd also have further to travel but would reach them, eventually.

Westland will likely arrive too late. We should already have taken control by then. Finally!

Kevin sighed out loud. Taking over the center of operations would deal the final deathblow to the United States of America.

After that, it would be down to mopping up some dissenters.

His thoughts drifted to the loss of Ben. It had hit Brenin hard. Ben was a special project. Only Kevin and a few others in Brenin's inner circle knew this. But Ben was gone now, likely gunned down on his last mission.

The mission you sent him to perform, Kevin — or did you forget that?

A flash of guilt quickly replaced the euphoria of a minute ago.

That school, the Ren... Their hour of justice is coming. Kevin made a fist as guilt became anger. He was going to make sure that vengeance was served cold and swiftly.

As a matter of fact, preparations were well underway. Rocko should be arriving first thing in the morning. Kevin was going to personally deliver Brenin's wrath. The optio he had sent out had made good travel time and was near the scene already. Kevin expected a situational report within a few hours.

Sage Peter had argued with Kevin when he announced his plan. The sage had suggested they send a few more fighting men, but that was nonsense according to the paladin.

We don't need a bunch of firepower. Just enough men to drop some bombs on that fucking school.

Peter had suggested that Kevin should not risk his personal safety on the mission, but Kevin had waved that away too. The truth was that Kevin needed this. He felt like he was about to burst. Being there and witnessing the destruction of this school and everything it represented firsthand? That was exactly what Kevin needed. Besides, it was going to be a breeze. They would fly in and drop their load before anybody in the school would even think about reacting. Then they would circle around for a bit and watch the barbecue.

Maybe pick off one or two of the stragglers. Or let Philip take care of that. The guy's supposed to be quite the sniper...

Tomorrow afternoon. By then he would be airborne and on his way.

Kevin smiled and congratulated himself.

Finally. Everything is falling into place.

Chapter 9

John

November 15, 7:00 P.M., The Ren.

"**W**hy can't I come?" Maria demanded.

John sighed. He had announced his plans to the entire community yesterday, after securing BB, Abi and Tammy as his team. He wanted to travel light and fast. Romy asked to come along, and their group had grown to five. She was a decent shooter and might be needed.

That seemed to be the end of it. Until the next evening. When, of all people, a child insisted on coming.

"Because you're a child." John regretted the words almost as soon as he'd said them.

Maria bristled. Joe quickly reached over and placed his hand on her shoulder. "I need your help here at home, Maria. You're our best scout."

She didn't buy the excuse. She shook Joe's hand off and scowled at him.

"This is bullshit!" The profanity rang through the cafeteria. John was oddly aware that there were no sounds of disapproval.

Ern was dead, and Nancy had abandoned them. *I'm not losing any more people. Not on my watch.*

His expression turned stern as he prepared to speak.

This isn't some fieldtrip. It was on the tip of John's tongue, but he swallowed the comment as he saw the desperation in Maria's face.

"I can handle myself out there." The girl looked anywhere but at John's eyes. She pouted and folded her arms.

"I know."

John's reply was not something she had expected. But it was true. John knew that Maria was aware of the situation out there. He also had no doubt that she could handle herself. John had actually been impressed by Maria's ability to cope with things. Here was a girl that had lost her entire family yet had grown into a useful member of the group. She was there, every time the call came for a volunteer.

And she has caused no drama. Very little, anyway...

That last thought snuck in his head as he looked beyond the teenage girl.

Very little drama. Not like some of the others... He allowed his eyes to drift over the people in the cafeteria.

He spotted Rachel arm-in-arm with Christine and the worse-for-wear Breanne, who looked oddly comical with her head so heavily bandaged. Then there was the always outspoken Michelle, who was flanked by the moody Romy.

Yeah. We've got enough drama.

"Huh?" John had missed something.

Maria frowned at him. "I said: Then why can't I come along?"

John smiled softly at the girl. "Sorry, Maria. I was lost in thought." He walked up to her. "Listen. I'm not as good as Craig at this. I just need you to bear with me for a little bit longer. This mission could be really dangerous. We have no idea what we are going to find."

Maria's body language made it quite clear that his speech was falling on deaf ears.

John knelt in front of her so that he had to look up. "I just don't want to put you in danger right now." He hesitated a moment before continuing. "I don't think that I could handle the guilt if something happened to you on my watch."

Maria's expression softened. "I can be careful," she replied somewhat hesitantly.

"We've already got five people. Can't take any more in the vehicle..." He thought for a moment. "I promise that you get to come on our next mission — assuming we know the risks of that mission and can manage them. Will you agree to that?"

Maria screwed up her face as John spoke. Her expression grew resolute, and she slowly nodded.

"You look tired," Maria blurted out.

It was unexpected. John had to admit that she was right, though. "Yeah."

The girl turned away. John watched her leave before getting back to his feet.

The room emptied few minutes later. Melissa, Joe and Mike stayed behind with John so they could do some final minute planning.

"Aren't you glad that I didn't throw a hissy fit?" Mike asked with a wink. The truth was that Mike was more than happy to sit this one out. As he had previously said, "I'm okay at driving, at best. I'm shit at shooting. But an AT RF1350? Hell, I can handle that like nobody's business!"

Melissa had heard enough banter. "Let's get to work." The former intelligence officer indicated the maps spread out on the table. "We've got a mission to plan."

John felt himself relax as his wife took charge.

Ten minutes later, they got up and started to head out of the cafeteria. Joe looked over at John as they walked.

"Maria was right, you know. You *do* look tired."

John grinned. "I'll take that under advisement, Doc. Frankly, it's the talking." He waved behind him. "That's what gets me tired. I'd rather be running out there with a gun in my hand than face any more drama."

Joe grinned back. After a moment, his expression turned more serious. "You did a good job with Maria. Craig would have approved."

"Fuck, I miss that guy."

The two men nodded in agreement.

Joe

November 17, 8:00 A.M., The Ren

Scattered clouds stretched across the sky. Out to the west, darker clouds loomed with the threat of another storm. It had been the same for the last several days. The promise of violent weather during the mornings and afternoons never materialized, though.

Maybe today... Joe shivered as he stepped out of the back door of the gym and into the crisp morning air. He carried a box toward the Humvee that was parked nearby.

The vehicle sat with its oddly shaped back hatch open. John met him at the hatch and took the box from his hands. He promptly handed the box to Abi, who had squeezed her tiny frame into the rear of the vehicle and busied herself organizing their supplies.

"Are you sure that's all?" Joe asked as he watched Abi place the cardboard box into a corner.

A slight grin cracked John's face as he nodded. "Yup. Won't need more than that." He leaned in closer to the big man conspiratorially. "I'll be surprised if we touch any of that stuff."

The box contained twenty MREs. It lay on top of a case of water bottles in the back of the vehicle. The small amount of food sat in sharp contrast to the large amount of ammunition. John wasn't preparing to eat a lot, but he sure was ready for a war.

"We'll be grazing," John said.

"Grazing?" Joe frowned in confusion.

"Yep. I am pretty sure that we will come across the odd grocery store or restaurant." He touched the side of his nose in a gesture of secrecy. "Just don't tell Melissa. She's got everything planned out, right to where and when we take our bathroom breaks."

"Oh!" Joe laughed. His deep booming laughter shattered the silence of the morning. He quickly swallowed his mirth, looking around him with an embarrassed expression.

"Frankly, I don't blame you." The big man admitted. "I was getting sick of MREs. Thank God for all the food we've found in the surrounding houses."

"Yeah. I hear you."

"Hey, if you happen to find a good bottle of whiskey..."

"Say no more, buddy. We'll be all over that."

"Assuming everything goes all right with your mission."

John nodded soberly.

Joe looked up as Tammy and Romy walked up with BB close behind. "Looks like you guys are pretty much ready to head out."

Joe grabbed his walkie-talkie and pressed down on the talk button. "Keith, this is Joe. They're ready to leave. Go ahead and open the gate."

"Got it. Jack and I are heading out now."

The expedition team settled into their seats. Joe could sense their nervous excitement. The bright eyes and flushed faces also gave it away.

Why do I feel envy?

He let the thought go as John closed the rear hatch. They walked to the passenger door together.

"Don't take any unnecessary chances," Joe said as John swung the door open. "I was just joking about the booze."

"Hey, don't worry. Caution is my middle name." John offered his hand and the two men shook.

"We should be back in four to five days. And we'll be in touch whenever we can, of course." John hopped into the passenger seat.

"Thanks." Joe leaned in slightly and addressed the rest of the team. "All y'all be safe out there!" He got a couple of okays and one, "You got it, chief " in return.

John closed the door and the vehicle started up. Joe slapped the back of the Humvee twice as it rolled away from him.

Good luck, guys.

N at could hear the roar of the Humvee starting up. Her rooftop vantage did not show her what was happening on the other side of the school, though. Besides, her eyes were on the men below.

Specifically, one man. She watched as he ran his hand through his hair, pulling the front of his dirty blond hair away from his eyes.

He could use a haircut.

As if on cue, Jack looked up at her. She felt her heartbeat race despite herself. She was falling for him. Hard.

It wasn't that he was a gorgeous example of masculinity or possessed the chiseled body and face of a model. It certainly wasn't his way with words — although that could still come if his father was anything to judge by.

Neither was it his experience and "tender" touch as a lover. He did not possess those traits yet. Nat smiled. This might be the first time that she was the more experienced of the couple. She reminisced about the last couple of days.

There had been their second ever kiss, two days ago. That one had hurt as they violently cracked their teeth together.

Passion 1, Common sense 0.

Then there was earlier today. When they were fooling around.

"You're not milking a cow."

That comment had hurt his feelings, but she diffused it quickly enough by laughing about it.

No, Jack wasn't some experienced Adonis.

In a way, it was the lack of experience that attracted Nat to him so much.

No. She corrected herself: It wasn't what he didn't have, but what he did have, which made him so attractive.

He was awkward, but true. He was beautiful in his innocence and sincerity. He was handsome in his bravery and intelligence. And while his touch tended to be rushed and rough, it was so fully committed and incredibly passionate that it made Nat's own needs and urges rise to meet his.

She looked down at him now, as he worked the chain on the gate. He cast a nervous glance around him, but Nat wasn't worried. She had already scanned the surrounding area and found it completely devoid of life.

Devoid of death, I guess.

The Humvee pulled around the side of the school, crossing the grass and the sidewalk to pop onto the driveway without losing a step. Nat was impressed. BB sure knew how to handle the vehicle. Although she did see somebody in the backseat reach for their oh-shit handle as they jumped the curb. John looked cool as a cucumber in the passenger seat.

The gate had been opened at this point. Nat quickly scanned up and down the street again. Still no movement.

Guess we really did clear most zombies out of this place.

The Humvee drove out and turned right, coming to a stop about ten yards from the fence.

That must be John. He's probably telling them to wait until the gate is secured.

Nat realized that she should be thankful for a guy like that. He wasn't a true leader; Joe had stepped into that gap rather nicely. But when it came to security, John was the guy in charge.

He just knows shit.

The gate was promptly closed, and the Humvee sped off without further ado. Nat watched them drive down to the next intersection and turn left.

Good luck, guys. She looked after them longingly. It was not the first time that she wished she had come along.

Nat stayed in position a while longer. The cold wind was a biting one, but she welcomed the sensation. It made her feel alive. She looked out over the rooftops and listened to the fading roar of the Humvee as it sped away. Pretty soon, the sound of the vehicle was lost to her.

Still, the world was not immaculately silent. There was the blustery wind, of course. It carried the smell of rain to Nat's nose and promised the future smells of wet earth and flora. Those smells would be welcome, especially with the constant presence of the sticky sweetness of rotting flesh.

We really need to do something about that.

She listened more intently and caught other noises. The sound of a door or a window slamming shut repeatedly — likely at the whim of the very wind that buffeted her on the rooftop.

Then other sounds. Unexplainable sounds. Sudden, irregular bangs, which sent Nat's imagination soaring. Were there people out there? Or was it zombies, with their morbid imitation of life?

Still, it was the lack of ordinary sounds which stood out by their absence. No dog barked at intrusion into its territory. No constant background drone of traffic from the surrounding highways. Even the birds were silent — although she knew that they were out there. She had seen the odd bird fly over. Nat considered that for a moment, then reckoned that any nearby birds were hiding from the wind and impending storm.

Nat sighed. The world they knew was gone — likely forever. Nat held no conviction that things were perfect before the syndrome. She wasn't ignorant to the fact that terrible things were going on, like pollution and starvation, but she felt that these were overshadowed by the good things.

Family. She knew instinctively that her dad was gone and had prayed that he had not joined the masses of zombies. She thought of her aunts and uncles, and her many cousins, and knew deep in her heart they were all gone.

Music. It had been her constant companion, matching her moods at the press of a button. Her life had played out to the beat of an eclectic soundtrack.

Coffee. There was a shopping mall near her college dorm. Nat never liked going out in public — but she'd braved the crowd at least once a day to get to Tony's. The coffee shop with its own roastery had a special place in Nat's heart.

"Americano. Large. No room," Nat said under her breath, repeating the order that she must have placed a thousand times. She didn't even mind that the staff hadn't been the friendliest, and that they had failed to recognize her after daily visits over hundreds of days.

No, that's not true, Nat. Be honest.

Secretly she had hoped that they would greet her the moment she walked through the door — like a loyal bar patron in some sitcom. Secretly she had hoped that they would start working on her Americano as soon as they spotted her, instead of making her wait in line with the other strangers.

Secretly you wanted acceptance.

She sighed again. Always her thoughts turned back to her insecurities. The moment didn't last long, as the wind buffeted her back to the present.

She looked out, her eyes scanning the empty street and abandoned houses.

What was that?

Nat was sure that she caught movement in one of the windows. She stared hard for a long moment.

Nothing. Nat lifted her rifle and stared through her scope at the spot where she thought she'd seen movement. She could barely make out the darkened interior through the glare of the window. She lowered the rifle in frustration after another moment.

You're imagining shit. Those places were cleared. Twice. First by the army and then by us.

It did remind her of the need to keep clearing houses. Joe had made such a promise to John. Clear the houses. Burn the bodies. No, the people remaining were not planning to sit on their laurels and wait for John to return.

She heard a sound behind her and looked over her shoulder. Jack was climbing onto the roof. He gave that goofy grin of his as their eyes met. Nat smiled. She loved his goofy grin. She turned away as Jack approached.

She felt a soft touch against the small of her back. Another thing she loved.

"What'cha doing?"

"Just... looking. And listening."

They were both silent for a few seconds. Nat swung her rifle over her shoulder, letting it hang by its strap. She reached out and held his hand. It felt incredibly hot to the touch.

"You're freezing." Jack nearly pulled his hand away. Instead, he turned Nat to face him and grabbed her other hand. His eyes lit up with a thought. "Here." He released her hands and unzipped his jacket, holding it open. Nat stepped in to hug her boyfriend, and he pulled the jacket closed behind her back.

You're in love. She couldn't suppress the thought any longer. She dug her face into his neck, feeling the heat of his skin against her cold nose. She wanted to cry as the senses of security and belonging that she had desired for so long nearly overwhelmed her.

They stood like that for a full minute. Nat slowly came to a realization.

The world has changed. We've lost so much...

Yet... I'm happy.

"Quork. Quork."

The sound of a single raven broke the crisp morning silence. Not a cloud hung in the pale blue sky. It was one of those sharp, cold mornings. One where a simple jacket and hat would not do — one where the cold even crept into gloves to produce aching fingers.

"Quork. Quork."

The raven called out again. It called to another — any other — raven. It had not seen any brothers or sisters in many days. So, it called out.

"Quork. Quork."

There was no answer. At least not from any other raven. Far beneath it, at the base of the tree, half a dozen zombies reached up. They circled the tree, seeking this thing they could not see or identify.

The bird called out once more. It sounded forlorn and sad. One of the undead managed to grab a low-hanging branch. The branch bent, then snapped with an audible crack.

Startled, the bird leapt into the air and spread its black wings. It circled once and flew off.

The zombies ambled around for a moment, trying to follow the direction of the sound. But as the sound dissipated, they slowed down their movement and stopped. Their programming instructed them to preserve their functions.

Then something happened. All six zombies turned their heads to stare in the same direction, although there was no sight to behold or noise to alarm them. A moment later, they moved off in unison. It looked like there was nothing to draw them. However, they all received the same command.

And they answered the call.

Chapter 10

Jack

November 17, 11:30 A.M. The Ren.

Jack was feeling good. He was quite sure that his expression was giving him away.

He greeted his friend as they met at the stairs. "Hey, Ethan."

"You got laid!" He imagined the words blurting out of his companion as they walked shoulder to shoulder.

Yes. Yes, I did. He had not expected it, but Nat had led him straight from the roof to his room. He knew that his mom would be gone for a while — preparing an early lunch for everybody — but still he had a healthy dose of nerves as she locked the door behind them.

Everything after that happened fast. So fast that his mind was still reeling from it.

"Huh?" he blurted, having missed what Ethan had said.

"Are you ready for this?" Ethan repeated.

"For what?"

"The house clearing." Ethan shook his head and frowned. "You ready?"

They reached the landing and shared a look.

He looks nervous.

"Oh. Yeah, for sure. We'll be fine." It felt funny for Jack to be the confident one. Ethan was the jock, after all.

"We're taking a bunch of people. Somebody will always have your back. Besides, you and I will probably just be dragging bodies."

He made a face at the smells and sights that were likely to accost him.

They arrived downstairs. Joe was in a flurry of activity as he organized people. He spotted the young men and pointed at the cafeteria.

"Go have something to eat. Get to the armory when you're done. We need to be geared up and ready to go within the next hour."

Ethan was about to ask his dad something, but the big man had already turned away. "Keith! A moment, please."

With a shrug, Ethan followed Jack into the cafeteria.

They picked up their meal and joined Emily at one of the tables.

"Heya, lads." She greeted them with a grin. They took the first few bites of reconstituted potato mixed with some form of meat. It was relatively tasteless, but then Jack had gotten used to that.

"Em, do you know what the plan is?" Ethan asked between bites. His eyes were as big as saucers.

"Kinda..." Emily said cryptically. She took another bite, leaving the two men hanging. "We're going to have a total of four teams. Two teams for clearing and two teams for mop-up." She looked up at Ethan and Jack. "You blokes will be mopping up."

Jack nodded. He had anticipated this.

"We're starting where John left off yesterday. One set of teams on each side of the street. Oh, hi." She told Nat as the young woman sat down.

Jack felt a hot flush as he saw her. Emily did not notice.

"Glad you're here, Nat. I think you and I will be providing taxi services today. With a side of security." She winked at Nat, then elaborated for the confused-looking Ethan. "We will keep the street clear. Take out any roamers."

"Oh." The spoon in his hand had frozen halfway through Emily's discourse. He seemed to snap out of it and rushed the food into his mouth.

"Don't worry, mate. We've still got Bill, Ben, and Keith. They're ace. All you guys have to do is carry the bodies out of the houses and pile them up.

"Right..." Ethan replied. Jack could tell that his buddy wasn't particularly hungry anymore. Neither was he, for that matter.

Chapter 11

Kevin

November 17, 12:00 P.M. Rosae Crucis Primary Domicile

Kevin stared at the radio, awaiting the report. "One vehicle left the premises several hours ago. A military Humvee. I counted a minimum of five people. At least two were military. They loaded up on supplies, and my guess is that they are going to be gone for several days." The tinny sound crackled slightly with interference.

Kevin lifted the handset to his mouth. "Good. Any other observations?"

"There are more vehicles in the lot. One Humvee and a minivan. The only other vehicles I can see in the parking lot are a flatbed truck and a school bus, along with a couple of burned-out vehicles."

Kevin mulled that over for a moment.

Signs of the battle. Just like Ben told us.

Then.

Fuck, Ben. What the hell happened to you?

Another burst of static from the radio brought Kevin back to the present. He moved on to his next question. "Any estimate on the number of people inside the school?"

"No, sir."

"Come on, Optio Philip. You must have some idea."

Philip was silent for a moment. "I did see some young people, including kids. My guess is that the fighting members of the group departed in that Humvee, leaving the civilians behind. My best guess is maybe a dozen adults and another half a dozen kids," he finally said.

"All right. I don't think they should pose a problem, given their best shooters are likely out on that road trip. Optio, you know the plan. Go get yourself into position. It should be a turkey shoot."

"Sir. Do I take out the kids as well?"

Know your enemy.

"Yes. Now, this might sound callous, but these youngsters need to be treated as hostiles. Are you clear on this?"

The answer came back immediately and clear. "Yes, sir."

Kevin nodded in approval. He looked at the man standing at his side. The Captain had a smug look about him and didn't seem the least fazed that Kevin had condemned children to their deaths. Kevin instantly decided that he did not like the man.

"Very good, Philip. We will be leaving here within the next couple of hours and likely arriving at your location around sunset."

"Sounds good, sir. If I may..."

"Yes, Philip. Go on."

"It looks like there is a storm brewing. Weather conditions might be somewhat adverse this evening."

"Ah. Don't worry about us, Philip. I've got a fine crew. It will take a lot more than some bad weather to cause problems for our helicopter. Now, go get into position. We'll see you tonight."

Kevin replaced the handset and turned to his captain. "Captain Michael, am I correct in saying that weather will not pose an issue?"

"Yes, sir. Not a problem at all," Captain John-Michael Dupuis responded.

Kevin looked at the man for a moment. He knew full well that his name was John-Michael, not Michael, but there was no crack in the man's countenance other than the tiniest and quickest sliver of annoyance.

"Okay. Let's walk." Kevin motioned for the Captain to follow him. They left the radio room and strode down the hallway.

"How much time do you need to get Rocko ready to fly?" Kevin asked without looking at the man at his heels.

"Aw, that will take no time at all, sir. No time. It will take longer to find my crew. You see, they're not the most competent with schedules."

"Very well. Go get your men and prepare Rocko. Be there within the hour. I'm going to make a quick stop at our armory and our fuel depot to get the supplies arranged."

The plan had occurred to Kevin just before his call with Philip.

He remembered seeing some old video, where people in a helicopter tossed bombs on a mountain top to trigger an avalanche. He quickly realized that they could swoop in and drop firebombs on that school before they would even know what hit them. Philip would take out the few that might escape from the burning building. He grinned at his own brilliance.

"It's going to be—"

He turned, but John-Michael had already left. The grin dropped from his face. Kevin looked around, but luckily there was nobody else in the hallway.

"—quite a surprise," he finished.

Chapter 12

Nancy

November 17, 5:30 P.M., Somewhere in the city.

Nancy sipped her tea.

It was cold, but it was her favorite kind, jasmine tea. She couldn't believe her luck when she'd found this place last night, with the front door wide open and nobody home. The stash of tea in the kitchen had made her day.

She crept toward the big bay windows and looked outside.

The overcast sky threatened to drop its liquid contents over the city once more. Nancy watched it and wondered if this was yet another false alarm. For all the clouds and gusting winds, it had been nothing but bluster.

Just like Ern used to be.

She'd lost count of the times that the self-proclaimed king of the jungle had threatened to blow his top, only to sizzle down to a simmering, grumbling little pussy cat.

More like an old gnarly tom cat.

One that can pout. The thought brought a grin to Nancy's face.

Tat—tat—tat. The sound of rain hitting the window broke her reverie. The wind had also picked up, and the clouds suddenly looked a lot darker and ominous.

Guess it wasn't all bluster. Nancy stared up at the swirling clouds. *Looks like I'll have to hunker down here for the night.*

Nancy didn't mind, though. She had no schedule. Besides, there was a whole box of tea to keep her company.

She heard a strange rumble and frowned.

84

Was that a helicopter?
Another rumble rolled across the sky.
No. Just thunder, I guess.

The sound of the helicopter was deafening. And the ride was rough. As if on cue, the helicopter dipped again. Paladin Kevin Wallace shot an annoyed look at the cockpit. He was starting to believe that blowhard, Frankie: Their pilot was incompetent at flying this fortress.

Frankie made his way over to the Paladin and held out a helmet. Kevin gave the man a quizzical look but laid his rifle down at his feet, accepted the helmet, and dutifully donned it.

"Mic check," said the speakers in the helmet. He gave Frankie the thumbs up. Frankie reached over to the side of Kevin's helmet and pulled down the microphone attachment.

"Check!" Kevin said, a little too loudly. Frankie smiled to hide his derisive frown.

"Okay. We can use these to communicate. Captain Dupuis — you got comms."

The combination of his heavy accent and the tinny sound of the speaker made it almost impossible to understand what he said. Luckily, the Captain's voice was intelligible.

"Paladin Kevin, we are less than two minutes out from our target. The plan is still the same. McLellan, Hershey. Get those barrels close to the door."

"Aye-aye." Two voices answered in unison as the marines started their way to the barrels. Kevin made his way to the door, from which these barrels would be launched. He wanted a front-seat view for the show.

I hope Optio Philip got set up. Kevin scanned buildings, despite the futility of the action.

The specialist would be setting up shop somewhere with visuals on the school, if he hadn't done so already. Once the explosions and fires started, the people inside the school would likely be running out the front door, and that would be easy pickings for a talented sniper like Philip.

"We're coming up on the target now, sir," the tinny speaker inside his helmet announced. Kevin looked out of the small window to observe their target.

You guys are in for a surprise.

B en sensed the gusts of wind. He could feel them through his fingertips, placed against the glass of the window. He watched the treetops swaying in the distance and could just make out the clanking sound of the metal clasp hitting the flagpole — its sound at once forlorn and weirdly threatening.

A solitary bird flew in the sky in spurts, getting tossed around by the winds.

The whole scene reminded him of something. It took him a moment to grasp the memory. He recalled a similar scene, at the airport.

He hadn't realized it at the time, but those moments had signified a change for him. A divergence from the doctrine he had followed since childhood.

Ben sighed. He didn't like it. Watching the approaching storm filled him with a strange sense of foreboding. He watched the bird until he lost sight of it. He supposed that the winged creature had struggled as it was pulled in various directions by the forces around it, but it had somehow made it to its destination.

These same winds pulled at the clouds high up in the skies. Lightning danced along the clouds in the distance. It was far enough in that he heard no thunder. The flashes of light made the nearest clouds appear as solid brown shapes moving in multiple directions.

Like a bunch of great brown snakes, twisting and turning around one another.

Ben moved away from the window and made his way out of his room. He heard people as soon as he entered the relatively silent bowels of the school.

Downstairs. The cafeteria, probably.

His instincts proved to be true as he traveled down the stairs.

A group of people had gathered in the cafeteria. They looked up as he entered. Their faces betrayed a nervousness that he felt as well.

"Tea?" Claire asked as Ben approached.

He replied with a smile and a nod. Ben had the strangest feeling that he was helping her and not the other way around.

Probably just glad to keep busy.

"I wonder how John and the others are getting along," Michelle said out loud. "Is this storm going to hit them as well?"

She got a few non-committal grunts in reply. The group preferred silent companionship to conversation.

Ben took his place at a nearby table, joining Mike, who was harboring his own cup of tea. He looked around the cafeteria and was surprised at finding almost everybody there.

Seeking comfort, I suppose ... Just like I am.

The storm drew closer. Ben could hear the wind swirling around the building with a continual noise, which rose from a low moan to a high-pitched howl. Sometimes the wind grew strong enough to rattle the storm shutters. Unconsciously, people crept closer together. Hushed conversations took place at several tables, their volume low as if in fear of drawing the attention and ire of the storm outside.

The first thunder strike caused several people to jump then laugh nervously.

Ben thought he heard something else, though. He frowned and looked at the face of the man across the table from him. Mike must have heard it too, as the veteran tilted his head, his eyebrow raised inquisitively.

"What is that?" somebody else asked. They all listened intently.

Several people gasped in surprise when Q ran in.

"There's a helicopter out there! I think maybe they're looking for a place to land," Q yelled excitedly.

Ben and Mike jumped out of their chairs and were first to leave the cafeteria. They needed a window. The main floor provided no view of the outside world, so they ran upstairs.

They entered the library with several others hot on their tail. Ben spotted Emily heading in their direction from the media room.

They got to the window and looked outside. At first it was impossible to spot the helicopter. Ben could only see dark clouds in a dark sky. Rain slapped the window in inconsistent assaults and further obscured his vision.

"There!" Jack's sharp eyes spotted the object. As if on cue, lightning flashed and lit up the flying vessel.

It was large. Much larger than Ben had expected. It was just about on top of them.

"Wait a second... I know these guys!" Mike pulled away from the window and headed straight toward the back of the library.

Ben followed, catching up to Mike at the roof hatch. "What do you mean?"

Mike started ascending the ladder toward the roof access. He laughed. "These are the good guys! It's Boston Frankie and his buddy, the chocolate bar!"

That only served to confuse Ben. He glanced at Emily. They shared an unspoken signal.

"If they were friendly," Emily said, giving voice to her suspicion. "How come they haven't tried to raise us on the radio?"

"Yeah. I don't like it," Ben agreed. Mike had already flipped the hatch and was out of earshot.

"I'm going up there for a closer look," Emily stated as she walked toward the ladder leading to the roof. Mike was up there already. She followed, but not before grabbing a rifle.

Ben thought about it for a moment before turning back. Ethan and several others passed him without a second look, intent upon the roof hatch.

Something's not right.

Ben rushed out of the library and ran down the stairs.

The helicopter hovered in the air, relatively steady despite the stormy conditions. Kevin made his way down to the open side door. Frankie and Johnny had gotten to their feet thirty seconds earlier, and Kevin could see the two Marines working on the fastenings that held their load secure.

"We've got movement on the roof," the voice said in Kevin's ear.

He got to the doorway and steadied himself against the fuselage with one hand while squinting into the heavy rains. One look told him that, indeed, a person had climbed out of an open hatch and was standing on the roof.

"I think he thinks we're friendlies."

Sure enough, the fool stood in plain sight, waving with both arms.

Kevin instinctively reached for his rifle. He held up his hand to the two Marines, who were maneuvering the first barrel closer to the door.

"Hold on with those barrels for a minute," Kevin ordered, as he checked the rifle and chambered a round. Next, he pushed the talk to button on his mic. "Hold her steady right here for a minute, Captain Michael. I'd like to deliver a personal message first."

He gingerly let go of the fuselage and tested his balance. Confident that he was not going to lose his footing, he raised the rifle sights to his eye.

"And I will strike down upon thee, with great vengeance," Kevin said softly as his finger found the trigger.

The wind blew past the open ceiling hatch, causing an eerie howl. Ethan closed in on the ladder, despite the protestations of his mom.

"No, Ethan! Don't go out there!" Rachel reached for Ethan's arm, missed, and tried a second time.

Ethan jumped away from her clutching grasp. "Mom. Chill out!"

"It could be dangerous, Ethan."

"Come on, Mom. Emily and Mike are already up there, and nothing has happened. Chris—" He motioned for his sister, who stepped in and gently pulled their mother away.

Without looking back, Ethan climbed the ladder. The wind and rain slapped at his face as he reached the top of the ladder and poked his head out. He saw Mike standing a few feet away, waving at a huge helicopter.

BLAM

The shot sounded clear above the storm. Ethan flinched. When he opened his eyes again, Mike was gone.

"Mike!" He heard Emily yell, somewhere to his right.

"Got him!" Kevin pumped his fist as he saw his target crash to his knees and slump over. The target was still moving.

"Ah! Another one!" Kevin yelled in excitement. Another person had poked a head up from the roof hatch and was scrambling onto the roof. "This is too easy," he said under his breath as he raised his rifle to take another shot.

He sighted the second target. "Those who would attempt to poison and destroy my brothers."

Ethan finally saw Mike. Their eyes met as Mike tried to drag himself toward the hatch.

"Geh ih-side," Mike whispered. Ethan had no time to figure out what was happening, as another gunshot rand — this one much louder than the one before.

For one hair-raising moment, Ethan was sure that he had been shot.

Then he looked up to see the helicopter spin and roll wildly.

Ethan thought he heard a scream in the distance and caught the brief flash of something falling from the helicopter before he was violently shoved aside.

"Out of the way!" Bill pushed Ethan and strode forward with the SAW.

He lifted the barrel and shot from the hip. It took a few rounds, but Bill found his mark. Sparks flew from the helicopter. Ethan flinched, expecting the helicopter to explode at any moment. Instead, the flying machine lurched once more and quickly sped away. Bill shot another volley after the retreating helicopter, but to no effect this time.

Ethan was soaked to the bone. He glanced from Bill to Emily, who looked past Ethan with a shocked expression. He followed her gaze to find Mike still crawling toward the roof hatch. Even in the wet and dark, it was clear that he was leaving behind a thick trail of blood.

F lashing lights and alarm claxons overwhelmed the inside of Rocko's cockpit. They had pulled away with all haste, knowing that their time in the air was going to be limited.

Captain John-Michael Dupuis was not about to crash Rocko, though. They'd been through too much together. He figured they could stay airborne for another minute or two, tops.

"Find us a place to land," he ordered his co-pilot. He had to raise his voice to be heard above the alarms.

The helicopter cleared the edge of the city. John-Michael just about felt the buildings dropping away behind them.

"Come on, Daniels. Find me a field." The control was slipping. Rocko needed to land. Now.

"We can land over there." Daniels pointed at an empty farmer's field. It was large enough and clear of obstacles.

"Hold on." John-Michael performed a tight circle around the area. "Johnny, can you spot any movement?"

"Negative, Captain," came the reply after they had circled the field twice. John-Michael looked over at his co-pilot. "What about you, DeAndre? See anything?"

The co-pilot shook his head.

"Okay. Setting Rocko down."

It was not a moment too soon, as another claxon joined the alarms. This one generally preceded a crash. John-Michael wrestled with the yoke and got Rocko into position before lowering the bird faster than usual.

They bounced once, a short, two-foot hop before the giant helicopter settled on the tall grass. DeAndre was first to move. He undid his seat belt, ripped off his helmet, and hastened through the opening leading to the back. John-Michael followed his co-pilot, rubbing his neck from the impact.

What he saw was shocking. Several barrels lay on their sides. One of them had cracked, and fluid leaked freely from it.

It took him another moment to find Johnny. The Marine knelt near the back of the fuselage over something. John-Michael approached quickly, and his fear was confirmed a short moment later. It was the prone body of Frankie. There was no sign of Paladin Kevin.

"What the fuck happened here?" DeAndre asked as he approached the Marine.

Johnny lifted his eyes from the man at his feet. His face was a mask of rage. "I should be asking you that."

"Take it easy, Sword Johnny." John-Michael approached behind his co-pilot. "Somebody on that rooftop got lucky. They shot the FLIR camera. Our helmets"—he lifted his for Johnny to see—"were fucked. We were totally blinded."

"Yeah." DeAndre added, "I'm still seeing a starburst. It was a miracle that we managed to get out of that roll." His eyes drifted to Frankie's body. "We were lucky not to go down."

"Not that lucky," Johnny said, his back still to DeAndre.

"What happened to Frankie?"

Johnny looked up at the captain he clearly despised. "Your little maneuver happened to him." His gaze returned to Frankie. John-Michael looked over his shoulder. Frankie seemed unharmed, except for looking cross-eyed. John-Michael frowned and leaned in for a closer inspection.

Sword Frankie McLellan was definitely dead. It took John-Michael a moment to realize that his helmet was cracked.

Crushed, John-Michael realized.

"Them barrels were loose as we were preparing to dump 'em on the school. But the paladin wanted to take a few pot-shots. Then all hell broke loose. It's a miracle that more of these barrels didn't bust open." Johnny put his hand on his dead comrade's chest. "Poor Frankie got his noggin' smashed."

He looked at John-Michael. His upturned face wore a strangely bemused expression.

"You'se also dumped our paladin out the door."

"Oh shit!" DeAndre looked around as if noticing the absence of the paladin for the first time, then turned to his captain. "Should we go back?"

"No," Johnny and John-Michael replied at the same time, albeit for different reasons. Johnny allowed his senior to speak.

"We have to fix at least one fuel leak and check on that hydraulic issue before we get Rocko back in the air."

"Besides," Johnny added, "our paladin would not have survived that fall."

John-Michael nodded. "At any rate, it would be better for us if he didn't."

The three men stared at each other silently for a moment.

"This is some freakin' mess we got," Johnny said as he got back to his feet. Nobody disagreed with that comment.

John-Michael turned away from the other two. "Let's get Rocko patched up and get the hell out of here." Nobody disagreed with that comment, either.

"**W**atch his head!" Joe called up irritably. Several steps behind him, Keith, Jack and Sarah struggled to carry the wounded man. They left a trail of blood behind.

Shelley met them at the door to the clinic. "Table is ready," she told Joe. "Go get scrubbed up."

Joe nodded and hurried to the second office to get ready.

"Put him in here." Shelley directed Keith and the others. "Place him on the table."

She watched as they carried Mike past her and into the room. Mike still had some color to his face, and even tried to smile at her. "I'll be all right."

Shelley wasn't convinced.

They laid Mike on the table as Shelley nodded her thanks. Keith and Jack were out the door in a heartbeat, calling out support to their wounded friend as they left. Sarah had not moved at all, though. The woman's eyes were on her own blood-covered hands.

Christine showed up then. She gently steered Sarah toward the exit. "You've done everything you can. Go get cleaned up now." She ushered the other woman out of the door and closed it.

Shelley was already working on Mike. Joe had not returned yet, so she asked Christine to help.

"Roll him onto his side," Shelley instructed Christine. She had already seen that he had been shot in his torso. She felt for his pulse with one hand, using the other to lift Mike's shirt.

There. The entry wound was high up in the abdominal cavity, but just below the rib cage.

She leaned over Mike's body to spot the exit wound. It was right above the pelvic bone.

Joe entered the room at that moment. "Shelley?"

"Pulse is good. The entry and exit wounds are clean and not pumping blood." She had another look, watching for the color of the blood that slowly seeped through the wounds. "I don't think that the bullet hit the liver."

Joe nodded. "Good." He looked down and met Mike's eyes. "That's a good thing."

Mike forced a grin despite his pain. "See? I told you I was fine."

Joe's expression turned serious.

"Let's have a closer look."

An hour later, Joe washed up and left Mike under the watchful eye of Shelley. He walked out of their improvised O.R. to find his son sitting in on the bench across the hallway. Ethan jumped to his feet as soon as he saw his father.

"Dad. How is he?"

"Hey, son. I think he might be in luck." He could see the agitation on his son's face. "Are you okay?"

Ethan nodded. "Yeah." He frowned. "Mike thought they were friendly..."

"Yeah. He told me that it was the same helicopter used to evacuate their group from the safe zone."

Ethan nodded knowingly. "Breanne told the rest of us about it." He shook his head. "Maybe it wasn't the same guys..."

Joe could see that something else was bothering his son. "What's wrong?"

Ethan's eyes started to shimmer. "It just... It happened right in front of me." He was going to say more, but his father had already wrapped him up in a big bear hug.

Joe held his son for a long moment. He knew Ethan well and released him once he felt the boy stiffen slightly. Ethan gave his father a thankful smile and wiped his face.

"Where is everybody?"

"Most of them are waiting in the cafeteria. I— I wanted to be the first to find out."

They walked to the cafeteria together. The buzz quieted down instantly as Joe walked in. He took a few steps into the room before addressing the crowd.

"Mike seems to be doing well," he started.

"See? I told you he'd be fine." Q punched Steve in the shoulder softly.

"Hold on, now." Joe put up his hand. "He's not out of the woods yet. I couldn't find any damage to his organs, so we flushed the wound and I stitched him up."

The faces turned serious and Joe was relieved that people seemed to understand the severity of the situation. "We need to wait and see if he heals okay. He's on antibiotics and painkillers and is resting. The next twenty-four hours are critical."

"Should we go out there and find the guy that fell from the helicopter?" Ethan asked.

"Maybe we should wait until morning. It's still bucketing down out there," Emily suggested. She had received a lot of praise for her quick thinking as she had snuck onto the roof with a rifle. Somehow, her single shot had nearly taken out the helicopter. She told people that she thought she'd missed the helicopter altogether and suggested that it was Bill with the SAW that had saved their butts. There was no denying the effect of her shot though, as the helicopter had rolled dangerously just after she'd fired.

"Good idea. It will be hard to spot other dangers out there in this weather," Joe said.

Just then, Jack had an observation.

"Hey. Has anybody seen Ben?"

Paladin Kevin Wallace stared unseeingly at the purple and dark-gray skies above him. Rain washed down upon his face, the droplets splashing into his open eyes and half-open mouth. His head rested at an odd angle, as did his legs. He had died on impact with the pavement.

Ben stood over the body and observed his former leader dispassionately. He knew that he didn't have much time, so quickly retreated to a thick stand of bushes. He crawled underneath the low-hanging branches and positioned himself. It might be a while, but he was sure that somebody was going to come check on the body.

This was this person he was after.

Ben had known something was up. He had run down to the armory to grab a gun and was just on his way up when the shooting had started. Through a window he'd watched as something sparked and the helicopter veered wildly, almost rolling completely onto its side. He also saw the man fall, although he had no idea who it was at the time. Ben determined that the helicopter was leaving and knew that his window of opportunity was limited.

He sprinted back down the stairs to the gym and out of the back door. The darkened sky and heavy rain provided great cover as he ran in a low crouch straight to the nearest fence, hopped it, and worked his way to the location where he had seen the man fall.

He recognized the dead man instantly. He had met the paladin several times during his optio training. This was not important to him, though. He knew that somebody else would come calling soon.

There was an optio out there. This optio would have observed the school for some time. That was the way the order operated.

The rain continued to come down in sheets, sometimes so heavy that it limited Ben's vision down to less than a hundred feet. It worked its way through the bush he was hiding under, soaking him from above and below at the same time. Minutes passed, and Ben regretted his choice of leaving the Ren without properly gearing up. He relied on his mental training and shut out the discomfort.

Twenty minutes later, Ben started to have his doubts.

There had to be another optio out there.

Think, Ben. What would you do? That train of thought comforted him. Ben would have carefully worked his way over to the area and lain low for a while in case there was an ambush waiting for him.

Just like there is now.

No more than a minute later, he spotted movement. Slowly the person stumbled into view. To his dismay, it was a zombie.

Shit. What if it finds me? He felt his carbine, secure and dry under his own body. He didn't want to use the weapon though, as it would surely scare off the other optio.

The zombie was joined by a second, and a third. They made their way in stops and starts toward the spot where Kevin Wallace lay dead.

Or are they heading toward me? Ben suddenly realized that he lay exactly on the opposite side of the dead paladin and directly in the path of the zombies. He could make out the face of the nearest one now, and it seemed to be looking right at him.

POP. One of the zombies in the back of the bunch collapsed to the ground, even as the other two veered to the side.

POP—POP—POP. Ben saw a shape detach itself from a house about fifty feet from where he lay and take measured steps toward the zombies. One of the zombies shuddered under the impacts but kept coming.

Ben noted the black-clad figure and the way he moved.

Optio. Male. Using a silencer. Ben recognized the sound, knowing all too well that it was still likely to be heard above the din of the storm.

POP. Another zombie fell backwards as the latest shot was true. The remaining zombie lurched forward, picking up speed. The optio stopped and aimed carefully. With another *POP*, it went down, falling at the feet of the person.

Quick, now. Ben found himself urging the optio on.

The optio rushed over to Paladin Kevin's corpse and knelt over the fallen leader. Ben couldn't make out what the man was doing, but it looked like he was rummaging through the dead man's pockets.

Ben watched as the optio straightened up suddenly and raised his rifle once more, aiming to his left.

POP.

The optio searched Paladin Kevin's body for another few seconds. He must have found what he was looking for, as he got to his feet and scanned the area. Ben dropped his face to the wet dirt in front of him, hoping to remain undetected. He waited for several seconds, then slowly lifted his face. Streaks of dirt washed down his forehead and cheeks.

Good. The man was on the move again.

Time to go.

John-Michael and DeAndre went through the start-up sequence.

"Hydraulic pressure is holding. Fuel okay." The final checks had all passed. It looked like Rocko was patched up.

Still, John-Michael was not going to take any chances. He lifted off and hovered a few feet in the air before setting Rocko back down on terra firma.

DeAndre gave him a thumbs up. John-Michael reached for his mic.

"Johnny — you still read me?"

"Yessir!" The response came back with the heavy crackle of static.

"We're taking off. Last chance to change your mind." He knew what the answer was going to be, though.

"Nope! I got something to set right."

John-Michael nodded. He looked over at DeAndre, who shrugged.

"Good luck. Summuh be with you, Sword."

"Ah. To be honest, Frankie and me, we never really bought into Summuh and all of that."

It was the kind of heretic talk that would get somebody kicked out of the order — or worse. DeAndre wore an expression of shock. This time it was the Captain who shrugged.

"Very well, Johnny. Go get your vengeance." John-Michael clicked his mic off. Out of the corner of his eye he could see DeAndre. It looked like his co-pilot wanted to say something.

John-Michael forestalled any comment with a raised hand. "Let it go, Dee. The guy is on a suicide mission." He had to yell at DeAndre over the noise of Rocko.

He turned his mic back on. "Let's get the fuck out of here. Find me the nearest base where we can set down and do repairs. I'm not convinced that we patched all the holes in Rocko."

To his credit, DeAndre answered without the slightest hesitation. "Affirmative, Captain."

P OP. The sound of the silenced pistol barely reached Ben's ears in the heavy rain. The thunder and lightning had lessened somewhat, but Ben didn't need the flashes of light to see his quarry at work. He was only three houses down and across the street.

POP—POP. Another zombie dropped to the ground in front of the house. The optio was dispatching undead with cool efficiency.

He's a good shot, Ben had to admit. He froze and dropped his gaze to the ground as the optio stared in his direction. From his peripheral vision he could see the man step back into the house and close the door.

Ben released the breath he was holding.

He had been staking out the house for the last fifteen minutes. The challenge was how to get in there undetected to neutralize his target. The events of the past minute had given him an idea.

Somehow, the zombies knew that this guy was in there. Several corpses lying around the house and sidewalk let Ben know these weren't the first visitors he'd received. He'd use the next one as a distraction.

Ben crept closer, first crossing the street to avoid being seen. He got to the neighbor's house and waited inside the frame of the front door. He was soaked to the bone but paid no mind to it.

His patience was rewarded about ten minutes later. A lone zombie was ambling along the road. Ben watched the creature approach, noting skinny gray legs and a tank top.

She died in bed.

She moved in a somewhat ungainly manner, weaving along the width of the road. For a moment Ben thought she might pass by his target house altogether. He shifted nervously on his feet, looking down as his foot touched something. It was a parcel. Delivered but never received. He bent down and picked up the parcel. It was just larger than his hand and had some good weight to it. Without hesitation, he stepped out of cover and launched the parcel into the neighbor's yard. It landed with a crack and continued to make noise as it rolled.

His action had the desired effect. The zombie made a beeline for the house. Ben quickly stepped out and made his way toward the back yard.

He waited at the fence for a noise and was rewarded a moment later as he heard a weak slapping sound. The zombie had reached the house. He lifted himself over the fence and quickly approached the back door, even as he heard movement inside the house.

The room was completely dark, except for the gray light that shot in through the open door. That gray beam barely reached halfway into the room, where it illuminated a shape on the ground.

Ben watched from the total darkness of a corner in the room as the optio opened his eyes. First slowly, carefully. Then shooting wide open in shock and realization. The man had been stripped down to his underwear and was lying on his side in the room. His feet were tied together at the ankles and his hands secured behind his back. He was also gagged. Ben watched the man struggle briefly against his bonds.

Ben had waited for this moment. He wanted to see if the optio had any surprises in store. They had been taught to be utterly resourceful, after all.

But this guy just struggled for a few more seconds and then seemed to give up.

Time to act.

"I'm going to sit you up. Don't try anything," Ben instructed, moving out of the corner of the room.

The man stiffened then craned his neck to see who spoke.

His eyes were wide with fear. He was smart enough not to resist as Ben lifted him into a sitting position and stepped back to the corner he'd come from. A moment later Ben returned, carrying a wooden chair and sitting across from his captive without another word.

They faced each other for a long moment. Ben was surprised when recognition crept into his captive's eyes. He started to mumble something into his gag.

"Don't say anything yet," Ben said. "Let me do the talking."

The optio nodded.

"My name is Benjamin Brown. I was an optio, in service to Brenin of the Rosae Crucis."

The gagged man nodded again. He started to mumble something, then stopped as he saw the warning in Ben's expression.

"I have seen what the Order has done to this world, to countless innocent people, and it made me sick." For a moment, the man was silent. He even cocked his head slightly, as if maybe he had misunderstood. "What Brenin has done is pure evil. I have switched my allegiance to the survivors. I have spoken to them. I know them, as I knew others. They are innocent souls. Now I protect them. Against the Order, if I have to."

The man started to shake his head and mumble again, but Ben lifted his index finger in reproach. The optio stopped moving and listened.

"I believe in the core values of the Order. But I also believe that we were misled by our leadership. Their designs are not to live in harmony... They just want to rule. They wanted a new order. This time, with them on top."

He was on a roll now and talked right over the mumbling.

"They want to enslave the common people that remain. How is that different from those same corporations and governments we were taught to despise? The few lucky survivors are just normal people. Some are ignorant, some are pompous... But none of them are evil. We're the evil ones."

The captive stopped trying to interrupt and sat in silence. This suited Ben, as he had more to say.

"We've committed the devil's work in the guise of saving the world. I've seen the results. Little children, suffering unfathomable pain. Lying in fetal positions as their insides get torn apart."

Ben shook his head ever so slightly, his eyes never leaving the other optio's. "I made friends. People I came to respect and love. I watched some of them die. I thought about their families, and their futures ... All gone."

Ben felt himself getting upset. He took a breath.

"I'll take off your gag in a moment. But understand this: I am no longer part of the Order."

With that, he got up, stepped around his captive, and loosened the gag. The handkerchief dropped around the optio's neck, and the man spat out the ball. He watched it roll away into the dark corner of the room.

"Huh. A dog's squeaky ball. Interesting choice," he said as he worked his jaw.

"You use what you can."

The optio nodded. Ben walked back to his chair and took a seat. "What's your name?"

"Philip." Philip winced as he turned his head this way and that. "Man, you really rang my bell."

"Philip," Ben repeated, ignoring the second comment. "What was your mission, Optio Philip?"

"Ha. Right to the point, eh?" Philip replied with a grin. Ben did not return it.

"Okay. That's fine. I was ordered to come to this location and observe the school. Apparently, there were some bad guys in there who ambushed one of our Captains and his team."

Philip cast a sideways glance toward Ben and pursed his lips. "They told me that you had also been killed. Guess they didn't get all their facts straight."

"Captain Shaw and his men attacked those people. I know that because I was supposed to support his raid. He executed their leader."

Philip merely nodded.

"Tell me more about your mission. About that helicopter."

"Not much to say, really. They loaded up the helo with explosives or something. They were going to bomb the school. I was in my forward position overlooking the front entrance. My order was to observe and pick off any stragglers." Philip looked angry. "But something went wrong. Did you know that our paladin, Kevin Fucking Wallace himself, was on that helo? Did you know that he was shot down, and is lying a few hundred yards away?"

"Yes."

"Of course you knew that. You were probably the one that shot him down." His eyes threw daggers at his captor.

"He wasn't shot. He fell." The excuse sounded weak.

"Dead is dead," was Philip's reply. He thought about that for a second, then started to smile. He chuckled. "Ha. 'Dead is dead.'

Not anymore, it isn't." He continued before Ben could respond, "I've seen plenty of the undead, Ben. I must have killed hundreds of them by now. I've killed some living folks, too. They got in the way. I had missions to complete." He looked up at Ben in defiance. "There are thousands of people in the Order. Those people rely on us. I happily do the things I do, for them."

"There are hundreds of thousands of survivors out there. Maybe millions. You tell me where Summuh ordained that all others should live in servitude to Rosae Crucis."

Philip shrugged. "Brenin knows these things. It's not for me"—he narrowed his eyes—"or *you* to question his decrees."

Ben regarded the optio for a moment. His own eyes narrowed, as he noticed the bound man fidget with his hands. "I guess that's where you and I differ, Philip. I interpret the testaments differently than you. In my opinion, we were always meant to question."

Philip started to argue, but Ben stopped him. "I can see that we are not going to agree on these things, Philip. I have more questions for you."

"Sure." Philip grimaced in derision. "And what happens after I answer your question? We both know the answer to that."

Ben nodded. "Yeah, that thought has occurred to me, Philip. I don't suppose you will take my word that I will set you free?"

Just then, an odd thing happened. Philip's face lit up ever so slightly. "I'll tell you what. Ask your questions. I will answer what I can."

"Okay." Ben reached into his pocket. He withdrew a large keyring with several plastic cards attached. "I saw you take this off the paladin's corpse. What are these?"

"Ah, so you did follow me." Philip shook his head slightly. "I had a feeling." He looked at the objects dangling from the ring. "Those are Kevin Wallace's personal set of keys. I received an order to retrieve them. My understanding is that he had access to any place in PD. He even had access to Brenin's private quarters."

"PD. What's that? The Order's main base?"

Philip frowned at Ben. "Did you live under a rock or something? Yes. PD is short for *Primary Domicile*."

The answer confused Ben.

Why wasn't I privy to this information? Did they know that I was going to turn on them?

"Hey Ben," Philip's voice drew him out of his reflection. "Do you think I could have some water?"

Ben considered for a moment. "Okay. Don't try anything." He stood up.

Philip laughed. "What do you think I'm going to do? He wiggled a little bit to emphasize his bonds. Ben nodded and stepped out of the room.

"When you get back, I'll tell you where to find PD. And I'll tell you something else. Something I suspect, anyway. It will blow your mind." Philip's disembodied voice followed Ben to the kitchen. He found a coffee mug and filled it with water from the tap.

He walked back down the hall and to the room. Ben took one step into the room and noticed that his chair was gone. In the next split second, he saw the chair swinging at his face.

Ben lifted his arms just in time to cushion the blow. Even then, he felt as much as heard the bone crack in his forearm. He held on to the legs of the chair and pulled, despite the sharp pain. Philip hopped forward, his ankles still tied together. He had somehow freed his hands, though.

The two struggled, the chair between them. Ben stepped to the side and rotated, never releasing the chair. Philip was now half turned away. He sprang at Ben, intending to knock his opponent to the ground. Ben moved backwards with the chair still between them, then he overbalanced and went down. Philip also lost his balance and fell onto his side.

Ben lay behind Philip now, the remnants of the chair still between the two combatants. Philip had bent forward and seemed to be sawing at the bonds around his ankles. Ben saw the handkerchief that had been used to hold the gag in place. It was still tied around Philip's neck.

He didn't think. He lunged forward and pulled on the cloth, hoping that it wouldn't rip. It didn't, and Philip gave a surprised shout as his head was pulled back.

They both lay on their sides, Ben pulling on the handkerchief while Philip still tried to get away.

Ben got his hand further through the loop and leveraged his position to twist the cloth and pull it tight. The reaction was instant, as Philip stopped pushing forward and straightened up instead. Ben let himself fall back, using the moment of slack to tighten his grip on the handkerchief. His adversary started to groan in distress.

Philip reached behind him with his right hand, and Ben felt a slight pull on this arm, followed by another pull along his side. Whatever Philip was trying wasn't working for him, so he swung a hand over his shoulder and tried to reach Ben's face. Ben dropped his head, just as Philip swung.

Something sharp sliced his scalp. Philip swung a second time and Ben felt a cut open from the top of his head to his hairline. He redoubled his efforts, the material straining in his hands even as blood gushed over his face.

Philip wheezed. He swung one more time, hard. Something stabbed Ben's skull, digging into the bone.

That was the turning point of the fight, though. The object slipped out of Philip's hand and clattered to the ground, leaving the optio weaponless.

Ben put all his energy into keeping the handkerchief tight around Philip's throat. Philip's actions became more erratic. He tried to buck off Ben a couple of times, but Ben held on. Blood had run into his eyes, blinding him.

Philip made his last, pitiful noises as he clawed at the handkerchief. His actions became weaker, and eventually his hands dropped. The sharp tang of urine rose to Ben's nostrils, and finally the Optio stopped struggling. Even then, Ben kept the pressure on. He didn't know how long he stayed in that position, but eventually he released his grip.

Ben grunted in pain as he experienced a mighty cramp in his hand.

He wiped his eyes and checked on Philip. The Optio was dead, his eyes bulged out and the whites red with burst blood vessels. Ben struggled to his feet and made his way to the kitchen. He spent the next few minutes trying to wash all the blood out of his face. He was unable to stop the bleeding in his skull, so wrapped a towel around his head instead.

He returned to the room and found the object that had caused his injuries. A razor blade lay a few feet away. Philip's hand was badly damaged as well, as several fingers were sliced to the bone or beyond. The acts of desperation.

"Of course." Ben spoke softly to the corpse at his feet. "The old 'razor blade in the seam of my underwear' trick." He shook his head sadly. "I would have let you go."

He felt the keycards in his pocket. They wouldn't do him any good without knowing the location of this PD place. He also wondered at the cryptic words Philip called out to him as he was getting water.

Something that would blow my mind.

A thin line of blood had started to leak through the edge of the towel. It ran down his temple and to his cheek before Ben grew aware and wiped it away with the back of his hand.

Seeing the blood stirred him into action. He had to go find this forward location that Philip had mentioned. He was sure that it would be one of the houses directly opposite the school's main entrance.

That's where he would have set up.

Ben turned and strode out of the room, leaving Philip's corpse lying in his own piss.

Chapter 13

Joe

November 17, 10:45 P.M., The Ren.

Joe was tired. Exhausted. Even the storm seemed to have run out of energy. The wind at times still buffeted the side of the school and rattled the storm shutters, but it was nowhere near as constant and violent as a couple of hours ago. Joe imagined that the storm was an infant — occasionally bursting out in throes of complaint and rebellion even as it was slowly lulled to sleep.

Joe would have loved to be lulled to sleep right now. But he simply could not allow himself to go to bed just yet. Besides, his body might be tired, yet his mind was anything but restful.

He wasn't the only one. Joe looked around and noted that only a few residents of the Ren had retreated from the cafeteria. He counted over half a dozen people sitting at the tables around him.

He saw the rifles laid out on the tables nearest the cafeteria exit. *It's no wonder nobody can sleep. We're expecting a war.*

Joe sipped the dregs of the cold tea in his cup. More out of habit and to keep his hands busy than anything else. He recounted the events of the evening as he swallowed the cold brew.

He'd gone back to check on Mike every half hour or so. It seemed unnecessary now, considering Mike was under the constant watchful eye of Shelley. Mike had been in good spirits, if that was anything to judge by. He had been regaling Shelley with stories about his youth and family, only complaining occasionally about the pain. The injured man had finally drifted off to a painkiller-induced sleep about an hour ago.

Mike was doing exceptionally well, it seemed. Joe, on the other hand, kept having those nagging doubts.

What if the bullet nicked an artery? No. We would have detected the blood flow.

What if the bullet shattered? The exit wound looked clean, though.

What if the wound wasn't cleaned properly? You checked four or five times before closing him up. All looked and smelled fine.

What if... Every possible scenario played through Joe's mind. He was going though all scenarios once again when Emily's voice startled him.

"May we sit?" Emily asked. Bill stood at her side.

"Huh? Yeah, sure."

They sat across from Joe. Their expressions were serious.

"What's wrong?"

Emily and Bill shared a glance before Emily spoke up. "Ben is gone."

That surprised Joe. "What?"

"We didn't want to raise any alarms, but yeah — Ben is not here anymore. We've searched the school, and best we can tell is that he slipped out sometime during the commotion."

Joe frowned and exhaled half a growl. "Do you think he was in on this? The timing was interesting — right when half our fighters are gone..."

Emily shook her head at once. Bill followed suit but seemed less certain. "No, mate." The English woman replied. "Ben's a good bloke. My guess is that he has gone out there to scout."

"Then why didn't he say anything?" Joe wanted to believe it, but he'd also seen where blind trust landed people.

Emily screwed up her face. "Maybe he didn't have time." She shook her head. "No, I'm sure he didn't betray us. He is on our side."

"I hope you're right." Joe suddenly looked up with alarm in his eyes. "What if they are preparing another assault?"

"I don't think so, Joe," Emily said. "Not this quickly. Whatever they had planned went tits up. I doubt that they had a backup plan. We've doubled the watch. If they do show up, we'll be ready. Now, as far as Ben is concerned, my guess is that he went out to find that bloke that fell."

They heard a disturbance at the cafeteria door and looked over. Ethan ran in. Several people jumped to their feet, ready for action. Ethan scanned the room until he spotted his father.

He made a beeline for Joe. "We've spotted somebody approaching from the front of the school. The person is taking the time to seal the gate behind him. He must have spotted me because he waved..."

"Ben." Emily was up from her seat in a flash.

Joe and Bill followed a moment later, but not before sharing a look and gesturing toward the table of rifles.

I t did turn out to be Ben.

He looked like a ghoul, all pale and covered in blood. He carried a powerful-looking sniper rifle, which he dropped unceremoniously as soon as he got inside the building. Ben was shaking on his feet and almost collapsed. Emily and Joe immediately helped him to the clinic.

"Are we about to be under attack?" Joe asked as he half-carried the wounded man down the hall.

"No. There are no others..." It was barely more than a whisper, but loud enough for Bill to hear. The soldier turned away at once. Joe heard him reassure the other residents.

Joe got Ben into the clinic. Shelley helped clean up the wounds, and several minutes later Joe started stitching him up.

"How's Mike?" Ben's voice sounded weak and far away.

Shit. He's lost a lot of blood. Keep him conscious.

"Mike is doing good. We won't know for certain until the morning, though."

Keep him talking. Joe thought of other things to say.

"You're lucky that I'm used to stitching up animals," Joe stated in a steady voice as he worked. "How's that?" Ben grimaced when the needle penetrated his scalp yet again.

"The hair. Most GPs would struggle with this mess."

"Ah." Ben was silent for a moment. "So, it's a mess up there?"

Joe didn't answer. It was a mess.

For over an hour, he worked on the wounded man's head. He'd enlisted Christine to keep Ben engaged so that he could concentrate on his work. Christine had brought some drinks and snacks with her as well, which seemed to help. Ben regained some color.

"I lost count ... Damn!" Joe berated himself when he was done. He held up a mirror so that Ben could see for himself, but the area was so covered in iodine, blood, and hair that it was hard to tell.

"At least seventy stitches." Joe's expression went from proud to thoughtful. "You're going to have quite a headache."

They weren't done yet. Joe thanked his daughter and sent her on her way. It was Shelley's turn to get involved.

"This thing is awesome." Joe patted the ultrasound machine as Shelley applied gel to Ben's arm. "It's got a setting for fracture sonography, which means we can check for bone fractures."

Ben didn't seem quite as excited about the technology, and Shelley was careful not to put too much pressure on the injured arm as she worked.

"There," she said about a minute into the session. The image on the screen meant little to Ben, but Shelley explained. "You've got a fractured ulna. It's hairline. I can't tell if it's a complete break. I think it is..." Shelley made a sympathetic face.

She turned to Joe. "Can you grab the SAM splint for me? It should be in the top drawer."

"Sam splint, Sam splint..." Joe rummaged through the drawer. "Never heard of the stuff. Oh. Found it." He turned back to the nurse. "Eighteen inches?"

She nodded and was applying the tape-like substance a few minutes later. She spoke as she worked.

"I'm applying an ulnar gutter splint," she said as she started bending the material. "This stuff gains rigidity as you bend it. It's pretty cool stuff." Shelley treated Ben to a lopsided grin. "The military always has the coolest stuff. But why the camouflage color scheme?" She held up the olive drab green tape for Ben to see.

The patient's head was covered in bandaging when he was finally released from the clinic. It gave him the appearance of a white, turbaned Sikh. He had also received painkillers, for which he must have been grateful. From the looks of him, the headache had well and truly started.

Both Joe and the wounded man longed for rest, but they agreed they had to do something else first. Ben needed to explain his actions. They walked into the cafeteria. Emily, Bill, Keith, and Melissa were there to listen to what Ben had to say. Joe was surprised that anybody was still up.

It must be two a.m. He grunted as he lowered himself into a seat, feeling physical and mental exhaustion.

"How's Mike?" Emily asked.

"Resting. He's looking good, though."

"Ben, tell us what happened." Melissa's expression was stern.

Ben nodded. "I knew that there would be an Optio out there. There was no way they organized this attack without coordination and communication. I knew that my best chance to catch this optio would be when I saw the guy fall and the helicopter retreat."

He gratefully accepted a cup of tea from Emily and took a careful sip of the steaming hot liquid.

"What, no milk?" He smiled at the British woman.

"All out, mate."

He took another sip, then placed the cup on the table in front of him, seeing the disapproving faces around him.

"Sorry. It's been a rough evening." At least he got a couple of the stern masks to crack at that.

"The guy who fell — he was a big shot in the order. His name was Kevin Wallace. His title was paladin." He turned somber.

"What?" Melissa leaned forward. "What are you thinking, Ben?"

"I'm thinking that we just started a war..."

Chapter 14

Jonas

November 17, 11:30 P.M., Primary Domicile

They clutched their jackets and hats against the manmade tornado and watched the helicopter lower itself toward the improvised landing pad.

Sage Jonas looked at his two companions. Sage Peter Torrance and Sage Wang Wei shielded their faces from the driving winds and the sting of the raindrops. There was no denying they were excited; all three of them were.

Paladin Kevin Wallace was gone. Fell out of the helicopter.

Fell from the sky. Jonas had a sudden vision of Icarus, the Greek mythological legend who had melted his wings by flying too close to the sun.

You sought personal glory and vengeance, Kevin. See where it got you?

He glanced at his companions. Jonas knew that neither was sad about the paladin's demise, although they wouldn't openly admit it.

As a matter of fact, they were quite relieved.

"His behavior was getting more erratic with every day that passed," Sage Wang had said just ten minutes ago as the three men strode through the compound on their way to meet the helicopter.

He'd said that under his breath, so that only the other two sages heard him. Sage Peter agreed wholeheartedly with that statement, showing none of the discretion that the Asian man had displayed.

"That's right! One minute he'd be all pleasant, and the next he'd be in a rage. He was unstable." The man talked excitedly, not even noticing heads turn their way as they passed.

"He was right about the spy, though," he added. "Inquisitor Stanley has had his hands full..."

"Well, he is gone now. This could be a chance for ... us." Jonas caught the slight hesitation in Wang's statement.

He means to take the title for himself.

They stepped outside into the cold, wet night and waited.

"They're down," Peter announced, breaking Jonas out of his reverie. The massive helicopter had indeed landed, its blades already slowing down from an invisible blur to distinguishable metallic scythes.

The three sages remained rooted to the spot, unwilling to near the aggressive looking beast. A few seconds later, the first man jumped out of the open hatch. He ordered some men into the chopper, then saw the three waiting sages and approached.

"Sages." Captain John-Michael Dupuis nodded in greeting.

"Captain Michael." Jonas took the lead. "Please explain what happened. We understand that Paladin Kevin has fallen."

"John-Michael. It's Captain John-Michael."

"Sorry." Jonas looked appropriately embarrassed. "John-Michael. Paladin Kevin called you Michael..."

"He did." John-Michael said no more.

"He fell?" Jonas prompted.

"Yup." Sword DeAndre had walked up to the group. He looked unimpressed. Bored, even.

"He fell," John-Michael confirmed. "He wanted to take some personal revenge. Changed the plan at the last minute and started shooting those civies." Jonas watched as Captain John-Michael shared a look with his crew member before returning his gaze to the Sages.

"He took a risk and paid for it. He also compromised the mission and cost the life of one of our crew."

As if on cue, the men John-Michael had ordered into the helicopter got out carrying a burden.

"Sword Frankie is no more. Guess I won't be getting called an 'emu' anymore..." Jonas couldn't tell if Captain Michael was sad or elated.

"One of us will have to inform Brenin of Paladin Kevin's demise," Sage Wang said.

Sage Peter chewed his lip for a moment. "I'll do it. He's pissed at me already." He shook his head and turned to leave.

"Captain John-Michael..." Peter hesitated as Wang spoke. "You had a crew of four men plus the Paladin when you set out. I only see two of you now... It appears one more member of your crew is missing?"

John-Michael snorted. "Yeah. Sword Johnny."

He looked down at the ground for a moment before returning his gaze to the Sages. The look in his eyes was one of pride.

"Hershey's gone hunting."

Chapter 15

Tammy

November 18, 7:00 A.M., Barney's Budget Motel and Bar, just
outside of Blue Ridge, Georgia.

The light that leaked in from the edges of the curtains started
to paint the room in shades of gray.

I feel color blind. Tammy thought to herself as she watched the
objects in the motel room. The chair in the corner was clearly visible, as was a desk and the TV that stood upon it. They did indeed
appear colorless. The TV screen looked like a gaping black hole
among its gray surroundings.

It was a black hole. Tammy realized.

I don't even miss it.

She scanned the rest of the room, which was sparse yet clean.
It sure beat the prospect of trying to sleep in some creepy barn —
or worse, the Humvee. Tammy was very pleased when they'd found
the motel last night. It was far enough away from any populated
place to be remote, so they checked it out. It turned out to be completely clear of zombies.

This probably wouldn't have been a bad place to ride out the apocalypse.

The hotel was approximately at the halfway mark to their destination. So far, the trip had been relatively eventless. Probably more
so than she had hoped. Her head had been filled with finding other survivors or rushing past hordes of undead when they'd set out
yesterday morning. The reality couldn't have been further from the
truth. Most roads were empty, especially once they got out of the

city. She had seen the odd humanoid shape in the distance, but Tammy could never be sure if they were living or dead.

A soft sigh coming from the other bed broke up her reverie. Abi was still asleep. Tammy watched the cocooned shape for a moment. She considered going back to sleep as well, but just then her bladder announced itself. For about a minute she tried to ignore the urge and drift back to sleep, but eventually the protestations of her bladder grew too strong.

Mildly frustrated, Tammy sat up and slid off the bed. She picked her way through the room into the bathroom, shutting the door before flicking the light switch. Light bathed the room.

Huh. This place still has power.

Tammy had more pressing matters to take care of. She rushed to the toilet. The feeling of relief when she emptied her bladder was almost enough to compensate for getting up. Almost.

She considered flushing the toilet when she was done, then decided against it. She wasn't sure that there was any running water, plus didn't want to wake her roommate.

She shut off the light and opened the door.

"Heya, Tammy. Good morning." Abi still lay in bed but faced Tammy from the depths of her comforter.

"Oh. Hi. Sorry if I woke you."

"Ah, no problem. It's probably time to get up anyway. Besides, I've got to pee like nobody's business." Abi threw off the blanket and sheets and swung her legs around to sit on the edge of the bed. Tammy couldn't help noticing that her feet were a long way from touching the floor.

"I didn't flush," Tammy stated as Abi hopped out of her bed. "Didn't want to wake you up."

Abi pulled open one of the curtains, allowing some light to flood the room. She turned back to Tammy with a smile. "That's fine. You're talking to an army girl. There's nothing that will gross me out."

Tammy smiled back at the petite woman as she rushed into the bathroom.

A minute and a flush later, Abi reappeared. She had huge grin on her face and a twinkle in her eye.

"You'll never believe this, but not only is there running water — there is hot water."

"No way!" Tammy instantly perked up.

"Yes way. Shower time." Abi grinned. "You go first. I'll grab something to eat."

Tammy wasn't going to argue about it. She was in the bathroom and stripping down before Abi had left the room. She left the bathroom open a crack and yelled out a hurried, "Thanks!" before stepping into the glass enclosure. Tammy heard the door slam shut and forgot about the rest of the world as glorious hot water burst from the shower head.

She luxuriated in the heat for a full minute before reaching for the soap. Tammy thought about the events of the last month as she scrubbed herself clean. She scrubbed hard, wanting to wash the memories away in some ritualistic cleansing event but failing.

Instead, Tammy's mood became somber. She thought about all the people she had lost and cried.

The door opened in the other room and she collected herself. Tammy considered getting out of the shower — but then spotted the shampoo. Without a second thought she reached for the mini bottle.

She was considerate enough to use only half the contents. It was enough. She thought that she heard another sound from the room just as she finished lathering. Her face was covered in suds, but she squinted through one eye.

The bathroom door seemed to be open further than she'd left it.

"Hello?" Her voice broke slightly as she called out.

She hurriedly let the water wash over her eyes and peered out again. The shampoo washed back in almost immediately, but not before she thought she saw the shape of a person in the doorway.

Tammy yelped and almost lost her footing. Somebody was in here with her! She didn't know what to do. She held the glass door closed with one hand while furiously trying to wash the soap from her face and hair.

For a moment, she felt pure panic. An involuntary wail escaped her lips before she finally washed enough soap from her face to open her eyes.

Nothing. There was nobody there.

Stunned, she finished washing the soap from her hair and peered out again.

The bathroom was empty. The door was open slightly wider than she had left it but might have swung open on its own. The bathrobe hanging from the door might have looked like a person.

Tammy turned off the water, shaking her head.

Get yourself together, Tammy. She jumped and let out a grunt as the door to the other room opened.

"It's just me!" Abi called from the other room.

"Ah. Okay," she replied quickly and just a little too loudly. She opened the shower door and reached for a towel.

"Brought you some coffee," Abi said, "and one of these wrapped pastries... Don't know what they put in those, but apparently it's still good!"

Tammy smiled, despite herself. "Just what I need."

Chapter 16

Nancy

November 18, 7:00 A.M.

N ancy took a sip of tea, silently thankful for the stash she had found days ago. She glanced around the room, realizing that she was starting to feel more comfortable in strangers' houses.

She cradled the cup and walked up to the window, hesitating a moment before slowly pulling the curtain aside. She hated these moments, and always imagined coming face to face with a zombie.

Thankfully, there was nothing to see. Just lots of garbage. Last night's storm had upended several garbage cans. All sorts of garbage littered the road and sidewalk. Nancy had to repeatedly steel herself as napkins and plastic bags moved with the blustery wind.

She lifted the cup of tea to her mouth for another sip. She needed the tea to calm her nerves. Especially after the night she had just experienced.

First, that storm had come rolling in a lot faster than she had anticipated. Before she knew it, her long gray hair was fluttering around her head as if she was a banshee crying out her rage. She fought against the strong winds, nearly losing her footing.

Then the rain came. Hard, and in biting sheets. Within a minute she was drenched. She had no time to choose a refuge and bolted toward the first open front door she could see.

She had shut the door behind her, locking out the storm and herself into the utter darkness of an unknown place. Her first reaction was to shudder in a combination of fear and cold.

Nancy had smelled the air and detected rot. It was hard to tell if it was the smell of foodstuffs wasting in kitchen or from a more sinister source.

She slowly crept forward, through the hall and into the open-concept living room/kitchen. The place was empty. Nancy expected the house to be abandoned. Any place with a wide-open front door was abandoned, in her experience.

Outside, the wind dashed around the house in a never-ending howl, from low to high and back to low. Rain hit the front windows in bursts, oddly reminding Nancy of the sizzle of bacon in a grease-filled pan.

The sound masked her own movement. For that she was thankful. She had no desire to get jumped. Nancy put her bag down in the kitchen and pulled the small but sturdy shovel from its strap. She had straightened the head yesterday, so it actually looked like a shovel now. Truth was, she lacked the strength in her old, arthritic fingers to hold down the latch and fold the head back, so she ended up leaving it as is.

Nancy crept toward the stairs, passing by a closed door. She carefully ascended the steps, stopping on the first-floor landing. If anything, the storm sounded even more powerful up here.

One of the bedroom doors rattled, startling Nancy. After a second rattle, she realized that it was the wind. The previous inhabitants of the house must have left a window open.

She opened the door and confirmed her suspicion. The room was used as an office, a desk set up in front of the open window. She spared a moment to observe the laptop and monitor. Icons of a past age, getting soaked by nature's fury.

She turned from the room and reached for the next door.

No. I'm not going back there! Nancy returned to the present in a flash.

She shook her head vigorously, almost dropping the cup of tea in her hands, and turned from the window to look back at the shovel, which lay on the kitchen counter. Its pointy end was still covered in human detritus.

Closing her eyes for a long moment, she shook her head again.

Why did I ever leave?

"*You know why, woman.*" She could almost hear Ern's amused voice.

"*You left because you want to go home. You want to sit with me on the couch, like we did just about every night. We'll have some snacks, and watch the news, and tut-tut at all the foolish people in the world.*"

Her imagination was interrupted by movement out in the street. Nancy slowly backed away from the window so as not to attract attention. At the same time, she carefully craned her neck to see what it was that had caught hers.

It was a dog. Nancy was shocked to see a living dog. It was the first one she had seen since the syndrome had taken all of them.

Well, not all of them, I guess.

She watched the dog run ahead several yards, then turn and look behind him. The dog did this several times, before a man came lumbering into view.

At least, Nancy suspected that it was a man. He was dressed in all kinds of armor.

She watched the man chase the dog.

No, wait. He's not chasing that dog. The dog is leading the man.

Nancy wasn't sure what to do. It looked like the man and his four-legged companion were looking for something.

Or maybe a place to hide. Like me.

She could make out more details of the man as he got closer. He was dressed in a mixture of armor pieces and had a sword, along with what looked like a massive club strapped to his back. He oddly reminded Nancy of a popular cartoon from the late 80s.

Heroes in a half shell. The lyric came unbidden to her mind. It had been a guilty pleasure for Ern and her in those days: Saturday morning cartoons.

The man was now within several houses, the dog still leading the way. Then a noise must have distracted the man, as he turned his head.

That was a mistake. The man stepped on something and did a flip. One moment he was moving in a low crouch, the next his feet were above his head, in some kind of fancy soccer kick. Except the man slammed the back of his head into the concrete ground with a crack loud enough to reach Nancy's ears.

It was unlike any flip Nancy had ever seen, and her first reaction was to burst out laughing. She caught herself a moment later, noticing that the dog had swung its head toward her.

Shoot! The dog knows I'm here.

She stepped closer to the window despite herself. The man lay spread-eagled on the ground. His helmet lay a few feet away. He lifted his head groggily, and Nancy thought for a second that he was going to be okay. However, his head dropped a moment later, and the man ceased to move.

The dog circled the man, sniffing at his face and anxiously lifting its nose to sniff the air. Nancy knew exactly what the dog feared.

"Not my problem," Nancy said softly, and she took half a step away. The dog seemed to look right at her.

"*Go. Help the lad,*" Ern ordered, albeit not unkindly.

"All right, all right," she told her invisible companion. She looked at her gear for a moment, deciding to leave her stuff behind before shuffling toward the front door.

Opening the portal as quietly as she could, she was surprised to find the dog there. It whined at her, circling twice before moving back toward its master.

The dog is afraid. It's afraid for its master.

It took away any reservations that Nancy may have had.

If the dog cares this much for its owner, then the guy should be all right.

Nancy stepped out of the safety of the building and out into the open. She immediately felt exposed. The dog seemed to sense her hesitation and came back to her. It circled her legs once and moved toward its master once more with a soft whine.

Nancy followed.

"Hey," she whispered when she got close. "Hey, are you okay?"

The man did not stir. She stood over him. He was young; probably in his mid-twenties, Nancy guessed. He was dressed like a circus freak.

Well, maybe not a circus freak. She checked out his armor and gear. *More like one of those anarchists.* Or at least what she pictured an anarchist would dress like.

Just then, a clanking sound rang out about a block away. The dog instantly whined again and nudged its unconscious owner's face with its nose.

The dog looked up at Nancy, who had taken a step back. Its eyes captured her, almost as if it were silently pleading for its master's life.

Please ma'am. Save him!

Another noise broke their locked gazes. Both dog and Nancy stared off in the direction of the noise. In the dead silence, she could clearly make out approaching footfalls.

Shoot. We have to get out of here. She reached down and grabbed one of the man's arms. Lifting it, she discovered just how heavy he was. Nancy highly doubted that she could carry a man this size.

Something got kicked up the street. She heard it clank and clatter.

They're getting close. She eyed the man one last time, trying to decide whether to abandon him or risk her life dragging him to safety.

What do I do, Ern?

Chapter 17

Brenin

November 18, Noon, Rosae Crucis Primary Domicile.

The audience chamber could almost be mistaken for a church or a medieval royal hall. Benches filled up most of the room, all facing the front, where, upon a stage, stood a large high-backed chair reminiscent of a throne. Several other chairs flanked this one. The fold-out kind.

Brenin's advisors sat in a half circle around him. They talked and squabbled and droned on endlessly. Brenin was barely listening.

For the moment, his mind was on other things.

Kevin's dead. Paladin Kevin had been his staunchest ally. As a matter of fact, Brenin had elevated his long-time friend right after his own rise to the top.

Well, as close to the top as you can get without burning off your wings.

Brenin had trusted Kevin. He'd known that Kevin would pose no threat to him and would never falter in his loyalty to the Sentinel of the Order. He glanced at the people around him.

None of you are fit to replace Kevin. For I do not trust you as I did him.

He didn't say those words. Instead, he sighed loudly. It was enough to stop the conversation happening around him. All eyes were on the Sentinel, waiting for him to say something.

"To lose a Paladin is no small thing. Yet I feel like we just lost ours over a trifling matter."

"Paladin Kevin sought to exact revenge for you. For the loss of—"

Brenin cut the man off. "I'm quite aware why Kevin did what he did." He frowned in distaste. "In the end, he was foolish. He paid the price for that foolishness. Pray that I am not surrounded by fools such as him."

Brenin slowly swung his gaze from one member of his council to the other, until all four had dropped their eyes.

"Sage Peter." Brenin kept his gaze locked on the fourth councilor. The Sage looked up and immediately blanched under Brenin's gaze. Brenin did nothing to mask his disappointment.

"Y—Yes Brenin?"

"You are the head of Intelligence. Yet you've provided me with very little *intelligence* since we started our campaign."

Peter dropped his head in apology. "I'm terribly sorry, Sentinel Brenin."

"Drop that title when you address me. I thought that I made that clear years ago. Also, spare me the excuses of communications issues and logistics. They did not stop inquisitor Stanley from doing *his* job."

"Yes sir." Peter looked up at his aged leader. "You're right. No excuses ... I have failed."

"Inquisitor Stanley and you do not get along." It was not a question.

"No, sir."

"You disagree with his methods. And you resent that he does not obey your commands, despite the fact that you are his superior."

Peter's nod was barely perceptible.

Brenin considered this for a moment. He took a deep breath and let it out slowly. "Kevin had his doubts about you, you know. He told me that you might even turn on us."

The barb had its desired effect. Peter turned a shade of red as he stammered, "I assure you, sir — just as I assured our Paladin, that I am a committed member of the order. I have d—" He stopped talking as Brenin raised his hand.

"Enough. You blabber like a woman," Brenin snarled. "I have half a mind to remove you, and let Stanley take on your position."

Brenin stared flatly at Peter, daring the Sage to complain or argue. The younger man was wise enough to keep his mouth shut.

"But that would be a waste. Stanley is our inquisitor, and he is too damn good at what he does." Brenin leaned forward. His presence was so grand that it gave the impression of looming over Peter. "You need to step up, Sage Peter. Bring me some good news, soon."

Just like that, the conversation was over. Brenin sat back into his chair and looked at the man standing beside Peter.

"Wilf. You are a loyal servant."

"Yes, my Sentinel." A scarred face gave Wilfred a wild look, only emphasized by the fervent devotion in his eyes. That made sense, though. The Legatis were Brenin's personal guard and Wilf was First Legatis. Brenin hated it when people called him by his title but chose not to correct Wilf.

His eyes drifted from Wilf to Peter. The young man looked ashamed and afraid, which pleased Brenin.

Good. Such are the tools of power.

"What do you make of Kevin's demise, Wilf?"

The First Legatis worked his jaw and scowled, deepening the scars on his face. Brenin knew that he was trying to choose his words. Wilf was frightening to behold and often needed no more than to look at a person to cow him or her. Wilfred had never liked Kevin, that much was common knowledge. It was suspected that Wilfred was jealous of the attention and trust that Brenin had placed in his Paladin. This despite his own undying loyalty to the Sentinel.

Wilf would lay down his life for Brenin without hesitation. Brenin knew this.

Too bad he's a psychopath.

Just then, Wilf had found the words he sought. "As you said yourself, my Sentinel, Kevin was a fool. He should have let real fighters do the fighting."

The two men to his left shifted uncomfortably. Wilf noticed and took it as disagreement. Without bothering to look at them, he continued, "A paladin is supposed to handle administration. Just look at Peter. He's struggling over in Europe, but he sure as hell is not risking his neck ... Leave the cutting to the Swords."

Brenin smiled softly. "Ah, yes. That old saying."

The Sentinel seemed to make up his mind then. He relaxed in his chair and addressed the group. "I have not been deaf. I have heard the rumors about our Paladin. Some admired him and others feared him. Some thought that he was an organizational genius." He glanced at Peter. "While others thought that he was losing his mind. Well, all that is done now. I will waste any more words on Kevin. Our Paladin is gone, and we have to pick up the strings."

He let that sink in for a moment, before continuing, "Tell me, Wilf. What have the Legatis been up to?"

"Our core mission is as it has always been. To protect you, Sentinel. However, I have sent half of our men to assist at the perimeter as you requested."

Brenin nodded. "Good. Who remains to protect me?"

"I do, of course." He glanced at the guard standing by Brenin's throne. "Legatis Charlie is at your side, and Legatis Aaron stands guard outside." He said the latter with a wave toward the door.

"We will try to keep at least one Legatis around you at all times," he concluded.

"That sounds reasonable. I require minimal protection. Especially here, in our primary domicile. What about the other Legatis? How do they fare?"

"They destroy the undead as they come. So far, our remote location has worked in our favor. Only the odd one makes it to the fence. They are disposed of quickly. We have coordinated with Captain Jason so that there are regular patrols."

Brenin picked up on this. "Then our location remains secure, but there are threats beyond our perimeter."

Wilf grimaced before continuing, clearly uncomfortable with the subject. "Captain Jason should probably be the one to speak of this, but as you know there are groups of undead approaching from the surrounding towns."

"You mean to say hordes of zombies." Brenin didn't expect anybody to respond to the attempt at humor.

Wilf hesitated a moment, then went on, "Yes, you are correct. Hordes of zombies. Sage Jonas is still trying to figure out how they know to come here — but they come. The Legatis have assisted the Captain and his men in excursions to eradicate these threats." His face screwed up again as he thought about it. "We try to meet them on the roads. They seem to stick to the roads... I have accompanied the men a couple of times. We have destroyed hundreds. Maybe thousands." He met Brenin's eyes. "They just keep coming. I am concerned that we will run out of ammunition before we run out of und—zombies."

Brenin nodded. "Yes. Captain Jason here has told me as much. He is thankful for the support of the Legatis. Wilfred looked over to the man sitting leftmost in the line.

The Captain nodded curtly and took a breath as he prepared to report. "We have scouts on the roads leading to five surrounding towns. We send out our mobile units when we get a call. It's messy, but highly effective. We haven't lost a single man, other than a few minor injuries. First Legatis Wilfred is correct in saying that we will run out of ammunition if this continues much longer." The Captain spoke as if he were reading a shopping list. The man showed no emotion, his only focus the security of their facility.

"Very well," said Brenin. "I am authorizing an expedition to the nearest military base for a supply run. Captain Jason, figure out the logistics and return to me by supper time with your plan."

The Captain seemed to perk up at the prospect. "Yes, sir."

"You are dismissed." Brenin was already looking at the final person facing him, and barely noticed the Captain get up, step off the stage and march out of the audience chamber.

Brenin waited until the door was shut. "Samuel." For the first time, the sentinel's expression softened to something approaching tenderness. "I need Summuh's direction. Now more than ever. What spiritual guidance can you offer?"

The Apostle nodded knowingly. "Yes, of course, Sentinel." Apostle Samuel's pitch of voice was rather high compared to the other men. He licked his lips before continuing. "Our teachings tell us that patience is required in times of adversity. You must control the things that you have the power to control, and trust Summuh's divine will in the things that are out of your control. To do otherwise would be a fruitless waste of energy."

Brenin nodded, eager for more.

"My advice is to name a new paladin as soon as possible and return the Order to its normal hierarchy." The Apostle stopped speaking as the person beside him harrumphed gruffly.

"Do you disagree, First Legatis Wilfred?"

The Apostle was clearly displeased by the interruption. Wilf scowled at the man.

"Speak your mind, Wilf," Brenin prompted.

Wilf turned to his leader, pointedly ignoring the spiritual advisor beside him. "I think that Samuel seeks the post of paladin for himself, my Sentinel." The Apostle bristled, although it was unclear if he was upset at the lack of ceremony with which he was addressed or the insinuation as to his motive.

"Yes," Brenin said. "I can see that."

Samuel's eyes widened in shock despite his efforts to remain impassive.

"But I can't think of a better person for the position," Brenin continued. He sighed loudly. "Let me think on the matter." He turned back to his Apostle. "What else do you have for me, Samuel?"

"The spirit of our people is strong. My fellow apostles have calmed the populace sufficiently in light of the recent events."

"You refer to the suicides."

"Yes, Brenin. Our people were dismayed and surprised by the ... events. Some of them started asking questions." He threw a look at Peter. "In that regard, Sage Peter has done an admirable job. He has quickly quelled any subversive talk and conjecture. It is crucial that we control — no, *guide* — our people's thoughts in these fragile times."

Peter's face remained neutral as Samuel spoke. It had indeed been a combined effort by the clergy and administration to achieve what the Apostle described.

Brenin frowned. "Bah. We made it quite clear to *all* our people that we were embarking on something drastic. I still think that we should weed out any fickle souls."

The Apostle nodded in understanding. "You are not wrong, Brenin. However, it is only understandable that people are confused in these trying times. We should take these poor souls by the hand and help them understand—"

"I will not abide dissidence!" Brenin growled. The Apostle hurriedly hung his head.

The Sentinel crossed his arms, his expression full of displeasure. Brenin was an old man, but he still cut an imposing figure. He possessed a vitality that belied his age, and the strength of his charisma made people want to do his bidding. Alternatively, people feared him when he was angry.

"I have heard a rumor that at least one of our satellite communities has cast aside the order. That Paladin Kevin had ordered that the news of these rebellious activities be kept secret, and that we are to consider these communities *lost*."

This information was shocking to at least one of the audience members. Brenin's eyes were on Sage Peter, whose expression of surprise was rather more subdued.

"Find the truth on this matter and report it to me."

"Yes, Brenin."

"We need to avoid any insurrection — especially here at the primary domicile. I want all of you to find the loudest objectors. Wilf, Sage Peter, work with Apostle Samuel on this."

Brenin thought it over for a moment. "We need Inquisitor Stanley for this."

"He is currently dealing with..." Peter hesitated. "Something. I will order him to cease his current mission and return here immediately."

Brenin nodded. "Go."

His audience immediately spang into action. They walked toward the door together, but their fellowship was for show only. Each man distrusted the others. Each man had vastly different opinions.

But for now, they were united under their leader. They had tasks to complete and would do so. For Brenin, their leader and Sentinel of the Rosae Crucis. Since only Brenin stood below Summuh.

Chapter 18

Tammy

November 18, 11:45 A.M., Bowmont, Georgia

They drove through a city. At least, the signpost stated announced it as a city.

Bowmont, Georgia was proclaimed proudly in bright, albeit weathered, letters.

And below that: *Population 855.*

"Can you call it a city, if it has so few people living in it?" Abi wondered out loud. Tammy had been thinking the same thing.

The city of less than a thousand souls lived up to expectations. They passed the Baptist church to their left and the library to their right, then the postal office again on their left, followed by a bank.

"This is where we turn north," John instructed BB as he read his map.

Tammy caught a quick glimpse of a grocery store and a fuel stop complete with a mini-mart. That was pretty much it — they were out of the city.

"Gas station back there," BB commented.

"Saw it," John confirmed. "How *are* we doing for fuel?"

"Half a tank. Plenty, for now."

John nodded in agreement. He traced his finger along the road map for a moment. "We've got less than ten miles to go." Several minutes later, he checked the coordinates again. "We're close. Weapons check then eyes out, everybody."

There was a flurry of activity in the vehicle. Tammy sensed the nervous energy and felt a flush of excitement herself. She had no

idea what they were going to find. The idea both scared and ex-
hilarated her. Her imagination ran wild. Were they driving toward
some cultist compound? Would they turn the corner and find some
massive church or religious building?

Or are we driving into a trap?

Whatever it was, it was in the middle of nowhere.

"Slow right down, BB." John ordered. He opened his window
and motioned for the others to do the same. "Everybody, eyes and
ears out." He took a moment to make sure his rifle was ready. Tammy watched him fidget with the rifle and felt a tickle at the back of
her brain. The tickle that warned her of impending violence.

"Take the next right. It should be..." John trailed off as they
passed a farm on their right and the view opened up. Tammy followed his gaze across the field.

"What is it?" She squinted as she tried to make it out. It was
an oddly shaped structure. BB slowed the vehicle down to a crawl.
Tammy's eyes remained fixed on the structure. It looked too small
to be a building.

Maybe it's one of those nuclear silos?

"I don't see any movement," John stated. "Take her in, BB."
BB sped up to the next intersection and turned right. The object
was only about two hundred and fifty yards ahead, but Tammy still
couldn't figure it out.

"I know what it is," BB stated suddenly. Tammy turned to the
gaunt-faced man in anticipation.

"We just turned onto Guidestone Road." He pointed ahead
with his chin. "Those are the Georgia Guidestones."

They all stared out of their windows as they approached the
concrete monoliths. The first thing Tammy noticed was that the
area was completely abandoned. She felt the tingling sensation
slowly ease. She had a closer look at the Guidestones as they continued to approach. The construction consisted of four rectangular

concrete slabs set upright in an X shape. A fifth block stood in the middle of the formation.

"Do you know anything about these things?" John nudged Tammy.

Tammy nodded, although her expression remained unsure. "A little. I helped out on a piece once, many years ago... Some people dubbed it 'the American Stonehenge.' It was built in the eighties. Nobody is exactly sure who built it." Tammy frowned as she tried to remember. In the meantime, BB was about to pull into the parking lot.

"R.C. Christian," Tammy blurted. "That's the name of the person who owns this. Obviously not his real name. He paid a guy named Fenton — or was it Fendon ... Fendley?"

She looked at John questioningly. John just shook his head.

"Anyway, this Fendley guy was the mayor of a nearby town, and he owned a construction company. He's the guy who built this monument."

They pulled to a stop in one of the parking spots. No other vehicle was present in the lot. John motioned for Tammy to continue.

"Uh, anyway..." Tammy frowned in concentration. "The stones have inscriptions in multiple languages. They talk about a future apocalypse and list rules for a better society."

She was about to say more, but Abi swung open her door at that moment.

"What do you say we find out for ourselves?" Abi didn't wait for an answer and hopped down to the ground. John gave Tammy a quick shrug and opened his door.

Chapter 19

Jack

November 18, 12:15 P.M., The Ren.

Lunch looked like a muted affair. Jack walked into the cafeteria and noted people hunched over their meals and lost in their own thoughts. Conversation was minimal. He followed suit, stepping up to the buffet table and collecting a plate wordlessly.

They had canceled all excursions for the day and kept the school locked up tight. Jack had kept himself busy on chores all morning, but even he could sense the nervous energy that pervaded the atmosphere. People were scared. Jack wasn't sure if he was scared. But he certainly felt nervous. There were too many unanswered questions.

Was there going to be another attack? Jack had had a terrible sleep last night and was sure that he hadn't been the only one.

Was Mike going to be okay? The news had seemed positive last night, but he had seen Shelley just an hour ago, looking even more concerned than usual.

And what the heck happened to Ben? The guy walked around like a mummy. He'd obviously been in a scrap.

Jack needed answers. He turned around with his full plate of food and looked for a place to sit.

There. He spotted Joe sitting alone at one of the far tables. *He'll have some answers.*

Jack had often been told by his mom that he'd inherited his inquisitive nature from his father. He was one of those people that simply needed to know. He'd go nuts speculating otherwise.

Boldly he walked through the cafeteria and up to Joe's table. Joe saw him coming. The big man smiled weakly. "Hi, Jack."

"Uh... Hi, Joe. Do you mind if I join you?" Jack sounded just as nervous as if he were asking some girl out on a date.

"Of course." Joe waved at the seat across from him.

Jack lowered himself into the seat and placed his plate on the table. Joe turned to his own plate. "Oh goodie. Yellow and brown slush with a side of green ... things," he said, giving up on trying to identify the meal. "Wonder why we're not cooking up the bounty we were finding in those houses..." He trailed off as he took a bite. "Tastes okay with salt, though."

Jack smiled politely. He wasn't too keen on the meal himself. He agreed with Joe. There was plenty of canned food — but every lunch still consisted of MREs. Jack guessed they were trying to conserve. Or maybe they were trying to eat the MREs before they went bad.

Do they go bad? Jack shook his head. He was here for different answers.

"Joe..." he began rather hesitantly.

"You want to know how Mike is doing," Joe finished for him.

"Um, yeah."

"You're only the tenth or so person who has asked me that." The smile on Joe's face belied any displeasure. "We sure are a curious bunch."

Jack waited.

"Well, to tell you the truth, I don't know." The smile faded. "I *think* he is doing all right, but he has developed a fever. Could be infection. Maybe we missed something when we cleaned him up. Or maybe it is just a natural response to the trauma." He seemed to be talking more to himself than to Jack. Joe mumbled a few other things under his breath before fading into silence.

Joe was lost in thought. Jack sat frozen through the pregnant pause. Joe finally snapped out of it and regarded the young man.

"I'm just not sure," he said with an embarrassed shake of the head. "We should know soon, though."

"Okay," Jack said softly. "Thanks."

Watching Joe go through such turmoil curbed Jack's need for answers. He decided to devote his attention to the meal in front of him instead. Joe watched the young man take a bite before turning back to his own lunch. They ate in silence for a minute.

"Peas," Joe blurted.

"Huh?"

"They're peas. The green stuff." He indicated the substance on his plate.

"Ah." Jack poked at the green portion on his plate.

Should peas be this color? He took a bite, but still wasn't sure if Joe's assessment was correct.

They continued consuming their meal in silence.

"We should grow our own," Jack commented between bites.

"Hmm?" Joe looked startled.

"Sorry. Peas ... We should grow our own peas."

Joe finished chewing the nondescript meat product that represented the brown bit of the MRE.

He swallowed his bite, nodding in agreement. "Yes. Yes, we should!"

Jack could see the wheels turning.

"We should make a run to a garden center. But first, we should figure out where to plant them. Guess it's too late in the year to grow anything outside ... Maybe we can set up some plants inside? One of the rooms upstairs, with lots of sunlight." His eyes lit up. "Oh, I know! We should gather some of those hydroponic systems, and those special lights." Joe looked around, patting his pockets. "I should be writing this down..."

Jack couldn't help himself. He guffawed.

Joe's expression went from shock to anger to confusion in a matter of two seconds. Jack's outburst shattered the silence that prevailed in the cafeteria and everybody else present looked over in surprise.

"Sorry!" Jack apologized to all. He turned and glanced around at the other diners, offering an embarrassed wave of his hand. The smile was still evident on his face when he turned back to Joe. "It's just that... Well, you really reminded me of my dad just now." The smile slowly faded.

It was Joe that started to smile then. "Why, thank you, Jack. I take that as a compliment."

"Your father was..." Joe bit his lip for a second as he attempted to come up with the right words. "Exactly the kind of person we needed, when we all got here." He nodded in agreement with his own statement. "He got us focused on things and helped us forget — or maybe get over — what had happened to the world outside. He was a great planner, a good organizer..." Joe reached across the table and grabbed Jack's wrist. He must have noticed that Jack's eyes had started to glisten. "He was the kind of guy everybody liked and respected. Thank you, Jack. Honestly, I've been trying to be more like him."

With his free hand, Jack wiped his cheeks. "Thanks, Joe."

Joe released Jack's wrist and leaned back. "You know, before all of this. Before this syndrome... I was all obsessed with the wrong things. Things like money. I was counting every dollar. One of the things that dominated my thoughts was getting the mortgage paid off on our house. I was constantly worried about the clinic turning a profit and putting the kids through college. Rachel and the kids were always going on about things they wanted. Stuff. Material belongings." He snorted in derision but smiled as he pulled at his shirt. "All I've got now is the shirt on my back."

His smile turned rueful. "I've had my belongings literally shrink to what I could fit into a bag."

"But the funny thing is, that I'm okay with that. At peace with it. Like, I've learned what really has value. Also ..." For the first time Joe looked excited. "I'm less stressed than I was a few weeks ago. That's right. There are goddamn zombies outside and I feel fine. You know what I mean?"

Jack did. "Yeah. I get that."

"Knowing what I know now, I should have been living my life differently. Less time buying stuff ... I should have been spending more time with my wife and kids."

"Dad was always pretty good about that." Jack stared down at his plate. "When I was younger, I always hated the family vacations. Resented the holidays we *had* to spend together." He met Joe's eyes. "Now he's gone and all I wish is to go back to those days."

"I'm sorry for your loss, Jack. We all are."

Jack swallowed, hard. He was trying to keep it together.

"Your dad knew what was important in life. That's a great legacy to uphold."

They sat in silence for a long moment, each lost in his own thoughts. Joe looked up and waited for Jack to do likewise.

"He also knew what made people tick. How to motivate them. I've learned some hard lessons over the last few weeks. Probably the biggest lesson was to get unstuck from my old behaviors and stigmas. Heck, those things don't matter no more in today's world.

"I was just like most people. Suspicious, critical ... greedy. I'd puff my chest out whenever I met other people. But I get it now. This isn't a contest to see who knows the most or who owns the most. There is no rivalry depending on what state you came from, what football team you supported, or even what president you voted for." The corner of Joe's mouth pulled up in a melancholy grin.

"It doesn't matter what the color of your skin is. Nancy told me that — and she was right. It's not about black and white."

"It's about the living against the dead," Jack said. Joe nodded.

"Yeah. Maybe. It's about staying alive, and the hopes of a future. Most of the things that seemed so important before the syndrome now mean little to nothing. To be honest, a lot of those things should have never been so important in the first place. I don't want to say it, but sometimes, in some way, I feel that the world is better than it was before."

It was Jack's turn to nod. He continued to nod as he chose his next words carefully. "You know ... when I first met you, I didn't like you."

He expected an angry glare in return, or maybe even a demand to know why. What he didn't expect was for the whole room to reverberate with Joe's deep belly laugh. If the sound of Jack's mirth had unsettled those around them, then Joe's outburst launched people out of their seats. It only made Joe laugh harder. One or two people even darted into the cafeteria to see what all the fuss was about.

Joe laughed for a long time. At one point he did seem to gather control of himself. He held up the palm of his hand to Jack, then promptly burst out laughing again when he saw the young man's face.

His laughter slowly died. First to intermittent bursts of mirth, then down to a chuckle and finally a few snickers that faded into silence.

"That," he said, "was an understatement." Joe threatened to dissolve into laughter once more but managed to hold it back this time. "I don't think *anybody* liked me during those first few days — not even my own family." He shook his head good-naturedly, then sobered up. "I always thought that I was a take-charge kind of guy. Somebody who took control of situations. But the damn truth is that I was scared and didn't know what to do. So, I lashed out... a lot."

Joe sighed. Jack waited, sensing that the big man had more to say.

"I've got to give it to your father. He helped me out. He set me straight."

Jack tried not to let his emotions overwhelm him. His father was special. Jack missed him. He tried to focus on the topic at hand. "I definitely think you've changed since then."

"Thanks." Joe shook his head. "But the truth is that people really don't change. Deep down, they stay the same." He thought about it for a moment. "You know, maybe the truth is that I — that many of us — were not really being our true selves before all this. Maybe we are truer to ourselves now ... Now that we worry more about our safety and less about our credit-card statements, or hair loss." For effect, Joe patted his receding hairline.

"High school was bad for that." He looked down at the empty plate before him. "Jocks and geeks and prom ... None of that matters anymore now."

"Exactly." Joe sighed as he stood up. "Okay, Jack. On your feet. John will be pissed if we haven't cleared any houses by the time he gets back."

He looked around. Quite a crowd had gathered in the cafeteria, so he addressed them all. "We can't live in fear, folks. I suggest we take charge of the situation and get on with our work."

Jack jumped up. He was eager to get back to it. He heard many sounds of agreement and saw the determination on many faces.

Just then, they all heard a different noise. Somebody was moaning in pain.

Chapter 20

Tammy

November 18, 1:30 P.M., Elbert County, Georgia.

Tammy was getting frustrated.

They had been at the Guidestones for at least an hour and still had not found anything connecting the site to Rosae Crucis. She'd studied every one of the granite slabs, read every piece of text — at least the ones she understood — and had even gone so far as to scour the ground around the monument.

She did find another stone just to the west of the Guidestones. She read the inscription:

Let these be guidestones to an Age of Reason.

Good luck with that. She shook her head. None of this was making any sense. Of course, it would help if they knew exactly what they were looking for.

"What the hell are we looking for?" she heard BB ask in frustration somewhere on the other side of the monument. Tammy smirked.

Guess I'm not the only one with that question.

She walked back to the vehicle. Romy sat on the front bumper. She looked pissed.

Did we just come out here on a wild goose chase? Tammy started second-guessing the cryptic note that Maddie had left behind. Romy met Tammy's eyes. Both women shook their heads.

"It's got to have something to do with the text." Romy scowled in frustration. "But what?" She slapped the bumper.

"I'm not sure." Tammy waved at the monolith. "Maybe this is just something to distract us from the real thing." Her statement felt weak, though.

"Well, we'd better find something quick. Let's do one more circuit before my patience is entirely gone." Romy stood up and stretched. It reminded Tammy of the way a cat would stretch. *Graceful, lithe, athletic. No, more ferocious than a cat. She has an element of unpredictability and danger. A leopard. Or a jaguar.* Tammy felt the slightest tinge of jealousy.

They walked a circuit of the Guidestones. Ten minutes later they were back where they'd started, and even more frustrated.

"I mean, I get those rules," Romy started. "I even agree with most of them. But what the hell do they tell us?" The question was rhetorical. "Is that what the Rosae Crucis are all about? Is that what this is telling us?" She shook her head.

Tammy shrugged. Romy stomped back to the Humvee and plopped herself onto the bumper once more. Tammy continued to walk to the back of the Humvee. She needed a bottle of water.

She found John there. He held the map against the sloped back of the vehicle, using it as a kind of tabletop. John stared at the map with furious intensity, as if trying to make the clues jump out at him through sheer will. Tammy approached silently.

"There's got to be something we're missing..." He traced the small X Jack had marked with his finger. "We're exactly on this spot."

Tammy could only agree. They seemed to be where they needed to be. John sighed in frustration and was about to fold up the map when Tammy placed a hand on his back.

"Hold on."

John looked over his shoulder at her curiously. "What is it?"

"Well, I can see that X marks the spot, but that's still a large area on a map of this scale. Do you have the coordinates handy?"

John nodded and produced a piece of paper. Tammy pulled out her phone and started up the GPS coordinate app. John dutifully read out the coordinates.

"Wait. What?" Tammy exclaimed. John started calling out the coordinates again when she shushed him. "We're in the wrong spot. The first coordinate, 34.2320 degrees north, is right. But the second coordinate is off. You said 82.8940 degrees west. We are at 82.8944 degrees west."

John frowned. "Okay, let me think. Four decimal places ... That's precise to eleven meters at the equator. Don't ask me how I know that," he added quickly.

Abi, Romy and BB had heard the sounds of excitement and moved closer. "You guys find something?" BB asked, only to get shushed. John was calculating.

"We should be about forty-four meters to the east of here." John pointed and they all looked. Nothing there. Just a farmer's field with a solitary tree.

A tree...

"The tree!" Tammy exclaimed and started jogging toward the lonely sentinel.

They hopped a fence and found themselves in a poorly tilled farmer's field. The tree itself looked as if it had withstood many struggles to survive. It was short and bent out of shape.

Tammy got within a few feet to stand under boughs that were as twisted as its trunk. Her gaze followed the trunk down to the ground, where time and a rock-filled soil had forced some of the roots to reach outward from the tree. It looked like the tree clung to the earth in desperation. She was at once awed by the sheer determination of life to hang on and filled with bleakness at the struggle.

"Look around the roots," Abi suggested. She was already poking around the twisted wooden objects.

And there it was.

Tammy could see a dark canister poking out from beneath a root as she circled the tree.

"Guys." She pointed.

John lifted his hand in caution and approached the object carefully. "Back up a few steps," he ordered.

Tammy and the rest of the team moved back and milled around, struggling to see around John's bulk as he worked at the object. Finally, John stood up and turned around. He grinned when he saw the concerned looks on their faces. "Sorry, guys, it's nothing dangerous."

With that he held up a tube-like item.

"It's a map canister," he explained. John walked over to the team and opened the top. "Feels empty." He said as he flipped the canister upside down.

A single item slid forward. John grabbed it and pulled it out, then held it up for the group to see. It was a map.

"Another map?" Tammy couldn't hide her frustration.

John placed the map on the ground, putting rocks on the corners to keep it from rolling up.

It was a map of America. There were a bunch of circled locations with text beside them.

"What the hell is this?" Romy asked the question on everybody's lips.

"Charlie." John put his finger on the map next to one of the circles. "Nova." He moved his finger to another circle. "Alpha."

He looked over at BB beside him and across the map at the three women.

"I know what this is. These are locations of Rosae Crucis strongholds. Each of these circles indicates the position of another one of their bastions."

"Hmm." BB bent over the map and pointed to another location. "They're all, like, Greek names. But this one is just called 'PD.' Wonder what that means ..."

"Here is Alpha." John pointed. "Near Tallahassee, Florida." They continued to study the map, pointing out the other locations. Most seemed to be some distance from any major city.

"Guys?" Tammy looked over at Abi. The diminutive woman had picked up the discarded map canister.

"There is more stuff in here." Abi had zipped open a pocket on the outside of the canister; she reached in and pulled out several pieces of paper. "It's a bunch of notes."

She sifted through them for several seconds before looking up at the rest of the group. Her eyes were large with excitement.

"It's Pedro!"

Tammy had taken ownership of Pedro's notes. The group took their findings back to the Humvee and sat around for lunch while Tammy sequestered herself into the back of the vehicle to read through the annotations.

The rest sat outside on a bench. The map was spread out on the tabletop and provided plenty of distractions as they ate, each taking turns to point out locations and wondering what would be found at the coordinates written next to the circled positions.

Half an hour later, lunch was over and the map thoroughly investigated. All that remained was for Tammy to share her findings. The sun had started to descend from its zenith. It cast shadows from the stone monoliths that slowly grew and stretched toward the group. The waiting was only interrupted once, when a lone zombie stumbled up the road toward them. John and BB dispatched the creature and dragged it off the road. By the time they got back, Tammy had stirred from the back seat of the Humvee.

"That thing is like a hot box," she commented as she stepped up to her seated audience.

Sweat soaked her hair and clothing, causing more than one surreptitious glance from the males in the group. Tammy was oblivious to it. The glint in her eyes betrayed her excitement at the information she was about to share.

"We had established that Pedro was helping Maddie. They were resisting the Order. From Maddie's diary, we figured that Pedro was nothing more than a willing accomplice." She held up the pages in her right hand, waving them slowly. "What this tells us is that he wasn't just an accomplice. He had a way more active role."

She lowered her hand and the pages to her side, her expression suddenly uncertain.

"I fear that Pedro got caught, shortly after hiding all this stuff. He might have given his life for that map and these notes..." She shook her head sadly. "In the end, it didn't change a thing."

"Okay, Tammy," Romy wore her frustration on her countenance. "Enough with the dramatics. Tell us what you've found."

Tammy studied the dark-skinned woman with some annoyance and shrugged. "Fine. I guess you're right." She pulled up the first sheet, her expression pensive. Then she stared to read.

'We're going to do something about it.'

Maddie's words kept ringing through my head as I drove away from the Jeffersons' farm that day. The conviction with which she stared at me — the belief — was so intense ... I admit that my first thoughts were that *mi dicha* was going to get hurt.

Then there was that other line she said. The one she overheard: "The end game has started." These words haunted me and instilled such a fear in me that it makes me shudder to even write them.

I hope somebody finds the map and these notes. I hope they find them before it's too late. They are going to murder many people. We're not sure yet how they are going to do it. Poison, or disease.

I know they're after me.

I have to stop them.

Chapter 21

Pedro

The end game has started. The ominous message rang over and over through Pedro's mind as he drove home from Maddie's place. That, and Maddie's words: *We're going to do something about it.*

Pedro went to his shop that very night. The shop had formerly been a garage. The tiniest hint of oil and chemicals still lingered in the air and was embedded in the concrete floor. Mixed with the scent of alcohol and fruit, the smell somehow made him feel at home.

He prepared his equipment, dumping out the batch of cider that was brewing to make room for the new apples coming in. The special apples.

He'd also cleaned the press, washed out the plastic barrels and gotten everything else ready. That next day he received his first shipment of apples and got started. He washed the apples before pulping them. Next, he ran them through his press.

Briefly he thought about adding sodium metabisulphite to the mixture to kill off any bacteria or molds but decided against it. He didn't want to take any chances in losing the antidote. The yeast went in next, and the waiting would begin.

He'd done the same thing two more times since then, and all his three barrels were currently in use. Once all was said and done, he'd have at least thirty bottles per barrel.

Ninety people saved. It sounded like a drop in the bucket to Pedro, but Maddie seemed really happy with it. Besides, she was baking her pies and smuggling away more apples. They hoped they could save a few hundred people.

That just wasn't enough for Pedro. He wanted to do more. He went along with Maddie's plans for the first two weeks, but then he got impatient.

More to the point, he got stupid. Pedro had resisted doing any investigating — largely because Maddie had asked him not to. However, one evening he couldn't hold his curiosity back any longer. He turned to his laptop and searched the internet. He spent hours on end, researching anything closely related to the Order. He went down dozens of rabbit holes and came up empty-handed every time. Pedro went to bed with a dozen hypotheses running through his mind and no way to verify any one of them.

He should have suspected that his browsing history might be visible to others.

Several days after his fruitless search, strange things started happening. Pedro drove to his shop one morning to find the door unlocked. He was sure that he'd locked it the night before. Pedro cautiously entered his shop but there was nobody inside. Suspicious, he had a look around. None of the equipment seemed to have been tampered with, and his stock of cases still stood against the far wall. Nothing was missing and nothing was out of place.

In the end, he shrugged it off and got to work.

He checked on the ciders. The last batch was ready to be bottled, so he spent the next two hours doing just that. He'd almost forgotten about the unlocked-door incident by the time he was done. His phone rang, just as he was putting the last bottles away. It was one of his regular customers — a liquor store from the next town over. He loaded up several cases of cider into his vehicle to make the delivery, never noticing that his glove compartment had been rifled through.

Two days later, Pedro was going about his business as normal. He'd not seen Maddie at all but had talked to her several times. He was driving home from making a delivery and gave her a call. His fiancée was holding up well and seemed to be focused on her plan. She had made her first deliveries already.

"Who are you giving it to?" There was no need to explain what 'it' meant.

"I started with some of our family friends and some of the other farms we do business with." Pedro heard her chuckle over the phone. "Mom thinks it's a marketing ploy of some kind — like I'm trying to get people hooked on apple pies. I couldn't figure out whom else to give it to, so I snuck a peak in my dad's address book. Took some pictures with my phone. Most entries were other people from the order. I did find some other candidates, though."

"Secret agent style," Pedro commented. Maddie's laughter sounded like music to his ears.

"Anyway, I'm going to be out of stuff pretty soon. Can I meet you tomorrow, to pick up the last bottles?"

"They might not be ready to drink yet," Pedro warned. He pulled off the highway, taking the exit into town. The sun was starting to get low in the sky. As Pedro shielded his eyes, he caught a flash in his rear-view mirror. A car was following him at a discrete distance. He frowned. Something about it didn't feel right.

"That's fine," Maddie said. "I'll tell them to eat the pie first."

"Okay, sounds like a plan." Pedro drove with one eye on the vehicle behind him. He entered the town and continued down the main drag, driving past the intersection where he would usually turn left.

The other car turned right at the intersection. Pedro released the breath he was holding.

"Pedro?"

"Oh, sorry, babe. Had to focus on the road for a minute."

"Well, you shouldn't be talking on the phone while driving anyway."

Pedro grinned. "Yeah, I know."

"I'm hanging up. Drive safe."

"Okay, Maddie."

"Love you." And she was gone.

Pedro smiled. "Love you," he replied into the dead phone.

His smile disappeared by the time he got to his house, though. The front door was wide open.

"What the hell?" He parked his car and strode up to the house. "Hello?" he called inside, but was met by silence.

Pedro pushed the door open and looked in. *"Mierda..."* He stepped into his house. The place had been turned upside down.

Pedro's first thought was that he gotten robbed. He walked from his living room toward his bedroom, picking up the baseball bat he had stashed near his front door for just such an event. He felt a moment of trepidation as he stood before his bedroom. The door was closed.

He took a couple of quick breaths, blowing them out violently. In one smooth motion he turned the handle and pushed the door open with the business end of his bat. The door swung to reveal his dresser and bed in an otherwise empty room. They showed evidence of having been rifled.

He checked his bathroom and the spare room before returning to the living room. The TV still stood there, and his laptop sat on the kitchen table. This puzzled him.

This was no robbery! Whoever had gone through his apartment had long since left. Yet Pedro could not let his guard down.

It's the Order... Pedro felt a cold sweat break out. For a moment he stood frozen in his living room, the baseball bat gripped tightly in his hands. He slowly lowered himself onto his couch.

"What do I do?"

Then he saw something out of the corner of his eye. *A piece of paper. A note?*

Indeed, a note lay on his coffee table. Full of misgivings, he reached for the paper.

The Order is watching and listening.

Check under pillow.

The note was signed: P

"What the fuck..." Pedro whispered, inhaling sharply.

The Order is listening.

He got up from the couch as casually as he could and moved toward the bedroom once again. Apparently, there was something under his pillow. At every step he felt as if he were being watched. Pedro glanced around, searching for hidden cameras or listening devices. Nothing jumped out at him, but then again, he had no idea what he was looking for.

His sheets and blankets had been jostled but his pillow lay exactly where it should. He hesitantly reached under it. His fingers brushed across a solid object and wrapped around it.

It was a phone. One of those cheapo disposable ones. He pushed the power button, and it came to life. The home screen appeared a moment later. To Pedro's surprise, he had a text message. He clicked on the icon and it appeared:

You have an ally. Was the first line.

Follow these instructions:

Wipe your laptop and destroy your phone.

Destroy my note.

Don't leave any evidence of your actions against the Order. Call the police and report this — not doing so will raise suspicion.

Stop acting suspicious! That part of the message seemed insistent.

They are monitoring you. Pedro looked around him, half-expecting a Rosae Crucis agent to jump out of his closet.

There are two bugs. Do not tamper with them! First one is just inside the heater vent of your bedroom, second one in your living room ceiling lamp. I will text you again shortly.

We will stop them.

P

Pedro stared at the message for a long moment.

They're watching me! Ran through his mind several times, but also: *You have an ally.* And *We will stop them.*

Pedro deleted the message and put the phone in his pocket. He couldn't help himself as he walked over to his heating vent and stared through the grill.

A dark metallic object was stuck to the galvanized ductwork, just below the vent. He stepped back carefully and considered it.

Okay, Pedro. Time to get to work. Pedro figured that he had no options but to follow the instructions of his unknown ally.

He stepped out of his bedroom. *Don't act suspicious,* he reminded himself.

"Damn meth-heads!" he grunted. "Breaking in here and messing with my shit."

He continued to rant as he made a slow circuit of his living room. He got to the window. The curtains were shut, just as he'd left them. The morning light tended to shine right in, and he hated nothing more than coming home after a day's work to cook in a sauna — so they stayed shut. That worked out well for him in this case. Nobody could look in on him. Pedro very carefully peeked out between the curtains.

There. The beat-up minivan stood out clearly to Pedro. After all, he'd lived on this street for nearly five years. He knew every neighbor and their vehicles.

Satisfied, but at the same time deeply concerned, he let the curtain fall into place. He stared up at the ceiling light.

There's a bug in there. He didn't need to see it to know it.

"Now I got all this mess to clean up," Pedro said. His mind couldn't be further from that activity, though.

What did "P" want me to do? Call the police.

It was with some trepidation that Pedro reached for his phone.

What the hell am I going to tell them? He stared at his phone for a moment before realizing that he didn't know what number to dial. "9—1—1" seemed a little excessive. He quickly looked up the number and dialed the local police station.

"Willemtown Sheriff's office." The call was picked up after the first ring and well before Pedro felt ready to talk. "Deputy Ruiz speaking. How can I help you?"

"Um, yes. Hi." Pedro swallowed quickly. "My name is Pedro Aragonez, and I live at 1218 Woodruff Lane East. My house... It's been broken into!" Pedro added emphasis at the end to make it sound more believable.

"1218 ... Woodruff. East?" Pedro could picture the deputy writing on the other end of the line.

"Yes, sir."

"Pedro Aragonez. *Eso es correcto?*"

"*Sí.*" Pedro answered. "I prefer English, if you don't mind."

"Sorry." Deputy Ruiz chuckled softly. Pedro thought that it might have been an embarrassed laugh.

"Is the perpetrator still on the premises?" The deputy's voice sounded decidedly less warm.

"No. I got here about five minutes ago, and they were already gone."

"Is the door or window smashed in?"

"No. I think they picked the lock. The door still works."

"How about the interior? Has there been any serious vandalism? For example, has your stove been tipped over?"

"No." Pedro frowned in confusion. "Looks like my stuff was tossed around. But the stove is okay."

"The reason I ask, Mr. Aragonez, is because a smashed-out window or door could provide easy entry to other criminals. And a tipped-over stove could lead to a gas leak."

"I understand. From what I can tell there is no real damage."

"Good. Somebody will come over to your place to investigate and take a statement." The way he said it convinced Pedro that there would be no investigating going on whatsoever. "We will call you at this number when we're on our way."

"Uh, okay. Do you have any idea when you will be here?"

It sounded like the deputy was walking with the phone. "We'll probably get to your case in a couple of days. Maybe tomorrow."

Pedro nodded, waiting for Deputy Ruiz to provide more instructions. The phone sounded muffled, like the deputy had covered the mouthpiece.

"Pedazo de mierda!" Pedro could just hear the man call somebody "a little shit."

"Uh, I have to go now, Mr. Aragonez." The deputy suddenly sounded rushed.

"Did you just call me a little shit?" Pedro could feel his temper flaring.

"Oh! No, sir. There is some kid spray painting our building. Look, I've got to go. Go ahead and clean up the mess. Just make a record of every damaged or missing item. Give your insurance agent a call."

As if I have insurance. Pedro shook his head in disgust. "All right. Thanks. See you in a day or two, then."

Deputy Ruiz hung up without another word.

"Fucking cops." Pedro didn't have to act as he put his phone away.

He stood in his living room for a moment, gathering his thoughts.

That went well. Now, what's next?

Wipe laptop, he told himself.

Pedro strode to his laptop and flipped up the screen. The power came on. He entered his password and considered what to do. He was about to check online for a solution but realized that this might alarm the people who were watching him. Could they see what he was searching? He decided not to risk it.

Instead, he opened Settings, figuring the solution to his problem might be there.

Update & Security. Try that.

Recovery. That sounds promising.

He had a few options at this point, but the option to "Reset this PC" sounded like the right one. The drop-down showed a "Get started" button, which he clicked.

Remove everything.

No way! Can it be this easy? Pedro clicked the button. A "Confirm" button confronted him. However, Pedro clicked the "Change settings" option first.

He scanned the options, not entirely sure what it all meant or what he was looking for.

Data erase. That's got to be turned on, I think... Pedro toggled the switch. He got back to the previous screen by selecting "OK" and clicked "Confirm" immediately.

That seemed to be working. Or rather, it was doing something. Pedro watched the screen for a moment, then got up. There were other things to do.

He went to the fridge and grabbed a couple of ciders. He poured the first one in a tall glass and pulled out his phone. He held the phone over the glass, intending to drop it — but changed his mind at the last second. He opened his phone and looked up Maddie's number. Pedro quickly pulled out the disposable phone and entered it.

Then he dropped his phone into the cider and walked away.

Deputy Ruiz might have a problem reaching me, he thought with some satisfaction.

Pedro knew what the high acid content of his brew could do to electronics. Opening the second bottle, he took a long draught. He started tidying up, occasionally making some comment for the benefit of those listening in on him. After a while, he turned on the TV. He made the volume louder than usual and sat on his couch. The note still lay where he had dropped it.

Destroy the note, Pedro reminded himself. He picked up the piece of paper and after a moment's hesitation did the first thing he could think of. He popped it into his mouth. It went down, with the help of a couple of gulps of cider.

Later that evening, he took apart his laptop and gave his hard drive a new home at the bottom of a bucket, topping it off with the contents of several more bottles of cider.

Finally, before he went to bed, he pulled out the disposable phone. He needed to get a message out to Maddie. He punched in her number and wrote a text.

Mi dicha. Be careful. They are watching. Delete this message and don't reply. I love you.

He sat there watching his phone for several minutes. He half expected Maddie to text or call back. He half hoped for it. But the phone remained inert. Finally, he went to bed. He slept poorly that night, expecting people to bust into his house at any time. When he did sleep, his dreams were troubled. Sometime in the middle of the night, and unnoticed by Pedro, his phone buzzed.

B arry's Pub, 1 P.M. today.
     He lay in bed and read he message from "Unknown" for the third time. He knew Barry's Pub. Charles, the actual owner and

manager of the place, was a regular customer of his. Pedro nodded. It made sense and would not look suspicious for him to make a delivery there.

Don't act suspicious. He remembered the first message all too clearly. He could see the warm glow from his living room, indicating that the sun was up.

Okay, Pedro, you can do this. It's just another day. He got out of bed and casually walked to his bathroom to have a shower.

Pedro went on with all the mundane tasks of his daily life. He got dressed, had breakfast, washed his dishes, left and locked the door behind him. He never even looked up at the minivan down the street as he got into his car and drove away.

He spent the morning in his shop, trying to go about business as usual. All the while, he had the feeling of being watched. He loaded several cases into his car just after noon and drove out to Barry's Pub. The drive was nice. He opened his window all the way and let the cool autumn air invigorate him.

At his destination, he drove to the back of the establishment. He carried a couple of cases to the door and knocked on the metal. Charles opened several moments later.

"Pedro? I didn't think we were getting another shipment until next week?"

"Ah, yes. That's right. But I was going to take some time off next week. Wanted to drop these off now." Pedro had worked out the lie on his drive over.

Charles nodded and stood aside. Pedro gave his old friend a grateful smile as he walked in. "There are two more cases in the trunk. Mind grabbing those for me?"

He looked over his shoulder to see Charles already moving toward his car.

Barry's Pub wouldn't open for another hour or so, and the main room was empty as Pedro walked in with his delivery. He placed the cases on the bar counter.

Now what? Just then, he felt the phone in his pocket buzz.

He pulled it out. The message consisted of a single word.

Bathroom.

Pedro quickly put the phone back into his pocket.

"Hey, Charles, mind if I use the washroom?"

"Sure." Charles paid him no heed as he carried in the other cases.

The bathroom was much like any bar's bathroom. The unmistakable smells of urine and bleach mixed in the air, and the tiled surfaces were covered in graffiti. A set of urinals adorned one wall with posters of advertising — usually including some hot model — hanging at face level. A couple of sinks and stalls sat across the way. The door to the first stall was open.

"Get into the stall," a disembodied voice instructed.

Pedro jumped, despite himself. He hesitated for half a second. He looked over his shoulder at the door.

Walk away now, and forget about all of this?

"Hurry," the voice prompted.

Before he knew it, Pedro had entered the first stall and pulled the door shut. His contact was in the next stall over. Pedro tilted his head slightly to see a foot. It was a large foot — larger than his.

"Before you say anything," the man started, "listen."

Pedro clamped his mouth shut.

"I am a field agent, in service to the Central Intelligence Agency. The CIA."

Pedro had expected something like this. The man's voice was neither deep nor high-pitched, giving him no clue as to what this guy looked like.

"I was part of a team which infiltrated the Rosae Crucis. This was over a year ago. There was some disconcerting information at the time. We thought that they were extremists. Thought that they might resort to minor terrorist activities ... We had no idea that it would be this big." The man sounded introspective for a moment. "I did not know any of the other agents, with the exception of my partner."

The man paused for a second. Pedro waited. He surmised that the agent sounded Caucasian.

"I suspect that all the other agents have been discovered and neutralized."

Pedro knew exactly what the man meant with that word.

"They're closing in on me as well. I have collected a lot of evidence but have no way to get it out to my superiors ... As a matter of fact, I don't even know if I can trust my superiors."

"You want me to deliver your evidence?" Pedro interjected.

"Yes. Listen. I am not done," the man admonished. "They are watching you, too. But they're spread too thin for some reason. I think you have a good shot at getting this thing exposed." Pedro heard the man shift slightly.

"We've only got a minute left. I will come to your house early in the morning, two days from now. I will hand you my materials and give you an address. It will be a long drive. Don't go straight to the cops — I don't think you can trust them. Don't raise any more suspicion. For now, they think you're just rebellious and they're keeping an eye on you. I want you to turn on your living room light and turn up your central heating to max. The heat generated from them will fry those bugs in about twenty-four hours."

The man's clothes rustles as he got to his feet. "You've got to go now. Our time is up."

"Wait." Pedro quickly lowered his voice. "What do I call you?"

The man hesitated for a moment. "Pope. Call me Pope. Now go."

Pedro had a million other questions. Instead, he flushed the toilet and opened the stall. He woodenly walked to the sink and washed his hands, never even attempting to look back to where Pope was.

He departed the bathroom and met Charles near the back door.

"You didn't leave a mess in there, did you?" Charles asked with a wink.

Pedro laughed. It seemed too loud in his own ears. "Nope!"

Usually, the two men would visit for a while. Talk about sports, the weather, and the latest local rumors. This time, Pedro just wanted to get out of there.

"Hey Charles, I've got to run. Got some more deliveries to make..." He watched his friend's face drop slightly in disappointment.

"Well, all right. We can catch up next time."

With a grateful smile, Pedro nodded and stepped out of the back door, starting toward his car.

"Oh, Charles?" Pedro pulled up short. Charles had just about closed the back door. "Try one of these ciders. It's—" He considered his words for a moment. "A new recipe. I think you'll like it."

Charles laughed. "I always do, buddy."

Good. Maybe you won't get sick.

Roughly an hour later, Pedro got back to his shop. He was relieved to see everything still in its place. Nevertheless, he pictured listening bugs or cameras in every corner of the place. It made his skin crawl.

He put on his gear and worked on his last batch of cider. Working seemed to be the only way for him to forget about all the shit swirling around him — even if only for a few hours. He kept glancing around, expecting to see dark metallic devices, though. Pedro stubbornly continued to work, presenting a calm exterior while on the inside he was in turmoil.

After a while, his thoughts drifted to Maddie. Was she still putting together baskets with antidote-laden pies? He figured that she would be. She had an unbelievable strength of conviction — one of the things he loved about her.

I hope you're safe, mi dicha.

Then he thought about the fact that the Order was watching him. Were they watching her as well?

Maybe they consider me the threat. He nodded as he worked. That made sense. She came from a respected family that had been part of the Order for generations. Her own father held the role of adept — a senior position.

Better for them to be watching me. Maddie, you do what you can.

His heart ached. She was the love of his life. He felt it in every part of his being. He wanted nothing more than to spend the rest of his life with her. She felt the same way. Their future was going to be great.

Now it looked like it wasn't going to be as simple as that.

Maybe we can still run away... The thought felt unrealistic, but he clung to it anyway.

Yeah. I'm going to find her, after this business with Pope is done. I'm going to get her, and we are going to drive away. Disappear. He had a little more spring in his step as he finished his work and went home.

The first thing he did when he got there was to turn on his light and turn up the heater. His place was already warm — probably needing air conditioning more than heat — but Pope had been very specific. He just hoped that it would work.

He sat in his living room that evening and had a few ciders. Pedro had the TV on but was hardly watching it. He kept glancing at the drawn curtains.

They're out there. Watching. His eyes drifted up to the light above him. *Listening.*

Pedro downed the bottle of cider and reached for the next one. He felt light-headed by the time he went to bed.

He awoke the next morning with a hangover. It was the first hangover he'd had in a long time. The heat in his place didn't help. Pedro knew what he had to do, though. He followed his regular morning routine and traveled to his shop. The sharp pain in his head slowly dulled over the course of the morning. Pedro made two more deliveries that afternoon, before calling it a day and returning to his place. He was assaulted by a blast of heat as he opened his door.

Shit. I don't know what's going to fry first. The bugs or me.

As he closed the door behind him, Pedro glanced at the ceiling. He'd left the living room light on all night and day.

Is that the smell of a chemical burning? He wasn't sure.

Pope was supposed to be there in the morning, that he was sure of. Pedro had filled up his car on the way home, remembering that Pope had mentioned a long drive.

He ate a quick meal, drinking several glasses of water instead of cider. It was not even seven p.m. when he retired to his bedroom.

I should get some sleep. He wanted to be rested for whatever awaited him in the morning.

Pedro was sure that he would not be able to fall asleep. That couldn't be further from the truth, as he drifted off within minutes.

He awoke early the next morning. The first thing he noticed that it was dark. Suddenly, he sat up straight in his bed. It was dark!

"Hello?" he called out softly. There was no response.

Pedro crept out of his bed and out of the bedroom. He flicked the light switch.

Nothing. He flicked it several more times.

Ah. The light bulb must have burned out. He sighed in relief.

However, he did not go turn on another light. His eyes had adjusted to the dark somewhat. Also, he figured that anybody watching his place would be alerted if a light went on.

Instead, he got dressed and took a seat on his couch.

P edro jerked awake at a sound outside. He silently admonished himself for falling asleep. He had no idea how long he'd been out. All he knew was that the glow of the sun's rays was showing around the edges of the curtains.

Just then the door opened, and a figure stepped inside. The person was backlit by the rising sun, making it impossible for Pedro to see any features. The man started as he saw Pedro on the couch.

Pedro blinked into the brightness. "Pope? Is that you?" He squinted to get a better look but couldn't see anything beyond the haloed outline of a person.

The man hesitated for half a moment before answering. "Yes."

As the man closed the door, Pedro got to his feet. It plunged the room back into darkness.

"Wait …" Pedro maneuvered himself around to the kitchen and turned on the light. The man had not moved from the door area. Pedro noticed that Pope's hand was behind his back.

Reaching for a weapon?

The man caught Pedro's stare and straightened up. "Sorry. Just nervous."

Pedro nodded. "Okay." He looked Pope up and down.

Pope was of medium build and height — even a bit stocky, compared to Pedro. He walked over to the window and drew the curtains open a bit, letting some more light stream in.

"Shouldn't we keep those closed?"

The man shook his head. "It's fine."

Pedro frowned. Something was definitely not fine.

Aren't we trying to stay out of sight of that van?

Before Pedro could ask his question, Pope spoke up. "Did you find the bugs?"

Pedro nodded.

"Show me."

That surprised Pedro. "I—I didn't move them."

He walked into the bedroom, trailed by the man. "I guess this one is the easiest to grab." Pedro knelt at the vent while Pope stood behind him. After a bit of pulling, he was able to dislodge the vent.

"Thing must have fried real good," Pedro said as he placed the vent beside him. "This thing's hot enough to fry an egg."

Reaching into the vent, he grabbed the bug between his thumb and forefinger. It, too, was burning hot. The bug came loose surprisingly easy, and he almost dropped it. Pedro got back to his feet and held out the bug in his hand.

"Doesn't look like much, does it?" he asked.

Assenting, Pope took the bug and put it into one of his jacket pockets. "Let's grab the other one." He moved out of the bedroom with Pedro trailing him this time.

Pope froze in place. It was so sudden that Pedro almost ran into him. He looked over the man's shoulder at another person who had just entered the house.

This person was taller than Pedro or Pope. His expression was one of shock.

"You!" Pope exclaimed, and reached behind his back.

Pedro could see the dull glint of something metallic. His eyes continued down to Pope's feet.

Of course! Pedro reached forward as the man grasped the item tucked into his belt.

Everything seemed to happen in slow motion then. The newcomer at the door — the true Pope — lunged forward. Pedro's hands clasped around the other man's wrist, just as he was about to pull out a handgun. The man twisted to try to free himself from Pedro's grip as Pope collided with both.

The collision sent Pedro flying back into his bedroom, where he landed in a heap right before his bed. He heard the loud clunk of something hitting the ground near his feet.

The gun! The weapon was lying there. He grasped it and jumped up. All the while sounds of struggle emanated from the living room. He heard the sharp crash of something breaking, followed by an impact and a grunt.

Pedro danced into the living room, holding the gun in front of him as if it were a sword. One of the men was just getting to his feet — the other lay below him, unmoving.

Pedro raised the gun.

"Put that thing down," the man commanded.

"Pope?" Pedro asked, still not entirely sure.

"Yeah. Looks like I got here just in time." He wiped his hand on his cheek, then examined it for blood.

Pedro's eyes drifted to the body. "Is he..." He met Pope's steely gaze and knew the answer.

"Yeah. Didn't leave me much choice." Pedro took a step backward, and Pope noticed it. "This is a life-and-death situation, Pedro. Don't quake out on me now."

About to argue, Pedro caught himself. He looked down at the corpse at Pope's feet and back up at the CIA agent. "You're right. What do we need to do?"

"Help me drag this guy into your bathroom."

They picked up the dead Rosae Crucis man. Pedro took the feet while Pope grabbed under his armpits. Pedro couldn't help noticing how the man's head lolled at an unnatural angle as they lifted him. He swallowed hard then got on with it.

"He wanted to collect the bugs," Pedro mentioned as they maneuvered the body out of the living room.

Pope nodded without looking back at Pedro. "Cleaning up any evidence. My guess is that this guy was supposed to dispose of you."

Again, Pedro swallowed.

They placed the dead man in the bathtub. They were about to walk back into the living room when Pedro suddenly started.

"The van! This guy opened the curtains." He looked ready to bolt.

"Relax. I took care of it."

"Oh."

"You know how to use that?" Pope pointed at gun on the coffee table.

Pedro had forgotten about the gun that he'd placed there moments ago. He shook his head hesitantly. "Not really..."

"Better leave it, then."

He turned to face Pedro squarely. It was the first time that Pedro got a good look at the man. He was tall and lean, with pale blond hair receding toward the crown of his head. Blue, emotionless eyes stared at Pedro below protruding brows. A heavy, square jaw covered in short stubble and a large nose completed the picture.

Pope sighed. Pedro watched his nostrils flare. "I'm afraid we don't have much time. Whatever the Order planned has been set in motion already."

"How bad is it?" Pedro felt his skin grow cold.

The emotionless eyes betrayed a flash of something else. Anger, or annoyance. "It's bad. Global. Something to do with nano technology. I never figured out exactly what, though." Pope continued to speak as he approached the front door, "Anyway, I've brought this."

A large tube stood there. Pope took it and turned back to Pedro, but did not present the tube yet.

"Here." He passed Pedro a note instead. "It's the address of my old office."

"Greenville..." Pedro read on the note. That was going to be a long drive, for sure.

"Yeah. You need to get this info to that place. Tell them 'This is A-grade steak.' They'll know what that means."

Pedro opened his mouth to ask a question, but Pope said, "I trust the people there. They'll know what to do."

"What are *you* going to do?"

"The only thing I can. Haul ass back to the satellite." Pedro wanted to ask what he meant by that, but Pope went on, "My cover isn't blown yet. The best thing for me to do is continue to work on the inside. Maybe I can find a way to reverse this nano thing..."

His expression told Pedro that the CIA man didn't hold out much hope for that.

"Listen." His eyes snapped to lock with Pedro's. "This thing — whatever it is — has started. We're out of time. I need you to take this info. It's a map. There are names and ranks written on the back. I've got other intel, but I couldn't get to it in time. This will have to do."

With that, he thrust the tube into Pedro's hands.

"You need to go. Now."

"Okay." Pedro took the tube. He stroked the leathery material with his thumb. "I—I'll do it. I'll get it done."

Pope merely nodded as if he expected no less.

Pedro collected his car keys and strode past Pope. His hand was on the doorknob when the agent spoke one last time.

"Now you know." He pointed with his chin toward the bathroom. "They're prepared to kill to keep this secret. We have to blow this out of the water."

It was Pedro who nodded this time. Without another word, he opened the door and stepped out into the sunshine.

Pedro drove for four hours, only stopping once to fill up. He got to the outskirts of Atlanta just after lunchtime and allowed himself a second stop — this time to grab a quick bite to eat and use the washroom at a roadside restaurant.

The sun was high in the sky. Pedro walked out of the restaurant and into the small parking lot. It was a pleasant day, the remnants of summer heat combining with the colors of fall. Pedro took a deep breath and admired the scenery. He was halfway to his car when he spotted the dark blue sedan. Something about the car — and more importantly the guy sitting in the car — made him feel on edge.

Why would a guy just be sitting there? Is it the Order?

All he wanted to do was sprint to his vehicle and peel out of that parking lot. He didn't, though. Pedro walked to his car with a calmness he did not feel. He got into the driver's seat and took a shuddering breath. Fumbling with the keys slightly, he managed to start the car and pull out of the lot. He made sure to never look at the blue sedan.

One eye on his rear-view mirror, Pedro merged onto the highway and drove.

There! He caught a glimpse of the sedan.

"Mierda." Deep down, Pedro knew that the Order was onto him. He briefly wondered if they had caught up with Pope. Then his thoughts turned darker.

Maddie!

Pedro started looking for exits. All he wanted to do was get back to Maddie and make sure she was safe. He spotted an exit up ahead and got into the right lane.

He took the exit, noting that the sedan had followed, a hundred yards back.

"Shit. I can't go home..." Pedro skipped the U-turn lane and continued to drive parallel to the highway.

I'd lead them straight to her. He glanced at the tube lying on the back seat. His best option was to try to lose the tail and continue his mission.

Two miles ahead loomed another highway exit. He slowed down, anxiously watching his follower. The sedan maintained distance. Another car had inserted itself between them.

The cars at the light ahead started moving. He slowed down again. The vehicle between him and his follower began encroaching. Pedro barely took note of the guy in a pickup waving his hand in a gesture of impatience.

The lights were just a couple hundred yards ahead now. Pedro slowed down some more. The pickup truck was really riding his ass now. The driver was losing his mind and about to have some serious road rage.

There. At fifty yards, the light turned yellow. Pedro floored it. He quickly left the pickup in the dust. The light turned red at fifteen yards, but Pedro was committed. He put the pedal to the metal and roared through the intersection, receiving a couple of horn blasts for his action.

But it had worked. The pickup pulled to a stop at the lights. Pedro could see the sedan poking out to the left behind the truck, trying to keep Pedro in his sights.

"I don't think so, buddy." Pedro took his next right. He sped down the road, easily going twice the speed limit. "Where are the cops when you need them?"

The sound of the horns faded quickly as he pulled into the oncoming lane to pass a minivan. He entered a wooded area.

You can do this. Pedro drove past the next turn, still going flat out. He passed several more vehicles, thanking his lucky stars that nobody was coming in the opposite direction as he executed his passing maneuvers.

He took the next left turn, followed by the next right. Pedro didn't allow the vehicle to slow down to a normal speed for the next fifteen minutes as he randomly turned at intersections.

It wasn't until an hour later that Pedro realized that he was totally lost. He also needed to relieve himself. Badly. For another ten minutes, he squirmed in the seat until he had to pull over.

Then he saw the sign.

As good a place as any. A mile later, he pulled into the small, empty parking lot of the Georgia Guidestones. He checked the map on his phone before leaving the car and was pleasantly surprised to find that he was still roughly heading in the right direction.

Pedro grinned. He was no secret agent, but he sure as hell had lost his tail. He'd take a quick piss behind the stones and continue the journey toward Greenville.

Barely giving the stones a glance, Pedro jogged around them. He had heard about them and was intrigued, but he had a much more pressing matter to attend to.

Thirty seconds later, Pedro sighed with relief as he watered the sparse grass.

He zipped up and turned around.

Wow.

The stones were an impressive sight. He stepped closer to look at the inscriptions on the massive slabs. It all looked like hieroglyphics to him. Then he turned, and then next slab was in Spanish.

Maintain mankind at five hundred million or less, in balance with nature.

Pedro frowned. *Huh. Wonder how they know that five hundred million is the balance?*

Manage reproduction — improve health and diversity.

He shook his head, unsure what the exact meaning behind that sentence was.

Unite mankind with a dynamic language.

Everybody speaking the same language made sense to Pedro. *Okay, that's one for three.* Curious, he kept on reading.

Rule passion, spirituality, tradition, and all things with moderate reason.

Protect people and nations with just laws and correct courts.

Let all nations rule internally, let a world court rule external disputes.

Avert frivolous laws and useless politicians.

Pedro snorted. *Useless politicians.* He liked that one.

Balance personal rights with societal duties.

Treasure truth, beauty, and love; seek harmony with the infinite.

I get the first part. But what's "the infinite"?

He read the last line and decided that he liked that one the best.

Don't be a cancer upon the earth. Leave space for nature.

Pedro nodded as he considered this. It was all very much in line with Rosae Crucis teachings — the ones he agreed with, at any case. He stared at the slab, wondering who'd built the monument.

Was it built by the Order? He shook his head. He'd never know.

Admiring the construction, Pedro walked around the concrete monolith. He stepped into view of the parking lot and froze.

Another vehicle had arrived. It was a dark sedan, parked right next to Pedro's car.

It's them.

Pedro considered diving behind the monument but could tell he had already been spotted. The driver got out of his vehicle and calmly had a peek inside Pedro's car before turning to him. They stood silently and stared at each other for a moment. The dark-haired man sported shades. He wore ordinary, nondescript clothing, with the exception of his long coat. Pedro knew immediately and without any doubt that this was one of the Rosae Crucis intelligence agents.

The man casually walked toward Pedro, stopping when he was about ten feet away. He took off his shades and put them into his pocket, leaving his hand inside.

"You almost got away from me. Luckily, we know where you're headed." His voice was rather high-pitched for someone who looked so ominous.

Pedro had a retort ready, but it slipped from his lips when the man took his hand out of his pocket. The sunglasses had been replaced by a handgun.

"I don't know who you are, but you're in a heap of trouble."

The pistol was pointed at Pedro, but the man held it rather casually. Pedro got the impression that the man knew how to handle the weapon.

Still, Pedro kept his mouth shut. The man took a couple of steps closer. "Hands up."

Pedro complied. "Turn around and walk to the back side of this thing."

Once again, Pedro complied. His eyes frantically searched the ground in front of him, looking for any means to defend himself.

"Don't try anything, or I will shoot." The lack of emotion in the statement made it all the more believable.

Just as Pedro stepped around the monument, something hit him in the back of the head. A starburst shot through his vision, and he felt a sharp pain as he crashed to the ground. He lay on his stomach and groaned, reaching to his head with one hand.

The man kicked him in the hip. "Turn over, traitor."

The kick alone practically served to flip Pedro. He rolled the rest of the way. Bright sparkles exploded in his vision as he opened his eyes and tried to see his attacker.

"Gonna need a name from you, right now. No name means pain. Understood?"

Pedro could only groan again. Before he knew it, he felt a sharp pain in his ankle as the man stomped down on it.

"Oh, this is going to be fun for me!" There was glee in the man's voice.

Slowly, Pedro's vision cleared. The man was standing over him. "A name. Now."

"Pope," Pedro managed to get past a thick tongue.

"You look a little messed up. A little concussed, as they say." The man leaned down to tap Pedro in the forehead with the barrel of his gun. "You sound kind of concussed, too." He drew himself up again. "Now, what did you say?"

"Pope. Pope." It came out clearer the second time.

"Who in the hell goes by the name 'Pope'?" He dealt a kick to Pedro's shin. "You're going to have to give me more than that."

"I don't know!" Pedro pleaded. "That's the name he gave me."

"Let's try this again. Name."

The malice was clear in the other man's eyes. He was putting the gun back in his pocket.

Pedro stammered, trying to think of something useful to say. The man lifted his leg, intent on stomping down on Pedro's knee.

Instinct took over. Pedro was no fighter, but he'd had his share of scuffles in his youth. He violently rolled toward the man and into his standing leg. The ankle buckled and the man yelped. He fell sideways and was unable to catch his fall, as his hand was stuck in his pocket.

CRACK!

The man's head hit the corner of one of the Guidestones. He collapsed listlessly to the ground, landing in a heap.

Pedro jumped to his feet despite the protestations of his ankle and approached the man.

Is he dead? Did I kill him?

Reaching for the man's neck, he felt for a heartbeat. He couldn't find one, but he was no expert at detecting life. He quickly extracted the gun from the man's pocket and carefully put his hand by his face.

There. The guy was breathing. He searched his pockets and found car keys. The sunglasses were busted.

Pedro acted quickly. It took five minutes, and a strength that he did not know he possessed, but he dragged the man by his feet to his vehicle, popped the trunk, and stuffed him into it. He looked at the handgun in his pocket for a moment, then tossed it into the far corner of the trunk and slammed the lid closed with some satisfaction.

He stepped up to his car, intent on getting in and driving away as fast away as he could, but then hesitated.

We know where you're headed, the man had said.

Pedro mulled it over. Would he be rushing straight into a trap? Did they truly know that he was heading toward Greenville? Did they know what he was carrying? His eyes traveled to the tube. He had to think of something. He pulled out his phone.

Time to get creative.

To whoever finds this.

       I hope you're the good guys. I don't know who to trust. Neither should the reader of this note.

My name is Pedro Aragonez. The information on the map is very important and must be brought to the authorities as soon as possible. This is a matter of national security. Maybe even global security. Many people are going to die if we can't stop them.

Hopefully it's not too late.

Sorry, I am ranting. The map was given to me by a CIA agent codenamed "Pope." I've added as much information as I could with my notes. The Rosae Crucis are a threat to our nation.

Good luck to you and to us all.

Tammy swayed on her feet slightly as she lowered the note. A combination of the afternoon sun beating down on her and reading out loud had taken her breath away. Abi was the first to react. She jumped up to her feet and quickly stepped over to the former news anchor.

"Here. Drink some water."

She held out her water bottle to Tammy, who took it with thanks. Tammy drank greedily from the bottle, not even noticing the water that spilled. She drank until the bottle was empty.

"Thanks," she breathlessly repeated, handing the bottle back to Abi.

The rest of the group had also gotten to their feet by then. They reluctantly stepped out of the shadow of the Guidestones and grouped around Tammy.

"That was interesting." John started. "Too bad they couldn't get the job done. Could have prevented all of this..."

"What I'm curious about is just who is this secret ally? Is he still around?" Romy said.

"Yeah, but we have no info on that. No name, way to establish contact." John frowned. "For all we know, they're all dead."

"I hope not," Romy said. "We need all the friends we can get."

"What about Maddie?" Abi chimed in. "My guess is that she and her family are at the nearest location to their farm." She pointed at the map in John's hand. "Maybe Pedro followed them to that place?"

"Good point." John motioned to the Humvee with his head. "Let's get going. The sooner we get back to the Ren, the sooner we can plan our next more."

Tammy followed the group. They all talked excitedly about what they had learned, but she was silent. One question dominated her thoughts:

What happened to Pedro?

Pedro

Ten minutes after stowing the map, Pedro was back on the road. The sun stood low in the sky now, occasionally dipping behind the treetops.

Pedro's destination was still Greenville. The CIA was his only hope of stopping the Order, so turning back was not an option. He'd stowed notes containing most of what he knew along with the map. He hoped that it was enough.

After checking a roadmap on his phone, he planned to get into town from the south instead of the east. Maybe they wouldn't be looking for him in that direction. It was a chance he had to take. His best shot was still to get to the address that Pope had provided him.

In the meantime, he had a call to make.

"Pedro! Where have you b—"

"Stop. Maddie, I need you to listen."

"This has something to do with the Order, doesn't it?"

"Please, Maddie."

"Okay."

The audible exasperation on the other end of the line made him smile a little.

Ah, mi hermosa novia. She really was his beautiful fiancée. Moreover, her beauty extended well below her skin.

"Look, I need you to copy something down for me. It's important. Do you have a pen and paper?"

"Just a sec ... Go ahead."

"It's just numbers. 342320 and 828940. Did you get that?"

"Got it."

"Repeat them back to me."

She did. Pedro sighed with relief, and finally allowed himself to relax a little.

"You're driving," Maddie stated. "Where are you going?"

"I just need to run one more errand, and then I'm coming back. I'll come over first thing in the morning, *mi dicha*. I promise." He tried to sound calm as he spoke.

"They're dangerous, Pedro. Please, be careful." He could hear the pleading in Maddie's voice.

I'm sorry, my love. It's too late to be careful. "Of course, Maddie. I'm always careful."

"What do I do with these numbers?"

"Ah, yes. We need to get those numbers out to the authorities, or anybody that will listen. Do you think you can get back to the library and post those numbers? ... Maddie? ... Hello?"

Pedro looked at his phone to see that the call had gotten disconnected. He was driving through a dead zone.

"Ah, damn!" Pedro tried to call Maddie back, but to no avail. Frustrated, he tossed the phone onto the passenger seat.

The countryside tore past him, going from open meadows and fields to wooded areas and rocky hills.

"Great. There ain't no reception in the backwoods." Pedro's attempt at a southern accent failed miserably. The sarcasm came through loud and clear, though.

Ten minutes later, the countryside dropped dramatically away behind him, and he found himself in a more urban setting. He grabbed the phone and was encouraged to see the bars. But one look in his mirror told him that he had a big problem. He was being followed again. It was the same car that had tailed him from Nashville to Atlanta. The dark blue sedan.

Pedro was out of ideas. *"Ya vale, su madre,"* he exclaimed. *I'm fucked.*

He looked at the phone in his hand. If they got a hold of it, then they'd know he had called Maddie. He couldn't let that happen. There was an interchange ahead, its elevated cloverleaf roads a gray monstrosity of concrete in the dimming light of day.

Pedro took the turnoff. The sedan was only a couple of vehicles behind him. He opened his window. A blast of wind assaulted his face. He hoped that the darkness would hide his action as he continued up the sharp incline of the overpass.

He waited until he got to the highest point and hurled the phone as far away as he could. He saw the tiniest flash as the phone caught a ray of light before it disappeared into darkness. Behind him, the sedan kept coming.

Not like it is going to reverse off the overpass. Pedro congratulated himself, but his joy was short-lived as he merged onto another interstate.

He still had the problem of his tail. He drove along, paying more attention to his rear-view mirror than to the actual road.

How am I going to get rid of you?

The answer appeared. A few cars back, a police cruiser drove along. Pedro immediately pulled into the same lane.

Now what?

He did the first thing he could think of. He swerved his vehicle from side to side. It elicited a couple of angry honks from other travelers. More importantly, the police cruiser turned on its lights.

"Fuck, yeah!" he exclaimed in triumph.

Pedro slowed down. He watched as his former tail drove by.

"See you later, asshole," Pedro whispered, and grinned as pulled his vehicle onto the shoulder and put it in park.

"Holy smokes. That was close."

He lowered his window and waited for the police officer to approach.

Now, what do I tell the cops? Maybe I can get these guys to take me to that address ... Pedro grinned at his sudden turn of luck.

"You're a sight for sore eyes." Pedro smiled up at the officer as he stepped up to the car. The man did not smile back. His hand was on his pistol.

"Turn off your ignition and step out of the vehicle, please."

"Yes, sir." Pedro turned off the engine and opened his door. "I was trying to get away from these people that are chasing m—"

"Turn around. Hands where I can see them."

"Sure..." Pedro obeyed. He was guided away from the open door and held up against the rear quarter of his vehicle. He felt his wrist being cuffed.

"You don't need to do that." Pedro was roughly shoved back into position.

"I'll be the judge of that."

His other wrist was cuffed.

"This the one?" the police officer asked. Pedro craned his neck to see who he was talking to.

A sharp-nosed, skinny man stepped into view. The man stared at Pedro maliciously through his circular glasses.

"Ah. Pedro Aragonez. Good to see you again."

Pedro had never seen the man before but knew who it was, nonetheless.

Oh, mi dicha. *I have failed.*

"We have some things to discuss, you and I," the man added.

The end game has started. Maddie's words shot into Pedro's mind as he was roughly led away from his car and shoved into the police cruiser.

Chapter 22

John

November 19 3:45 P.M., Bowman Minimart, Bowman, Georgia

"Where is everybody?" Tammy asked as they stepped out of the vehicle. They had pulled up to the gas pump, right in front of what looked like the general store of the town.

City. John corrected himself. The sign as they drove in said as much.

A city of all but eight hundred people.

Tammy was right, though. There was not a soul in sight. *Where did they go?*

Clack.

They looked toward a house set further back in the block. At first, they saw nothing. Then:

Clack.

Abi gasped as a pale hand slapped the small window high up in the door. Something was in there, and it wanted to get out.

Clack.

It seemed too weak to break through the glass, so John let it be. He scanned the area, squinting in the afternoon sunlight.

Nothing. No one.

"Let's not waste time here. BB, see if you can get the pumps going. Tammy, you stand by the pump here. Romy, watch that angle." John made a chopping direction toward the northeast. "Abi." This time he chopped his hand toward the south. "Go."

The team broke up, each heading in a direction. John's head was on a swivel, watching BB's back and the area across the street in turn.

He need not have worried. BB found the store to be abandoned, and a generator in the shop next door. A minute later, the generator hummed to life, and Tammy was able to start filling the gas tank. There had not been a single incident by the time that the Humvee's twenty-five-gallon tank was filled. Just the occasional *clack* in the background to break the silence.

BB had a surprise for the team as they drove out of Bowman several minutes later. He'd brought a cardboard box with him from the minimart. Tammy tallied off the items from the back seat as she pulled them out of the box.

"Georgia Nuts." She took several bags and placed them beside her. "Ah, of course: Twinkies!" She grinned at a mostly full box of the cream-filled pastries from the container.

"And lastly, booze."

The passengers of the vehicle spontaneously cheered.

"Apple brandy," Tammy read the bottle as she lifted it out of the box. "Can't say I've tried that before."

She rummaged for the last bottle. It was a one-gallon glass jar with the classic finger slot in the neck. There was no label.

"Somebody scribbled on this bottle with a marker. It says, 'black cherry shine.'" She looked up at Abi in the front seat. "Moonshine?"

Abi glanced at BB. "Yeah, I'd say from the look on BB's face that it's moonshine."

"I ain't Bill, but y'all hear me: We gonna have us a good ol' party tonight!"

Everybody laughed at BB's poor attempt at a southern accent. All thoughts of zombies were momentarily out of mind.

Roughly twelve miles to the southeast, most of the former residents of Bowman trudged along the highway. They were packed together tightly, forming a somewhat solid mass of undead. Most stuck to the pavement, but some were forced to stumble along the shoulder or the verge. The ones forced to the outside were the unlucky ones. They would often lose their footing on the uneven surface, and it was not uncommon to hear the sharp crack of a snapping limb as the horde traveled. Some were slowed enough by their injuries that they lost touch with the main horde, limping, crawling or dragging themselves along from a few yards to over a mile behind the rest.

In sharp contrast to these slow movers, several jogged or lurched in front of the main group, only to come to a halt when they got too far ahead. They would then wait until the horde caught up to them before lurching on. Observers might think that these undead were impatient, but they would be wrong. The undead knew nothing of impatience.

The same observers might note that the main group moved in a consistent pace. Nothing was left of the starts and stops that had been their trait for the first weeks of their existence.

They had evolved, if you could call it that. Moreover, they had direction and purpose.

Observers would note that any exposed skin had turned tough — impermeable, almost. They would also see that many of the zombies appeared to be shedding their hair. Most disturbingly, the eyeballs had shriveled inside their eye sockets. In fact, the eyeballs themselves were being shed as well. This seemed to happen out of the blue. An eyeball would detach as they walked, to land with a rubbery splat onto the pavement. The zombies seemed not to mind.

A few of the zombies displayed some damage, though. This ranged from cuts and abrasions, which oozed pus, to deep gashes that appeared as dark maws. They exposed innards that had long since dried up.

The stragglers way behind the horde were even worse off. Their wounds included dull ivory shards that broke the skin on every step. Some were missing limbs altogether. Their lot was to fall ever further behind, moving stiffly and often stumbling, but they would continue to travel. At least until the aegis of their skulls were breached.

The lead elements of the horde approached an on-ramp. Secondary Highway 172 met primary Highway 72 here. This was also where the Bowman horde would merge with the tail end of the Corner horde and the lead elements of the Eberton horde.

The Bowman zombies stepped onto Highway 72 and walked shoulder to shoulder with former rival high-school football players and fans. All animosity was now a thing of the past. If there was such a thing as animosity, it was directed at "the others." The ones that were already surrounded by thousands, but still out of reach.

It would be frustrating. But zombies could not feel such an emotion.

They marched on, as fast as they could, to answer the call. They were going to march another fourteen miles before they reached their destination. After that, they would mill around, waiting for a sign. They would occasionally press in on the obstacles in front of them — especially when one of the others made their presence known.

Eventually, those obstacles would fall. Crushed or pushed over under the combined weight of the host.

Then, they would be able to continue their approach. Find the others. Complete their programing.

For the others must be silenced, and their brightly shining auras must be snuffed out.

Chapter 23

Christine

November 19, 11:45 P.M., The Ren.

"Ooooooohhhh ... Ooohhhooooohhh!"

The wailing never seemed to stop. Or rather, it seemed to start up again with renewed energy whenever there were a couple of minutes of blessed silence.

Christine felt awful for Mike. The poor man was suffering in terrible agony as his wounds festered. But his cries made getting sleep a near impossibility. She sighed as his latest cries slowly faded into a moan that finally stopped. Christine let her eyes close and tried to clear her mind.

Please, sleep. Come now.

But it was not to be, as Mike moaned in pain once more.

With a frustrated growl, she threw off the covers and got up from the small couch. Christine thought about opening the door and begging Mike to shut up but knew that it would do no good. Mike was delirious with fever. Instead, she walked out of the small office that was her post and shut the door behind her.

Not like anything is going to change in the next few minutes. As if on cue, Mike's latest moan drifted down to a whisper. Christine hesitated for a moment, trying to decide whether she should return to the couch and try to catch some sleep. She made up her mind with a small shake of the head and continued out into the hallway.

She walked past the main office and entered the cafeteria. Just a couple of lights were on, standing out like islands of brightness in the otherwise darkened room. The fact that they had lights at all was thanks to Ern and Jack.

Christine shook her head. She didn't want to think about Jack. She walked to the back of the cafeteria, where the buffet counters were. Several pitchers of water had been placed there, for those who needed hydration. Christine helped herself to a glass of water.

Another thing for which we can thank Ern, she realized as she sipped the filtered rainwater. She never would have drunk rainwater before all this. But not only was it necessary, it tasted fine. Christine figured that this was because no factories were spewing clouds of chemicals into the skies. Missing were the chemtrails of planes in the air, and the fumes from many millions of car exhausts.

It was kind of funny to Christine. Hundreds of years of pollution seemed to be reversed in a matter of weeks.

"Oh." She spun around as another figure approached.

Keith stepped into the pale light. "Mind if I grab a glass of water?"

"Sure." Christine stepped aside for the Asian man. Her eyes never left him as he filled a glass from the pitcher and finally turned to face Christine. "Couldn't sleep?" she asked.

He shrugged noncommittally. He took a deep draught of the water. Christine watched his Adam's apple work as he swallowed.

"I think that I know the answer to this, but how's Mike?" he asked.

Her expression grew troubled. "Not good. The infection has spread too far." She shook her head sadly. "I'm not sure how much longer he's going to hang on."

Keith sighed. He put the glass down and leaned back against the counter. Christine took a step forward, her hand reaching for him. She pulled up short as she saw the look in his eyes.

Shock, and fear. Like a cornered animal.

Christine knew the look. She sighed and dropped her hand. "You can relax. I'm not going to make a move on you."

Keith did relax. A little. To his credit, he looked slightly embarrassed. "Sorry, Christine. I'm just not..." His voice faded as he searched for the right words.

Much to his surprise, Cristine chuckled. "It's okay, Keith. I've been on that side of the equation many times." She stepped next to him and also leaned against the counter.

They stood there for a long moment, sharing a not uncomfortable silence.

Keith took another sip of his water and turned his head to look at Christine. "Why the sudden interest in me? I mean, it's not like you were interested when we first got here."

Christine thought about it for a moment. "To be honest, I don't think I *am* interested in you." She added with an apologetic smile, "Sorry. I'm not trying to insult you. I guess it's more that I just didn't want to be alone."

Slowly nodding, he stared ahead once more.

"I have been thinking about it," Christine continued. "It's like I've been reacting blindly, but instead of lashing out at those around me, I've been trying to latch on to anybody." Christine made her hands into claws and drew them toward her chest in a grasping gesture. "I can't remember a time when I wasn't with somebody. I'm not good at being alone."

"Maybe you're just out of practice. Maybe you should give yourself a chance first."

That comment took her by surprise. "You know what? I think that maybe you're right about that." She pushed herself away from the counter and faced him. "You're smarter than I gave you credit for."

"The Dude abides." Keith's deadpan expression gave little away.

"That's some movie quote, isn't it?" Christine laughed. "You are a weird duck, Keith. Weird, but good." She stretched out her hand. "Friends?"

"Friends." They shook hands.

They hung out for a while. Keith shared a story about Cindy, and Christine talked about Matt. It felt good for her to talk about it, and some of her anxiety melted away. As she listened to Keith, her mind drifted to Jack. As had happened with Keith, her interest in Jack had been nothing more than the need for attention.

I should talk to him.

A moan of pain drifted out of darkness, and Keith and Christine turned their heads to the cafeteria exit. The moan faded away. Mike was silent once more.

"Poor guy," Keith said.

Christine agreed. She'd liked the old soldier. She had not spent a lot of time in his presence, but he had impressed her as a calm, kind man. She had not seen him lose his temper once. He was more prone to disarm arguments. Something her dad could learn from, she realized.

Keith drained his glass of water and placed the cup in the dish tray on the counter. "I think I'll try to get some sleep now."

"Hey, Keith." Christine also put her glass away. "Thanks. This was good."

Keith nodded and tipped his imaginary cap. For once he did not have a movie quote at hand, so he just grinned and walked away.

She watched him leave the cafeteria and stood in the dimly lit room for a long moment, just enjoying the silence. That silence was breached moments later.

The sound of terrible suffering stirred her into movement.

Chapter 24

The dead

The world was darkness. It enveloped all, like a shroud. It mattered not to the being. Its eyes were no more — a necessary action to keep the host mobile and functional.

Yet it could see.

The images came into its awareness as little more than muted flashes of color, appearing beyond the mist of shapes in its immediate vicinity. It was enough to keep the host from running into obstacles. And it lit up the others.

But sight was not its highest sense.

It heard moans and cries, as muffled as they were. It knew not the difference between a moan, or speech, or a dog's bark. But sound indicated the energy it sought to extinguish. Hence it came, drawn on by its programing.

It had arrived here with one other. There was a third, but that one was slow. They left it behind. It would continue at its own pace, never giving up, never quitting. None of them did. They knew their program, or the end of existence.

Both hosts cocked their heads in unison, picking up a new sound. They were drawn to the sound, but the obstacle held them back. Its companion beat at the obstacle in fury, seeking to destroy what was keeping it from its purpose. The noise it generated was distracting, so it was ordered to stop. The lessons of a thousand others entered its consciousness, and as one they reached up with their hands and grasped the chain link fence.

Chapter 25

Tammy

November 20, 7:30 A.M., A private residence

John walked into the atrium.

"Do I smell coffee?"

Tammy nodded and pointed at the counter with her chin. "Right there." John's eyes lit and he walked up, rubbing his hands.

"You can thank Romy for that, by the way," Tammy added, winking at the dark-skinned woman sitting beside her.

"This place is a fucking gold mine," John said enthusiastically as he poured himself a cup.

"This place," was a mansion. They had stumbled across it on their journey toward the Guidestones and promised themselves that they would come back and stay the night on their return. The mansion was quite secure, with a high cast-iron fence around the perimeter and all windows with bars.

Once inside the gate, they still had the challenge of getting into the mansion. It was locked tight. Finally, they had to resort to parking the Humvee underneath a second-floor balcony and encouraging the reluctant BB to pull up his slender frame. Five minutes later, he had opened the front door with a flourish. Their luck held, as the place was abandoned.

"Ahhh." John sighed as he sank his frame into a chair and luxuriated in the flavor of the black liquid in his cup.

Tammy had only gotten to the atrium a minute before John but was already halfway through hers.

"Where's Abi?" John asked after taking another sip.

"Still sleeping."

They had all partnered up for the night. Tammy had shared a king size bed with the diminutive but quite restless Abi. She reminded Tammy of an old boyfriend who tossed and turned his way right out of their relationship.

"What about BB?" she asked.

"Same. The kid took the late watch, so I figured I'd let him rest."

They drank their coffee in companiable silence, lost in their own thoughts.

"Have we had a chance to look around this place?" Tammy wondered. They hadn't done much apart from making sure the house was clear the previous night.

Romy nodded excitedly. "Yeah. There's some good stock in the pantry, which includes an actual wine cellar."

Tammy snickered. "I didn't picture you for a wine girl."

"Yeah, I suppose you're right," Romy replied without losing a beat. "But a girl can't be too picky these days."

They all shared a small chuckle at that.

"I also found an indoor pool down the other wing." Romy pointed behind her. "What's more, it's got a working hot tub and one of those ultra-fancy showers with like sixty settings!" She was clearly exaggerating, but Tammy sat up straight, nonetheless.

"No way." She turned to John. "Do we have some time, before we have to leave?"

"Yeah," he said. "We should let BB sleep for at least another hour."

Tammy finished her coffee with one large gulp and got up.

"Where are you going?" Romy asked her.

"Hot-tub time. I'm going to grab a towel. Who is in?"

"Hell, yeah." Romy said, and also got up.

"Sorry, John. Girls only!" Tammy called over her shoulder as she left the atrium.

Tammy quickly walked down the hall and to the suite she shared with Abi. To call it a bedroom would do it a disservice. It even had the type of fancy seats and large, ornate writing desk that she thought was the stuff of movies.

I should keep it down, Tammy told herself as she approached the door. Abi had been fast asleep when she left the room five minutes earlier.

The only thought in her mind was the en-suite bathroom and the towels inside, so Tammy opened the door carefully and stepped through. Then she heard a noise.

Tammy looked up and froze.

Abi was sitting on the writing table, naked. Her back was arched, her arms holding her upper body up even as her legs wrapped around BB's waist, clenching him tightly as he thrust into her. BB was still dressed except for his pants, which were down at his ankles. The skinny man had claw-like hands on her hips and buttocks, pulling her into him hard with every thrust. His eyes were shut and his mouth open, his face tilted up toward the ceiling, the large Adam's apple standing out in his throat.

Too stunned to say anything, Tammy stood in the doorway as the two lovers grunted with animal desire. She realized that she had not been seen yet, so silently backed up into the hall and shut the door with infinite care.

She walked back toward the atrium and right past the surprised John.

"No towel?" he asked.

"Maybe there are some at the pool," she hurriedly answered as she strode past.

Chapter 26

Joe

November 20, 8:00 A.M., The Ren.

J oe tended to be a light sleeper. Lately, he wasn't sure if he had been sleeping at all, which was taking its toll on him. He was tired all the time, and that led to making mistakes.

He lay in the cot he shared with Rachel, careful not to move around too much and rouse his slumbering wife. Joe figured it was nearing dawn. He was starting to be able to see shapes. He let his head roll to the side and watched the shape of his wife's shoulder and back, just making out the gentle rise and fall of her breathing.

She had a good night, for once.

Joe had been sure she would have another episode, especially when he'd shown up last night covered in blood. Yet it didn't trigger a trip into psychosis. Or nightmares that ended up with him having to defend himself.

Carefully he got out of the cot. Rachel mumbled something but quickly fell back into deep slumber. At the sink, he washed his face then the sink itself, as there were still traces of blood in it.

He really should have washed up in the clinic the night before. But he hadn't been able to face it.

Mike's dying. It's your fault. He couldn't face Shelley's impossibly large eyes. *What went wrong?*

Joe frowned, wondering how he had missed the perforated intestine. The bullet had a clean entry wound and a larger but similarly clean exit wound.

The frown brought his own injury to light. He gingerly touched the nose, inspecting it in the mirror.

Healing well...

Invariably, his thoughts turned back to Mike. *What did go wrong?*

Were there bullet fragments left behind? Or maybe the bullet chipped a bone, turning those shards into miniature daggers. He pictured those tiny daggers shredding Mike's bowels.

One thing was certain: Mike was in bad shape. Joe had little hope that the man would survive much longer, if he had even made it through the night.

Christine or Shelley would have told me. Mike must still be alive. And if he is alive, there is hope.

Joe finished washing up and got dressed as quickly and quietly as he could. He watched Ethan, fast asleep in his own cot. Only his face was exposed from the cocoon he'd constructed. The boy's face still looked so young. Angelic, even. Joe smiled at the sight, glad to give his son a few more moments of peace before the harshness of the real world wiped the innocence from that face.

Joe quietly let himself out of their room. He could hear signs of life once in the hallway, as some people stirred awake while others were up and at it already. He had just gotten to the stairs when the alarm rang out.

Oh my God! It's them. The Order. The hair on Joe's neck rose as he rushed down the stairs and toward the noise.

Jack was ringing the alarm. Nat stood beside him, already armed with a long rifle. Joe was the next person on the scene.

"What is it?"

"We've got at least one zombie inside the fence." Jack turned from Nat to Joe as he spoke. "We were just up on the roof ... Wanted to watch the sun come up. Anyway, we heard a noise. When we looked, there was a zombie on the ground just inside the fence."

As if on cue, they heard a bang against the front door.

Jack's eyes opened wide. "Must be a fast one. Nat was going to shoot it, but we spotted another."

Nat shrugged. She seemed much calmer than Jack.

Big rifle like that gives anybody courage.

Emily and Bill arrived just then. They were trailed by Ben.

"What's the commotion?" Bill asked. The twang in his voice combined with the melodic way he spoke made Joe think of Elvis.

He lives.

Joe desperately wanted to make a comment about it but knew this wasn't the time. "There is at least one zombie inside the school grounds. At least one more at the fence."

The soldiers nodded.

"Can you go grab rifles from the armory?" he asked Bill. "We'll need four. Jack, give him a hand, please." Bill and Jack were off by the time he turned to Nat and Ben. "Can you guys get back to the roof? We can use somebody up there to spot and cover us."

"Sure thing, Joe." Nat began moving.

Nearly a dozen others arrived.

"Mel!" Joe spotted the limping woman working her way down the stairs and waved her over. Before she got to him, he saw Shelley. "Shelley, please go check on Mike." The nurse gave him a curt nod and left.

Joe quickly explained the situation.

"I'm going to slip out the back and circle around the building. I'm taking Emily, Bill and Jack with me. We should be able to sweep them away from the school."

Mel nodded, approving the plan. She grabbed Keith by the crook of the arm and told Joe to add one more to their squad. Keith took it all in stride.

Maria was just wiping the sleep from her eyes as she descended the last stairs.

"I'll set up a couple of spotters and let the rest know what's going on." Mel turned toward the crowd and raised her hands.

Joe gave her a grateful smile. "Okay, Em, Keith; Let's go bust some zombie heads."

"Right, mate." Emily fell in step with him as they walked down the hallway toward the gym. Behind them, Mel was ordering the rest of the residents around.

"Blimey. Glad I'm not staying there," Emily remarked as she heard Mel take charge.

A minute later they were joined by Bill and Jack. Keith grabbed the axe sitting just inside the armory door. "This will do for me," he stated as he hefted the weapon. Nobody doubted him.

"Good." Joe said. "You take it out with that axe if there is just one of them inside the fence. That way we don't accidentally shoot at the school ..." Keith nodded, his face expressionless.

How does this guy keep his cool? I'd be shitting myself.

Joe had no time to ponder this as they slipped out of the rear door of the gym. The coast was clear on this side of the school. They turned to their left, deciding to circle around the school the short way. They were blasted by cold wind when they got around the corner. None of them had thought of wearing jackets.

Emily blew out her lips. "It's brass monkeys out here," she whispered to the rest of the group.

"Huh? What the heck does that mean?" Jack raised his eyebrow inquisitively.

"You don't say that here?" Emily shook her head in disbelief. The far corner of the gym was several yards ahead. "You know, it's cold. Cold enough to freeze the balls off a brass monkey."

Joe would have guffawed if he wasn't so damn scared.

They turned the corner and got into the formation that John had drilled into them. Joe could hear the zombie irregularly beat at the school door. They stepped toward the middle of the parking lot, getting a better position and a first look. Joe also spotted Nat and Ben on the roof now. Just below them, Maria stood at the library window. She pointed at the door. Then she held up her hand, fingers spread apart, and pointed at the school fence, followed by pointing at her eyes.

Good girl. "Maria's spotted five at the fence," Joe whispered. "Let's take out the one at the door. Keith..." Joe indicated for Keith to take position at the front of their formation.

They could see the zombie clearly now. It was completely naked and of a sickly pale color. Joe could not make out whether it had been a man or a woman in life. He waved at Nat and Ben to get their attention. Joe mimicked a shooting action, then pointed toward the fence. He received a nod in affirmation.

A second later, Nat and Ben took their first shots directed at the fence.

The zombie at the door swung its head around, disoriented by the sound. Joe moved his team closer. He realized that he was in the "rabbit" position of their formation. His companions had already stepped away, leaving him feeling like it was just him and the zombie. He swallowed, hard.

"Over here, asshole!" he called out.

The zombie turned immediately and started moving toward him. It was faster than the shambling forms that he had gotten used to, and Joe took an involuntary step backward.

The zombie slipped on the steps leading down from the school door and tumbled to the concrete sidewalk. Its face remained turned toward Joe the whole time, the darkened holes where the eyes used to be still seeming to regard its prey. It was utterly terrifying.

Joe realized that he had slipped into silence. *Come on, rabbit!* "Uh... Come and get it!"

The zombie got back to its feet and started toward Joe. Its loping gait reminded Joe of primates he'd seen on TV.

The zombie got to within fifteen feet of Joe before Keith stepped behind it and whacked its legs from under it. He reversed the grip on the axe and chopped the sharp end down on the back of its head. The skull burst under the impact, and Joe could hear the loud *CLACK* as the axe hit the sidewalk.

There was no time to be disgusted, though, as there were more threats to take care of. Joe signaled to Nat and they stopped shooting. He then led his team to the fence, where two zombies still stood.

Shooting these zombies was relatively simple. Joe took the responsibility of shooting one of them, unaware of the approving glances he received from the rest of his team.

Several minutes later, they were dragging the corpses to the burn pile they had set up half a block away. They encountered one more zombie as they did this. Emily performed her job as shooter, destroying the thing while the rest of them dragged bodies.

It was too windy to start a fire, so they left the bodies on the pile. Joe shuddered as he looked at them, stacked like firewood on top of the other bodies. He recalled seeing a similar image in a very disturbing documentary about the Second World War. He looked at the faces of his team. Their expressions were a mix of disgust and sadness.

"All right. Let's get inside," he prompted.

They walked back to the Ren, lost in their own thoughts. Joe waited while Keith and Bill shut and secured the gate.

"That was well done, mate."

Joe started slightly, then glanced at Emily, who had snuck up beside him.

"Uh, thanks."

"You kept your cool. Nobody got hurt. Not much more a soldier can ask for."

Joe felt color creeping to his cheeks. "Thanks."

"Nobody got hurt, but I could use some clean pants," Keith said as he walked away from the gate. He indicated the fresh stains on his legs.

"Shouldn't have chopped down so hard, mate." Emily grinned as she spoke. "Not only do you need new pants — you've got a dull edge to mend." She indicated the axe.

That helped break the tension. They entered the school and were glad to be out of the cold, but Joe realized that it wasn't time to relax yet.

He handed his rifle to Bill and made his way to the clinic.

Shelley looked up from her chair as he walked in. He could tell from her expression that the news would not be good.

"How is he?" He had to ask, anyway.

Shelley shook her head. "The fever is getting worse."

"Damnit."

"Is that Joe?" Mike called from the bed. The voice sounded like that of an ancient, tired man.

Joe walked over so that Mike could see him. "Hey, Mike."

Mike smiled weakly. "Guess I'm not doing too well."

"No. I'm sorry..." Joe's voice broke and he lowered his head in shame.

"Hey." Mike waited for Joe to meet his eyes. "It's not your fault. Even if it was, I forgive you. I can feel myself, sort of ... slipping."

Mike reached out. Joe clasped his hand.

"Just promise to look after the kids. I mean Abi and Willy. I know they're in love with each other." Mike shook his head weakly and smiled. "Been trying to hide it from me for months." His gaze turned serious. "Joe. Promise me that you keep those two from getting distracted. They need to survive this."

"Okay, Mike. I promise."

"Thanks." Mike smiled softly and closed his eyes. All recognition was gone when he opened them again. "Dan? Where are you? Private Dan McKenzie. Get over here."

Joe reflected for a moment, then answered, "I'm here, Mike."

Mike seemed to believe that. "Ah." Again, he smiled. "You're a good kid, Dan. You've got to lay off the candy bars, though!" Mike laughed at his own comment.

"I will, Mike," Joe said softly. "I will."

Slowly Mike's eyelids drifted shut.

"I will," Joe whispered to the fading man.

Joe felt something on his cheek. When he wiped it with the back of his hand, he realized that it was a tear. He looked over at Shelley and she too was crying. They locked eyes over the sleeping form of Mike and shared a moment of utter despair.

There's nothing we can do...

Joe needed to do something. He felt it in his bones.

"Can you stay with him?" he asked the nurse. She gave him a weak smile and nodded.

Joe walked out of the clinic, leaving Shelley to stand vigil over the dying man. He headed straight to the armory. Bill was still putting stuff away when he walked in.

"We're going to need some of that," Joe said.

Bill looked at him in surprise. "How's that?"

"It's time we continued the work that John started. Let's round up a few volunteers and clear zombies."

Chapter 27

Mark

November 20, 9:00 A.M., Nova

"Is it gone?"

Mark jumped slightly, startled by the sound. He had been so focused on the scene outside that he had not noticed Alan's approach.

He turned back toward the other man, annoyed at the interruption as much as at his own brief show of weakness.

"Fuck, man. Don't sneak up on me like that."

"Sorry, Sword Mark." Alan dipped his head slightly in apology. If anything, it annoyed Mark even more. "I was just wondering if it's left yet..." the sage continued.

"Yeah." Mark looked out of the tiny window once more to be sure. "It's gone. It trudged away a couple of minutes ago. I think it's standing just around the corner at that coffee shop." He turned back to the adept with a slight wave over his shoulder.

"Coffee." Adept Alan repeated. "I would just about brave those monsters for a fresh cup."

With that, Mark could agree.

"Okay, let's head back downstairs."

He walked out of the small administrative office and stepped out into the semi-darkness of the warehouse that had been their group's safe haven for the last several weeks.

Mark looked around at their austere habitat. The warehouse wasn't very large — only about eighty feet wide by one hundred and twenty feet long. Of that space, only a fraction was useable.

Their miniature tent city was spread out over the back half. It looked about as disheveled as it felt with one, two- and four-man tents set up around pallets and large crates of materials. Electric lanterns sat on some of those crates, casting bright light in some areas and rather strange shadows in others.

Thirty-nine people were scattered around those crates.

Add yourself and Adept Alan here, for a grand total of forty-one. An island of the living in a sea of the dead.

Not for the first time, Mark wondered if they were truly the only survivors in their city of nearly two hundred thousand.

It just can't be ... Can it?

He knew that the Order had been behind the syndrome. He immediately thought of the term genetically modified when news of failing crops had reached his ears. At that time, he'd cheered the news. He hadn't been the only one.

That was just one day after they arrived at their new sanctuary. They'd numbered twenty-five that first day, and it had felt more like the start of an adventure than the end of the world.

The news coverage had quickly turned several shades darker. Mass extinction of animals followed the failure of crops, and mankind had turned ugly. Even these things were cheered on by his companions, albeit rather less enthusiastically. Humanity, with its religions, politics and insatiable hunger for material goods, was showing its true colors. The first shots were fired, and the first people died.

There were supposed to be over seventy people staying at Satellite Nova. Not all these people had answered the call of the Order, or they had been waylaid in their travels. A few more people trickled in over the course of the next couple of days, after which they were forced to bar the doors as best they could. That was because the riots had started.

Even in their sleepy city.

Mark remembered several close calls, when crowds of people scoured the city, looting for all they were worth. The funny thing was that their decrepit warehouse was not even deemed worth looting, as they were passed by time and again. Mark guessed that the newer warehouses down the street looked more appealing — and thanked his lucky stars.

The only time anyone had tried to force entry was about a week after all the riots, when people had crawled into their homes and holes to die. When the dead were already outnumbering the living.

Mark and several others watched from their hidden location as a family of four arrived. They had tugged at the door ineffectually, while Mark and his colleagues questioned their own morals. Soon enough, cries of alarm alerted both the family members and their unseen observers that zombies were approaching. Mark had to physically hold back one of his own men as the family fought desperately to gain entry.

They finally gave up and ran away. It was rather disturbing when most of the zombies did not give chase but milled around the front of the warehouse. Mark had ordered everybody to the back of the warehouse then. They had stayed back there for a full twenty-four hours, afraid to make any noise.

That was some real fear. Mark recalled. He also recalled the relief when the coast was clear that next day.

It was the push they'd needed to bring out their radio and erect the antenna on the roof. Unfortunately, theirs was not the tallest building, and communications were intermittent at best. What little they heard caused them much concern and confusion.

Apparently, their group was holding up quite well. They had suffered no breaches and no casualties, had their full stores of food and water, plenty of equipment and survival gear, and more batteries than they knew what to do with — thanks to a discovery when they opened one of the crates.

Mark knew that the hand of censorship was heavy within the Order, but even then he heard that many satellites were being plagued by zombies. He feared that some of the satellites might even have been overrun. This was not a stretch of the imagination when considering the defensive qualities of their current shelter.

The area around their warehouse seemed to be abandoned, and within days people started getting bored. Or, rather, curious. Mark wanted to know what was happening outside of their limited field of view, as much as anybody. So he had sanctioned an excursion.

How long ago was that? Time seemed to lose all meaning in their eighty by one-hundred-foot world.

He'd led the team himself. They'd traveled slowly and cautiously. It took them nearly half an hour to travel just over one block. Then they were spotted, and it took less than five minutes before they were all hiding out at the back of the warehouse again. Mark had made the executive decision that there would be no more excursions after that.

Odd how they approach whenever we venture outside. Like they're blinded by this building. Mark felt like he was on the verge of a discovery.

A tap on his arm shook him from his musings. "You coming?" Alan looked at him askance.

"Huh? Oh, yeah." Mark replied, slightly embarrassed. "Lead the way." He gestured for Alan to go ahead of him.

They went down the stairs and navigated through the tent and crate jungle to the back of the building, where the common area and kitchen were set up. They'd even found some patio furniture to complete the picture. From the smell of it, breakfast was ready.

"Mark. Alan."

They stopped their approach of the kitchen counter, where a large pot of porridge bubbled away. Adept Mary sat at one of the patio tables, alongside Quincy, their tech guru and appointed radio operator. Mark veered off to meet them right away. Alan followed after a longing look at the porridge.

"You've got to hear this." Mary told them, opening her hand to Quincy. The bearded, bespectacled man dipped his head before turning to his new audience.

"I made contact with Onyx. The people over there were freaking out. Apparently, the zombies were stacked five or six deep around their building ... Like the zombies knew they were there."

"They do know. They sense the living," Alan supplied as he lowered himself into a lawn chair.

Quincy once again dipped his head, like he was ducking under a beam. "Yes. PD confirmed that as well. It's like they have a built-in radar or something. What's more, PD states that they can communicate."

"What?" Mark saw the look of incredulity on Alan's face and knew that his own matched it.

"Seriously. It's true." Another dip. "Sage Jonas came on the radio personally to tell everyone."

Jonas Enright. Mark was impressed.

The top science dog. Well, maybe not, if Vicky Hohndahl has anything to say about that.

"Onyx is in serious trouble. They said that there were hundreds of zombies outside, pounding on the walls."

"I really don't get it." Sage Mary played with her porridge, pushing it to one side of her bowl with her spoon and watching it slowly roll back into place before repeating the process. Unbeknownst to her, both Mark and Alan also watched the lava-like flow of the porridge intently. Their minds were not on the breakfast meal, though. Mark's was stuck on the mental picture of hundreds of bloody fists pounding on concrete walls.

"Why aren't they coming here?" Mary stabbed her meal with the spoon, watching as it stood for just a moment then drifted to the side of the bowl. "I mean, if they can sense us and talk to each other and everything ... Why not attack this place?" She shook her head in disgust, pushing the bowl away from her. "We're hardly defensible. There are like six entries, and half of those doors are so old and rusty they could fall in on themselves."

Mark nodded in agreement. He was also confused.

Why are they not bursting in here? Surely those monsters have been aware of us several times.

He pursed his lips, reconsidering. *Perhaps I should be thankful. If they actually tried ... Well, we'd be toast.* Mark held little to no confidence in their ability to withstand an assault.

"Maybe it has something to do with the metal?" Alan suggested. "I mean, those doors are all metal."

"Yeah, but the walls are just brick and mortar," Mary said dismissively. "Maybe they just don't like blue," she added, referring to the color of paint that covered the warehouse.

The place had been painted many times over during its existence. The latest attempt had involved a kind of aqua blue. It stood out like a sore thumb, even in this industrial district.

We chose the oldest, ricketiest, most garishly painted warehouse to hide out in. And nobody's found us. For some reason the thought amused him, and a smile crept into his face.

Alan saw the smile and grinned back. "Shit, sounds like all we have to do is paint ourselves in blue — and the zombies will just ignore us."

"Like that group of blue men," Mark said.

"Don't forget blue women and children!" Mary said.

"Damn," Alan responded. "We're going to need a lot of paint."

The leaders of Nova and their chubby technical guru sat in silent retrospection for a moment.

"Radio," Quincy mumbled, then looked up with an embarrassed smile at the others. "Sorry, I was just thinking. I need to get on the roof to make the radio work. There is too much interference inside."

Something clicked for Mark just then. He looked up sharply. "Maybe whatever is causing this radio interference is also blocking the zombie radar thing."

Mark thought back to the lone zombie outside. It had just been standing there. It had faced Mark's building straight on, which concerned the sword greatly.

Like it sensed us for a brief moment, before losing us again ...

Quincy's head bobbed several times in quick succession. "That makes sense."

They all looked at each other excitedly. They knew that they were onto something.

But what?

Chapter 28

Tammy

November 20, 2:00 P.M.

They had been driving along in silence for quite some time. The scenery hardly changed, lulling each member of the team into their own daydreams. They passed by fields, farms, stands of trees, and more fields. It was monotonous. This was the heartland.

Tammy split her time between looking out the window and at the two lovebirds in the front seat. She suddenly became hyper aware of the looks that passed between BB and Abi.

How did I not see it?

She caught Abi smiling at BB and had to smile herself. She certainly didn't begrudge them their fling.

No. Not a fling. Tammy could tell that this was more. Meant more. These two had been working together for a long time, and the relationship they had built was deeper than a sexual liaison. These two loved each other, at least as much as they desired each other.

She started to feel self-conscious and guilty for spying on them, so looked out of the window instead.

What? She started as she saw a single individual stand in a field in the distance.

"Somebody is out there," Tammy warned and pointed at the figure. BB slowed down the vehicle and came to a stop on the shoulder.

"Can't tell..." John jumped out of the Humvee and took his binoculars. After a moment he put them away and got back into the car, a wistful look on his face. "It's a zombie." He motioned to BB, and the vehicle started to move again.

"Weird that they just kind of stand around when they're on their own ..." Tammy mused.

"When they're in groups, they seem to be moving around with greater purpose," Romy finished for her.

Tammy shuddered. Somehow the sight of that single zombie in the middle of nowhere disturbed her more. She pondered this for the next fifteen minutes as they traveled.

"Coming up on the city."

BB's remark broke Tammy out of her reverie. One glance ahead told her that they were indeed just entering the outskirts of the city.

"We've made great time. Good work, team," John remarked.

Tammy shrugged. She hadn't done anything. The roads had been barren except for the occasional abandoned car or wreck. BB had done all of the driving. They had barely seen any zombies. Tammy wasn't sure if she was happy or disappointed about it.

Concrete replaced fields, and structures replaced shrubs and trees as they entered the city. The outskirts looked absolutely normal, apart from the lack of cars and people. Tammy could picture herself walking into this coffee shop or that fast food joint.

Suddenly John pointed. "Over there, BB. Take this exit."

BB slowed the vehicle down. "What is it, chief?"

"It's a place worth stopping at," John replied with a mischievous grin.

He continued to point as BB steered the Humvee down the ramp and onto the parallel road. He appeared to be pointing at a strip mall.

"Oasis," Romy read the sign. She gave Tammy a dubious look as she added, "John, I don't think that there are going to be a group of exotic dancers holed up in there. Also, I don't think your wife would approve?"

John laughed. "No, man. Over there." He pointed again. "Ah."

"Come to Papa." John reached into the display case. Tammy watched him with amusement. "Should I leave you two alone? You're making me uncomfortable."

John grinned and winked at her.

"What is that thing, anyway?"

He held up his prize as if affording Tammy a better view would help her identify it.

At her lack of recognition, he explained. "This is a Bushmaster Adapted Combat Rifle, and it is possibly the best combat rifle in the world."

Tammy pursed her lips and nodded, trying to look impressed.

John noticed. "Ah," he said, and approached Tammy with the weapon.

"It's okay. I don't need the lesson," Tammy said, but it was too late. What was worse, BB had drifted over and seemed interested.

"I used to have one of these puppies." John cradled the gun to his chest like it was some long-lost, fragile baby. "Spec Ops turned a blind eye to how we wanted to arm ourselves, so I swapped my M16 out for one of these."

"So, what's so special about it?" BB ventured.

"Glad you asked," The chiseled face of the ex-soldier broke into a grin. "This guy can fire multiple calibers. Handy for operations behind enemy lines." He wasn't done. "Check this!" He held the rifle up for a closer look.

Tammy had no idea what she was looking at and told him so. That didn't faze John's enthusiasm one bit.

"It's a modular design. You can swap out barrels." He pointed at the showcase that he had just raided. Two barrels lay on top of the thick glass surface. One of them looked serious.

"That one looks like the SAW," Tammy suggested.

John's eyes lit up. "Exactly. I can make a SAW out of this. The stock, handguard and trigger unit are also adjustable."

"Hmm." Tammy nodded, then pretended somebody had called her and slunk away from the conversation.

Unperturbed, John continued the explanation for BB. "Interesting fact: The Bushmaster is actually called the Remington, and it used to be called the Masada."

Even from the other side of the room, Tammy could still hear him clearly. She looked toward Romy, who also seemed like a kid in a candy shop.

The team continued to plunder the shop over the next few minutes. Tammy gladly accepted the role of mule, running boxes and cases to the vehicles outside. She almost envied Abi, who had remained at the vehicles as the lookout.

The harsh sound of a gunshot reminded her that the young woman was doing more than just watching. Surprisingly, Abi had only fired her weapon twice so far. Tammy had figured there would be more zombies in the area than that.

Did they all move off or something? she wondered as she stacked the latest load inside the vehicle.

The Humvee was getting full, and her arms were getting tired. She was just about to complain about it to Abi when the short woman popped her head back out of the hatch. The look on her face told Tammy that something was wrong.

"Get John and everybody back here on the double. I got a transmission from the Ren. They've been attacked."

Chapter 29

Emily

E mily replaced the headset and sighed.
  Finally, a break.

She got up and rushed out of the media room. Ethan was in the hallway.

"Oy!" she cried.

Ethan turned toward her in surprise. Emily jogged over.

"Where's your dad, mate?"

"He's still in the clinic. Been there all morning..." Ethan's concern was plain on his face.

Right. Mike.

"Thanks, lad." Emily jogged past Ethan.

"What's going on?" he called after her.

"John and them lot are on their way," she said over her shoulder. Emily started down the stairs.

"Mmmaaaawwh!"

The moan of pain came from downstairs. From the clinic.

Ah, Mike. Mate... Emily shook her head sadly as she descended the stairs.

She heard another moan of pain as she got to the bottom. Emily looked to her left and spotted Sarah and Claire near the cafeteria entrance. Clearly, both women were distraught by the situation taking place down the hall. They clung to each other and cringed at every cry.

Emily had no time for words of encouragement though, so merely nodded at them before turning away. She had to talk to Joe.

Nevertheless, she unconsciously slowed her pace the closer she got, and it was with some trepidation that she knocked on the door to the clinic.

"In," Joe commanded in a harried tone.

She opened the door and was immediately assaulted by several things.

First there was the sound. A cacophony of noises, which seemed to be amplified by the confined space, blasted Emily upon entering. The clanging of equipment and groaning of the bed were accompanied by the angst-filled voices of people and, of course, the continuing cries of pain.

Then there was the sight. Christine and Shelley moved like angry bees, delivering clean bandages or removing soiled ones, handing over wet cloths and various instruments. Mike squirmed on the operating table while Joe frantically moved around him. Joe wore long gloves, but the spatters of blood and other bodily liquids were evident on all his clothing.

Then there was the smell. The rich, metallic smell of blood was nothing but a hint. It was trounced by the sweet-sickly smell of infection, and the acrid smell of shit.

Finally, and most profoundly, there was the sheer intensity of emotions. Joe and his assistants tried to keep their cool. They wore expressions of concentration. However, Emily could sense the almost overwhelming cloud of fear that hung over them.

It took her a moment before she realized that Joe was looking right at her.

"What is it, Em?" he demanded for a second time.

"Oh! Sorry. It's Abi ... I've made contact."

Joe straightened up suddenly. He motioned for Emily to meet him in the far corner of the room. He motioned for Shelley to take over for him and stepped aside. Emily caught a glimpse of a sliced-open belly and many wads of bandaging. Most of the bandaging was already soaked through.

"Tell me," Joe urged.

"I got lucky. Our setup doesn't really reach very far, but sometimes the signal will bounce off buildings and such. At any rate, I was able to contact Abi." The stress inside the operating room was infectious, and Emily felt herself blabbering. She took a breath to calm herself — immediately regretting it as the smell almost made her gag.

"Go on." Joe seemed impervious to it.

"They're on the other side of town. They should get here within a couple of hours."

"What about their mission? Did they all make it back?"

"Yeah. They're all in fine fettle. Didn't talk much about the mission."

Joe nodded. "Right. Guess we'll find out when they get here."

Mike cried out in pain behind them, and Joe looked over in concern.

"Is he going to make it?" Emily hadn't wanted to ask that question but couldn't hold it back.

Joe took a shuddering breath. For a brief moment, it looked like the big man was about to tear up.

"His ... Mike's condition is deteriorating rapidly." He took another breath, gaining control of his emotions. "We caught the smell of infection late this morning. We had no choice but to open him up. What we saw ... There must have been a ricochet, or a bullet fragment. It perforated his intestines in several places." Clenching both his fists and his eyes, Joe breathed out sharply through his nose. "We should have opened him up yesterday. Right after he got shot. We knew there was a chance of this, but didn't want to risk operating with the limited equipment we've got. Damnit! I should have known better."

As fast as the outburst came, it left. Joe opened his eyes and seemed in control once more. "Listen, Em. I've got to get back to Mike."

"Okay, Joe. Thanks." She reached for his arm but stopped short. "You're doing brilliant, mate. Keep the faith."

Joe turned back to his patient.

Emily let herself out of the clinic. Shutting the door to the sights, smells, sounds and emotions that had nearly overwhelmed her.

Chapter 30

Tammy

Their vehicle raced through the city, the sound of the engine bouncing off buildings and through the valley, creating a cacophony that was hard to pinpoint.

They had quickly piled into the vehicles after Abi's message. It was a small miracle that she had received the call at all, as they were supposedly out of range. It must have had something to do with industrial buildings, radio towers and maybe some repeaters that were still operational.

The gist of the message was severe: *We were attacked.*

The original plan was to follow the ring road around the city. This plan was quickly abandoned for a more direct approach. The main thoroughfares were not completely empty, with vehicles parked haphazardly here and there. So far, their luck had held and there were no blockades.

Tammy sat in the back. Her face was drawn with worry, as were those around her. The tension was palpable. She stared out of the window without truly seeing anything, the cityscape passing by in a blur of shapes and colors.

What do they want from us? Was this revenge?

Tammy felt that itch impossible to scratch. That itch of needing to find out more information. Of needing to find out the truth.

What is it going to take to stop them?

Annoyingly, they had been unable to raise the Ren on the radio since that one message had gotten through. She figured that they would be able to reestablish contact once they got to the other side of the downtown core.

They passed through an intersection; it afforded her an unobstructed view far down the road. She barely registered the multiple shapes moving in the distance. The bodies were packed so tight that it almost looked like the entire surface in the distance rolled like a wave.

"Did you...?"

She turned to John, who sat beside her. He didn't acknowledge her. John stared stoically forward, lost in his own thoughts. She looked over her shoulder at Romy, who sat in the very back. Romy was intently cleaning her handgun and hadn't even bothered to look up.

Tammy looked out her window again, but they had passed the intersection.

Maybe I imagined it?

She waited intently for the vehicle to pass the next intersection, hoping to get a good view down the road. However, that street ended abruptly at a park only a couple of blocks away.

Tammy sighted in frustration.

I must have imagined it.

The sound of the radio squawking a moment later broke everybody out of their personal reveries.

Chapter 31

Nancy

"Here. Found you a Pepsi."

Nancy looked up to see a bottle of the beverage dangling in front of her face. Dean's smiling face hung beyond it. He looked more like a smiling raccoon, what with his two black eyes and bruising all over his forehead. Nancy couldn't help but return the smile.

"Thank you, dear." She took the bottle from his hand.

He stood up proudly, waiting for her to pop the cap and take a drink. She gladly obliged. Pepsi *was* one of her weaknesses, after all.

She took several sips and allowed herself a satisfied "ahh." It made Dean's smile broaden all the more.

He's a people pleaser. Nancy smiled back at the athletic young man.

I'm glad I saved him.

"How's your head?" she asked after another sip.

"Ah." He reached up as if to touch the back of his head, but froze several inches away. "Hurts to touch." He admitted, letting his hand drop. "But other than that, I feel fine."

"Well, you ought to feel rested, at least." Nancy grinned up at the young man. "You slept long enough."

"Hah!" Dean walked to the couch on the other side of the room. "I feel like I could sleep some more."

He grabbed his flanged mace just below the head, withdrew it from his belt and leaned it against the furniture before lying down. The man was so large that his feet dangled well past the far armrest. Nuggets immediately hopped onto the couch and lay down between the his legs.

Nancy's eyes shot to the weapon, and her mind drifted back. To stepping through that door, away from the safety of the house and out into the street.

Goodness. Was he ever heavy!

She remembered putting her hands in his armpits and putting all her body weight into it. Still, she was barely making progress. She was not even halfway to the steps leading to the house when she heard a crash down the street.

It was too late. A zombie had spotted them and was lurching over.

Nancy's first thought was to drop the guy and run back inside the house. Then she saw the dog. It stood a few feet away, hackles raised. It faced the threat and gave no indication of leaving its master. Eerily, the dog did not growl at all.

That's when Nancy spotted it. The club, with a vicious metal ball and cutting edges on the end of it. It lay right on the edge of the curb. She knew instantly that it belonged to the unconscious guy.

She let go of the man, wincing slightly as his head hit the ground, and quickly went to collect the weapon. The zombie was almost halfway to them by now.

The weapon was heavy — so much so that she needed to use both hands to lift it — but it also felt strangely comfortable. Deadly.

And deadly it had been.

The dog had been a great help as well. It literally tripped the zombie so that it landed right at her feet. All she had to do was swing down. The weight of the weapon did the rest.

Nancy shook her head. It was an ugly memory.

"Are you okay?" Dean looked over with concern.

"Yeah ... Yeah. Just remembering using that weapon of yours."

"Ah. My one-shot kill." He picked up the weapon and held it aloft. Dean handled the mace quite casually.

The thing must way close to forty pounds. Yet he's handling it like it's a golf club. He placed the mace on the ground beside the couch.

"Thanks again, for saving my ass."

Nancy chuckled. Dean looked at her quizzically, so she explained, "I remember my first thought after I had finished pulling you into that place."

"Oh?"

"I closed the front door, saw you lying in a heap in the hallway, and thought: 'Is he actually still alive, or did I just risk myself to drag a corpse in there?'" She chuckled again.

"Hah!" Dean turned to stare at the ceiling. Nuggets lifted its head up from Dean's thigh and looked at its master quizzically. "Luckily I fell on the hardest part of my body."

They were both silent for a moment, lost in their own thoughts.

That was two days ago, Nancy realized. She remembered checking to see if he still had a heartbeat and being relieved to find one. Next she'd managed to drag him onto the living room carpet.

Then she'd thought: "Now what?" She racked her brain as to what to do with head injuries. All she could recall was that she was supposed to put him in a straight line — keeping his head in line with his spine. So she did.

After that, she just did what she thought was right.

She cleaned up the scratches on his face and applied cold cloths to his forehead. Then the nervous brooding started. She had no idea what to do next other than wait.

It was several hours later when she tried to get him to drink some water. He choked on his first sip, so she quickly abandoned that idea. Another thirty minutes before a memory came back to her. It was from some romantic movie she'd watched with Ern — much to her late husband's chagrin, she recalled.

The protagonist had wet cloths and got the unconscious hero to drink water that way. She put on her best Florence Nightingale performance and did likewise. The crazy part was that it worked.

After a while, he came to. That was when she managed to get him to swallow some aspirin and a bit of broth. That was also when she found out his name, and that of his four-legged companion. A few hours later, he was well enough to sit up and eat some solid food. And a few hours after that, they beat a hasty retreat as a congregation of zombies arrived.

It had taken all of Dean's energy to make it to this place. He promptly found a bedroom and slept for nearly twelve hours. Nancy had to wake him up out of fear that he had slipped into a coma or something.

This place is all right. They'd been at this house for over twenty-four hours, and still there wasn't a single sign of a zombie.

Dean had assured her that they could not stay there for long though.

"They are able to communicate." He'd frowned with severity as he said this. He went on to explain that he'd seen them in action. "One person by himself doesn't seem to draw much attention. But small groups ... It's like they are able to triangulate the position of living people somehow. No matter how well the people hide."

Strangely, that made sense. How else could she explain the recent attack by hundreds of zombies at the Ren? That was when Nancy had told Dean where she'd come from.

Nancy came back to the present as Dean spoke up. "I was thinking about what you said yesterday. About your plan of going home."

He looked over at her and continued. "I can help get you there, if you want."

Nancy thought about it. Only her hands moved, stroking and chocking the soda bottle. It betrayed her conflicting emotions.

"Funny. I was thinking about what you said yesterday as well," she finally said. "All those people I've left behind. They mean a lot to me. More than the ghost of Ern. More than the memories that may or may not await me back at my old place."

She dropped her gaze to the floor for a moment, before lifting it once more to meet Dean's.

"I'm not so sure that I want to go home anymore. I think you're right about all that triangulation stuff. And when you told me about that big horde you'd seen, and the direction they seemed to be going ..." Nancy grimaced. "My gut feeling is that my friends are going to be in trouble." She squeezed the bottle tight. "But will they even want to see me again, after what I've done?"

Dean considered this. He turned his head to stare at the ceiling and chewed on his bottom lip. "Well, the decent thing to do would be to warn these folks." He frowned slightly before nodding. "Yeah. That's what Sophie would have wanted me to do. Right, Nuggets?"

The dog wagged its tail upon hearing its name and tried to crawl closer to Dean's upper torso, intent upon delivering a few licks. Dean lifted his hand.

"It's okay, boy." Nuggets put its head down. Its eyes never left Dean's face, though.

Loyalty. Dedication.

The thought came, unbidden, to Nancy's mind as she watched Nuggets and Dean. She got up from her chair. The half-full bottle of soda was all but forgotten.

"What's on your mind?" Dean asked.

Nancy smiled down at the young man. "Just ... It's nice to see how dedicated you and Nuggets are to each other.

Nuggets looked up upon hearing his name but swung his gaze back to Dean immediately. Dean was quiet for a moment as he contemplated. He rested his hand on the dog's head. His expression had grown serious.

"We're all that we've got."

They regarded each other in silence. Nancy started moving toward the table.

"Well, we'd better get you up on your feet," she said over her shoulder as she approached the kitchen table, where all their gear lay. "We've got to get over to the Ren and warn my friends." She started putting stuff back into the packs. Dean slowly got off the couch. Nancy paused her packing when he joined her. She looked up into the young man's face. Hers was a mask of conviction.

"*They* are all that I've got." She choked with emotion.

Dean put his hand on her arm and waited for her to look up at him.

"You've got us, too."

Chapter 32

William

Time unknown, location unknown
William was confident.

He hadn't seen a freak around his house for almost a whole week. Of course, he had spent most of that time in his basement. He sat on his couch, which doubled as his bed, and looked around at his surroundings.

It was dark in his sanctuary. The only light came from the glow around the covered windows and through the doorway at the top of the stairs. His eyes had gotten used to that by now. Besides, he knew the exact layout of his place. It had been his home for his entire life.

Forty years ... Or am I fifty?

William shrugged. He didn't care.

He jerked upright on the couch as a sharp pain shot through his jaw.

"Aw, fuck!" He rubbed his jaw with his hand. His eyes widened and shot to the stairs leading up to the rest of the house. He held his breath for an angst-ridden moment.

But there was no angry yell from upstairs. No heavy footfalls tracking toward the door up there.

William sighed in relief. A moment later, he remembered.

Right. She's dead.

"You're dead," he said aloud, daring his mother to argue with him. He waited anxiously for a moment, despite that fact.

The pain in his jaw slowly subsided. He continued to rub it as he got to his feet. The light was poor, and he stepped on something. A plastic wrapper crunched under his foot. It was one of the causes of his current predicament.

Momma didn't like me eating no candy ...

She'd get angry whenever he asked for some sweets. Then there were the times when she caught him sneaking some.

William shuddered with the memory of cowering under a whirlwind of slaps to the face and head. Those were the lucky times. He also recalled those open-handed slaps being fists on occasion. Then there was that big wooden spoon she was so fond of.

One time, she got so mad that she had physically dragged him to the stairs and shoved him down ...

He ran his hand over the hard lump on his arm, remembering the loud CRACK and the excruciating pain. Momma had been sorry after that. She'd said so. She'd wrapped his arm tightly, pulling on his hand to keep that lump down. She'd even brought down some treats for him later. The same treats that William had tried to sneak, no less.

William opened and closed his hand. His arm hadn't healed quite right. He couldn't grip very well with the hand, and things seemed to slip from his grasp every now and then. That just got Momma mad at him again ...

The pain in his jaw had faded and William remembered that he was hungry and thirsty. He eyed the light streaming down the stairs suspiciously for a moment. He knew that there was a lot of food up there.

So is Momma.

She should be sitting in her big chair in the living room. Staring at a TV that was turned off. She would be wearing her favorite dress, her face covered in the bright make-up she loved so much.

William should know. He had dressed her, applied the make-up, and placed her there. That had taken a lot of effort. Momma outweighed William by a good hundred pounds.

But he knew that this is what she would want. She loved that chair and her TV. She liked her make-up and her dress, too, often encouraging William to tell her how pretty she was.

She sat up there, now. Dead. She'd had a bad tummy ache. It got so bad that she was screaming almost nonstop. William didn't like that screaming. He'd begged her to be quiet. Especially when a freak showed up and started pounding on the wall.

William tried to shush her. He found that she got quiet if he put the pillow over her face. It wasn't quiet enough, so he put another pillow on top. And then another. And then he lay down on top of those pillows, whispering to his frantic mother to be quiet.

He remembered her blue-tinged face and her bloodshot eyes when he pulled the pillows away.

She must have been really sick.

He shifted his focus back to his hunger and thought of the pantry just beside the kitchen. It was a treasure throve. So full of food that you could barely walk into the room. Boxes of canned stuff stacked from floor to ceiling. Most of the food was still packed in grocery bags, though. There was a shelving unit in there, some-where. You couldn't see it for the mountain of food. Some of it stank so bad that it made William's eyes water. But he knew all too well there were plenty of tasty things in there as well.

There was lots of stuff upstairs. Too much, according to some people.

He remembered that one time, when some stranger had visited. He remembered having had to shower and dress in clean clothes, and only answer yes or no to the questions. Momma had drilled him on those questions and answers, threatening him with a beat-ing if he got any of the questions wrong. But William need not have feared. That stranger's attention seemed to be on Momma more than on him.

Hoarder. That's what the stranger had said several times. It had upset Momma terribly.

Momma had been real nervous for a while after that.

She continued to make William shower every few days, and dress in clean clothes — which was a challenge, as he only had two pairs of pants and a handful of t-shirts. She had even allowed William to stay upstairs for most of those days. He got to sit by her feet and watch TV, if he didn't say a word or move around too much.

Whatever she expected to happen did not happen, so life went back to normal after that. William didn't mind that too much. He found the shows on TV to be confusing and sometimes even scary.

He also hated showering.

William's stomach growled, and he looked up at the stairs again. He thought of the pantry and Momma sitting in her chair.

But you can't stop me no more.

Emboldened, William stood up. He crept toward the bottom of the stairs, listening intently for a moment before placing his foot on the first thread. He skipped over the second thread, recalling how many times its squeak had betrayed him in the past.

Slowly, he crept upstairs. He paused again when he got to the top, waiting so that his eyes could adjust to the brightness. He craned his neck and stuck his head past the doorframe. He looked down the hallway, to the kitchen at the end. To the right of the kitchen, an open entryway led to the living room.

Momma is there.

William crept forward, avoiding the stacked boxes in the hallway. The kitchen loomed ahead, and he got his first look out of the window. All he could see from this angle was the top of the neighbor's house and a cloud-covered sky.

Hunger spurred William into the kitchen. He couldn't help but look to his right as soon as he had entered. His deceased mother sat in her lazy chair, exactly as William had left her.

Well, not exactly. Her head had lolled sideways and forward. William knew that she would not have approved of this. He quickly walked over and tilted her head back into a normal position. The head immediately lolled sideways again, so William had to employ a small pillow. He breathed through his mouth; but even then he struggled not to gag.

"I'm a good boy. I'm a good boy," William repeated the mantra as he worked. "I'm a good boy."

Finally satisfied, he turned back to the kitchen.

William ignored the fridge, making straight for the pantry. Within moments, he had found a box of cookies and started munching. After several cookies, he spotted the rounded plastic of a soda bottle. His eyes lit up and he lunged into the mountain of food, coming out with his prize proudly held aloft.

He quickly twisted the cap off and drank several large gulps.

CLACK.

William froze mid-gulp.

What was that. Is it a freak?

Lowering the bottle, he replaced the cap. He carried the bottle into the kitchen. The window showed him an ever-increasing view of the world outside as he approached. He saw the edge of the neighbor's house again, and that gray sky. Then the trees in the neighbor's back yard, and then the fence.

CLACK—CLACK. William's eyes opened wide, and the bottle of soda slipped out of his hand to bounce off the linoleum floor as a face stared at him through the gaps in the fencing.

It's a freak! Ohmygod!

The zombie slapped the fence violently yet ineffectively, attempting to get at its prey. It slammed its head into the wooden fencing in apparent frustration. It had smashed its nose and had a large gash in its cheek when it next looked at William.

It scared William. Badly. He turned, kicking the bottle of soda in his hurry. William ran for the stairs, screaming in terror. He got to the doorway but clipped one side with his shoulder, spinning off balance.

His right foot connected with a step and then nothing but air as he launched down the stairs. The next part of his body to hit the stairs was his back. The blow knocked the air out of his lungs, and William blacked out.

He came to moments later, although he had no idea how much time had passed. He lay on his belly, his head a mere inch from the bottom step.

"Ah!" he gasped as he moved. He had landed on his arm, and his hand hurt. He rolled off his arm and raised it, staring in horror as his pinky finger pointed in the wrong direction. He whimpered.

Then the sound of something outside his house made him gasp in fear again.

William eyed his couch. He crawled toward it, taking care not to use his right hand. His eyes had gone funny too, as the couch seemed to move in small circles. He yelped in surprise as something slammed into the side of the house. He was halfway to the couch.

He didn't remember making it to the couch, or the cry that escaped him as he lifted himself onto the furniture.

T*hirsty ...*
    William came to and carefully lifted the blanket away from his face. He hurt all over and moaned softly. He cast his gaze toward the stairs. Light was still shining down from upstairs. Then he remembered his fall and the ensuing crawl to his bed.

"Ah!" he yelped as he got into a sitting position. He lifted his hand in front of his face to get a better look, then moaned again in dismay as he saw the strange angle at which his pinky sat. The digit had turned an angry purple and was swollen to the point of making his skin shine.

The pain in his hand paled in comparison to a sudden stab of intense agony. William reached for his jaw and howled in pain, starting at a high-pitched shriek and ending in a low groan.

Instantly, there were several impacts into the side of the house. William's eyes grew wide as he looked around him in fear.

"G-go away," he stammered.

William ignored the pain in his hand as he lay back down and pulled the blanket over himself.

"Go away," he repeated softly. The pounding on the sides of the house continued for another minute, before slowly coming to an end. William sighed underneath his blanket and eventually fell asleep.

It was nighttime by the time William woke up again. All the hurts were definitely making themselves known to him. There was his finger, and his tooth. But now he also had a splitting headache.

And he had to pee. Badly.

Taking his time to get up, William was careful not to use his bad hand. Thankfully, his toothache had subsided somewhat. He shuffled in the dark, feeling his way with his feet. Some limited light was still coming in from upstairs — William figured that it was moonlight.

What if there's freaks?

His bladder told him that there would be no holding it. He was too afraid to climb those stairs, though. He shuffled his way past the steps and toward the far corner. He pissed against the wall, sighing with relief. At the same time, the sound of splashing set off a serious craving for William.

So thirsty! There was nothing to drink down here.

William shuffled back to the stairs. He looked up longingly, knowing that a nearly full bottle of soda lay just at the end of the hallway. Before he knew it, William was ascending the steps. However, he'd forgotten about that second thread. It squeaked loudly as he put his weight on it.

The effect was immediate; William heard something moving. It did not sound like it was coming from inside the house, but he quickly backed down the stairs and returned to his bed.

The noises continued for several minutes as William lay in fear. He pulled the blanket over his head once more and tried to shut the world out.

It was dawn by the time William woke up again. He could tell that it was dawn by the glow around his window. His momma had covered the window with aluminum foil. A little while ago, she'd brought home some metal siding that she'd found, and they mounted that in the window, too. William couldn't see outside, but somehow the sun still came in. In the mornings, when the sun shone just right, it looked like the window had an aura of light. William used to love to wake up to that sight.

This morning was different. William felt pain everywhere. His back, his knee, his head — and especially his finger. William lifted the injured digit to his face so he could take a look. He groaned at the sight. His pinky finger had swollen to an impossible size. Holding it up, he could make out that it had turned from reddish purple to nearly black.

William was so terribly thirsty that he ignored the pains and complaints of his body and got up. He stepped toward the stairs and ascended them, this time mindful of that second thread. Before he realized it, he had entered the hallway and caught sight of the bottle of soda. He rushed to his prize and twisted the top off with his good hand.

PSSSSSSSSSSS. The bottle emitted a loud fizzing sound as pressure was released. Immediately, there was a banging on the walls. William wailed in response, retreating down the hall with the soda bottle clutched against his body.

"Go away." William could muster barely more than a whisper. He inadvertently squeezed the bottle and spilled soda all over himself and the floor.

"Go away!" he called out as he neared the stairs. The assault on the house only seemed to intensify with his demand.

William had taken the first couple of steps down the stairs when he heard a crack.

"GO AWAY!" he screamed, and rushed down the stairs.

As he got back to his couch, he continued to wail and yell. He threw the blanket over himself, heedless of the soda he was spilling all over. He heard more cracking noises and peeked out of the blankets. Shadows played across the window as something moved out there.

William screamed then. He screamed as loud as he ever had. The bottle of soda lay on the ground, forgotten, its contents leaking out in waves.

The door upstairs caved in over his screaming. He stopped screaming and covered his mouth with both hands. William could hear heavy footfalls upstairs.

The stomping around reminded him of something.

"Momma?" he called out tentatively. The footfalls seemed to multiply and go in various directions.

"I'm a good boy. I'm a good boy," William repeated, even as shadows appeared at the top of the stairs.

Chapter 33

John

M ike was dead.

They'd received word as soon as they got within radio range. Abi cried out upon hearing the news and immediately burst into tears. They pulled over and John switched seats with her. John tried to focus on the radio but couldn't help hearing Tammy comforting the fragile young woman. Even the usually aloof Romy must have felt for her, as John could hear her attempts at soothing the heartbroken girl.

Not that John wasn't upset, but he was experienced with these types of things. He'd deal with his sorrow later. This was not the time to lose focus. He glanced at BB beside him. The young man's face was twisted with emotion, and tears rolled freely down those gaunt cheeks. Credit to him, he continued to drive like the professional he was.

John kept communicating with Emily, getting all the intel.

Mike had passed away half an hour ago. *Rest in peace, brother.*

There had been no more attacks. *Thank God. Mel...*

Ben had snuck out right after the attack and tracked down a Rosae Crucis operator. The operator had been neutralized. *Did he do that to protect us or himself?*

They had shot down a Rosae Crucis VIP. *Fuck. We're getting into a fight that we can't win.*

They made it into the community and continued to drive toward the Ren. They stopped only once, when John spotted a roamer. BB asked to take the shot. John understood, and let the young man take out his grief and anger on the zombie. A single gunshot barked, and they moved on.

John nodded at BB as he got back into the vehicle. "Good shot, son." The real message was slightly different. *Glad you found a release. Just don't get used to killing. It gets to be too easy. Eventually, it creates more emotional problems than it eases.*

John had given Emily the heads up, so it was no surprise that several people were outside to meet them. Other than Bill at the gate, John spotted Keith nearby. He saw the business end of a rifle sticking out from the edge of the roof and surmised that Nat was up there, providing cover.

They drove through the open gate and Bill quickly closed it behind them. He'd barely raised his hand when John waved at him. John watched him from the passenger seat and the young soldier's face told him volumes.

BB pulled into the lot, parking at a random angle. Nobody moved or spoke for a moment after he shut down the engine. They all sat in the sudden silence, preparing themselves. John heard one of the women in the vehicle take a deep breath and exhale in a loud sigh.

Joe and Mel stood at the school entrance and started walking toward the parking lot as soon as they pulled in. They now stood several feet away. John realized that none of his crew had moved.

"Okay, guys." He reached for the door handle. "We're home."

Joe started to say something the moment he stepped out of the vehicle, but John waved him off. He went straight to Mel and drew her into his arms.

They held each other for a long moment, communicating through touch.

I'm glad you're okay. I missed you. I don't want to leave you, ever again.

They buried Mike that afternoon. John followed the somber procession through the gym door and to the all-too-familiar burial ground. The service was short. BB and Abi placed the sheet-wrapped body of their former commander into the freshly dug grave, with the assistance of Tammy and Ben.

About half a dozen people said a few words. John barely heard them.

He did stand at attention as the grave was filled with dirt, while most of the other folks turned back to the school. A mound of dirt and a freshly made cross marked Mike's final resting place. Still, John waited. It was only after Jack, Keith and Bill slung their shovels onto their shoulders and retreated that John stirred.

He released Mel's hand and approached the grave, kneeling at the foot end. John dipped his head and said a silent prayer. With a final nod, he got to his feet, stuck out his hand for Mel to take, and walked away.

He didn't get far before he heard somebody call his name. It was Joe. The big man had also remained at the grave and came walking up to them now.

"I need to talk to you." His face betrayed that this would not be a pleasant conversation.

John was about to tell him to lay off, but Mel released his hand and nodded.

Go. See what he wants, was her silent message.

John watched her move away.

Her limp is already fading. What a woman ...

"All right, Joe." John turned around and faced the big man. "What is it?"

Joe opened his mouth to speak but then shut it again. John could see that he was struggling. When he did say something, it was barely more than a whisper.

"I'm sorry."

John's eyebrows pulled together in confusion. "What do you mean?"

Joe's hand shot to his nose, and he gently touched the injured appendage. His eyes darted around before settling back on John. "I lied to you. To all of you."

John stepped closer. "What are you talking about?"

"Rachel is sick. She has ... mental health disorders," Joe blurted out at last.

It wasn't as if John hadn't suspected something like this.

"She needs medication."

John nodded. "Okay."

"But that's not the worst. I've been taking meds from the clinic. I didn't know how people would react if they knew that Rachel was sick." The big man watched Mel enter the gym, leaving the two men alone outside. "I don't know how they're going to react."

Knowing that Joe had more to say, John waited.

"I panicked when Shelley found out. It was easy to put the blame on somebody we don't know." He hung his head. "That was wrong. The kid's a pain in my ass, but he doesn't deserve that."

"At least you're coming clean now — before we had a chance to confront Q," John said.

"Yeah." Joe took a deep breath and blew it out. "Yeah."

The two men were silent for a moment.

A faint noise in the distance broke the silence. They looked toward the direction of the sound. John thought that it might have been a gunshot. He shook his head. "Whatever that was, it was far away."

Joe grunted in agreement. His mind was back on other things. "What do I do?" He wasn't talking about the gunshot.

"First of all, *we'll* tell Shelley the truth. We'll tell her about Rachel's condition, but I want her to keep your stealing of medications to herself."

Raising his hand and opening his mouth to argue, Joe seemed to disagree. But then he grunted, and lowered his hand. "You're probably right. No need to stir everybody up about this." He considered it for a moment longer. "But folks are bound to need some of that medicine at some point. What do we do then?"

"We go and get some." John grinned. "There are a bunch of hospitals, clinics, and pharmacies around here. Any of those are likely to contain the things you need. Let's check out the maps and come up with some candidates. I felt that we should gather up some meds and stuff anyway. Kind of a priority in these days." His wheels were already turning. No sooner was one mission complete than the next one kicked off. "Do you think you can make a list of stuff we need?"

"I'll do you one better." Joe smiled down at the warrior. "I'll go with you."

John's own smile faded at that. "Look, Joe... It's not that I don't want you to come with me, but... You don't really have any experience with this." He was about to elaborate when Joe placed a hand on his shoulder.

"I owe our group this. I owe Rachel this." He chewed on his lip for a second before continuing. "I owe Mike this. I might have saved him if I had the right materials ..."

"Okay." John sighed. "I'll ask for some volunteers to accompany us. I'm thinking we go in with a four or five-man team, max. Get to the place and scope it out. If it looks good, we go in, find the supplies, and fuck off. In and out." He met Joe's eyes. "No last-minute side missions."

"No, sir. I'll prepare a list of what we need." Joe turned and strode toward the school as John watched; Joe seemed to have a bit of spring in his step.

Eager to redeem himself? Or just excited about this mission?

John looked back at the slight mounds and crosses that marked the graves and hesitated one last second, admiring how the late afternoon sun shone on those crosses. *Almost like they're lit up. God is embracing you guys.* John smiled, liking that idea, then he followed Joe.

T wo hours later, they had a big meeting. Just about everybody attended, the exception being Ethan and Jack — who had drawn lookout duty — and Christine and Rachel for lesser known reasons. Only Joe, Shelley and John knew why.

Tammy got to go first. She recapped the excursion to the Georgia Guidestones.

There appeared to be no consensus on what to do next. Some of the group thought that it was too late to do anything significant and suggested to leave well enough alone. Rosa, Sarah and Claire were the most supportive of that train of thought.

Others wanted to take the fight to Rosae Crucis. Breanne, Q, and to a lesser extent Romy were behind that idea. They looked ready to fight anybody at the moment.

Most just wanted to get on with more pressing matters, though.

"We still have to clear the community of zombies," Melissa suggested to the group. "Maybe our immediate safety and wellbeing should be the priority."

Keith raised his hand. "We still have to finish work on our water collection system." He referred to the rainwater collection system he had built with Ern. The plan had always been to source a few more barrels, along with the materials for a filtration system.

Melissa nodded emphatically in agreement. "Exactly. *That's* the kind of stuff we should be working on." She looked around. "Didn't somebody mention something about preparing the ground for a garden outside?"

"Hold on." Joe had gotten to his feet. All eyes turned to him. "There is another priority item that we need to take care of."

His expression turned troubled, and he lifted a hand to his face. He caught himself, however, when he looked up and spotted his audience. Awkwardly, he dropped the hand. He spotted John nodding imperceptibly in encouragement and continued.

"We didn't have the right equipment to save Mike. Now, I'm not sure if we could have saved him — but I am sure that we would have had a better chance ..."

Joe trailed off as Abi started to cry. BB put his arm around her, and several people moved closer for support.

"Ahem," Joe cleared his throat and tried to continue where he left off. "I've started a list. We need equipment. But most of all, we need more meds. We need antibiotics, painkillers etcetera."

He could see the agreement in many faces.

"So, I want to propose another expedition. I've already spoken with John, and the two of us will go. We could use a couple more volunteers."

People spoke up at once. Joe held up his hands to stall the comments, and the crowd fell silent. "Please see John after this meeting. I'm leaving the selection up to him."

That, effectively, was the end of the meeting. Several people immediately left the cafeteria. Others followed John out, pleading their case to join the expedition. It surprised Joe to see so many people willing to risk themselves for the good of their group.

He walked over to the far table. The map that John's team had found was laid out there. Ben was already intently studying the map.

"What do you think?" Joe asked as he joined Ben. "Was it worth the effort?"

Ben looked up. "Difficult to say."

He looked down at the map again. His finger traced several marked locations. "I mean, it's not like we can alert the authorities anymore. Nor can we mount up a strike team to take them out."

"Yeah. I suppose you're right." Joe took place beside Ben and the two men studied the map some more. "Looks like they were spread out all across the country." Joe commented.

Ben nodded, the white turban on his head bobbing up and down. "Yeah. I heard there were thousands of people in the order, and that was just in America."

"How the hell did they keep all of this secret..."

Ben met his eyes. "The Rosae Crucis are a very secretive bunch. I don't even think that *I* know enough to scratch the surface."

The men turned their gazes back to the map. After a moment, Joe pointed down at one specific location.

"Hmm. I get these other names. Alphabetic, and all that. But what is 'PD'?"

Ben stared at the map intently for a moment. He inhaled sharply as realization hit him.

"I know what that means. PD stands for 'Primary Domicile.'"

"Primary Domicile?"

"Yeah. It's their home base. It's where I—we—can find Brenin."

Chapter 34

Nancy

A group of zombies, several dozen strong, marched down the street. Very little was left of the stops and starts that had characterized them for the previous two weeks. It was like they knew where they were going. A terrifying sight.

"The only good thing," Dean whispered in her ear, "is that they're less spread out. You don't run into individuals as often."

Nancy nodded, although she had a hard time seeing the good thing in that.

So we will run into a horde of the things instead of singles. Great.

They had just started to travel back in the direction of the Ren when Nuggets gave them a silent warning.

They're coming. Everything about the dog's body language stated that simple message.

They heeded it.

Dean and Nancy snuck into a house with minutes to spare. They picked the house with the wide-open door. It made sense. Whatever had been inside that house was no longer there. A closed front door might harbor a surprise, whether it be alive or dead.

Now they stood in a living room full of overturned furniture, watching a large group of zombies trek down the street.

Silent Screamers.

That's what Dean called them. It seemed a fitting name for them.

She felt a light pull on her arm and allowed herself to be taken back through the living room. Dean led her to the kitchen, which was located near the back of the open-plan layout.

"We'll have to wait them out. Either that or we sneak out of the back and circle wide," he said. Nancy agreed, but it frustrated her to no end. She'd wanted nothing more than to fly back to her people at the Ren once she'd made the decision to return there.

Stubborn old bat. Ern would have said, although the inflection on his voice would tell Nancy that he meant no harm. *There never was any talking you out of it when you decided you were going to do it.*

She smiled softly. Dean raised an eyebrow in confusion.

"Ah, it's nothing. Just thinking about what my Ern would say."

"Hmm." Dean pursed his lips.

He looks sad.

"You miss your Sophie." Nancy placed her hand on Dean's arm. "I get it. I'm sad too. But I think of Ern like he is still here."

Nancy smiled again. "We were the typical old couple. Always nagging each other. But we secretly liked that. So I try to think of what he would say. It's like he is the angel on my shoulder. Or maybe the devil." She snickered at the thought. Dean could do nothing but join in her amusement.

"I suppose you're right," Dean said after a moment.

"Then what would your Sophie say to you right now?"

Dean considered it for a moment. "She'd say that I should stop bumping my head." He grinned and touched the lump on the back of his skull.

"Smart woman. I think she'd also give you hell for not showering." She waved her hand in front of her face in mockery.

"Hey! I did shave." Dean grinned good naturedly.

"Well, you're not getting any sponge baths from me." Nancy cackled.

Some of her first words to the young man when he woke up had been, "You need a shower!" She'd teased him later, telling him that she was about to give him a sponge bath, conscious or not. Dean had turned several shades of red, which had greatly amused her.

They both tilted their heads as they heard a different noise. Their eyes met in recognition.

"That was a gunshot," Nancy said.

"Not very close."

Both adventurers silently speculated on the source of that noise.

Somebody's last stand. Nancy concluded, then berated herself for her negativity.

"So... What do you think we should do?" Dean brought her back to the present.

"They're heading to this Ren of yours," he continued. "I'm sure about that." Concern was etched on the young man's face. "Should we keep going?"

"Yeah. Yeah, we should. Especially now that we know." Nancy shook her head immediately after that statement. "But we shouldn't risk everything. Let's wait for them to pass. Maybe we can get around them somehow."

Dean nodded in agreement, stepped out of the kitchen and made his way to the window. He observed the scene outside for a moment before turning back to the elderly woman.

His expression was severe. "I hope we make it in time."

Johnny was hauling ass.

He sprinted down the street at top speed, never even looking back.

Fuckin' hell! That was way too close.

He turned right at the next intersection and forced himself to slow down to a manageable run. Back in boot, they could run like this for hours on end. Johnny figured he could keep up this pace for ten minutes or so.

Should be enough to put some serious space between me and them zombies.

He had been too confident. He'd survived plenty of engagements in the past. Him and Frankie, together. The Boston Bruisers — that's what their squad was called in honor of the two Massachusetts natives.

Massachusettans? Massechurians?

Johnny kept running. The Boston Bruisers got into some serious pickles — but they always made it out again. This, though ... This was different. The undead didn't follow rules of engagement.

He'd come across a group of about two dozen of them. He'd hid some distance away, allowing them to pass without so much as a glance in his direction. He'd stepped out of cover overflowing with confidence. This was going to be easy — especially if zombies were sticking together in clumps.

But then he'd run across a straggler. A crawler, to be exact. The pathetic creature noticed him at once and started crawling toward him. It was gross, dragging a trail of bodily fluids behind it, like a snail.

He made short work of the creature, slamming a brick onto its noggin and splashing brains all over the pavement.

Apparently, it communicated with the rest of its group the moment that it became aware of him.

Somehow. It must have.

Next thing Johnny knew, a couple of zombies were running toward him.

Not limping. Not lurching. Fucking running.

Johnny's training took over. He immediately knew he would not have time to shoot both, so he raised his rifle and took aim at the nearest one. He didn't rush his shot, letting the nearest zombie get to within fifteen feet. Johnny didn't want to miss.

BLAM. He let the rifle recoil with the shot, bringing his sights up from where he aimed. It was an old trick he'd learned many years ago. It worked to perfection.

One moment the zombie's face was there: eyeless and with mouth agape. The next moment a large crater appeared where nose and brow used to be, and a gray splash behind the head a millisecond later as the bullet blew through the back of its skull. The zombie flipped backward with the momentum of the shot.

Johnny had no time to appreciate it, already reversing the grip on his rifle as the second zombie got to within fifteen feet. The one thing about zombies was that they were predictable. It just ran straight toward Johnny. He sidestepped the thing's lunge effortlessly and swung into its back with the butt end of his rifle. Something cracked, and the thing was suddenly not so fast anymore.

Any sense of victory was short-lived as he looked down the street. More were on their way. Many more.

He hauled ass out of there, driven by pure fear. Now it was nearly ten minutes later, and he was getting tired.

Time to find a hidey-hole.

Chapter 35

Joe

November 21, 8:55 A.M., The Ren

Joe waited. He impatiently checked his watch every minute, waiting for his companions to show up. It was nearly nine a.m. He looked up at the windows, set high in the wall. The sun cast a soft, golden glow inside the gym. It had risen almost an hour ago. Joe had peeked outside earlier and noted the clouds moving in. That sunshine was not going to last.

"Been waiting here for long?" Joe looked up and saw John approach. Shelley and Bill followed in his wake. John had his new weapon slung over his shoulder.

Bushmaster. Joe remembered John boasting about it the night before.

"Oh. Hi, guys." Joe smiled at the approaching threesome. "Yeah. Guess I'm just impatient to get going."

John grinned at the big man. "All right, Joe. Let's get cracking then."

Joe looked his companion up and down. In addition to the new rifle, John had seriously armed up. He was carrying a backpack that Joe suspected was filled with all kinds of goodies. One of those entrenchment tools was attached to the outside. He also wore a pouch on his belt. Joe could see magazines poking out of some pouches.

Always ready to fight a war, that John. He grinned back at the ex-soldier and looked beyond him at the other two companions.

He met Shelley's eyes as she stepped up. "Are you sure you want to come along? It could be dangerous."

Shelley's large eyes had always been windows to her emotions. Right now, they showed nervous excitement mixed with determination. "I'm sure, Joe. You've done so much for us already. I want to do something to help you, now."

Joe didn't trust himself to speak. He smiled at the nurse thankfully.

Bill and Shelley had been briefed on Rachel's condition. Joe worried over them learning of his theft of medications. They had taken it in stride, though.

And you would do it again in a heartbeat.

His companions had passed him by, yet Joe remained rooted in place.

This is really it.

He checked his own gear quickly. An M4 was slung over his shoulder, and he had several spare magazines in his pockets. He'd also picked up a nine-millimeter pistol, which was secured to the utility belt he wore.

"Shall we?" John called from the gym door. With a nod, Joe followed the rest of his team.

They stepped outside into the sunshine. The school fields stretched out before them, the grass tall and lush. Their immediate objective stood parked a few yards away. The Humvee had been topped up and was ready to go.

Surprisingly, Shelley had volunteered to be the driver. John had quickly agreed, as it left the shooters with their hands free. Bill hopped into the passenger seat. John and Joe entered the back seat from opposite sides. Joe watched as John placed his backpack on the middle console.

"Didn't you have one of those on your excursion to the Jeffersons'?"

"Sure did. Nancy took that one when she left." John glanced meaningfully at the backpack. "Hope she's getting good use out of it."

Chapter 36

Nancy

November 21, 10:15 A.M.

C lack. The shovel on Nancy's backpack caught the fence as she tried to crawl through.

Nancy stopped, halfway through the gap. Up ahead, Dean's head was on a swivel as he scanned the area for movement. Nuggets, in contrast, was frozen in place. After what felt like a lifetime, Dean signaled for her to continue. She carefully crawled through the gap in the fence, making sure that the shovel didn't catch on the wooden planking a second time.

"That darn shovel! It keeps getting in the way," she grumbled as she made it to the athlete.

They stood in the gap between two houses. The plan was to cross here, straight to the backyard of the house across the street, and so on. Because, for one thing, the zombies tended to stay in the streets. For another thing, they couldn't climb fences. At least not very well.

"Do you want to leave it behind?" Dean asked.

"Huh?"

"The shovel." He pointed over her head. "Do you want to ditch it?"

Nancy shook her head. "It may come in handy. Besides, I stole this pack from John. I'd like to return it intact."

Dean screwed up his face. "I think a baseball bat would suit you better.

"I don't think so, Dean. That's your sport." She grinned.

"You've got a point there. I like one-shot kill, though." He lifted his eyebrow good-naturedly.

"What position did you play, anyway?"

"Short stop."

"Oh?" Nancy looked pensive for a moment.

"You have no idea what that is, do you?"

A sharp, short bark from Nuggets alerted the humans.

Three zombies stepped around the front corner of the house. A fourth trailed a few feet behind.

"Ah sh-oot." Dean remembered to watch his language at the last moment. He pulled the mace from his belt.

Nancy knew what was expected of her. She backed off to give the big man room. Removing her pack, she placed it to the side and tugged the shovel free. It had caused her grief moments before, but now it just might save her life.

She stepped away from the pack, giving herself room. She remembered her role and waited.

Dean took one practice swing with the mace. It made a slight whistling sound as he swung it.

The next swing ended with a *thunk*. The first zombie took the impact in the side of the face. Pieces of meat flew off as the zombie crashed heavily into the wall of the house. Dean did not hesitate; he used the momentum of the swing, leaning back and spinning the weapon over his head. On the next swing, he stepped forward and caught the second zombie just under its reaching arm. Nancy could see its chest cave in, impossibly deep. It shot sideways to land in a heap behind the first victim.

But therein was the problem. The zombie took the mace with it as it fell. What was worse, the zombie was not done. The handle of the mace stuck out of its chest like a thick arrow shaft. Despite this, it was still moving.

Nancy was halfway to Dean by then. The third zombie had lunged at Dean, who held it at arms' length. The two performed a macabre dance as Nancy got to them.

"Get the other one!" Dean grunted as he struggled with his assailant. The big man easily held the zombie off but didn't want to let go of it either.

The other one. The other one. Nancy didn't know which one Dean had meant. She turned to the closest one. It had gotten to its feet but stood rather shakily.

Nancy screeched and put all her strength behind the swing. The zombie could not lift the arm on its injured side and Nancy made contact flush with the zombie's head. The entrenchment tool cut cleanly through its skull, the tip entering just behind its eye socket and exiting out the of opposite temple. Nancy nearly lost her footing, spinning a complete circle as she met less resistance than she'd expected.

When she looked down, she almost gagged at the sight. She heard a yip from Nuggets and turned to face the last zombie. It was being harassed by the dog, which ran circles around it. She watched anxiously as the zombie reached down and nearly got a hold of the dog. That spurred her into action. She quickly stepped forward, turning the shovel half a rotation as she did so. Nancy was on the zombie before it appeared to register her presence.

She swung hard, spurred on by fear. Nancy caught it on the side of the head with the shovel, sending it spinning away and to the ground with its head caved in. She yelped in pain and dropped the shovel as the violent reverberation shot through her wrists.

"Are you okay?" Dean ran over. Nancy saw the unmoving body of the zombie he'd been wrestling with. It looked like he had smashed its head repeatedly into the fence post, as evidenced by the dark stain that ran down its length.

"Yeah. Fine." Nancy was breathing hard. She picked up the entrenchment tool.

Dean jogged over to retrieve her pack. "We've got to move. More will be coming."

Nancy nodded. They ran across the street, feeling terribly exposed, then up a driveway and squeezed between the garage and the fence to the neighboring yard. It was a relief to find the area empty. A minute later, they crossed the back alley, traversed another yard and were once again ready to cross a road. Dean took one look at Nancy and wisely called for a short break. He handed her backpack to her, and she gratefully pulled out a water bottle.

"That was some good stuff back there." Dean said. "You've got a lot of power."

Nancy gulped down some water, then gulped some air. She forced herself to slow down and finally managed to get her panting under control.

"Thanks. You should see me with a pan."

Her attempt at humor made him snicker.

He's so nice that he won't even make fun of my jokes. See, Ern?

"I take back what I said about that shovel thingy," he remarked. "Thing must be very sharp ..."

Nancy realized that she was still holding on to the entrenchment tool. Its head was covered in human detritus, including a chunk of meat and skin with hair attached. She struggled to hold down the water she had just drunk.

After wiping the shovel on the grass, she could detect a slight silvery tint to the edges. "I think John sharpened the edges." She swallowed, hard. "I cut through that guy's face like it was a piece of cheese ..."

"First of all, it wasn't a *guy*. Secondly, you did what you had to do. You saved my ass back there. You and your mad shovel skills." Dean ended his statement with a disarming grin.

Nancy smiled back somewhat half-heartedly. "Yeah. I guess I did."

"You and me, we're an unstoppable force," Dean continued.

Nancy guffawed at that. "I'd rather get back to the Ren, and let you do your Conan thing with John. Or Keith." Nancy took another drink of her water and put the bottle back in her pack. She slid her arms through the straps and indicated that she was ready to continue.

The entrenchment tool stayed in her hand, though. She was going to hold on to it for a little while longer.

I think John would approve. She smiled again as she followed Dean and Nuggets.

Chapter 37

Joe

November 21, 2:00 P.M., Nearing Healthlife Hospital

Joe was on edge. This was the first time he'd ventured out on an expedition. He felt especially exposed once they'd left the perceived safety of their walled community behind. Not knowing what to do with himself, he got into the habit of checking his weapon, his pockets, then staring out the window for a few seconds.

Weapon, pockets, window. Weapon, pockets, window.

"Hey, Joe?"

Joe twitched in surprise.

"Sorry. Didn't mean to startle you," Shelley said.

Joe looked at the rear-view mirror and into Shelley's impossibly large eyes.

"No, it's nothing Shelley." He forced himself to smile, trying to make it look soothing rather than manic.

"I was just thinking... What if this place is like the other ones?"

The smile melted from his face. It was something he had considered as well. He put the smile back on. "We'll figure it out, Shelley. Don't worry."

"Maybe we should try for another pharmacy."

"Yeah. Maybe we will. But you know what? I think this place will work out." He glanced out the window. "This whole area looks deserted." He wasn't exaggerating.

And then, there it was.

Healthlife Hospital stood like a solitary tombstone in the landscape. The area was a new development, the only completed buildings being the hospital and a hotel about two blocks away. The rest was a combination of unfinished construction, pavement, and grassy fields.

They drove past the beginnings of what seemed like an office building, the metal beams of its skeleton reaching into the gray skies in apparent supplication. Joe's gaze drifted up to the clouds and back down to the hospital, which now loomed in front of him and his companions. The building's exterior, darkened by the shade, exuded an ominous look, and Joe couldn't help but shiver at the sight.

John noticed. "Nerves?"

Joe was about to make an excuse, then thought the better of it. "Yeah. This place, it looks ... Spooky."

"Yeah, it does." John looked out his window as Shelley pulled their vehicle into the parking lot. "Abandoned," he added.

It did look abandoned. The lot was completely empty, other than a couple of ambulances and a police cruiser. It still looked spooky. Especially seeing that police cruiser with its front doors wide open. There wasn't a person in sight.

Suppose I should be thankful for that.

John appeared to pick up his thought. "We might have gotten lucky here. It sure beats Memorial."

Joe could only agree with that. Their first stop, Memorial General Hospital, had looked more like a warzone than a place for health care. They'd driven past that place and noted all the barriers and military vehicles, conspicuously parked on the street side of the barriers.

Meant to keep stuff in, not out.

Then they'd seen the tank. Its turret was pointed toward the hospital. A pile of debris where the front entrance used to be showed evidence of its use. The pile of human detritus strewn between the hospital and those barriers left little to the imagination.

They'd seen movement in that debris and beyond, inside the hospital.

They'd quickly driven on.

It hadn't been their first stop today. It had actually been their third. The two pharmacies they'd considered Plan A and B both stood in ruin. The first place had burned to the ground, along with the rest of the mall it was attached to. Joe wasn't too disappointed about that. He had seen too many horror movies about zombies and malls.

The second pharmacy had seemed to be the victim of repeated lootings. The team had spent a solid fifteen minutes scoping out the place before making a run inside. Their reward had been a small plastic bag full of sundry items, but the closest they'd gotten to any medication was a roll of throat lozenges. They'd quickly decided that pharmacies were not going to yield much. Joe remembered hearing about all the lootings that had occurred just before the world truly went to shit. Malls, big-box grocery stores and pharmacies had been the first targets of the scared masses. They had drawn up plans to try a hospital right then and there.

Then the zombies had shown up, and they had had to hustle back to the vehicle. Joe could tell that John was pissed. They had let their guard down and allowed zombies to approach from all angles. In the end, they'd made it back to the Humvee. It had been a lot closer than Joe liked.

On top of that, he'd gotten lectured for the next ten minutes about fire discipline, proper aiming and managing ammunition.

In the past, he would have bristled. *Fuck you and your magazine! So I dropped it. So what?* he would have said. Instead, he'd nodded and promised to do better next time. Five minutes later, as they discussed plan C, it had occurred to Joe that he had changed.

Guess that's what four weeks in the apocalypse will do to a person.
Plan C had been Memorial. Plan D was their last stab at success. This place was a new hospital in a mostly undeveloped new area. They hoped that less people meant less zombies. Actually, they hoped that less living people had made a run to the place. Zombies didn't steal medications.

The Humvee jerked to a halt, stirring Joe from his reverie. They had arrived. Joe leaned over to look out of the front window at their destination. If anything, the silence made the place appear more ominous.

"Quick check out your windows. Holler if you see any movement," John instructed.

Joe performed his duty. From his window he could just see the far-right side of the hospital. No broken windows marred the building's face. Beyond the hospital lay an empty lot. The hotel stood roughly two blocks away. It was hard to tell distances without any true landmarks. Joe saw no movement, other than the soft waving of the calf-length grass growing in the field between the two buildings.

Joe turned his head to look straight out to his right, as well as over his shoulder.

Nothing. It's like a ghost town.

"Clear on my side," John stated.

"Um, all clear on this side, too," Joe responded.

"Clear," Shelley and Bill added.

John told the rest to stay put for a moment. He quickly opened his door and hopped out of his seat, closing the door immediately behind him.

He's doing that for our safety. It wasn't the first time that Joe felt a special appreciation for the former special-forces man. He watched John glide away from the vehicle, his weapon in lockstep

268 MARCO DE HOOGH

with his eyes. He seemed satisfied after a moment and returned to the Humvee.

"We are all clear." John grabbed the belt of magazines he'd brought with him from the floor of the vehicle. "Take your gear and step outside. Shelley, you know what to do."

Shelley nodded, her eyes still wide.

"Don't worry," John stated upon seeing this. "You've got your walkie-talkie. We'll only be a minute or two away."

Shelley smiled slightly and nodded again, although her eyes still told a different story.

John had gone through the roles as they traveled. Shelley was to pop the top hatch and keep an eye out for approaching zombies. She wasn't supposed to raise any alarm unless there were more than half a dozen of them, or if they approached to within fifty feet.

John had also made it very clear that she was not to use the walkie-talkie until she absolutely had to. "Silence is key here, guys," he had said. "We want to be in and out without attracting any attention."

Joe stepped out of the Humvee and immediately felt cold wind bite through his jacket. He closed the door, the cold metal of the handle stinging his fingers. Winter was around the corner. He looked at his clothes and those of his companions as they strode to the front of the vehicle.

"We're going to need some winter gear soon," he whispered.

John looked annoyed for half a second before giving him a curt nod. "You're right. But now it's time to focus." With that he stepped toward the front entrance of the hospital. Bill and Joe flanked their leader, several steps back and out to the sides as they had been instructed.

Joe glanced over at the police cruiser. It sat with its front doors wide open. *I wonder what made them abandon the vehicle like that?*

They slowly approached the front doors of the hospital. Once they got within fifteen feet, they could tell the doors were sealed shut, impeded from opening by some strange device.

"The military did this," John whispered.

He signaled for the team to head to their left, to the emergency entrance where two ambulances awaited them. The ambulances were parked one behind the other in the driveway. Joe scuffed his shoe against the pavement, which seemed excruciatingly loud in the deadly silence.

For a second, he thought that John was going to berate him for his blunder, but the ex-military man was all business. He motioned for the others to spread out some more as they approached the first vehicle. In contrast to the police cruiser, the ambulances' doors were all shut. John still took extreme care in approaching though. He appeared to study the ground for a moment, then with infinite patience he got to the rear door of the first ambulance and put his ear to the portal.

What is it?

John faced Joe, listening at the ambulance door. Joe frowned as their eyes met and gave a curt signal with his hand.

Right. Focus outward. Joe turned away and kept an eye out for any movement.

Behind him, the ambulance door opened. He was sorely tempted to turn around and satisfy his curiosity but managed to maintain discipline. He became aware of the smell of decaying flesh a few moments later.

Out of the corner of his eye, he saw John emerge from the vehicle and move toward the second ambulance. Joe stepped forward, as did Bill from his side near the hospital. The scene remained eerily quiet. After another minute, John had checked the second ambulance and the emergency entrance. He gestured, and the threesome stepped away from the hospital.

"Emergency doors are sealed, just like the main doors. We're going to have to go in through another door or bust a window."

Joe and Bill nodded. They had kind of expected that after seeing the main entrance sealed.

"Found a dead cop," John said.

"Was that what you found in the ambulance?" Joe asked.

"Found some scuff marks and blood on the driveway. Somebody dragged him to that ambulance and placed his corpse inside. It's been in there for a while. Weeks, I'd guess."

Shuddering, Joe shook his head. John noticed Joe's reaction and shook his own head in response. "That's not the worst of it. I had a quick look at the wound, and it looks to me like this guy was executed."

"Holy shit."

"Yeah." John looked down at the pavement for a moment, lost in his own thoughts. "Anyway, you can go check the ambulances for supplies. If you can stand the stench. Bill, you keep a look out. I'm going to walk a circuit of the hospital to see if there is another way in."

"You really think we should bother? I mean, if the military came in and blocked all the exits..." Joe trailed off.

"I know what you're thinking." John seemed annoyed at Joe's comment. "That the hospital is chock-full of zombies. Well, I don't think it is. Maybe the military put up those barriers to keep people out, not in. Besides, I haven't seen any zombies at all in this area." He pointed toward the hospital. "I haven't seen any zombies slamming themselves into the windows. I mean, that front entrance is all glass. I didn't see a single zombie inside."

Inviting Joe's questions by raising his palms, John nodded when the other man stayed silent. "This is our last shot. We don't go in there, we won't be hitting any place today."

"Yeah. You're right, John," Joe agreed.

"Okay, then enough chit-chat. We're pissing away daylight." With that he turned on his heel and marched back toward the school.

Joe and Bill exchanged a look. Joe snorted at the other man's expression.

"Dang." Bill shrugged.

"All right. Let's go raid some ambulances."

The ambulances were treasure troves. Joe looted the second vehicle first, the smell of the rotting corpse in the first one almost enough to make him gag already. Eventually, once he had built up enough courage, he also looted the first ambulance. He did throw up, and from the sounds nearby so did Bill.

They had stashed the loot in the Humvee. It included several jump bags and one fully-stocked medication bag. Joe had also packed some of the gear, including a couple of bag valve masks, a cervical collar, and a spinal board. He was sorely tempted to grab the wheeled cot as well, but space inside the Humvee was at a premium, and he reluctantly left it behind.

John had also returned by then. He had found a busted-out window around the side of the hospital. It was a high window, so he had to pull himself up for a look inside.

"It leads to a bathroom. Whomever took out that window made sure to remove all the shards so as not to cut themselves on their entry. They knew what they were doing." He looked at his companions. "We're going in."

"Should we climb in through that window?"

"Not a good exit if things get hairy in there. No, we'll go in through the front window. It will be noisy, and we will not have a lot of time." He turned to Shelley. "Can you pull up the Humvee closer to the front entrance? Back it in so that we can get away quickly."

The nurse nodded and turned on the vehicle. John followed her and retrieved something from the back seat.

"Call us on the walkie-talkie if you see any zombies coming this way," he instructed before he shut the door and walked to the waiting men.

He passed them without a word and started toward the main entrance of the building. Bill and Joe looked at each other and shrugged. They had no choice but to follow. Curious, Joe quickened his step to see what John had grabbed.

"These are double-glazed, toughened glass windows," John said as they walked up to the building.

He pointed at one of the windows to the left of the barred entrance with the object he had retrieved. It was a hammer. John handed the hammer to Bill as he pulled on gloves.

"Many folks don't know how to break through shit like this."

"I bet you do," Joe said.

John merely smiled at the big man as he reached for the hammer once more.

"Stay back. It will be messy and noisy." He approached the window, standing to the side of the pane. "We're going to have to move quickly. Joe, get to the reception desk and see if you can find a layout. We need to find the dispensary. Bill, you cover the area to the left and down that far hall. I'll take the right." He waited for both men to acknowledge his instructions.

Joe was prepared for the noise. Nevertheless, he jerked in surprise at the sharp crack and the ensuing crash as the window shattered into a million pieces and fell to the concrete. John had struck the pane near the bottom corner, which surprised Joe; he had figured that John would need to strike it dead in the center. He had no time to admire John's handiwork as Bill moved beside him.

This is it. Go.

Joe clutched his weapon as he stepped through the window frame. He had to catch himself as he skidded slightly on the fragments of glass that littered the polished concrete floor. When he looked down, he found he had not only slipped on glass — bullet casings lay scattered about.

Another step, and Joe skidded again. Neither Bill nor John took notice.

They're in the zone.

Get in the zone, Joe.

The glass crunched under his boots, making the noise that always made him cringe and clasp the back of his jaw. Joe was determined not to let it bother him this time. He shook off the feeling and quickly but carefully stepped forward.

He was surprised at the lack of noise inside the building. In sharp contrast to his expectations, no zombies stepped out of the dark background to assault them.

"Clear," Bill whispered over Joe's shoulder, just loudly enough for the other two men to hear. "Affirmative. All clear on this end, too," was John's response.

Joe had arrived at the front desk, quickly stepping around to the business end of it and scanning for a map. He was rewarded with a laminated sheet several moments later.

"Got a map," he whispered as he stepped back around the desk.

John gave Bill a hand signal and the two men quickly met up with Joe. The map was focused for hospital guests, highlighting the departments and common areas. Nevertheless, Joe was able to decipher the approximate location of the dispensary. "It's not indicated, but I figure that it's one of these rooms here." He traced a hallway with his finger. "That's my best guess." He looked to John for confirmation.

After agreeing, John took a look at the map to orient himself and made a cutting motion toward the area Bill had been guarding.

"Down that way." Then he did a radio check. "You read me, Shelley? Over."

Shelley was already backing the Humvee up to the hospital. It jerked to a stop and Joe imagined the flustered nurse putting the vehicle into park to reply.

"Yes. I hear you. I mean, I read you. Over," she said.

John and Joe shared a grin.

"We're heading into the hospital now. Radio silence unless you see something. I'll let you know when we're on our way out. Over."

"Okay. Good luck." There was a short pause before she remembered "Over. Sorry."

"Like we planned," John told the others. "Joe on the right, Bill on the left, me in front. Looks like there has been a fight here, so stay sharp." John waited until the others acknowledged him before starting off.

They had been instructed in the car ride how to position themselves as they moved down corridors, and Joe was secretly proud of their execution — his own included. He felt silent and deadly.

Enough light still radiated from the lobby behind them, but at a signal from John they turned on their flashlights. Even the direction of their beams had been carefully explained by John. He was not one for taking unnecessary chances.

They silently slid down the hallway until they hit the first intersection. "Left here. Then right again," Joe whispered after another quick look at the map. He inwardly cringed, as his voice seemed unnaturally loud in the oppressive silence.

I wonder if the place is abandoned. They had not encountered a single corpse, moving or otherwise.

He knew that it wasn't though. Joe had seen the dried-up blood stains on the main lobby floor. People had died here. A second clue was undeniable. The unmistakable smell of rotting flesh hung in the air like a blanket.

They turned left, then right. But not before they caught a glimpse of something irregular in the distance. Joe couldn't help himself. He lifted his flashlight. The military-grade flashlight seemed to stab through the dark hallway, illuminating—

Bodies. Oh, God. They're stacked like firewood! Joe stood frozen in place by fear, scared to move the flashlight beam away from the bodies. He was sure they would move as soon as the light did. Would tumble to the floor, get up, and charge them. He could see it clearly in his mind's eye.

He felt a presence beside him. Still, he could not take his eyes off the bodies. The presence reached out and firmly grasped his wrist, slowly forcing him to point the flashlight away. Only once the stacks of bodies were out of sight and all remained silent could Joe turn away.

The stern expression on John's face was enough of a message.

Get with the program.

Joe assented once, in embarrassment and acknowledgement. John turned and took up his position once more.

They continued down the corridor in absolute silence, the hair on the back of Joe's neck rising as he imagined bodies getting up and following them in the darkness.

The assault never came. After a minute, Joe started to relax.

While Bill and Joe were tasked with keeping their flashlight beams pointed in one direction, John's moved around more sporadically as he read signs above doors. His flashlight beam found its target near the end of the hallway.

Dispensary

The first thing Joe noticed was that the door to this room was wide open. Every other door he had encountered in the hospital had been shut. John must have noticed as well, as he approached the threshold cautiously, his weapon raised.

Bill and Joe waited several steps back as John shone his flashlight in, popping his head around the corner a moment later. He scanned the room for a few tense seconds, then signaled for the other two men to move forward.

There was a body in the dispensary. The rotting corpse of a uniformed police officer lay splayed out between the wall and the first shelf of medications.

Joe ushered the other two men in and silently closed the door. Next, he placed his flashlight on a file cabinet. He lay the flashlight so that it was facing outward, effectively lighting up the room with the industrial-strength instrument.

He took a deep breath. "We should be all right to speak, as long as we keep our voices down," he whispered.

Joe didn't trust himself to say anything, so merely nodded. He turned off his flashlight and put it in his pocket. Bill did likewise. Intrigued by the corpse, Joe walked over to have a better look. The officer's head was all but gone, but his mouth and nose were still intact. His pistol lay about a foot away from his hand. Joe shuddered.

"Looks like suicide," John said softly. He had stepped up beside Joe.

Just then, something else caught Joe's eyes. The body had slid down slightly, but between its legs was the tell-tale white of several sheets of paper.

"What's this?" He gingerly reached between the dead man's legs. The pages wouldn't come free. He had to put his hand on the corpse's shoulder to get some leverage and yelped as the body slid onto its side.

"Sorry," he told John, who was still standing beside him.

At least the pages were no longer held down by the corpse. Joe quickly scooped them up.

"Looks like this guy wrote down a bunch of stuff..." Joe started to look at the first page, but John put a hand on his arm.

"No time for that now, Joe."

"Of course," Joe hastily folded the pages and stuck them in his pocket. "Sorry."

John turned to the shelves. "What do we need to take?"

For the first time, Joe took in the dispensary. Three rows of shelving units occupied most of the room, a portion of their shelves angled downward to let gravity assist in keeping the products close at hand.

Joe stepped up to the first shelving unit and started to scan the products. After a moment, he grabbed the front of a shelf and tugged. It rolled forward.

"Cool," Bill said.

Joe looked at the soldier, then past him to the far corner of the room.

"Bill, grab that box. Dump everything out of it, then bring it over here." Joe knew they had brought a duffel bag with them, but that wouldn't be enough. "We've definitely hit the jackpot here."

They spent the next ten minutes packing every medicine that Joe even suspected they might need into the two containers. Their shadows danced across the room as they moved down the shelving units. By the time they got to the last row, the duffle bag was so full that the zipper wouldn't close, and the box was close to overflowing.

"Shit. We've got to run this to the Humvee. Maybe we can make a second run."

Joe reached down for the duffle bag, catching John's gaze as he did so.

"Did you get what you need?" John asked quietly.

Joe knew exactly what John was referring to. Meds for Rachel.

"Yes. Enough to last a long time." Joe felt the emotion rise and quickly turned to Bill. "Let me carry the box. You keep your hands free in case we run into trouble.

"Sure thing, boss." Bill grinned. He reached down for the shotgun. "Mossberg 500. Nice." With that, he slung the weapon over his shoulder.

John pulled out his walkie-talkie. "Shelley. We are on our way out, over." He waited for a response but got none. "She's maintaining radio silence." He mumbled to himself before lifting the duffel bag.

Carefully John opened the door and scanned the hallway. He nodded back at the other two men, and they followed him out. They would only be using two flashlights, as Joe had his hands full.

The box of assorted medicine must have weighed at least forty pounds. Joe was easily able to lift it, but his arms started to feel the strain before they were halfway down the first hall. He refused to say a word, though.

These guys are sticking their necks out for me and Rachel. He stoically kept putting one foot in front of the other.

The hallway was luckily still deserted. Joe didn't even bother to glance down the corridor to where he knew many bodies lay. He did feel awfully exposed, nevertheless.

They carefully navigated their way back down the second hallway. Joe almost sighed out loud in relief when they turned the last corner and could see the sun-lit reception area once more. Bill and John immediately turned off their flashlights and stowed them away.

Just then the walkie-talkie attached to John's belt came alive.

"—ear me, over?" Shelley's urgent whisper came from the walkie-talkie. Before John could put down the duffel bag, Shelley spoke again. "Guys you have to get out of there. They're here!"

John retrieved the walkie-talkie. His other hand was already reaching for his rifle. "Shelley, I hear you. What's the SITREP? Over."

"Oh, thank God! You didn't respond. I thought you guys were in trouble. A couple of zombies walked past me and into the hospital, and—" There was a slight pause. "At least another ten coming this way. You have to hurry! Over."

"Got it. We're coming out shooting. Get ready to drive. Out." John threw a quick look at his companions. "Shit. The noise must have attracted them. Joe, can you take this bag? I'll need my hands free."

"Sure. One moment."

Joe knelt and quickly dumped a few things out of the duffle bag. He zipped it up, the noise eliciting some movement in the reception area. The men looked at each other as they heard the unmistakable sound of glass crunching underfoot. Somebody was coming this way.

Quickly swinging the bag onto his back, Joe put his arms through the loops. Next, he reached down and lifted the box. He nodded at John, and they started forward.

John took the lead. He signaled to Bill, then lifted the rifle to his shoulder and stepped forward. Joe couldn't help feeling impressed by how the man and his rifle seemed to move as one. Just then, John stepped past the end of the hallway and into the reception area. He immediately swung to face something out of view for Joe. The sound of his weapon firing was deafening in the enclosed space.

A moment later he fired again.

"Move!" He signaled for Bill to come forward with him and they quickly stepped outside, flanking the vehicle. They immediately started shooting. Joe brought up the rear. He spotted two corpses on the floor. One of them had been a teenage girl in life, the bright colors and glittering material of her clothing in sharp contrast to the gray skin and the darkened hole where her face used to be.

This could have been Christine, a few years ago.

Joe would have shuddered as he walked past, but he was already shaking with the effort of carrying his load.

"Move, move!" John called out between shots.

As he stepped up over the lip of the window frame, Joe almost lost his balance. He was near the end of his strength but refused to call for help. He carried his load to the back of the vehicle, but John had already opened the rear passenger door.

"In here!" John said.

Joe put the box in, spilling a bunch of the contents, then took off the duffle bag and tried to swing it over the back seat and into the storage area behind. It clipped the top of the backrest and distinctly heard several bottles smash as the bag's momentum carried it over. He hopped into the back seat.

"Okay, in!" John ordered.

Bill was already in the seat beside him by the time Joe pulled his door shut. Joe watched John shoot another zombie then curse, as he had only winged it.

"Start her up," Bill said.

Shelley pushed the button and the engine roared to life. John jumped into the front seat, and they were off.

Two minutes later, they were out of trouble and on the road.

"That was smart driving, Shelley," John said. Joe couldn't agree more. Shelley had kept her cool and weaved around the zombies rather than plowing into them. She got them out of the parking lot without clipping a single zombie.

Maybe she just didn't want to hit them.

"How did you keep them from noticing you? Those ones inside must have walked right past you," John asked.

Shelley shrugged. "I just made myself as small as possible. Hid down by the gas pedal. I saw those two coming for a while and tried to warn you ... Maybe I wasn't using the walkie-talkie correctly?" she asked, concern and guilt evident in her expression.

"No, you didn't do anything wrong. It's these walkie-talkies. The hospital must have some reinforced walls or something because the signal didn't penetrate very far."

"Oh. Sorry, I didn't know."

"Not your fault, Shelley. You did good," Joe croaked from the back seat, still not quite recovered from the effort. "And would you please stop apologizing."

Shelley cast an embarrassed smile at him through the rear-view mirror. "Sorry. Habit."

"You're doing it again," John reminded her with a grin.

They drove in silence for a bit. The streets seemed utterly abandoned. Joe looked out the window and couldn't see a single zombie.

Where are they?

"So, you hid. Still odd that those two that walked past never noticed you," John continued.

"I watched them approach to within about twenty feet. Their eyes were ... gone." A slight frown played across Shelley's face. "I moved really slowly and quietly too."

John digested that. Joe could tell that the veteran wasn't fully satisfied with that answer — he wasn't either.

There's got to be something we're missing.

They drove for another minute in silence before Shelley ventured another comment. "Looks like you guys managed to get a lot of loot."

The box still sat between the two passengers in the back seat. It reminded Joe that he had spilled some of the contents. He reached down to the floor at his feet and felt around. He was rewarded with several bottles, tubes and small boxes and started to place them back into the box.

"How did it go on the inside? I didn't hear any gunshots," Shelley said.

"We did see some signs of violence, but it looked like the ground floor had been cleared," John said.

"You saw signs of violence? The place looked abandoned ..."

"People got shot in there. I also saw evidence of drag marks." John thought for a moment. "My guess is that the military came in there and cleared the place out."

In the back seat, Joe nodded slowly. "The dead were stacked in some of the hallways. The only body that seemed out of place was that cop..." Just then he started and reached into his pocket. "He left a bunch of notes behind. Maybe there are some clues as to what happened in these." He brandished the pages that he had fished out of his pocket.

"Read them aloud, will you?" John suggested. "We've got a bit of a drive here, and frankly I'm curious too."

Joe unfolded and straightened the pages. It took him a moment to figure out which was the first one. It ended up being the one with blood splatter on it. Joe started to read. "'My name is Ralph Becker. If you've found this note, then I apologize about the brains.'"

Chapter 38

Ralph Becker's Story

M*y name is Ralph Becker. If you've found this note, then I apologize about the brains.*

Ralph chuckled as he read the line. Jenny would have admonished him for his crude humor. A sob escaped him as he thought about his wife and newborn child.

Now she'd be giving you the gears about being melodramatic.

He took a deep breath as he pulled the pen away from the paper. He sat against a wall, his legs splayed out so that his feet nearly touched the shelves across from him. A million multi-colored boxes and bottles stared back from the shelves, which ran wall-to-wall across from him.

So many drugs. So much salvation.

But no, Ralph had already dismissed the notion a while ago. He doubted that he could even get up after that last spasm of pain.

Don't want to come back as one of them.

He wasn't sure if he would turn into a zombie now that he had been bitten, or if the syndrome had something to do with it. But either way, he was going to end it on his terms.

A bullet will be quicker — albeit messier. That reminded him of the report he was about to write. Something inside him made him want to do it. Maybe it was a way to rationalize the things he'd done. Maybe it was a way to ask for forgiveness.

Maybe it's habit.

"One last police report..." Ralph sighed again as he brought the pen back to the waiting paper.

Chapter 39

Ralph

October 23, 7:15 P.M.

"It will be okay, Ralph. Deloris and I are safe and sound. You just do your job — and be safe! We'll see you soon." And with that, she hung up.

Oh, God. I hope so, girl. Ralph stared at the darkened screen on the phone in his hand.

They had been talking about the news. None of it seemed to be good. As if it weren't bad enough that most of the crops had failed, all the cattle were now dying as well. And to top it all, people had started getting sick.

The world seemed to be going to shit around them.

What a time to have a baby!

"How's she holding up?"

A voice behind him broke into his thoughts. He turned to see Sergeant Dijkstra walk around the back of the cruiser toward the driver's side. He was cradling a brown paper bag with the logo *Bennie's Dogs* in the nook of his arm.

"Fine. But she always says that ... I can't believe that I missed the birth of my own daughter." Ralph put away his cell phone and reached for the passenger door handle just as his partner reached the driver's side door. The two men exchanged a look over the top of the police cruiser.

"Look. That wasn't your fault. I actually thought that it was a good idea to isolate the maternity wards. Protect them from this thing that's going around." He looked like he was ready to get into the vehicle but changed his mind. "Becker."

He waited until Ralph met his eyes.

"Don't beat yourself up about it. And Jenny? Jenny's tough as nails — you know that. Also, she's got a good head on her shoulders." Dijkstra's expression changed to a smirk. "Wish my partner was more like her."

Ralph grunted and got into the cruiser. Dijkstra maneuvered his large frame into the driver's seat and placed the bag that contained their supper on the console between them. The first grease stains were starting to darken the brown paper already.

"Okay, partner. Dig in before it gets cold." Dijkstra's large mitts opened the bag with deft experience, and he thrust into its contents like a toy crane at the county fair.

Dijkstra was a beast of a man. Ralph studied him as he unwrapped his hot dog. The sergeant was in his late fifties but looked a lot younger with his baby face and tufts of blonde hair peeking out under his cap. He had an easy smile, which usually disarmed any situation — that is, if his two hundred-fifty-pound, six-foot-four frame didn't do so first.

Ralph knew that the big man had a first name. Leonard, or something like that. But everybody called him Dijkstra.

Just like they call you Becker. Wonder if that's an army thing? A lot of the officers in their department had a history in the armed forces. Ralph knew that Dijkstra had been kind of a big deal in the army. The sergeant was still in pretty good shape, although his beer belly had been growing steadily recently.

The radio chirped in the background. Thankfully, it wasn't their unit being called into action.

"World is going nuts," Dijkstra commented between bites. Ralph grunted in agreement.

"K-9 unit is pretty much wiped out. Last of the healthy dogs got sick today, I heard." Dijkstra reached into the brown bag blindly, coming up with a handful of fries. He stuffed the fries into his mouth but continued to speak around the mouthful. "Big cities got riots breaking out all over the place ... Lootings ... It's starting here too, you know."

He chewed for a moment, then swallowed before going on.

"You don't need to worry about Jenny, Becker. She probably couldn't be in a safer place—"

Dijkstra grimaced, then groaned. Ralph watched him cringe in pain and rub his lower belly.

"You all right, chief?"

For a few seconds, Dijkstra continued to rub his belly, then he nodded sharply. "Yeah, just a cramp." He looked at the hot dog in his hand. "Probably from eating this shit."

It didn't stop him from taking another bite, though. Dijkstra chewed his hot dog, staring out of the window thoughtfully. Ralph shrugged and followed suit, taking a bite of his own meal.

"Does this taste ... *off* to you?" Dijkstra still stared at the hot dog in his hand, then at his partner. Ralph shook his head slightly. He didn't know.

Just then, their radio chirped. Sure enough, dispatch was calling their unit.

The two men put away their half-eaten meals with well-practiced dexterity. Time for some law enforcement, as Dijkstra was fond of saying.

The night that followed went by in a blur. Ralph and his partner drove from emergency to emergency. Robbery, arson, assault and battery ... The list went on. They even responded to a 999

call, which meant that an officer was down. By the time they got there, the perpetrator had been shot. It was messy. The other cop, a guy named Nunes, was practically in shock. Ralph stood near enough to hear him talk about it.

"The guy just kept coming ... I emptied my whole clip, and he just kept coming ..."

The body had been covered up, but there was no hiding all that blood and gore. It spread out from the blanket in all directions.

They were still going by the time the sky lightened above them.

"What a fucking shift." Ralph felt exhausted as they pulled into the station parking lot. Dijkstra only grunted in agreement.

Twenty minutes later, Ralph was toweling off. He'd needed that shower. It certainly was way more enticing than the paperwork that awaited him upstairs. As he got dressed, he reached for his cell phone. A few seconds later he frustratedly put the phone down.

"What's wrong?" Espinosa asked from a few lockers over.

"I tried to call the hospital. Can't get through."

Espinosa nodded knowingly. "Yeah, I bet they're pretty busy too."

Ralph finished getting dressed but could tell Espinosa was still observing him.

"Hey, Becker."

Becker turned to the constable.

"Don't you worry about that girl of yours. I heard that the national guard arrived last night, and they went straight to the hospitals. She's in good hands, bro." Espinosa was a good-natured fellow. One of those guys who wanted everybody to get along and stay positive.

Sometimes Ralph wanted to give him a high-five. Sometimes he wanted to choke him. He was too tired to do either of those things this morning. Ralph nodded with a half-hearted smile, then turned away.

He traveled to the main floor and entered the bullpen — a collection of desks and cubicles that contained the seemingly ever-shrinking work environment for him and his fellow police officers.

Well, the ones who actually warrant a desk. He recalled the days when he was a junior member of the force and looked at those desks longingly. It all didn't seem so great now.

But he had paperwork to do.

After that, he was going to see Jenny.

That day turned out to go any way but as planned. He was still filing reports when Dijkstra came around to collect him.

"We've got trouble, partner." He gestured for Ralph to get up and follow him, not even looking over his shoulder to make sure that the younger man complied.

"What's going on?" Ralph asked, putting on his gear as he followed his colleague through the cubicle jungle.

"Take your pick," Dijkstra said with a hint of annoyance. He listed a series of codes. They included shootings, fights, civil disturbances, public intoxications, a fire, and a riot.

"We're heading to the 10—34. Dijkstra said, holding the door open for his partner. "Riot at the Pharmacy Barn on 80th and Stone. Looks like we're pulling a double shift."

Adrenaline took over for Ralph, and the next fifteen minutes went by in flashes of lights, howls of sirens and screeches of tires. The only thing that he remembered from that drive was the lady they almost hit. Dijkstra just managed to swerve around her, nearly side-swiping a parked car in the process. The sergeant swore up a storm, which was very unlike him. Ralph looked back at the woman, who stared after them with a shocked expression.

The scene at the pharmacy was pure chaos. Ralph had never experienced anything like it — the closest thing to it was a disturbance at the university football stadium a couple of years back.

Drunken students and sore losers.

This was different. People drove haphazardly though the parking lot and street. Ralph witnessed at least two fender benders and one good-sized crash before they even got their cruiser parked across the street.

"Holy shit..." Ralph exclaimed as he watched people run to and fro, pushing shopping carts in front of them at ramming speed.

The two officers sat in their cruiser in stunned silence, caught up in the spectacle outside. Ralph didn't know where to look.

A woman got pushed to the ground as a man attempted to rip the shopping bag out of her hands. The woman hung on with fierce determination, causing the bag to rip and its contents to go flying. He watched as two cars collided head-on, neither giving way in the congested driveway of the parking lot in a badly executed game of chicken. People were rushing into the pharmacy through the busted-out windows, pushing and shoving each other out of the way in their rush.

"Gun," his partner said.

He looked at the sergeant and followed his gaze to the far corner of the parking lot, where a looter was being liberated of his stolen goods at gunpoint. But it was the sight of a man swinging his baseball bat that stirred the two police officers into action.

"That nutjob is going to hurt somebody," Dijkstra stated as he took off his seatbelt and reached for the door.

Sure enough, Ralph saw the man swing and connect with the shoulder of a teenager. The boy was sent skidding into the pavement. Ralph got out of the cruiser and oriented on the nutjob. He seemed to be walking around in random directions, threatening anybody and everybody who got in range. Ralph watched as he swung at another person, who quickly dodged out of the way.

"Thank God you're here!"

Both men turned around at the voice behind them. An elderly man approached from the sidewalk.

"Not now, sir," Dijkstra said, and started to turn back toward the scenes of violence on the other side of the street.

"My wife. She got sick. But now ... She's gone crazy!" the old man continued, unperturbed. Ralph stepped over to him, making a calming gesture. He watched his partner step out into the street from the corner of his eye.

"Sir, we have to go deal with this," Ralph gestured toward the chaos across the street. The old man looked at the scene as if registering it for the first time, then turned back to Ralph.

"She attacked me. Bit my finger clear off." He raised a bloodied hand in front of him. The top half of his pinky was gone. "I locked her in the bedroom. Then I called you."

"You should get yourself to a clinic for that hand, sir. I'm sorry, but we have to go and deal with this situation first."

Ralph turned away from the old man and hurriedly followed Dijkstra, who had already crossed the street. He looked over his shoulder once to see the old man still standing there, his hand still raised in front of him.

"Sorry," Ralph apologized again over his shoulder, then jogged over to Dijkstra.

Dijkstra's presence had its desired effect on the scene. A lot of people fled the scene instantly, and Ralph noticed that the gun-wielding gangsters had also melted away. The guy with the baseball bat was still wandering around aimlessly. Dijkstra made a beeline for the short, stocky individual. Ralph followed.

"Sir, you need to put that bat down," Dijkstra waited until the man had turned to the sound of his voice. "Right now."

The man shook his head. "N-no. No, no, no. Can't do that. They'll get me." He did not hold the bat in a threatening manner but had hugged it to his body.

"Sir. You're scaring everybody else here. Now, I'm only going to tell you once more. Put the bat down."

Ralph tensed as he heard the threat in his partner's voice.

The man started to shake his head again. "Y-you don't unders—" He never got to finish his sentence, as Dijkstra lunged at him. Ralph was already moving before the two men hit the ground.

The two experienced officers had disarmed the man, rolled him onto his stomach and cuffed his hands behind his back less than thirty seconds later.

Ralph looked up from his kneeling position and noted that the parking lot had practically emptied since they had arrived on the scene.

A little show of force goes a long way. That was one of the things the captain always said.

Guess he was right about that.

They got the perp back on his feet and marched him to the cruiser. He babbled nonsense at them the whole time. Ralph was accustomed to people coming up with all kinds of outlandish lies to get out of trouble, so he largely ignored the man.

That was the first time he heard the term "zombie" uttered, though.

"They're out there, man. Zombies. They're dead and they want to kill us too."

"You can tell us all about it at the station, sir."

Dijkstra maneuvered the nutjob into the back of the cruiser. Ralph walked around his side and noticed that the old man was gone. They had barely started the cruiser up before the first person darted through the parking lot across the street again. Dijkstra and Ralph exchanged a look.

"Ah, damn. I'm not in the mood for guard duty." Dijkstra reached for his radio to call it in, just as it chirped. It was a code that they had not expected.

"Emergency. All units in the first and second district. Mass disturbance at city hall. Officers in need of assistance."

Dijkstra responded immediately and they were off.

The scene at the pharmacy was a Sunday stroll compared to what was happening at city hall. Dijkstra had to park his cruiser several blocks away, as a seething mass of people blocked the street. They cracked the window slightly for the perp in the back seat and continued on foot toward city hall.

This was very different from the march that had taken place a couple of days ago. Ralph observed the people around him as he walked.

It seemed there were several groups of thought within that mass of humanity. He recognized the looks of confusion and anger. Most of the people didn't know what was going on and figured the authorities did. They wanted answers. Others were looking for the government to protect them. There was the usual anti-establishment element here and there too, evident by the dark scowls that were thrown his way as he walked past. Then there were the opportunists. People who liked trouble. People who used civil unrest as an excuse to commit crime. This last group was the one Ralph was most wary of. These shifty-eyed individuals tended to melt into the crowd whenever he spotted one.

He heard several terms that were unfamiliar to him. "Safe zone" was one of them. Ralph almost asked somebody about it after the third time he caught it being said.

What the hell is a safe zone?

Then gunshots rang up ahead and all thoughts of safe zones disappeared. Ralph and Dijkstra froze for a second, hands on their own sidearms, as they tried to locate the source of the shooting.

ITINERANT

Another volley of shots made it clear: It was coming from city hall.

The street erupted in noise. People yelled in confusion or screamed in alarm. Many people turned on their heel and ran away from the source of the gunfire. The curious and stupid continued toward the noise.

What does that make us? Ralph thought as he and Dijkstra trotted toward the disturbance. They got within sight of city hall. Hundreds of people were still packed tight in the open plaza in front of the building and to the sides. Ralph was somewhat relieved to see at least a dozen police officers on the steps of the building. He noted they were all looking off toward his right as he got closer.

"Something over there." Dijkstra had seen it too.

The big man veered off to the right. Sure enough, several more shots were fired. Dijkstra reached for his service revolver. Ralph followed suit. This was about to get real.

They headed for the altercation but couldn't quite see over the heads of the crowd. It felt like swimming upstream as people fled the violence. For the first time, Ralph noticed a common look on the faces around him. Fear. Wide-eyed individuals ran past him, some sobbing in shock. Ralph's training as a police officer kicked in. He picked up speed and ran toward the trouble.

The volume of people around them lessened, then disappeared completely as Ralph and Dijkstra emerged into an open area. Three police officers stood with their guns drawn. A fourth lay at their feet. Their weapons were pointed in the opposite direction, down one of the side streets. Several people lay in the street. Some screamed in pain and writhed around. Others were deathly still.

Oh, no. Ralph and Dijkstra drew their weapons.

"Friendlies!" Dijkstra warned the officers up ahead. Ralph could see the look of relief as one turned to see reinforcements arrive.

"999. Officer down, officer down," one of the officers said into his shoulder microphone.

Ralph and Dijkstra lined up with the other officers, pointing their weapons down the street. Ralph could see people fleeing in the distance. There seemed to be another altercation about a block down the street, where four or five individuals were engaged in a brawl. His immediate attention went to the bodies on the ground directly in front of him. He counted seven people down. A couple were still moving, moaning in pain and crying for their mothers.

One of the officers knelt over the fallen policeman. "Hang in there, Phillips." The woman was unresponsive.

"What happened?" Dijkstra asked.

"We were working our way through the crowd, trying to get to city hall. A fight broke out. We went to intervene when the crowd turned on us. This guy — he was a real wack job — he was only wearing underwear. No shoes, nothing..."

Ralph looked down the street and quickly found the pale figure.

"He just kept ramming her head into the pavement. She got her gun out and shot him like five, six times." He made eye contact with Ralph. "It hardly seemed to faze him! I pushed him off and shot him through the face. People went nuts after that."

"Yeah, good thing Espinosa and I showed up just then. Managed to pull these two from the brawl." Ralph looked over and recognized Espinosa and his partner.

"I fucked up. I just kept shooting around me blindly." The kneeling officer looked out into the street. "I did that..." His voice broke with emotion.

"Get up, officer. Go check on that ambulance." Dijkstra took charge. He pulled the man to his feet and turned him toward city hall. The plaza, which had teemed with activity just a minute before, was nearly abandoned.

"That guy is in real trouble."

Ralph and Dijkstra were walking back toward their cruiser. The rioters had quickly dispersed, leaving about twenty shell-shocked police officers on the scene. Dijkstra and Ralph hung around for a bit, but the place stayed deserted.

Dijkstra recalled the perp they had in the back of their cruiser, and they decided to leave this mess for the one they were already dealing with.

"Real trouble..." Dijkstra repeated, his thoughts apparently as far away as Ralph's.

"Yeah." Ralph agreed. He knew exactly what guy Dijkstra was talking about. The officer who had opened fire on the crowd.

"Constable Roberts," Dijkstra added.

"Guess he almost took out Espinosa in his panicked state."

Espinosa had lost his shit the moment Roberts was out of sight.

"That fucking guy shot at me!" he had said as the rush of adrenaline ended and left him shaky on his legs. They sat him down on the curb to keep him from keeling over. He sat there, looking at his own hands tremble. "I came running in. There was a dogpile on top of him. I kicked a guy off of him." He looked up at his partner. "Maybe that was a mistake. He got his hands free."

Ralph knew that he meant Roberts with that last statement. Roberts had pulled his gun out and started shooting after that.

"I called out for him to cease fire, but he just turned the gun on me. The look in his eyes was fucking wild! I dove out of the way just in time..." Espinosa rubbed his elbow as he remembered the event. Ralph could see the scuff on the material of his jacket and imagined Espinosa diving onto the pavement in order to avoid getting shot.

"That fucking guy..." Espinosa was going into shock as he kept repeating the scene in his head. Ralph could tell. He'd seen this before.

Dijkstra pulled him aside shortly after that, and now they were making their getaway.

Ralph felt sorry for Roberts. The guy was relatively new to the force with only one year's worth of field experience.

Now his life is going to be turned on its head.

There were plenty of stories about officers discharging their weapons in the line of duty. Wrong or right, something like that usually did a job on the officer. This one was going to be many times worse than any story he'd heard. Roberts would never be the same.

Heck, Espinosa might never be the same.

"Ah. What the hell?" Dijkstra's exclamation brought Ralph back to the present. The sergeant picked up his pace as he spotted their cruiser.

"Damn," Ralph growled in dismay as they got closer.

The vehicle had been vandalized. The first thing he noticed was that the windows had been smashed. That included the back-seat windows. There was no sign of the baseball-bat-wielding nutjob.

The damage didn't stop there, though. The body was covered in dents and scratches, and no light seemed to be left in working condition.

The worst discovery was when Dijkstra opened his door. "Ah!" He leaned in for a closer look, then jerked his head back. "They pissed all over the seats." He shook his head in disgust.

Dijkstra's look of disgust turned into a grimace of pain, and he rubbed his chest.

"You okay, Dijkstra?"

The sergeant continued to rub his chest but straightened up. "Yeah. Not having a heart attack if that's what you're thinking, rook."

Ralph smirked. The last time Dijkstra had called him that was when he'd been an actual rookie.

Half a lifetime ago. Before I ever met Jenny.

That reminded him, and he fumbled in his pocket for his phone. He never did get to use the phone, as a police cruiser chose that moment to appear. Dijkstra flagged them down and the partners caught a ride. Ralph put his cell phone away as he got in.

"Holy fuck, Dijkstra! I thought I saw you in the middle of the action. Did you see what happened?" one of the officers asked excitedly.

All four officers in that vehicle were still high on adrenaline as they busily compared notes about the events at city hall. They didn't stop talking about it until they got back to the station.

It was going to be one hell of an inquest, so they all decided to get their stories straight ASAP. To Ralph that meant more paperwork.

By the time he finished the paperwork, Ralph was beyond exhaustion. He'd been on his feet for nearly twenty-four hours straight. The room actually spun a little when he stood up.

"Easy there, Becker." A colleague had come to his aid.

"Let's get you to the quiet room."

Ralph didn't even know who was leading him away, but the quiet room was exactly what he needed. There was a room just for sitting around and another with several cots set up so that those burning the candle from both ends had a place to really crash.

Ralph crashed.

A noise somewhere nearby woke him. Ralph felt heavily disoriented, and it took him several long moments to remember where he was. He rolled up to a seated position and reached for his boots in the dim light. As he put them on, he noticed that all the other cots were occupied, with various sounds of snoring and heavy breathing emanating from the dark corners of the room.

Guess I'm not the only one that had a hellish shift.

Then he remembered.

Jenny! He quickly tied his boots and left the room, trying not to make too much noise but reaching for his cell phone before he was out of the door all the same. The harsh light of the screen elicited a groan along with a few select words. Ralph hardly heard it as he stepped out and brought the phone to his ear.

He walked up the stairs as he listened to the phone, held it away from his face, and hit redial. This time he didn't get a busy signal.

"You have reached the general information desk at Healthlife Hospital. If you know the extension you are trying to reach, then please enter i—" Ralph hit 0.

The line rang four times before another automated message started.

"Fuck." Ralph punched the red phone icon with his thumb.

He walked into the bullpen, heading straight for Dijkstra's office. It wasn't actually Dijkstra's office — space was too precious for that. No, Dijkstra had to share that office with two equally graying and gruff sergeants.

Ralph could recall stepping into that office on many occasions to find two or sometimes three larger-than-life personalities vying for the upper hand in whatever the argument of the day was. At times he wondered how they managed to get into that small office with their massive egos.

A recent memory came to him as he reached for the door. They were up to their usual "my arrests were more important than yours and my war wounds are larger than yours" argument.

Ralph had said something along the lines of being surprised that they could fit their massive dicks behind their desks.

He immediately forgot about the memory when he saw Dijkstra. The sergeant appeared to have collapsed on his desk while still seated.

"Sarge. Dijkstra," Ralph called out from the door, then sighed in relief when the big man stirred.

Ralph entered the office. The other two sergeants were gone, the only sign of their presence being the overflowing stacks of paperwork on their desks and the colored tape on the floor which marked their personal borders.

Dijkstra turned his head and faced his approaching partner. "Hey, Becker."

"You okay, Dijkstra? You look like shit." Ralph wasn't exaggerating. Dijkstra looked terrible.

"Yeah. Just didn't sleep much." The sergeant rummaged through the paper jungle on his desk and reached for one of the ever-present bottles of pain meds. He shook the bottle and was rewarded by the clacking of some pills inside. He dumped an indiscriminate amount into his large hand and popped them into his mouth. It always amazed Ralph how his partner chewed those things like they were candy.

"Got the place to yourself, for once." Ralph indicated the vacant chairs.

"Yeah. Anderson is out there somewhere. Got his hands full, would be my guess. Miller called in sick."

That made Ralph raise his eyebrows. "You guys aren't going to let Miller live that down."

Dijkstra scoffed in agreement. "Guess his dick's not that big after all. What was it you said to us the other day?"

It was Ralph's turn to scoff. "I said that I was amazed that you guys had chairs."

The sergeants had stopped their argument and stared at Ralph in utter confusion. Ralph had waited for dramatic effect and followed up with: "Because if your measurements are accurate, there is no way you can sit with dicks that large." It was one of the rare times that the room burst out in laughter rather than insults.

"Ah, yeah ... dicks that large." Dijkstra laughed at the memory, albeit somewhat weakly. "That was a good one, Becker."

Dijkstra tried to push the organized chaos into piles and got up from his chair, groaning like a bear. He got to his full height and rubbed his back, neck, and head in succession.

"Twenty-two years, I've been on the force. Jumped straight from one uniform into this one." He pulled at his shirt, a wry expression on his face.

"You sure you're okay, Sarge?" He looked anything but.

"Yeah." Dijkstra stood silently for a moment, thinking about it. "Yeah. Good to go." He turned away from his desk and walked past Ralph.

"Let's go see what the captain has in store for us."

Dijkstra opened the door and stepped out, not bothering to see if Ralph was following. Ralph hesitated for half a second. Dijkstra was definitely off. But then again, Dijkstra wasn't called a typical stubborn Dutchman for nothing, despite being third-generation American. Ralph shrugged and followed his partner.

The captain had no good news for them. Fred McPherson was a twitchy, nervous, and devious man in the best of days. He often kept his cards close to his chest — so close that his own men didn't know what was going on half of the time. Ralph detested the man and wished that old Captain Gordon was still around.

"Ah, Dijkstra." He never bothered to acknowledge the lower-ranked Ralph, and his first move was to make a show of looking at the clock. "Last ones to report."

Fuck you, dude. I haven't seen my own family for two days! Ralph put his hand in his pocket and fingered the smooth surface of his cell phone. He was going to get a hold of Jenny as soon as they were out of McPherson's office.

"You guys all rested up?" It wasn't really a question. "Good. We've got all hell breaking loose out there, and our own men are dropping like flies."

Ralph jerked forward at that statement.

"Dropping like flies?" Dijkstra beat him to it.

McPherson waved the question away. "Not what you think. District two lost that officer — you guys were on the scene for that. No, a bunch of our guys called in sick today." He said the last with a look of distaste.

Screw you. You're the one running us into the ground. Ralph could feel his ire rising.

"Anyway, I've got a job for you," McPherson went on. "You two are to travel to State University Hospital. All of the hospitals are being evacuated and—"

"What do you mean?" Ralph blurted out as he took a step forward.

McPherson didn't like being interrupted. He hated that almost as much as he hated any sign of insubordination. "Back the fuck up, Constable." He put heavy disdain in the tone of his voice.

As Ralph opened his mouth, the view changed from the captain to a broad back as Dijkstra stepped directly in front of him.

"My partner's wife is in a hospital. Can you tell us what's going on?"

Ralph stepped around Dijkstra. McPherson's face swung from Dijkstra to him. His expression was worrisome.

"Um ... that's ... unfortunate."

"What does that mean?"

The captain seemed about to answer, then changed his mind. "Becker, your wife is fine, I'm sure. The army is moving all hospital personnel for national security reasons. We're supposed to help out with traffic control and such."

"My wife is a patient, not personnel." Ralph tensed up.

McPherson looked uncomfortable for a moment but recovered quickly. "Yes, of course. I meant the patients, too. What, you think they were going to leave the patients behind?"

McPherson shook his head and smiled. It was altogether unconvincing to Ralph. He could feel the heavy weight of Dijkstra's hand on his shoulder, gently pulling him away.

"Who is slated to go over to that new Healthline Hospital?" Dijkstra asked. "Maybe we can switch with them."

"Healthlife," Ralph corrected.

"No-can-do. I've got enough shit to coordinate here." McPherson waved at his desk which, truth be told, looked even worse than Dijkstra's. "You guys grab some new keys — yes, I've already heard about how you got your cruiser destroyed — and head out to State University Hospital. Not fucking Healthlife — *State*. You got that?"

Ralph didn't respond, but apparently Dijkstra must have nodded, as the captain continued.

"You are to keep the streets clear so that these army guys can do their job and get back on the road. Think you can do that?" Again, it wasn't a question. He turned to Ralph. "You can go see your wife when the job is done. Understood?" Ralph nodded out of force of habit before he could stop himself.

Five minutes later, they had requisitioned a new cruiser and were walking through the parking lot. The sun was shining. It looked like it was going to be a nice day. To Ralph, it was too bright outside — it felt disorienting.

Must be overtired. The last time Ralph had felt this way was after a long-haul flight back from Hawaii. The time change had really messed him up. This reminded him of Jenny, who had been right beside him on that flight. She'd moved her legs to the side so he could stretch his out.

I'm coming to get you, girl. Today. I promise, he vowed to the blue skies.

"Ah. 288. That's us." Dijkstra pointed at the number on the trunk of one of the cruisers. He popped the trunk and they dumped in their combat gear. The captain had said that they would probably need it. Dijkstra did something very uncharacteristic next, as he tossed the keys to Ralph. "You drive. I've still got that killer headache."

Ralph caught the keys and stared at his partner with a raised eyebrow. "You sure, Sergeant?"

Dijkstra nodded and walked over to the passenger side.

"Yeah. Just don't let it get to your head. And don't fuck it up!" he added with a grin.

They got themselves settled into the cruiser. Dijkstra turned on the radio to check in with dispatch and was assaulted by a cacophony of sound. He grimaced and turned off the radio.

"Too much shit going on out there." He turned to Ralph. "Besides, the captain made our assignment pretty clear."

"Fuckwad." Ralph couldn't keep the comment in.

Dijkstra's face turned serious. "Hey, that's no way to address our captain," His face broke into another grin. "Besides, everybody knows that he is a dickwad, not a fuckwad."

They smiled at each other in their moment of solidarity. Ralph inserted the key and turned the ignition. The cruiser came to life with a satisfying roar. Dijkstra patted the dashboard with a nod of approval.

"I think I read once that the number eight is lucky in China or something. Seems like we got an eight for each of us," he stated, referring to their cruiser number.

"I don't know what astonishes me more," Ralph replied as he backed the cruiser out of its stall. "That you know about lucky Chinese numbers"—he threw the car into gear and put on his best shit-eating grin—"or that you read."

Their moods had changed considerably by the time they got to State University Hospital.

First of all, people were nuts. They observed more looting and violence in that thirty-minute drive than they had seen in most of their careers put together. It was pure anarchy out there.

At one point, they drove by a mom-and-pop grocery store which was being looted. They slowed down and turned on their lights, but the only reaction they got was angry stares from a dozen or so hoodlums. Dijkstra had called it in, but dispatch ordered them to proceed to their assignment. Ralph remembered sharing a look with Dijkstra as they were stuck in indecision. This went against everything they had stood for — everything they had been proud to fight.

To the looters, it must have looked like weakness. They stood their ground and dared the police officers to try to break things up. It was only a few seconds later that the first rock flew in their direction. Ralph reluctantly moved on, much to the satisfaction of the crowd. He was pissed and swore up a storm. Dijkstra didn't react. His headache only seemed to be getting worse.

This wasn't even the craziest thing they saw. They watched people fighting in the streets — a couple of times it looked serious, with entire groups of people attacking each other.

They saw cars on fire, and at one point spotted billowing black smoke rising into the sky in the distance, indicating a much larger fire. By that point they had given up on calling things in. There just weren't enough emergency services to take care of all the emergencies.

The whole situation was giving Ralph heartburn. He reached into the dash for the bottle of antacid, then swore a string of curses as he realized that this wasn't their regular squad car. The usually puritanical Dijkstra didn't even blink.

They arrived at the hospital, pulling into the main lot, but were promptly halted by several soldiers. Their black armbands had the white letters MP printed on them.

"Military police," Dijkstra said as they came to a full stop. He rolled down his window and one of the men approached. "Sergeant." Dijkstra nodded as he greeted the man.

"Officer," the soldier responded.

"We're here to provide traffic control for the evac," Dijkstra said.

The soldier pursed his lips. "Not gonna need that, now. Situation's changed."

Dijkstra frowned. "What do you mean? We were told explicitly to come out here and escort hospital personnel and patients to a new, secured location."

The soldier had started shaking his head halfway through Dijkstra's protestation. "We ain't escorting anybody out of there. As a matter of fact, men are sealing it up right now. The place is a death trap."

Oh, my God ... Jenny!

Ralph was out of the car before another word was said. He looked over the top of the cruiser at the soldier. "You're not making any sense. Tell us what's going on!"

"Hey. Take it easy, man." The sergeant took a step back from the vehicle. The other three soldiers had noticed and moved a bit closer.

"Just tell me," Ralph pressed, slightly less aggressive this time.

The sergeant put his hand up for the other men. "It's okay, fellows."

Ralph watched from the corner of his eye as they released their grips on their weapons.

"Sorry. My guys are a bit trigger-happy after the shit we just went through. Okay, I'll tell you what's going on." The soldier licked his lips. "Listen, man. There is some kind of outbreak in the hospital. People went nuts or something. One minute we were here for traffic control — the next, all we could hear was weapons being fired inside that place. A few minutes later, the order came down from HQ. Lock the place up. Nobody in or out."

Ralph had walked around the cruiser. The MP leaned down toward Dijkstra conspiratorially. "The guys that got out of there ... They were talking about zombies! I heard at least two guys talk about emptying entire clips into them."

"Bullshit." Ralph couldn't bring himself to believe it.

The MP glanced up at him sharply. He stiffly drew himself up to his full height. "Whatever, man. I'm just trying to warn y'all. Believe what you want to believe — but that hospital over there was a warzone and is now locked up tight."

They all looked over at the sound of heavy engines. Two personnel carriers rumbled along the street behind them.

"They're pulling out," The MP stated as they watched the large military vehicles drive off. "Heading to the next hospital, I guess," he added. "We'll probably get the order in a minute."

He stepped away from the cruiser then and signaled to his team. Ralph noted the military jeep a few yards away.

"Wait!" Ralph took a step after the sergeant. "Do you know if the army has gone to Healthlife Hospital?"

The MP shrugged. "No idea. All I know is that the orders changed about an hour ago — and that we've got to move fast."

"To contain those so-called *zombies*," Ralph finished for him.

"No, man. We've got to move fast because our guys are dropping like flies. This syndrome thing ... It's hit the armed forces, hard." He reached for his gut and winced slightly. "All of my guys got it, too. Feels like my insides are getting torn apart."

"Syndrome? Is that what they're calling this flu?"

The MP shook his head. "Where have you been, man? Do yourself a favor and turn on a TV. This syndrome thing — it starts in your gut and ends badly. Like, you turn into a zombie."

"Bullshit." The comment had little to no conviction behind it this time.

"Believe what you like. I've seen the fucking body bags moving like a bunch of worms." He shuddered.

The radio squawked inside the jeep just then. One of the other MPs jogged over.

"That will be our call to move out. Don't go near that place." He waved at the hospital behind him as he strode toward the jeep.

The vehicle started with a roar as the soldiers piled into it. Ralph stood frozen in place as the jeep passed them and pulled out of the lot. A minute later, they were the only people left.

The sound of engines had faded enough for Ralph to detect other sounds. He looked up at the hospital. People were banging on windows. Dijkstra had gotten out of the cruiser and stood beside him. He pointed at one window. It was liberally splattered with what could only be blood.

"We've got to get to Healthlife. I've got to get Jenny and our baby."

Ralph shot into action. He ran back around to the driver's side of the vehicle. Dijkstra got in with a groan.

"This freaking headache has got me seeing double."

Ralph turned on the radio as soon as he started driving. Not their police radio — the AM-FM one. It wasn't hard to get information, as none of the stations were playing music.

"Reports are stating that people are dying, only to get up and attack the living. I repeat: We are receiving legitimate, reliable reports that the syndrome is actually a malignant organism. It activates in the intestines but travels to the brain. This causes varying symptoms, from bowel irritability to heartburn, chest aches, neck aches and finally headaches. The syndrome organism takes over the host's brain at this point, causing the immediate death of the person and subsequent resurrection ... I can't believe that this is true, folks — but its right here in front of me."

"Holy shit." Ralph fiddled with the dial. He found the next station a moment later.

"—iddle east, as Iran has openly declared a jihad, or holy war, against the Zionists in Israel. This in response to the destruction of Gaza and the apparent nuclear response to Egypt."

"Nuclear?" Ralph shook his head.

"The UN has called for an immediate ceasefire, and there has been a statement from the White House that the president has sent a similar message to all involved parties, just like he had done during the India-China nuclear exchange."

"Change the channel." Dijkstra grimaced, his face in his hand. "Something in this guy's voice is making my head burst."

Ralph obliged. He only half watched the road as his attention was drawn to the radio.

"There have been all kinds of rumors. All unsubstantiated." An authoritative voice claimed. *"Listen,"* the voice continued, *"we need to stick to the facts. What we do know is that the syndrome is a real, serious virus of some kind. It has already killed millions. It also seems to cause a form of psychosis, which turns the victim violent."*

"How do you explain the multiple, often lethal wounds that don't seem to affect these victims?" another voice asked.

"That's all part of the psychosis. These people have no more comprehension of their wounds. All they know is their need for violence. And that's my point. There are many people out there, on the streets of all our cities. They are making things worse with their rioting. I mean, have we learned nothing from Africa? That entire continent is in a blackout right now because they couldn't get their people to listen."

The other person tried to interrupt, but the expert spoke over him as if he did not exist.

"People need to respect the law. People need to stay home. Sick people, especially, need to stay home! Have some faith in the authorities."

"Enough." Dijkstra turned off the radio. "Sorry, Ralph, but it's like the radio waves are going through my brain." He leaned back in his seat and closed his eyes.

Ralph wanted to hear more.

What else have we missed over the last twenty-four hours? Nuclear exchanges? Holy fuck, it's Armageddon out there! He wisely kept his mouth shut and continued to drive.

Fifteen minutes later, when they were getting through downtown, they were forced to stop.

"What the..."

Dijkstra and Ralph could only stare, open-mouthed, as a full-blown battle seemed to be playing out in front of them. A group of at least a hundred people were fighting. Ralph watched as armed individuals charged into unarmed people. Baseball bats, two-by-fours, and machetes rose and fell as people were literally slaughtered. Some people tried to defend themselves, their hands reaching up to ward off the brutal attacks.

Something beyond the fight drew Ralph's attention. An armored military vehicle had turned onto the road. Without warning, its mounted machine gun opened up.

"Holy shit!" Ralph ducked as bullets fizzed by.

"Get us out of here," Dijkstra moaned. Ralph hit the gas and turned down an alley.

"We've got to reach headquarters." Dijkstra turned on the police radio but only got static. "Ah!" he exclaimed at the white noise, and dropped the mouthpiece.

Ralph quickly turned off the radio.

"We've got to get back to the station," Dijkstra managed between groans, his hand on his forehead.

"Nuh-uh." Ralph shook his head vigorously. "We've got to get to Jenny."

Dijkstra sighed. "We've got a job to do, Ralph. They nee—"

"I don't care what they need, Dijkstra! I'm going to get Jenny!"

The sergeant sighed. "Kid, I don't have the energy to argue with you. Fine. We'll go to that hospital. But we're heading straight back to the station after that."

"Deal." Ralph pressed on the gas pedal some more.

Ralph drove fast but cautiously after that. He turned off the road whenever he spotted a group ahead. Eventually, they zigzagged their way through the rest of downtown and got to a less populated part of the city.

Still, they could not avoid all scenes of violence. Here and there people were running — seemingly in random directions. They spotted another brawl down one of the streets, accentuated by gunshots. Ralph looked at the sergeant, but Dijkstra merely shook his head.

A few minutes later, a woman ran alongside their vehicle screaming for help. Dijkstra ordered Ralph to pull over, but before Ralph could even comply, she pulled out a gun and pointed it at them. He hit the gas instead. They heard the gunshot, but she must have missed. Then Ralph checked his rear-view mirror. The woman was shooting other people on the street.

"This city has gone nuts!"

Dijkstra could only grunt in agreement.

Three blocks later, they watched dumbstruck as a church went up in flames. People danced and laughed in front of the house of worship as if the blaze was a bonfire at the fair. A block beyond the fire, they dodged around a half-naked madman who lumbered down the center of the street. The guy even tried to lurch in front of their vehicle as they got close. Ralph quickly maneuvered the vehicle up the sidewalk and around the crackhead. At least, Ralph was pretty sure he was high after seeing his expression.

"I've got to call this in ..." Ralph reached for the radio. He tried to contact headquarters again — much to the consternation and personal discomfort of Dijkstra — but it was to no avail. They weren't answering. Ralph stopped paying attention to the chaotic events around them after that. He tried to, anyway.

Twenty minutes later, they finally pulled into the parking lot of Healthlife Hospital.

"Place looks deserted," Ralph commented.

Dijkstra glanced up and mumbled something indiscernible. Ralph parked the vehicle and the two men got out. Ralph saw the sheen of sweat on his partner's face and put a hand on his arm. "Hey, Dijkstra. You don't look too hot. Do you want to wait in the car?"

"Nah. Starting to feel better."

They got to the front entrance only to find the doors locked. On top of that, a heavy device sat across the doors, preventing them from opening.

"Military's been here. That's one of them hydraulic locks," Dijkstra commented.

The device seemed to consist of two vertical bars with metal wedges inserted underneath and above the door, along with a blocky mechanism in the middle. Ralph fiddled with the mechanism, but nothing seemed to happen. Dijkstra had backed away from the building. Curious, Ralph followed him.

"What is it?"

Dijkstra did not respond. Ralph tried to detect what Dijkstra was looking at. There didn't seem to be anything wrong. He scanned the windows and saw nothing at first. Then he saw it.

Somebody was slapping at one of the windows. They could only see the palms of hands as they repeatedly slapped against the glass. Disturbingly, there was blood on the window as well. It spattered onto the glass with every slap.

The slapping continued, smearing the blood.

"Good god ..." Dijkstra crossed himself.

"We've got to get in there. Jenny is up there." Ralph started to walk to the main entrance again.

"Hold it," Dijkstra ordered. "Nilsson, that's an order."

"Huh?" Ralph turned in surprise. "Who the fuck is Nilsson?"

Dijkstra frowned. He shook his head, then looked at his partner again. "I'm ... confused."

"Shit. Let's get you back to the cruiser." He led Dijkstra away. They only got halfway to the vehicle when Dijkstra suddenly doubled over in pain.

"Ah! It hurts!" He clawed at his face, gouging bloody furrows in his forehead with his nails. Ralph tried to stop him, but the big man was much stronger.

"Dijkstra, stop it!" He hung on to Dijkstra's elbow.

Suddenly, Dijkstra struck him with his free hand. The blow caught Ralph in the shoulder but was forceful enough to send him sprawling to the pavement. Dijkstra dove on top of Ralph, driving the air out of the younger man with the impact. The two men wrestled on the ground, trying to get a hold of each other.

Dijkstra was older, but he was also heavier, stronger, and more experienced. He maneuvered himself behind Ralph and managed to get his forearm under Ralph's chin. Ralph knew that he was in trouble.

With a good lock-in, Dijkstra started to squeeze.

"Gggggh! D—Dijkstra! ... S-Stop. Pleasss ..." Ralph felt himself going light-headed.

Suddenly, the pressure was off. Ralph gasped for breath, his vision full of stars. He could just make out Dijkstra's shadow standing over him.

"This is madness," Dijkstra said. "Becker, are you okay? I—I don't know what came over me."

Ralph started to recover. He lifted a hand. "Yeah ... Just give me a minute. Fuck, man. I think you've got that 'syndrome.' You're losing your mind."

"I think that I need help." Dijkstra looked scared.

Ralph had just gotten into a sitting position when Dijkstra flinched, his hands going back to his head. He clasped his forehead with his right hand, groaning in pain. Ralph watched in horror as Dijkstra's fingernails dug into his forehead.

As quickly as the attack came, it was over again. Dijkstra dropped his hand and took deep breath. He looked down and saw Ralph.

"I've spent my whole career trying to bring order to the world, then this city. And now some goddamn syndrome is going to mess it all up." Blood ran freely from his wounds, creating small red rivulets that ran past his brow and down his cheeks. "Well, not on my watch. And not on yours either, soldier!" His eyes were manic once more. "On your feet, Nilsson."

"Damnit, Dijkstra. It's Becker!" Ralph pleaded as he got to his feet.

"It's collateral damage. You know it is." Dijkstra stared off into space. His eyes were wild when he turned his face to Ralph. "You leave this out of the OPREP. We'll be in a world of shit if you don't." He seemed to plead with Ralph.

"Dijkstra. It's me, Becker. Your partner." Ralph tried to keep his voice calm and soothing, but Dijkstra didn't even seem to hear him.

Suddenly, Dijkstra's service weapon was in his hand, the business end pointed at Ralph. "I can't let you do it, Nilsson. Those people,"—he waved his pistol toward his right—"they got in the way ... But we're at war here!"

With his hands up, Ralph was still talking to his sergeant. The big man did not seem to hear him, though. He pointed the gun at Ralph's face.

"Sorry, brother." Dijkstra was crying as he spoke. Tears blended with blood on his cheeks. Ralph could see him start to clench his trigger finger.

Ralph shut his eyes tight.

But the shot never came. Instead, Dijkstra exclaimed in pain and bent over. He dropped his weapon and brought his hands to his face. "My head!"

Ralph's instinct and training took over. He drew his own weapon, took three quick steps, and shot Dijkstra in the top of the head.

The single gunshot seemed to echo forever. Ralph stood over the corpse of his former sergeant and partner, his ears ringing. He lowered his hand slowly but still did not move.

"Dijkstra ... What the fuck, man ..." He paused and looked down at the pistol, then back at the body of his friend. "What the fuck!" He dropped the pistol as if it had burned his hand. Ralph took three quick steps back from the scene.

He stood there for a long minute. The only sounds he heard were far off in the distance. He thought that he could spot the shrill ringing of an alarm. But no sirens approaching, signifying his brethren coming to take him down.

Another noise made him turn around. He couldn't see it from this angle, but somebody was slapping ineffectively at a window somewhere above him.

He almost ran back to the cruiser then, intent on getting the hell out of there. But hesitated after one step.

Get yourself together, Ralph. You're here for Jenny and the baby.

He stepped forward and again stood over the body of his former partner. He saw the damage he had done: a relatively small entry wound just at the base of the skull. When he turned the body over, he saw what was left of the face and nearly vomited. Gone was the easy smile. The only thing that looked familiar were the blond locks of hair.

"Fuck, Dijkstra. I'm sorry, man." Ralph looked around and saw the parked ambulance nearby. He grabbed Dijkstra under his armpits and started to drag the body. "I shot you for — for nothing." After about six feet, he stopped. "No. That's not true. Not for nothing. For Jenny, and the baby."

Grunting with the effort, he started to drag the body again. Dijkstra was much heavier than him, so he had to use all his strength and body weight, stepping back then leaning backward to drag the body.

"And" step — drag

"you were losing" step — drag

"your mind ..." step — drag

Ralph was out of breath after several minutes. He stumbled away from Dijkstra's body, glancing up at a familiar noise. Those palms were still slapping at the window. The slapping sounds were now accentuated by a sharp tap. To Ralph's horror, he could see the white of bone sticking out near one wrist.

Right. This syndrome thing is real. People are going nuts. Or dying — I don't know.

"But I've got to find Jenny," Ralph repeated to motivate himself.

His body was shaking with the effort by the time he got to the ambulance. He almost cried in relief when he found that the door was unlocked. Getting Dijkstra's body inside was another serious — and messy — effort.

Ralph had to take a breather once he shut the ambulance door behind him. He sat down on the curb and took several long breaths, wiping the mixture of sweat, blood and gore off his forehead. As he sat there, he observed the massive blood stain that led right up to the ambulance from the murder site.

Not going to take a detective to figure out where that body is hidden.

He let his gaze slide upwards, from the red-stained gray pavement up to the gray skies. It looked like it was going to rain.

That's good. Wash away the blood. He looked down at his hands, still covered in Dijkstra's blood, and realized that no amount of rain was going to wash away that sin. Ralph lay down and gazed up. At the top of his view, he could see the hospital walls reaching skyward. The off-white seemed to join the gray sky seamlessly.

No, not quite. Ralph realized. A gutter hung from the edge of the roof. Its dark gray color stood out and created a physical border between the building and the sky. Ralph imagined that it was the border between heaven and earth.

There are not a lot of people capable of crossing that border, he surmised as he thought about what he had witnessed recently.

I won't be.

R alph awoke with a start. The sky was darkening.
How long have I been out? he groaned as he got into a sitting position. His back was sore. There was another pain evident, though. He felt it up in his stomach and chest. It burned.

Gingerly Ralph got to his feet. He wobbled unsteadily for a bit and had to hold on to the side of the ambulance for balance. Then it all came back to him.

Jenny!

He turned around and surveyed the emergency entrance. The doorway was blocked off by another steel device. Beyond the glazed doors there was no movement. Ralph knew people remained in the building, but the main floor appeared to be abandoned.

Reaching for his sidearm to shoot out one of the massive panes of glass, he found his holster empty. He looked around in a panic for a moment before spotting the black device on the pavement, halfway between him and the cruiser.

Ralph had changed his mind about shooting out the window by the time he gathered his weapon. He figured there would be another way in. One that was less ... loud.

At the first corner of his circuit around the hospital, he spotted a possible way in.

Smaller windows, about seven feet up. Bathrooms.

His mind made up, he ran back to the cruiser and retrieved the window punch tool. *Zak tool, or something.* He knew it had a name, but it escaped him. He also grabbed several other items, including his flashlight and a heavy blanket. Finally, he put on his combat gear.

Back at the window, he silently congratulated himself on bringing the heavy blanket. He placed the blanket over the glass and quickly smashed the window, muffling the noise. He made sure to knock out all the edges, having seen folks cut themselves in these situations all too many times. Finally, he removed the blanket, shook it out, folded it several times, and draped it over the windowsill. Ten seconds later he was inside. The whole operation was silent and flawless. Well, unless you counted the landing. Luckily, Ralph had had the foresight to also don gloves.

He took a moment to orient himself. *Ladies' room.* Four stalls sat opposite four sinks. He got to the door and listened for a moment. All was silent.

That doesn't mean one of those crazies isn't nearby. In his mind, he pictured several of them just on the other side of the door. It took him a lot of self-assurance to finally twist the door handle and crack the door open.

At first, all he saw was darkness. The power was out, even the emergency power. As he kept looking, he started to see a bit more detail — especially where light from other windows penetrated the building. There wasn't a lot of it, as just about all doors were shut. Most of the light came from the reception area, way down the hall.

Ralph decided against using his flashlight. He took his time and let his eyes adjust to the darkness. Once he stepped out, his sidearm was already drawn. Nothing moved. The sound of people scrambling toward him occurred only in his imagination.

He inched his way forward. There was an intersection just up ahead. Around that first corner he made a discovery that shook him to his core.

Bodies. Many bodies.

He fumbled for his flashlight with his left hand, finally getting a good grip on the tool and pressing the switch.

Ralph gasped in alarm. It looked like dozens of bodies were piled up along one side of the hallway. Ralph crept closer. He leveraged his police training and studied the bodies.

He spotted everything from multiple gunshot wounds to missing limbs. But they all had one thing in common — one thing that likely was the cause of death: massive head trauma. There didn't seem to be a single head left intact. Some of the bodies had massive craters where their faces used to be, indicating that they were shot through the back of the head. Ralph wasn't sure if that was better than the ones that did not get shot through the face, as he spotted many eyes and mouths wide open. They all seemed to be screaming in fear. Ralph had to swallow hard, several times.

Eventually, he made it to the end of the bodies. Ralph did a quick check down the rest of the hallway and found that all doors were shut.

The army's come in here and cleared this floor. That made sense. He knew that it would be a different story upstairs. Quickly he doubled back and made his way down his original hallway. The reception area was lit like a beacon compared to the pitch-black of the rest of the hospital. Ralph rushed to the light despite his better judgment.

He forced himself to stop at the end of the hall and scan the area. The reception was deserted. He started forward and was quick to spot the blood stains. He also saw the multiple casings on the floor.

People were shot here. Maybe the same people I saw back there ...

He continued to the far side of the reception area, where he found an information desk. He stepped up to the desk and stopped, his eyes searching furiously.

Bingo. He reached across the counter and pulled out a map. Ralph studied it for a minute.

Elevators down this hallway ... But the power is out. He continued to scan the map. He needed to find a stairwell. Jenny was on the third floor.

Stairwell ... Stairwell. After a few more seconds, he spotted them. This hospital did not have a main stairway, but two emergency stairwells were located on opposite sides of the building. Ralph now had all the information he needed to get to his wife.

You're coming with me. Ralph stuffed the map under his vest and stepped toward the darkened hallway. He left his flashlight off, trying to get his eyes accustomed to the darkness, but was forced to turn the flashlight on after taking the first turn, as it just got too dark.

The hallways all looked the same — especially with all doors shut, and Ralph referred to his map often ... He spotted a sign after his second turn.

Dispensary. Maybe I should drop in and find something for this gut ache.

Ralph passed the door without a second glance. He was this close to finding his wife and their baby, and wasn't going to let any distraction get in the way.

A few minutes later, he found the stairwell. He reached for the door with some trepidation.

Are there more nutjobs in the stairwell? Is the door locked? The doubts shot through his mind as his hand hesitated mere inches from the handle. Ralph took a deep breath and grabbed it.

To his surprise, the door swung open silently and without resistance.

Of course. The maglocks no longer work due to the power being down.

If the hallway was dark, then the stairwell was pitch-black. Ralph shone his flashlight into the stairwell.

Just in case ... He spotted a fire extinguisher and pulled it off the wall, placing it in the door jamb to keep it from closing. It made a slight clanking noise as he put it down.

He stepped back into the stairwell and hesitated. *Did I hear something?*

"Hello?" Ralph's voice barely cracked above a whisper, but it sounded like a shout compared to the dead silence that hung in the air.

The result was instantaneous. Ralph took an involuntary step backward as he heard noises somewhere above him. Ralph drew his pistol and held his flashlight aligned with the weapon. The noises were drawing nearer. Somebody, or some people, was rushing down the stairwell toward him.

Two people. Maybe three. Ralph estimated.

"Come down slow and with your hands up!" Ralph warned. The approaching noises only became more frantic.

He raised his pistol, aiming at the first landing. "I *will* shoot!"

However, when a person appeared there, he hesitated. The man's eyes were wild, his mouth wide open as if screaming, although he uttered no noise.

Both of his arms were broken, the wrists and hands dangling. The white of bone showed as a fibula pushed through meat and skin.

"Stop r—" Ralph never got another word out as the man launched himself down the stairs toward him. His instinct taking over, Ralph pulled the trigger.

BANG. The sound was painfully loud in the confined space of the stairwell.

BANG. BANG—BANG. Three more shots followed in short order. He aimed center-mass, exactly as he had been trained. Ralph was distinctly aware of the viscera flying from the exit wounds to splatter in violent patterns onto whitewashed walls.

His last shot might have gone high — he didn't notice — as a second person emerged on the landing.

The first man crashed at his feet and rolled into his shins as Ralph raised his sights toward a second man. He didn't have time to assess the person — barely registered the horribly smashed-up face and punctured eyeball before firing.

Only two of his three shots connected, the third shot missing as something pulled at his leg and threw him off balance. Ralph looked down. The first assailant was still alive! He clawed at Ralph's leg, staring up at him with malice. The third shot had indeed gone high, as a large portion of his neck and part of his jaw was gone.

"Fuck!" Ralph fired off another shot at point-blank range. The bullet took his assailant through the forehead and the man instantly let go of his leg.

He had no time to celebrate as he was bowled into. The flashlight flew from his hand, falling to the hallway floor behind him and spinning wildly. He punched, hitting the person on top of him. It did not seem to have any impact.

As he felt the person try to bite him through his jacket, he yelped in alarm. Ralph panicked, yelled out a string of curses and bucked to get out from under his assailant. He reached down and got a handful of hair. He pulled up, just as the flashlight spun back in his direction.

A horribly damaged face hung, suspended by her hair, several inches from his chest. Ralph exclaimed in shock and horror. He pushed the woman's face away from him and rolled. Freed from his assailant, he scrambled to his feet and ran into the hallway. Ralph picked up his flashlight and shone it at the woman as she crawled toward him.

Her ankle had broken, her foot twisted at an unnatural angle. Ralph forced his eyes away from her and tried to locate his gun. It lay halfway between him and his attacker. He knew that he needed that weapon.

Ralph strode forward. The woman reached out for him as he got close. He kicked the arm away and followed up with another kick. Blood flew as his boot found her face, but disturbingly it seemed to have no effect. Ralph quickly picked up his pistol. He aimed for the disfigured face and fired twice. Blood, brains, and bits of bone exploded outward.

Ralph stood frozen for a moment, his pistol still aimed at what remained of the woman's head.

"Fuck ... Fuck, fuck, FUCK!"

His eyes traveled to the gaping hole of the stairwell. Involuntarily, he retreated until his back hit the opposite concrete wall. His pistol was still aimed in front of him.

Ralph felt his arms and legs starting to shake. He listened carefully for any more sounds of movement, but thankfully all was quiet. Satisfied, he lowered himself to the ground and sat with his back against the wall.

"Fuck ..." Ralph muttered. It took him several minutes to calm down enough to think straight again.

"Zombies. They're fucking zombies." There was no doubting it. He had shot the first guy four times, and still he had kept coming. He thought of Jenny.

Oh, my God. Images of his wife fighting off similar monsters shot through his mind.

I have to find her! But first ... Ralph forced himself to his feet. He stepped over to the woman, grimacing in disgust as he grabbed one of her arms and dragged her away from the stairwell door. Ralph left the dead man inside the stairwell and silently shut the door.

Roughly half an hour later, he once more stood before the doorway. This time, he felt ready.

Ralph was now armed with a shotgun. He had traveled back to the cruiser to collect it. He still wore his sidearm on his belt, along with his baton. Having found a roll of duct tape, he'd attached the flashlight to the shotgun, and then taken it a step further by applying generous portions of tape to his pantlegs and forearms.

Bite through that, motherfuckers.

He reached for the door handle but suddenly doubled over in pain when a fiery stab of pain shot through his gut.

"What the fuck?" The pain ended as abruptly as it had started.

What the hell is going on with me? The answer was apparent almost immediately: *It's the syndrome.*

Ralph considered the situation for a moment. Was he going to go nuts, like Dijkstra had? Was he going to die, only to rise again as a zombie? Ralph sighed.

Whatever. He clenched his jaw. *I'm not going to let it control me.*

Ralph had a mission. He was going to find his wife and baby. He needed to know what had happened to them. Ralph would put them out of their misery if they were zombies. He opened the door and stepped into the stairwell.

Up, he coached himself. *Third floor.* That was where the paternity/neonatal and pediatrics departments were.

He crept up the concrete steps, choosing his steps carefully to avoid stepping on the human detritus that decorated the first landing. He knew from experience now that silence was key. Ralph paused at the door to the second floor and listened carefully. It was deathly silent, but he guessed there were zombies on that floor.

The one Dijkstra and I saw earlier. The one slapping the window. That one had been on the second floor.

Ralph wondered for a moment if zombies had enough intelligence to turn handles. He looked around but found nothing with which he could block the door, so moved on. Before he knew it, he was in front of the next door.

Third floor. This is it. Still, Ralph hesitated.

Man up, Becker. He opened the door and stepped through in one smooth motion.

Immediately he heard noises. They came from both ends of the hallway. Ralph swung his shotgun in one direction. Multiple shapes were moving toward him. They were too distant to take out with a shotgun, so Ralph swung in the other direction.

A woman in a hospital gown was almost upon him. Ralph fired and the woman fell backward, her upper torso and face riddled with shot. Another gowned person stepped around the first woman. She received the same treatment as the Mossberg 500 roared.

Ralph did not see any more zombies behind the two he had just taken out. After a moment to get his bearings, he realized that he needed to go in the other direction. Groaning inwardly, he turned around. At least four figures moved into the flashlight's beam. Ralph spotted several more in the shadows behind. He racked the next round and stepped toward them.

He fired into the crowd, keeping his aim at head height and trying his best to ignore the resulting carnage. It got hairy for Ralph when he fired the last of his nine rounds to find two more zombies stumbling toward him. He quickly jogged back to the stairwell door to reload but was met there by another zombie. The stocky female showed no shame as her hospital gown hung from a single arm. Her pendulous breasts swayed as she lunged at him. Ralph shoved her to the ground and drew his pistol, only hesitating to shoot for a second when he realized that she was probably a new mother.

A minute later, Ralph loaded nine new shotgun shells into the Mossberg. His hands shook and he fumbled one of the shells.

Come on, Ralph. Focus on your mission. He took a deep breath. His hands had almost stopped shaking.

MARCO DE HOOGH

The hallway was cleared less than a minute later. Filled with newfound confidence, Ralph continued his journey.

His confidence proved to be short-lived when he entered the maternity ward. Noises came from several directions as he got to the central desk. He scanned the board for his wife's name but had a hard time making out the chicken scratch. Leaning in closer, he squinted as the beam of his own flashlight bounced off the whiteboard.

Then he hit the ground hard as something slammed into him from the side.

With a burning pain down his throat, he kept a hold of his shotgun and swung the barrel, knocking something off him. He just had time to see several zombies close in. They piled on Ralph, knocking the shotgun out of his hand. They frantically clawed at him, hitting each other as often as they hit Ralph.

He tried to protect himself. Even then, he felt somebody bite down on his calf. He caught the glimpse of a woman's face as she lunged toward his. Ralph turned away just in time but felt a stinging pain as the woman bit down on the bottom part of his ear. She viciously shook her head, tearing the bit in her mouth away.

BLAM. Ralph's hand had found his sidearm. His scream was drowned out by the sound of his weapon.

BLAM. BLAM. BLAM—BLAM—BLAM. He blindly fired around himself. At least one of his shots found their mark, as he suddenly found himself freed. He kicked out at the ones clutching his legs and fired several more times in the half light.

Back on his feet, he fired more rounds. He didn't stop firing until all rounds in his magazine were spent. His hand shot to his ear. A chunk of it was missing, and the exquisite, sharp pain of touching an open wound made him gasp. He took a few quick breaths to calm down and push back the pain, inserting a new mag into his sidearm at the same time.

Collecting his shotgun, he shone his light on the carnage. The remains of four women lay at his feet. Thankfully, none of them had Jenny's coppery-brown hair.

Even so, he had to swallow hard to keep from vomiting. One of the four corpses had been highly pregnant. He thought that he spotted movement under the skin of her belly and heaved the contents of his stomach all over the floor.

Ralph could hear several more noises coming from deeper in the ward. It sounded like pounding on doors. He quickly stepped back to the whiteboard.

"Come on, Jenny. Where are you?" Ralph got more frustrated with every second.

Hold on. Ralph froze, then almost palmed himself in the forehead.

Pediatrics. I need pediatrics, not maternity. The rattling and banging on doors continued for long moments after his departure.

Several minutes and one incident later, he stood before the pediatric department door. He hesitated as a face stared at him through the small window set in the door.

"I'm coming for you, Jenny."

His gut burned, but Ralph wasn't going to let that stop him. He pulled the door open violently. The woman, who had been a nurse in life, crashed to the floor as the object she had been leaning against fell away.

"Sorry, lady." Ralph opted for his sidearm. He put his boot on her back, keeping the zombie down as he carefully took aim.

The pediatric department was sparsely populated, much to Ralph's relief. Only one more zombie roamed the single hallway. From the sounds of it, several others were stuck behind doors that they did not know how to operate.

Ralph's heart skipped a beat when he saw the board. "Jenny Becker" was noted next to Room 2. Ralph was nearly overcome with emotion by the time he stepped up to the door to Room 2. He feared what he would find inside. Even deeper down, he knew what he would find inside. It had been ever present in the hospital.

She's dead. Ralph squeezed the tears from his eyes as he faced the truth.

He psyched himself up and opened the door. For a brief instant he was blinded by the light shining through the window in the late afternoon. He blinked, then looked again.

Empty!

The room was abandoned. Ralph rushed in. He searched the room then the attached bathroom. Some of Jenny's things lay scattered around, but of his wife there was no sign.

A plethora of thoughts ran through Ralph's mind. Where had Jenny gone? Had she been evacuated? Was she hiding somewhere else in the hospital — maybe with their baby?

He stood stock-still for a moment and gathered his thoughts. Where to next?

Nursery. Maybe she is there. Maybe our baby is there. Ralph immediately turned around and left the room.

And walked straight into another zombie as a half-naked woman lunged at him. Ralph just managed to lift his hand to shield his face, and she bit down on the back of his upper arm instead. Ralph yelped in pain and tried to shake her off, but she held on to him. The pain was incredible. It overwhelmed Ralph's mind, and he couldn't think straight. He continued to try to shake her off, to no effect.

Then he punched into her face with his other hand. He smashed her nose on the first punch and dealt her a glancing blow off the forehead on the second, breaking one of his fingers in the process.

She released his arm after that second blow. His third punch caught her right in the mouth. Teeth cut into his knuckles and sprang from her mouth. The violence of the blow sent her reeling back and Ralph followed it up with a kick to her midsection. The zombie shot backward and landed in a heap.

"Bitch!" Ralph snarled and reached for his pistol. She had just gotten into a seated position when he shot her. She fell back once more as the shot took her high in her chest. "Fuck!" Ralph snarled once more, this time in frustration. He stepped up to the zombie and shot her twice through the face.

Breathing hard, he stood over the destroyed zombie. His arm pulsated with pain, as did the index finger on his left hand. Blood dripped from the cuts in his hand and from the side of his face. His thoughts drifted to the zombie movies his wife had liked so much.

They turned into zombies after getting bitten ...

That wasn't important right now. He had to get to the nursery.

Ralph tried his best to pull the broken finger straight. The bones were more or less aligned after the second try. He contemplated taping it against the next digit but quickly changed his mind. He needed his fingers free for action.

He picked up the shotgun and strode to the ward entrance. After a quick scan of his map and a check through the window, he stepped back into the darkness.

The nursery was just down the hall from pediatrics. Fifty feet, tops. It nevertheless took eight blasts from his shotgun to get there. More zombies seemed to be converging on his position.

For once he was not confronted with a zombie when he pulled open the door. He quickly stepped through and shut the door, finding himself in a short, empty hallway. His flashlight caught the glint of a large sheet of glass along his left side.

One of those viewing rooms. A couple of days ago he would have expected to be standing out here with a few other nervous and incredibly proud new fathers, but that was not meant to be.

A door to his left led into the viewing room. It was locked.

Full of trepidation, Ralph ventured forward and shone his light into the room.

What he saw nearly broke his heart.

The babies were dead. He looked closely at the nearest one, then scanned the rest. None of them had the open eyes and mouth of the zombies he'd encountered. Instead, several were rolled up tight in the fetal position, and on all the faces he could clearly read pain and discomfort.

"These babies starved to death," he whispered. "Oh God, no..."

Ralph rested his forehead against the glass and let the tears come. Even the first drubbing against the door could not stir him. One of these babies could be his.

Not yet ready to find his own child, Ralph turned away from the viewing room. Three rooms faced him on the opposite side of the hallway. One was clearly a small office. The other ones, he wasn't sure about. He opened the first door and shone his light in. A dead woman lay on her side beside a glass box. Ralph gingerly approached. It looked like this woman had died but not turned into a zombie. One quick look into the glass box told him that this baby had also perished. His gut twisted with a sharp pain, as if in response to his anguish.

He left the deceased mother and child alone, closing the door to their tomb and marching woodenly to the last room. The pounding on the nursery entrance had slackened. Ralph was thankful for that. He was also thankful to find that last room empty.

Ralph stepped back to the viewing room window and forced himself to read the names. His search came to an end at the fourth crib.

Jenny. Our baby ... She's dead! The tears came a second time as Ralph collapsed to the floor in grief.

"Deloris. Your name was Deloris," Ralph managed to croak. "It was my mother's name ..."

He cried until he ran out of tears. Even then, he did not move. He felt lost. It wasn't until a violent slam into the door caused him to look up that he became aware of his surroundings once more.

Deloris is dead. But Jenny might still be alive. It was feasible. He had not found her body, after all.

"Maybe she got evacuated." He struggled with the rationalization, knowing that Jenny would never leave Deloris to such a terrible fate.

Maybe she didn't have a choice.

His ponderings were interrupted by a violent spasm which doubled him over in pain. His cries of drew a response from those outside the door as the poundings increased. Slowly the spasm faded.

Ralph took steady breaths until the pain was completely gone, and considered his options. His eyes sharpened with focus as a decision came to him.

"I can still find her," he stated to the empty hallway.

He got to his feet and reloaded his shotgun.

Ten minutes later, he was back on the main floor of the building. His travels back downstairs had been a blur to Ralph, interspaced with faces coming out of the darkness, blasts of a shotgun, and bouts of heartburn.

The pain was getting bad, and Ralph decided to stop at the dispensary. Once there, another spasm of pain hit him so hard that he fell to the floor, writhing in agony. The spasm lasted several minutes, and by the time it faded Ralph knew that he wasn't going anywhere.

He crawled to the desk and pulled down a bunch of paper and a pen. This was going to be his last report.

I don't know if these bites will turn me into a zombie, or if the syndrome is going to make that happen. But I won't let it happen. Better to end it now. Anyway. Last words.

Jenny and Deloris, the loves of my life. I'm sorry that I let you down.

Dijkstra, you went crazy. I hope you can forgive me for killing you.

Ah, shit. My last words should have been for Jenny and Deloris. I will see you soon.

Joe reverently folded the pages and put them in his pocket. "I think that I should give these to Tammy."

Beside him, Bill nodded in agreement.

They drove along in silence for a while, lost in thought. Joe's thoughts were firmly directed toward the deceased officer.

Poor guy. He imagined the despair that Ralph must have felt.

He thought about the absolute loss of hope that had pushed the man to take his own life. *He must have been hurting something awful. I hope you found your peace, Ralph.*

They got back to the gate without incident. It loomed in front of them as they pulled up to it, looking like an oversize prison door to Joe.

"I knew somebody that committed suicide," Shelley said.

Joe snapped his head to Shelley, who looked over briefly before turning her gaze back to the street. Her pained expression was mirrored in her shimmering eyes.

"It happened about a month before ... all of this." She gestured out the window with her hand. She put her hand back on the steering wheel and drove on in silence. However, all three men in the vehicle knew that she had more to say and waited.

"I guess that's only a couple of months ago ..." She trailed off again.

They pulled up to the community gate. Shelley put the car in park, but nobody moved. After a moment, she turned to face John, before craning her neck to meet Joe's eyes. Bill, who sat directly behind her, could not see the anguish on her face.

"Mona was a dear friend, you see." She wiped a tear from her cheek. "Sorry."

The men stumbled over each other in their attempts to assure and comfort her.

"It's okay." John looked clearly uncomfortable but nodded encouragingly.

"Hey, we're here for you." Joe's eyes had started to shimmer in response to her sadness.

"Poor thing." Bill reached out and patted Shelley's shoulder. "Y'all let it out if you need to talk about it."

Shelley smiled at the caring response and cast them an embarrassed smile. Once more she was silent for a long moment. She was gathering her thoughts.

"Mona was the most vibrant, cool person I knew. She worked at the same hospital and started there on the same week as me — albeit in a different department. We hit it off at once and tended to have lunch together whenever our shifts were the same." Shelley's smile grew at the memory of Mona. "She kind of drew me out of my shell. Got me to do all kinds of things that I'd never do on my own. We went camping." Her eyes flashed. "That was out of my comfort zone.

"But that was nothing! I had no idea." Shelley laughed. "Mona was a real health nut. She used to make me go with her to the gym. She worked out so hard, it put most guys there to shame. We would go out to the bars whenever our nights off lined up. That girl was fearless. She was pretty, but it was her attitude that got her whatever she wanted. She was always smiling." Shelley paused for a second. "Always telling jokes and being funny..."

Her smile slowly faded. "I remember thinking: *How can somebody who looks so happy get to such a bad place?*" A tear rolled down Shelley's cheek unchecked. "How could she do anything to hurt herself ... She had the world at her feet!"

This time she was silent for a long moment. Bill exchanged a look with Joe and they both looked out of the side window. A lone zombie was approaching. Joe shook his head slightly. The dead could wait.

"I got the call from a mutual friend. We were all in shock. Disbelief. That next morning, I got up and it took me a while to realize that it had really happened." She shook her head. "I still find it hard to accept that somebody I knew so well was harboring all these dark thoughts. Deep under that bubbly, confident surface she was lonely and sad. Maybe afraid. She spiraled into that depression, and I wasn't around enough to see it, or smart enough to recognize it."

Shelley had spotted the approaching zombie. Bill moved instantly, opening the door. "I'll take care of it. One moment. You need to finish what you have to say." He shut the door behind him before Shelley could argue.

The nurse watched as the young soldier took careful aim, but she still jumped at the gunshot. Bill ran ahead and opened the sliding gate, waiting patiently as Shelley moved the Humvee through it. He was back in his seat a minute later.

Shelley had managed to compose herself by then. She smiled softly at her companions. "Thanks for listening."

"You feel guilty that you didn't save your friend." Bill startled her with his statement.

She nodded after a moment's hesitation. "Yes."

"Y'all need to get over that guilty feeling. I've been there too — a long time ago."

Everybody's attention was on the normally soft-spoken man in the back seat now.

"The thing is, death ... It's"—Bill frowned as he tried to find the right word— "Well, I guess it's final. One thing that I learned was that it's the living who seem to go on with all that second-guessing. We're the ones left with doubts and guilt. But that ain't right either. Shelley, you should remember all the good times all y'all had together. Because you've got to go on living."

"Wow, Bill," John looked over his shoulder at the man. "And here I thought you were a simple country yokel!" he said with a wink. The group burst out laughing — none harder than Bill.

Their laughter came to an abrupt end as a bang sounded behind them. A solitary zombie had reached the gate. They weren't sure if it watched them through its remaining eye, but it was definitely aware of them as it reached through the bars. It tilted its head slightly. Joe shuddered as he observed the creature. It looked like it wanted to swallow them whole with its mouth so wide open and its shrunken back lips.

"Guess I was wrong." Bill commented. "Guess death ain't so final no more ..."

They watched the zombie in silence for a moment. In frustration, it beat the bars keeping it from its prey. The sun was getting low in the sky, casting a long shadow of the creature at the gate. For some reason, Joe didn't want that shadow to reach their vehicle.

"Let's go home."

They drove off, leaving the zombie alone with its shadow.

Chapter 40

Stan

November 21, 4:15 P.M., Horus

"Stan! STAN!"

Lauren pulled at Stan's shoulder. Slowly, he tore his eyes away from the perimeter fence.

"We've got to get out of here!" his wife pleaded.

But where can we go? Stan stared at his wife, uncomprehending. He looked back at the fence. It swayed back and forth, seemingly further with every motion. What really caught the eye were the undead.

There are hundreds of them ... The sheer volume of zombies was enough to strip away all hope. Worse was that Stan knew it was the same on every side of the compound. They were completely surrounded. There was no escape. Camp Winnatonga had turned out to be the exact opposite of the haven they thought it had been.

It was a deathtrap.

The camp had been a perfect front for the Rosae Crucis, providing an out-of-the-way location capable of housing hundreds of members. When the call came through, Stan, Lauren and nearly a hundred other members of the Order loaded up some stuff and drove out. A sense of optimism prevailed at first, and people enjoyed the setting. They hung out at the small lake during the day and roasted marshmallows over campfires at night. It had felt more like a vacation than the end of the world.

The sturdy fence around the perimeter was the only sign they had in those first days that this was not a vacation. Apparently, the entire perimeter had been fenced in the last year. Stan wasn't sure if that had been good luck or good management.

The mood at Camp Winnatonga got more somber as the days went by and the news from the outside world got worse. Several pets in the camp died, along with millions of their kind. Luckily, people remembered the "special medicine" they had all received upon arriving at the camp. Three dogs were saved that way.

Those same dogs were barking their heads off right now. Stan couldn't see them, but he sure as hell could hear them.

Maybe feeding them that medicine hadn't been a mercy, after all.

"Stan. Please!" Lauren continued to cling to him, like a drowning person to a piece of flotsam.

She wants me to save her. But I can't.

Gunshots rang out nearby. The last of the ammunition was being used up in one last desperate attempt to clear a path of escape. Stan had heard the call but neglected to answer it.

We're all doomed.

Those bastards... He thought about Adepts Vincent, Gail and Deedee. They called for help yesterday and assured them that the Order was on their way to save them all.

But it was immediately apparent there wouldn't be room for everybody when the helicopter arrived this morning.

Still, they could have taken a few of the children ...

Instead, they'd saved their own asses. They even shot the old guy, Ken. *Who used to be a sage, for fuck's sake!*

They flew off, leaving over a hundred souls to fend for themselves.

Sword Tanya tried to put on a brave face. They were going to load everybody in vehicles, clear a path, and make a run for it. But Stan had lost the will to fight, just as a few others had. They walked back to their cabins and waited for death.

Then the gunshots started and the curious amongst them, Stan and Lauren included, couldn't resist taking a looksee.

One of the posts bent with an ugly metallic sound. Stan snapped back to reality. He felt Lauren's hands around his bicep. She had given up trying to run, it seemed. "We've got to do something," she muttered under her breath. She, too, was entranced by their impending doom.

"Shit." It was the first word Stan had uttered for minutes. Lauren's tear-streaked face turned to her husband, a question forming on her lips. He met her eyes and shrugged. "I've had an idea."

Without hesitation, he turned toward the stairs of the porch, his hand instinctively finding his wife's. He rushed around the side of the cabin and onto the pathway. They passed another cabin to their right. A woman and her daughter stood on their porch. They held each other tightly, their expressions trancelike. Stan was afraid to turn and follow their gaze for fear of seeing a huge tidal wave sweeping toward them.

"Where..." Lauren began, but soon enough it became obvious. The office.

Stan and Lauren jogged across the small field, even as the sounds of gunfire and screams intensified in the distance. Somewhere out there, a dog yelped. For some reason, that disturbed Stan more than the other sounds of violence.

They made it to the office and walked up the steps. Stan tried the door and found it to be locked.

Fucking Gail, Stan fumed.

Lauren yelped in alarm as Stan put his fist through the glass. He'd cut his hand, but that wasn't going to matter much in a while anyway. He reached in and unlocked the door. They walked in and he locked the door behind them.

Might buy me another minute.

Lauren's confusion was complete. "Stan, what are you doing?"

He walked around the counter. He reached down, lifted the object he'd been searching for and watched as recognition flashed in her eyes.

"We're going to make some calls of our own. It's time the other satellites find out what has happened here."

"But the Order—"

"Fuck the Order! Fuck Brenin, and his grand plan, and especially fuck Vincent and those two bitches!"

Lauren stepped backward, lashed by the intensity of Stan's anger. Stan meant to apologize, but instead he looked down at the radio transmitter.

Blood dripped freely from his hand as he turned on the power and started twisting the dial. The electromagnetic sounds of the radio filled the small building, while sounds of terror were closing in.

Chapter 41

Pedro

November 22, 7:00 A.M., Location unknown

"**H**ow about now?"

The voice sounded reasonable. Pedro tried to open his eyes. Only one of them obeyed.

The speaker was a skinny man dressed in a clean and trim suit. His receding hair was slicked straight back, making it appear like he was wearing a thin black helmet. A sharp hooklike nose holding up circular glasses and a gaunt face completed the picture. He looked like he belonged in the corporate world.

The man did sound reasonable. However, he was anything but. He was flanked on both sides by two other men. In sharp contrast to his clean clothing, they wore blood splattered t-shirts and jeans.

Pedro moved his tongue inside his mouth, feeling the loose teeth as well as a few gaps. He felt a sharp jab as he cut his tongue on the sharp edge of a broken tooth and the cold rush as blood filled his mouth. Pedro wanted to spit, but he couldn't operate his thick lips. He had to settle for letting the bloody spittle drip from his mouth and onto his own lap.

"Disgusting." The man made a face.

His henchmen stepped forward, but he raised a hand, delaying the next beating. "I need him able to speak."

They looked back at their leader.

"Not the face, or the torso." He seemed to consider for a moment before his eyes lit up. "How about the feet?" He seemed to be asking Pedro.

No, thanks? Pedro wasn't sure how he was supposed to respond, so he stayed silent.

The man sighed. He turned his back and took a few steps away. Pedro didn't bother turning his head to track him. There was a scraping sound and several seconds later the man returned, dragging a chair. The twin to the very chair to which Pedro was currently tied.

Placing the chair six feet from the shackled and beaten man, the stranger wiped imaginary dust off the seat before sitting gingerly.

"You guys take five. Stay nearby," he told his henchmen.

Once they were out of the door, he stepped out of view for another moment, returning with a bottle of water.

I'm thirsty. Pedro only had eyes for that water as his interrogator sat down and took several large gulps.

"Thirsty?"

The man went to offer the water bottle. He held it out in front of him. Pedro raised his hand despite himself, about a foot off his lap before his chains refused to allow any further movement. The man smiled in satisfaction. The image of a rat came unbidden to Pedro's mind.

"Tell you what ..." He put the cap onto the water bottle and placed it at his feet. "You tell me everything that you've done, and I'll give you the rest of this."

It sounded like one hell of a deal to the parched Pedro.

Would have been a good deal — if he didn't know with absolute certainty that the man was lying.

Still, Pedro nodded ever so slightly.

"Good."

Chapter 42

Theodore

November 22, 7:15 A.M., Lower parking lot at Olympus

"You should take more people with you."

"For the millionth time, Winston: I don't need more people. I need a fast car and a good driver." Theodore tapped the jeep with his right hand and the rather apprehensive-looking Private Fred Keensley with his left. "I got both, right here."

The jeep would have to do. There was nothing faster at Olympus anyway.

Maybe we'll hit a Ferrari dealership on the way to our destination, Theodore considered before continuing to speak.

"Are you sure that you're healthy enough to travel?" the young man persisted.

The old Theodore would have given some gruff answer. Probably treat it like an insult. Something about the look in the boy's eyes made him swallow his reply.

"I'm fine, Winston. We've wasted enough time, at any rate. Those guys will be waiting for me as it is." He lifted his hand to quell any further comments. "We'll be just fine. Besides, it's this place that needs protecting." He turned to the man beside Winston. "Sergeant Laughton, that task falls on your shoulders."

"Sir." Ken Laughton had more than earned Theodore's trust. He was a good man. Loyal. And ruthless when he needed to be. Exactly what Theodore required. Theodore had promoted the corporal on the spot. He even looked the part, what with his scarred face, ever-present scowl, and wad of tobacco up a cheek.

Heh. A sergeant without a squad.

He turned to the next man in line. "Sergeant Harris." Theodore shot a glance at Laughton. "You are to second two of your team to Sergeant Laughton." The sergeant nodded. "Your best 'soldiers'" Theodore added.

"Yes, sir."

"That leaves you with ... What? Four men?"

"Three, sir."

Theodore nodded. "Enough to keep your operation going?" It wasn't really a question.

"Of course, sir."

"I want you to meet with Senator Williams every day to go through all communications. Every one of them," he added for emphasis.

The sergeant nodded in acknowledgement. It reminded Theodore of something else.

"Speaking of the good senator, his daughter approached me earlier this morning. She used to be ANG." Upon seeing the look of confusion on Harris' face, he explained, "Air National Guard. Anyway, she wants to help. Let her join your crew."

He turned away before the sergeant could respond.

"We're off. Fred!" he called over his shoulder as he approached the jeep.

Fred jumped into the driver's seat and Theodore walked around the vehicle. He was reaching for the door when he felt a light touch on his shoulder.

"Please be careful, sir." Winston's eyes had grown large with emotion.

"Don't worry, kid. I've gotten quite good at this cheating death thing." Theodore tried to smile at the young man, but his face still hurt too much, so it came out more like a grimace. He turned back to the vehicle and opened the door.

"President Clarkston chose wisely," the young man stated. Theodore need not have turned around to see the glistening in Winston's eyes. He could hear the emotions in his voice.

"Thanks, Winston" he replied, not trusting himself to turn and face his aide. Theodore wasn't an emotional person but nevertheless felt a slight pull on his heartstrings.

He hesitated, his mind elsewhere for a moment.

The last time he'd cried was the last time he'd seen Agatha alive. She had drawn him into a hug and stroked his head, comforting him even in her dire state. The only other time he had shed a tear was when Russel died. He'd become a hardened person since then.

Which explains why you received so few visitors and get-well cards. He hadn't cared at the time. If anything, he was ready to die and finally be with Agatha again. But then he didn't die. He'd never know whether it was the chemo or radiation or any of the other injections he received, but he didn't die.

While the world around you did.

"Sir?" Winston said hesitantly behind him.

Theodore snapped out of his reverie. He looked back at the young man.

Are you my new Russel?

He stepped back from the door and turned to his aide once more.

Face it, old man. You've grown fond of the kid.

Theodore stared at the young man. Winston looked nervous. He pushed his glasses over the bridge of his nose. Finally, Theodore smiled.

"You take care, Winston ... Winny. That was what the president called you, wasn't it?"

The young man nodded.

"Winny," Theodore savored the name for a second, then shook his head. "No. To me, you're Winston." He smiled again. "Is that okay with you?"

An array of emotions played across the young man's face. "Of course, sir!"

He held out his hand. "Good luck, son." Slightly taken aback, Winston shook the hand.

Only wincing slightly at a multitude of aches and pains, Theodore turned and sat in the passenger seat. He shut the door and addressed the man at the wheel.

"I've been told that you're a hell of a driver, Fred."

The private looked back at Theodore and swallowed. "I'm all right. I guess... Sir."

"All right, eh? Well, let's find out how fast you can get us to Yorktown." He had strapped on his seat belt and pointed.

Fred hit the gas.

Theodore looked straight ahead as they drove out of the small lot. He couldn't keep himself from glancing at the side mirror in hopes of catching one last glimpse of the men and women he was leaving behind. He didn't see anything but imagined them standing there, watching the jeep speed away.

He wasn't worried about himself. That wasn't in his nature anyway. But he couldn't deny the trepidation he felt in regard to his people.

Stay safe, he wished as he viewed a retreating hillside in the mirror.

Chapter 43

Christine

November 22, 8:30 A.M., The Ren

Christine walked into the cafeteria, offering a few waves and good mornings to those already seated for breakfast. She headed to the buffet counter and helped herself to a plate, piling on some reconstituted eggs and a meat substance that she thought tasted okay. She grabbed cutlery and a glass of water, then turned around to look for a place to sit down.

Her mom and dad were sitting at one table, but she was not in the mood to join them. Melissa sat with Shelley nearly on the opposite side from her parents, and she decided they would be better company.

"Hi, ladies. Mind if I join you?" Christine asked as she approached them.

"Sure!"

Shelley's large eyes and bright smile made her feel instantly welcome. Christine couldn't remember ever finding the nurse not in a positive mood. Shelley was always pleasant, respectful, and caring.

Especially caring, Christine realized as she smiled back at the nurse and sat down.

Shelley had always been one of the first to help when help was needed. She'd patched up almost half of the residents of the school by this point, and always did it with empathy. And then there were those eyes. Those large, expressive eyes were a true window into the woman's soul.

She really is a wonderful person.

346

"Thanks."

Christine placed the plate in front of her and reached for the salt, which sat next to Melissa's plate. Melissa passed the saltshaker with a smile of her own.

"How are you healing? I don't see you at the clinic anymore," Christine said.

Melissa nodded ever so slightly, her lips pursed as if she were impressed. "Honestly? Better than I expected." She grinned. "And I put a lot of expectations on myself."

"I checked her wounds last night, and they're pretty much healed up already," Shelley added. "It's amazing."

Melissa glanced over at the nurse before looking back at Christine. "I got lucky, I guess."

"She's been up and walking already for days. Your dad told her that she was not to strain herself," Shelley added with a sharp look at the woman beside her. "But there seems to be no stopping her."

"Hey. I listen ... A bit."

The three of them shared a chuckle.

"Well, I'm glad that you're getting better so quickly. We need you," Christine stated. Shelley nodded enthusiastically across the table from her.

They started eating their breakfast, sharing some small talk.

A few minutes later, Christine looked up as newcomers entered the cafeteria. It was Jack, hand in hand with Nat. She watched them walk toward the buffet table together.

"What's wrong?"

Christine jerked at Melissa's question.

"Oh. Sorry ... Um, it's nothing."

"Yeah, right," the middle-aged woman responded. "You don't fool me."

Christine squirmed uncomfortably under the scrutiny from the other women. Shelley seemed curious and compassionate at the same time, while Melissa had more of a knowing look.

"Fess up, sister. Did you have something going with Jack?"

Staring at the last of her breakfast, Christine sat willing it to catch fire and distract the others. She felt her temperature rise and her cheeks blush. What was worse, her eyes started to brim.

"It's my own fault," she said. "I've been leading him on. Playing him ... Then he hooks up with Nat."

Anger and disbelief crossed her face, even as a solitary tear streaked down her cheek. She was silent for a moment as she thought things through.

"It's not Jack's fault. Or Nat's. I just got really angry. Jealous, I guess. I'm no good at being alone. Then there was Jack ... And then he was with Nat."

"I thought that's what I saw." Shelley nodded, her expression not altogether unkind.

"Yeah ..." Christine's voice trailed off. "I've been a total bitch. And clingy. I practically threw myself at Keith." She couldn't help breaking into a grin at that. "I threw myself at that geeky Bruce Lee lookalike and bounced right off."

"He's a weird duck," Melissa agreed.

The three women snorted, enjoying their moment of levity.

"Anyway, I probably just need to move on," Christine concluded before stabbing the last of her eggs with her fork.

"Hey, there are plenty of fish in the sea," Melissa prompted, which resulted in more snorting.

Shelley decided to try her hand at a pick me up. "You've still got your family and your health. As do we. We can be thankful for that." Her companions nodded in agreement.

Shelley frowned then, her mind obviously on something else.

I've never met a person with more expressive eyes, Christine thought before the nurse spoke.

"I haven't figured out why I didn't get the syndrome."

"Maybe you are immune or something," Christine offered.

Shelley shook her head. "No, that can't be it. From all the information we've got, we figured out that these nanobots attached themselves to our bowels and stayed in a dormant state until activated. Most people reported pain in their lower stomach as one of the first symptoms, which makes sense now that we know those nanobots started drilling into our body cavities."

She shuddered and met the eyes of each of her two companions in turn.

"But I never had any symptoms at all. Nothing."

"Maybe it was something you ate?" Christine suggested, remembering that it was something she ate that cured her. Shelley looked doubtful.

"Maybe it was your job," Melissa said, her expression thoughtful. "You worked as an X-ray tech, right?"

"Yeah." Shelley struggled to see the connection.

"Well, maybe you were exposed to radiation. Maybe that radiation messed up those nanobots."

"Holy shit. That makes sense!" Christine said excitedly. "Ethan told me that Keith thinks he got cured by electrocution. Maybe these nanobots get fried by radiation and electricity."

Melissa nodded. "I had a theory about all of those radio operators ... It was along the same lines."

"Of course!"

Several people from other tables turned at Christine's raised voice.

"Radio waves are also kind of a radiation, aren't they?" she added in a lower tone.

It was too late, though, as people were now listening in. She looked away quickly when she saw Jack's face turn her way.

"Well, you know our story already. Maddie Jeffersons saved my family." She indicated Melissa with her chin. "And yours, too."

"Yeah. That's the thing. John and I don't know the Jeffersons at all ..." Melissa frowned in frustration. "It's kind of pissing me off."

"Well, there has to be some link," Christine suggested. "Maddie's dad was in the army. It's got to have something to do with that. What was his name, again?"

Christine looked up and caught her father walking to the buffet counter, cup of coffee in hand.

"Dad," she called out.

Joe deviated from his path and approached the three women. "What's got the three of you so excited?" he asked.

"Never mind that. Do you remember the name of Maddie's father? Melissa is trying to figure out if she knew him."

"Uh. Give me a sec." Joe stopped and squinted, trying to remember. "Randall. Yeah. I think his name is Randall."

"Randall Jeffersons ..." Melissa's own squint resembled more of a frown. "I think ..."

Her eyes opened wide in surprise. She nearly knocked over her cup of tea.

"RJ!" she exclaimed.

Several people drew near, curious at the commotion.

"Yes! I know who that is. RJ ..." She savored the name and the memory for a second. "RJ was the Lonely Ranger."

The outburst got the attention of almost everybody in the cafeteria. Many people left their breakfasts behind and approached so they could hear.

"Tell us what you know," Joe asked, a serious expression on his face.

Mel blinked and shrugged, unsure where to start. "It happened a long time ago. Twenty years, at least ..."

Chapter 44

The Lonely Ranger

Melissa scanned her ID badge against the reader. The satisfying sound of a maglock releasing reached her ears as she twisted the handle. She had another door to get through — this one requiring a security code along with a second badge. After that she would still need to sign in at the security desk.

Is it going to be Carl or Sandra? She wondered which security guard would be on duty. Either way, there would be light flirtations.

Getting through the second door gave her the answer to that question. "Ah, somebody let the sun shine in."

Mel smiled despite herself. "Hi, Carl."

The slightly overweight and slightly older soldier leaned over his desk, craning his head to see better. Mel endured the leer, unconsciously wanting to draw her jacket further over her bosom. Still, she preferred Carl's attention to that of Sandra, who was a lot more direct and aggressive.

"Some shit going down," Carl whispered conspiratorially. "Lots of buzz in the ops center today."

Mel nodded as she signed in. She was aware of an operation that had kicked off roughly twenty hours ago. She processed Carl's response.

Something must have gone wrong.

She wasn't going to tell the security guard about it, though. Carl was also smart enough not to ask.

Down the long hallway, she passed several doors without a second look. She'd been there for well over half a year now, and the server room, equipment storage and maintenance room did very little to tweak her interest. No, it was the room at the very end that held her attention — and had since the day she started. The operations room was commonly called The Brain, and for good reason. Very little occurred in the military world without The Brain being aware of it, if not influencing events directly.

She entered the door and sensed the buzz that Carl had referred to.

Yes. Definitely something wrong.

She got to her desk. Richard looked up at her and shook his head. "Hey, Adams." He turned back to the monitor and proceeded to log off. "Intel report is over there." He gestured with his chin as he wrote.

Melissa reached for the folder. She and Richard had perfected their hand-off routine after months of being partnered up. She could tell by the sound of his voice and the stiffness of his posture that something bad had happened.

She opened the folder, aware of the mission objective: Eliminate Volkov, whose weapons dealings had armed several known terrorist organizations. The unfortunate thing was that Volkov enjoyed a protected status in Belarus. On top of that, Belarus relations with the US were icy, at best.

"Operation terminated?" She immediately saw the stamp at the bottom.

Richard nodded, clearly frustrated. He stood, giving the seat to his partner. "Brass pulled the plug after some chatter was picked up. Mission's compromised."

"Shit ..." Mel continued to read the report and lowered herself into the chair. "Says here that they got Volkov."

"Yeah. The operation was executed flawlessly." He scratched his head. "Belarusian intelligence must have been watching. Waiting for us to take the bait. Which we did. Luckily, we picked up on the chatter. Warned the team to get the hell out of Dodge. Had to cancel exfil, though."

Mel read the last entries of the report, then pushed it to the side as she logged into the terminal. "Cancel exfil?"

Richard grimaced. "Belarus is trying to catch us with our pants down. It was a trap ..." He placed his fingers on the report. "They don't give a fuck about Volkov — never did. All they wanted to do was catch our assets in their territory and kick off an international shit storm."

Clearly frustrated, he picked up the folder and dropped it on the desk. "The guys are on their own."

"Damn." Two four-man teams of Rangers had been deployed for operation Razorgrass. They would have known the risks — as they did with every operation. Still, this felt harsh.

Disposable heroes. She remembered overhearing somebody say that once. Nobody would ever know that they were heroes — not even their families.

"What's their protocol?"

"They've got to hoof it. The border with Lithuania is thirty miles to the west. We've got Lithuanian cooperation, so getting through the border is no problem. Getting there, though ..." He shook his head. "The planned route will be through Narachanski National Park. Rough terrain, but sparsely populated."

"Do we have eyes on them?"

Richard shook his head. "We did, but Han ordered us to stand down."

"What?"

"Major Han ordered us to cease all communications as well. Doesn't want to take any chances."

"So those guys are on the run and we can't help them?"

"Yeah. I don't like it any more than you do, Adams."

"What's the effective time of the order?" Mel was already reaching for her headset.

Richard checked his watch. "Technically, you've still got ten minutes."

"Okay, thanks. Go get some sleep."

Richard dipped his head. "Okay, Adams. Just watch yourself. Han won't like it one bit if she finds out you're contacting the team." That said, he turned on his heel and strode toward the exit.

Melissa multi-tasked, pulling up satellite images even as she spoke into her mic. "Mothership to Blade. Come in, over."

The reply was almost instantaneous. "Mothership, this is Blade. Over."

"What is your current status and location? Over."

Some specialists went out into the field with chips embedded just under their skin. They could easily be geo-tagged to a specific location. But on operations like these, all possible evidence tying the Rangers back to the US was removed as a precaution. It gave the US government plausible deniability. It also made it challenging for operators like Mel, who then had to rely on more traditional methods for gathering operational intel.

"We're about a mile west of Myadzyel, just north of lake Narach. We've had to ditch the vehicle we had appropriated since our last check-in. There are roadblocks set up all over the place." Mel sensed a slight hesitation on the other side of the line. "We thought that we were flying solo. Does this mean we can plan for exfil? Over."

"Negative on the exfil, Ranger. My orders are to stand down as well. I have a five-minute window left for communication only. Over."

That definitely disappointed the Ranger. "This is fucked up, operator. Over."

"I know, Ranger. Let me see if I can provide you with some intel ..." Mel scanned the satellite imagery intently for a few seconds. "You'll need to find a hole to hide in for the day. I think that I've located you guys. You should be hitting a creek in a few hundred yards. Follow the creek to the north. It curves back to the west eventually. Keep following the creek for another mile and you'll find a building. Might be a hunting lodge." She noted that the roof had partially caved in but switched back to infrared just to be sure. "Definitely abandoned. You should be able to hide out in there for the day.

"From there, you head straight west. Skirt south of the town of Narac, then travel west by north-west all the way to the border." Mel did another quick check. She was good at this. This was her game. "Best I can tell, Belarus forces are focusing their search around Svoboda." Svoboda was where the hit had taken place. "Some of the chatter we picked up implied they believe you're heading toward the town of Pastavy — that's about five miles north of you. Over."

There was another brief pause. She imagined that the Ranger was taking notes. "Got it. Thanks, operator. Over."

"Wish I could do more, Ranger. I will keep an eye on you, but that's about all I can do. Over." It felt like it would not be enough to get the men out. Not even close.

The Ranger seemed to take it in stride. "Hey, you've helped us lots. We've got some talent on our team. We'll make it out." He seemed to be trying to convince himself. "Tell you what," he continued. "Just hearing your voice made us feel better." Some unintelligible banter was happening on the other side of the line. "Just what a lonely Ranger needs at a time like this."

The Ranger spoke again after another round of banter. "What's your name, operator?"

This went against regulations and procedures. But their conversation had been far from proper protocol in the first place.

"Melissa. What's your name, Lonely Ranger?"

She could hear him chuckle as he spoke. She could also hear a couple of lewd comments in the background. "RJ. They call me RJ. I kind of like this Lonely Ranger thing, though. Maybe I should make that my nickname." More apparent ribbing followed.

Mel checked the time. She needed to end the call within the next thirty seconds, or she would be in direct violation and face far heavier sanctions than just a reprimand. "Our time is up, RJ. Good luck to you and your team. Over."

"Thanks, Melissa. Over and out." Melissa smiled as somebody in the background called out, "I love you, Melissa!" in a high-pitched voice.

These guys were unreal. There they were, in a strange land and surrounded by hostiles. Completely cut off from support. But they still managed to be ... guys. Melissa smiled as she took off her headset.

Her smile faded quickly as she realized the daunting task ahead of RJ and his team. The odds were stacked against them.

M el wanted to approach Major Han and request that the termination order be rescinded. However, she knew that this would be pointless. Major Han was a stickler for rules — and despised insubordination.

Instead, she spent the next several hours on mundane jobs. She had paperwork to complete and several other menial tasks to perform. She got handed a training module at the team meeting and invested her energy into that. Mel had a love-hate relationship with training. It felt to her that their entire corps spent more time training than doing actual hands-on mission stuff.

But today, it gave her something to focus on. Something to draw her mind away from the events occurring over four thousand miles or seven time zones away.

No, eight, she had to remind herself. Belarus kept the same time as their close ally, Russia, despite their geographic location. That simple thought broke her concentration, and her mind was back on RJ. Mel stared at her screen. At the mouse icon that hovered over the next training file.

Fuck it. She closed the training program and pulled up operation Razorgrass.

She leveraged one of the satellites flying over Belarus to sneak a peek. This at least allowed her to watch their progress. Mel breathed a sigh of relief when she found their heat signatures in the abandoned building she had directed them to.

Good. Hopefully they will remain undetected for the day. The rundown building in the middle of nowhere should keep them out of sight. Satisfied, she closed down the windows and got back to her training.

Mel spent her lunch hour at her desk. That in itself was not out of the ordinary. Even the fact that she appeared to be working was not out of the ordinary — the world around them didn't take breaks, after all.

But Mel wasn't working on her assigned tasks. She was scanning Narachanski National Park. Specifically, the roads leading in.

What she saw was disheartening.

She had captured a few images and enhanced them.

Trucks. Could be used for moving troops. Another image confirmed it. *Those are personnel carriers.*

She followed the convoys. A couple of trucks pulled into the town of Myadziel, almost four miles southeast of RJ's location. One personnel carrier continued north and set up a roadblock near the northern edge of the park. The rest continued west. To the town of Narach and beyond.

Shit. RJ and his men are going to have to find a way through that net.

Mel continued to track the Belarus army units, watching them set up roadblocks at multiple intersections to the south, west, and north. She widened her search to find that similar troop movements were taking place all along the Belarus western border.

They've cast a wide net. That was both comforting and worrying. Comforting in that the search appeared to be blind and without focus. Worrying as to the sheer size of the operation. They really wanted to catch these guys.

I've got to do something. Before she knew it, Mel was halfway to Major Han's office.

The door was open. Mel knew that she'd chicken out if she hesitated, even for just a moment. So she walked in.

A low, mumbled conversation drew to an abrupt stop as Mel entered. Major Linda Han was not alone; she stood with another officer.

A colonel. Mel spotted the eagle on his chest. She almost turned around on the spot. This was many levels above her paygrade. But then she thought of RJ and his team. She clenched her jaw and stepped forward.

She saluted sharply. "Major Han, ma'am, we have a situation."

Major Han looked displeased at the interruption. She dipped her head apologetically at the colonel. "My apologies, sir."

The colonel, a man in his late fifties, seemed to take it in stride. "That's fine, Linda." He gestured for Mel to speak.

For a terrifying moment, Mel did not know which officer to address. Finally, she turned to Major Han. "It's the Rangers, ma'am. All support has been withdrawn a—"

"Yes. Their mission has been compromised, and our adversary is paying attention. We needed to withdraw all drones to keep this situation from escalating. This is protocol."

Melissa started to nod but turned it into a shake of her head. "We can't simply abandon these men, ma'am."

She caught the flash of anger in Major Han's eyes. "You have no idea of the political game that is being played. Now, I order you to drop it and drop this mission. Do you un—"

"Hold on, Linda." It was the colonel who interrupted this time. "Is this Operation Razorgrass?" He waited for the major to nod in acknowledgement before turning to Mel.

"Who are you? Name and rank, soldier."

Mel stood at attention. "Intelligence Sergeant Adams, sir."

The colonel nodded. "And how old are you, Intelligence Sergeant Adams?"

"I'm twenty, sir."

"Twenty ..." The colonel huffed. "You're still a kid. What the hell do you know about life?"

It wasn't a question. Despite that, Melissa had an answer ready. "Not much, sir. But I do know that those men will all die if we don't do something."

Major Han bristled, her eyes and nose flaring at the same time. She was ready to reprimand Mel on the spot but stopped when the colonel chuckled. She turned to the colonel and waited for him to speak.

The chuckle was short-lived. "They knew the risks when they signed up. They knew the risks of this operation."

It sounded logical, and Mel's brain urged her to agree completely. Instead, she set her jaw and looked the colonel in the eyes.

"I cannot accept that, sir. There has to be a way to get our men out and still not risk an escalation."

The colonel opened his mouth to answer, then closed it again. He tilted his head slightly, as if she had given him something to ponder. Finally, he smiled.

"Yes. There has to be a way. And you're going to figure it out."

Mel was shocked. Her expression must have shown it. The colonel chuckled again.

"Intelligence Sergeant Adams, I task you with this. They will need to make it across the border, on their own. You can communicate with them, but under no circumstances are you to interfere directly. We will not be sending reinforcements, or drones, or ordering air strikes. Is that understood?"

It was all Mel could do to nod weakly. "Yes, sir."

"Very well. Dismissed."

Mel bolted like a startled deer. She could hear the colonel chuckle again. However, she had also seen the expression on Major Han's face.

I'm in serious shit!

But that was for another day. She got back to her desk and started typing before her ass hit the chair. She pulled up a screen and quickly assessed what satellites would be flying over RJ and his team.

Good. She ran a time-lapse. *Good. Only a couple of small gaps.* She could stay with RJ and his team nearly continuously for the next few hours.

Mel entered a set of orders. A few seconds later, she had a clear view of the building where RJ and his men were hiding out. She was relieved to see no signs of violence.

They're not there yet. Mel widened her search and switched to thermal imagery. Her relief turned to distress. She immediately reached for her headset and reconnected the dead commlink.

"Mothership to Blade, come in, over."

"Mothership, this is Blade. Good to hear your friendly voice, over." She could hear the relief in RJ's voice on the other end of the line. She had no time for niceties, though. "RJ, I have eyes on you. You have multiple bogies incoming. Southeast of your position. A hundred and fifty yards and closing. I count ten to twelve individuals. Prepare your team to engage. Over."

"Roger that."

Mel knew that the rangers would be scrambling into position. She switched back to the satellite feed, noting that it was raining heavily.

Good. Mel knew the weather conditions would be a distraction.

She could see several bright shapes moving around inside of the building. The Belarussian soldiers were clumped together as they approached the building. They were still a hundred yards away when Mel watched RJ and his team set their trap. They snuck out the back of the building and edged around the walls in two-man fireteams.

Now they just need their prey to step into the trap.

The Belarus soldiers were disciplined, but only human. They sent in a couple of scouts to see if the building was empty. Mel could see them do a cursory scan of the area around the building, obviously not spotting the hidden rangers.

Otherwise, I'd be watching a firefight right now.

The scouts entered the building. Again, RJ and his team must have hidden all clues to their presence well. She saw one of the scouts stand at the entrance to the building and imagined him calling out to his comrades.

Sure enough, the men approached and entered the building. She could see RJ's men inch into position. Mel held her own breath in anticipation.

Time to spring the trap.

However, nothing happened for several minutes. She watched in amazement as the Belarus soldiers started a fire.

Must be cold out there. Then she realized that she was thinking about northern Belarus in late winter.

The fire had been going for several minutes now, and the Belarus soldiers crowded together for heat.

Now is the time to strike. She flinched at the sudden explosions of light as a barrage of bullets flew. It was over in a matter of seconds. A few more shots were taken to ensure their prey was downed. The bodies were already cooling and fading from her thermal-enhanced view.

"Blade to Mothership, come in, over."

She jumped, despite expecting the call. "Blade, this is Mothership. What is your SITREP, over."

"Our SITREP is ... Well, you saved our asses. Ten tangoes down. No shots fired by the opposition. Over."

Mel sighed in relief. She figured that RJ and his team had used suppressors. The Belarusians would not be alarmed. Yet.

"You're going to have to move quickly, RJ. Stick to the plan that I outlined yesterday but expect more traffic. We're still under orders to not interfere, so you're on your own. They've cast a wide net to try to catch you. The longer you stay undetected, the longer that net doesn't get tighter. Over."

"ACK. We're going to tidy up a bit here, then roll out ASAP. We'll go silent, but chirp if you need me. Over."

"I'll have eyes on you the rest of the way out. Good luck. Over and out."

Mel had to chirp the radio once, shortly after they had circumvented the town of Narach. Another group of soldiers threatened to intercept RJ and his team. Thanks to Mel's warning, RJ's team hid, and the platoon of enemy soldiers passed two hundred yards in front of their position without so much as a pause.

They continued without incident and were halfway to the village of Lyntupy when the corpses of the ambushed soldiers were discovered at the abandoned building. Mel immediately warned RJ that the gig was up.

Mel had checked the terrain and distances several times by that point. She knew they were a mile from Lyntupy, but that they would be traveling through some rough terrain. Lyntupy was only a mile away from the Lithuanian border, though. RJ's team could not risk the road and would have to cross several farmer's fields — but they could move at a significantly faster pace than in the forest where they were now.

Of course, they would also lose a lot of their natural cover.

But they can do this. I think they're going to make it!

Mel looked up from her desk then over her shoulder to Major Han's office. Her spider sense must have been tingling, as the major was watching her through the glass. Her mood dropped at the expression on Han's face. Han was going to make her pay for this — she was certain of that.

Fuck that. And fuck you. She flashed her most winning smile toward her superior and turned back to her desk.

For a moment she lost sight of RJ as a satellite slipped out of range. This was one of those gaps she knew was coming. The minutes ticked by as another satellite slid over the Baltic Sea and over the west coast of Lithuania.

Mel immediately searched the last location for RJ and his team when the satellite was in range. They were only a hundred yards from the village. Then she spotted something that made her heart sink down to her shoes.

The satellite had detected air traffic. At least one military airplane had flown over the area, and several helicopters were crisscrossing the park. It would only be a matter of time until RJ and his team were spotted.

Mel chirped the radio. "RJ, you guys are going to have to haul ass. There are helos incoming to your position."

She received a chirp back. "ACK," RJ whispered.

RJ's team approached Lyntupy. Mel knew that a roadblock had been set up there. In fact, she could see a four-man team standing on the side of the road.

RJ's team crept closer.

Oh. Fuck, no! Mel could do nothing but watch as one of the Belarusians opened fire. RJ's team returned fire immediately, pinning the soldiers down. One of the rangers flanked the position and opened up on the three remaining men. The fight was over in seconds, but the cat was out of the bag.

The team wasted no time. They crossed the road and immediately stepped into a farmer's field. Two of the men paired up. Just behind them, three men appeared to move in unison.

Shit. Somebody's hurt.

RJ's next message confirmed her fear. "Mothership, we're going to need medics when we get across the border. Over."

"Roger." Mel immediately started typing. The problem with these requests was that her senior officer would have to approve the support. She feared that Major Han was feeling anything but supportive at the moment. She kept the request as simple and to the point as she could.

Medical support immediately requested for multiple wounded at 55.03694, 26.23361.

Mel didn't even have time to leave her desk and make the plea in person, as the next satellite images showed a helicopter approaching.

"RJ, you've got a bird bearing down on you from the east." She tried to keep her voice calm, despite her racing heart. The Rangers picked up their pace. They still had nearly a mile to go, though, and the helicopter was only minutes away.

Every image showed the helicopter closing in, while the Rangers got closer and closer to the border.

"Helo at one mile and closing." She figured that they could probably hear the approaching helicopter.

They caught a break just then, as the helicopter hovered over Lyntupy. Apparently, they were trying to figure out where the Rangers would have gone after the firefight. Somebody on the ground must have waved them into the proper direction, as thirty seconds later the helicopter sped off after the Rangers.

"Fuck. They're not going to make it." Mel's outburst caused several operators to look up out of curiosity or annoyance. She didn't care. "Come on, RJ ... Run!"

They weren't going to make it. The helicopter was almost on top of them, and they were still at least a hundred yards short of the border. Mel imagined the guns on the enemy aircraft spinning up.

Just then three helicopters rose to the sky, straight ahead. The Belarus helicopter hesitated. It hovered in position even as RJ and his men continued to run. There must have been some communication back and forth as the helicopters faced off — and the Belarus crew must have gotten cold feet, as the aircraft turned and sped away from the scene.

"Holy shit! We made it!" RJ's statement was music to her ears.

"Those helicopters, were they the Lithuanian military?" Q couldn't help himself. He was on the edge of his seat, as were several others.

Mel smiled. "Yep. They intimidated their Belarus counterparts and allowed our troops to escape across the border. They never physically crossed the border, and both countries decided to shove the incident under a carpet."

"But how did they know to get there? I thought you had just asked for medical assistance?"

"Yes, I did. That's a sharp observation, Q." The young man beamed with pride at the compliment.

"You see, what I didn't know was that Major Han and the colonel were watching my every move. The good colonel decided to request more than a medevac at the border. Han opposed the idea but was overruled." Melissa smiled at the memory. "I remember finishing my call with RJ and turning around. I expected to see Han, glaring at me from her office. Instead, the colonel stood there. He grinned at me and gave me a thumbs up. That's when I knew that he hadn't been sitting idle either."

Her audience made approving noises and nodded at each other.

"Cool!" Q stood up and gave her a salute. "You're the shit, Mel!"

Melissa smiled. "Thanks, Q. I actually did get a medal for that. But it also got me transferred within six months. Major Han wasn't going to let my insubordination slide." Her smile turned introspective. "It wasn't the last time, either. No wonder my career never really took off …"

Several people spoke up in her defense at that point. Joe put it best when he simply stated that she did the right thing. She couldn't disagree with that.

People noticed the time then and started to disperse. Mel got a few pats on the back and words of appreciation from some of the folks as they left. Tammy waited until the crowd had dispersed before approaching her.

"Wow." Tammy shook her head. "Just wow. That's the kind of stuff movies are made from." She added, "It's certainly more exciting than most of the news I get to read."

"It's all true," Mel stated, trying not to sound defensive.

"Oh, no!" Tammy lifted her hands. "I believe you! As a matter of fact, I'd like to record it."

Melissa looked up with a confused frown.

Tammy took a step closer. "Look ... Can I sit?"

Melissa shrugged. Tammy took that as a yes.

"I've been compiling peoples' stories. I already have half a dozen of them."

"Why do you want to do that?" Melissa's confusion turned into suspicion.

Tammy bit her lip for a second as she considered her words. "I don't know what our future holds." She met Mel's eyes as she continued. "Things could fall apart here. Or zombies could kill us all. And of course, that 'Order' could come here and wipe us out."

"Is this supposed to convince me to share my stories?" Mel was truly confused now.

Unperturbed, Tammy continued. "On the other hand, maybe we survive this. None of us know the future. But we all know our past. What happened to people — what are the stories that link us together."

"What if there is nobody left to read these stories?"

"What are we without hope?" was Tammy's reply.

That stumped Mel, but she still wasn't convinced.

"Regardless of what happens to us, I think it's important that our stories get told. I'm trying to collect enough stories to give somebody in the future an idea of what really happened. What people went through. Your story was poignant. It teaches us about doing what we believe is right, which through some chain of events put you here in this place. Alive."

Mel nodded ever so slightly. Tammy took a deep breath. She was going to try one last time.

"My job was always to present stories. I had to park my emotions and just deliver the facts. But those stories"—Tammy screwed up her face— "were about real people. About their striving and struggles. Their sorrow and their outrage. But I couldn't pick sides. This time, I want to put a human face on it. Forget about being impartial. Tell it all and include the emotions."

"I can relate to that. Heck, my career was all about suppressing emotions."

"I think a lot of us can. Or could. But the truth is that we aren't human without emotion. I want to record our stories, and our emotions. You've been through a lot, and I get the feeling that there are some valuable lessons in your stories ... They might help somebody."

Mel nodded more firmly. "It might even help us. Okay, let's do it."

"Jack."

Jack pulled up short on the landing of the stairwell. He recognized that voice. He'd dreaded a confrontation with its owner.

Christine stood at the top of the stairs. Jack remained frozen in place on the landing despite his instinct, which told him to turn around and run.

The young woman slowly descended the stairs. Jack couldn't help but see her ample breasts as they pressed into the army-issue t-shirt she wore. Her hair had grown a bit since they had all arrived at the Ren. The straight hair had started to curl, hanging in dark ringlets in front of her face. She pulled the hair away, exposing her green eyes.

Jack swallowed. "That was quite the story from Mel ..." He tried to make small talk. Christine wasn't interested in that, though.

"I'm not used to being cast away," she said as she stepped onto the landing.

"I—" Jack was about to stammer some sort of apology but was cut short as Christine raised her hand.

"Hold on. Let me say my piece first."

She went close to Jack. For a brief moment, he thought that the woman was about to slap him in the face, a dramatic homage to all the love-lost scenes he had seen on television and in movies.

What actually happened came as a surprise. "I'm sorry." Her eyes started to sparkle as tears threatened to fall. "I toyed with you. I thought there were no other women worth any attention and was too confident that I had you wrapped around my little finger."

She hesitated, but he said nothing.

"Arrogant," she added. "For that, I apologize. And you ... You hurt my pride."

Jack did not trust himself to speak yet, so just nodded.

"I'll admit. I did not understand what you saw in Nat." She gave a wry smile.

"She ... We're friends." It sounded lame, but Jack couldn't come up with better words to describe it.

Christine stared flatly at Jack for a moment. "Yeah. I suppose that can be true. Anyway, I wanted to let you know that I'm okay with it. At the end of the day, it's your loss." She threw him a knowing look and then a mischievous wink to let him know that she wasn't entirely serious.

Jack shook his head in confusion as he continued up the stairs. *Girls...*

He headed to the media room. It was time for him to put in a shift there. As he neared it, he heard the sound of conversation and frowned in confusion.

That's a woman's voice — but it's not Emily! He rushed into the room just in time to hear the voice again.

"Oh my God who is this?"

"This is Romeo Echo November One," Emily replied. Jack could see by the glint in her eyes how excited she was, yet somehow Emily was still able to remain calm and professional. "We are a group of survivors. Who are you, over?"

"Oh, my God! I'm so happy to hear another person! My name is Margot Dubrovski, and I'm calling for help. I've been taking a ladder to go from roof-top to roof-top—"

Emily turned to Jack as the woman kept on talking. "Go get Joe!" Jack shot out of the room as she turned back to the radio.

"—trying to find more supplies for the rest. I saw the antenna on the building and hoped that this was a radio station. I wasn't even sure how to operate the radio, but luckily for me it had been left on! There are some batteries in the room here. Oh, shit! What if they run out?"

"Slow down Margot." Emily coached. "Can you tell me where you are?" She could tell that Margot was a civilian, so refrained from using proper radio protocol.

"We're a group of about forty people, and we're stuck at the safe zone. There are zombies all over! They told me to find supplies. They're..." She paused. Emily was about to reply when she continued. *"I've been traveling from rooftop to rooftop in the safe zone, using a ladder to cross over. I saw this building yesterday, so made it over here today."*

"Which safe zone is she at?" Joe had burst into the room and caught the last statement.

"It's got to be the one in the city, mate," Emily replied. "Radio range is limited."

"Right. Okay." He thought about it for a moment. "Tell her we need to discuss this with our people. Don't make any promises of help yet. Ask her to wait for us to call back."

Joe had already turned and was heading toward the door. "Tell her we will call back in one hour!" He called over his shoulder as he rushed out of the room.

"We have to do something." Michelle hit the tabletop for emphasis. "These are fellow survivors — and they need our help!"

Half a dozen discussions promptly started. The buzz of voices was overwhelming for Shelley, and she was reminded of that first day — when the doors of the Ren were closed.

Except we don't have Craig around to calm us down this time.

Joe stood on the small stage in the cafeteria. He raised his hand for silence. That didn't have the desired effect, so John stepped up onto the stage and took a position beside the big man. "HEY!" he bellowed.

The effect was immediate as the silenced crowd faced them. John took a step back and looked at Joe, allowing him to speak.

"Let me start out by saying that we will do what the majority wants. What I don't want is for us to spend hours debating this. So let me make my argument, and if somebody is completely opposed, then you will get to state your counter argument."

For once, the crowd waited patiently for Joe to continue.

"My vote is that we plan this thoroughly but mount a rescue mission as soon as possible."

There was a murmur of surprise. Joe raised his hand for silence.

"Only so many living people are left. We need to come together and stand together against the threats."

A few people nodded. They understood that the undead weren't the only threat out there.

"If this is a new start for us, as Rosa states"—he indicated the Latina woman, who nodded back at him—"Then we should do the right thing. Those people need our help. We have a duty. We have to rescue these people."

After a moment, his solemn face broke into a grin and, much to the surprise of those around him, he started laughing.

"Sorry," he said when he was finished. "It's just that this would be the last thing I would have said, just a few short weeks ago ... I guess Craig left his mark."

He looked at John. The former special operator appeared amused.

Joe turned back to the rest of the group. "Okay, guys. That's my opinion. Is there anybody that is dead-set against mounting a rescue mission and wants to state their reason?"

Surprisingly, the room remained silent. Joe could tell that some of the people in front of him disagreed, but apparently nobody felt strongly enough about it to say something.

"I have a comment." Shelley seemed to surprise herself by speaking up. Her large eyes grew even larger as people turned to stare at her.

She hesitated for a moment, building up the courage to speak.

"I am in favor of attempting to rescue these people. But not at any cost." She surveyed some of the faces around her. It steeled her resolve, as she stood a little straighter when she spoke next. "My vote is that whoever goes on this rescue mission does not take any unnecessary risks. Don't risk your lives if there is no way to rescue those people. Sorry."

Joe smiled warmly at the nurse. "No need to apologize, Shelley. I totally agree with you. The safety of our own people should be our top priority."

He waited for a moment, to see if anybody else had something to add. Nobody did.

"Let's just go ahead and vote. Raise your hand if you think we should try to rescue these folks." Over twenty hands shot up in the air, followed by a couple more after a moment of hesitation.

Joe smiled with satisfaction. "Good. That's settled."

John had been ready and waiting. The brawny man stepped forward.

"Can I get a hands up of people willing to come along on this mission?"

John scanned the room, counting the hands but also noting to whom they belonged. Shelley could see the look of mild surprise on John's face as Joe also raised his hand. John gave him an appreciative nod.

"Can the volunteers please stay behind in the room? We've got some planning to do."

The non-combatants got the hint, and the cafeteria was cleared quickly. Nearly a dozen people remained in the cafeteria. Shelley looked around the room and found the usual suspects. Everybody with a military background was present, including Mel and Emily. The civilians included Keith and Joe, but also, surprisingly, Rosa.

One look around told Shelley that people were equally surprised to find her still present as well.

"Thanks, everybody." Melissa was already taking charge. "I think we will need eight to ten people, tops."

She walked over to Rosa and Shelley. Rosa jumped off the tabletop on which she had been sitting. "I was going to volunteer in case we didn't have enough." She still wore bandaging around her hand, but her other injuries were mostly healed.

"Thanks, Rosa. I appreciate it." Mel stepped aside to let the other woman leave. She turned to Shelley.

Shelley wasn't quite as prepared to give up her spot. "You could probably use somebody with a medical background ..."

"True. But we don't need two." Smiling, Mel gestured toward Joe. "Besides, I need somebody with me to keep this place running."

"Okay." Shelley was never the type of person to create drama. "I'll stay behind."

Mel dipped her head in thanks as Shelley strode toward the door. The nurse watched over her shoulder as Mel addressed the rest of the group. "Whatever we do, we need to do it as a team, and we need to do it fast."

Shelley heard mumbled sounds of agreement from the rest of the group.

"I think I've got a strategy for this," Mel added.

That was the last thing Shelley heard as she left the cafeteria. She smiled. Mel was definitely back.

Chapter 45

Emily

November 22, 11:30 A.M., West gate.

This feels familiar. Emily thought as she maneuvered the bus through the gate.

The sound of gunfire shifted her attention from the gate behind her to the Humvee in front. The area around the gate was mostly deserted, but not entirely, as about half a dozen zombies approached from various angles. Somebody shot from the top hatch of the Humvee, and she noted that John had refrained from using the mounted SAW in favor of his new weapon.

She eased the bus forward, allowing enough room for the rear Humvee to make it through the gate.

"Open her up for a sec, Em," Bill asked as he strode up to the bus exit.

Emily stopped the vehicle and opened the door. Bill stepped out and immediately took aim.

BLAM. She grimaced as, thirty yards away, a zombie's head seemed to explode.

"Another one to the left, mate," Emily warned her companion as another zombie stepped around a dumpster. Bill already had it in his sights.

Ah. Another child. Emily hated the sight of zombie children and felt a wave of sadness as Bill ended its existence.

"Time to roll." Bill stepped back into the bus as they heard the gate close with a loud clanking sound.

Emily closed the door and Bill returned to his seat. Up ahead, John took his last shot.

"Gate is shut. Car two ready to move out." Emily recognized the deep boom of Joe's voice.

"All clear. Car One moving." Abi's high-pitched tones came through in sharp contrast.

The convoy started moving forward once more.

Emily followed the front Humvee at a distance of about fifty yards. BB drove that vehicle, completing a three-man crew with John and Abi. She glanced through her side mirror, catching the second Humvee following. Keith drove that vehicle. Joe manned the radio and Ben acted as gunner to complete that crew.

In the bus, it was just Bill and her.

They hadn't wasted much time. They had called Margot back and geared up, checked the vehicles and topped up the fuel. The convoy pulled out within two hours and were at the west gate less than fifteen minutes later.

Mel had figured out a route for the team that would keep them on the highways as much as possible and thereby probably avoid any groups of zombies. The only tricky part was getting out of the community and to the nearest highway. The east gate was busted, so the only direction that really made sense was to go west. Emily focused on the road as they left the safety of their gated community behind them.

Seven blocks. That's how far they would have to travel to get to the nearest on-ramp of one of the ring roads.

This was the first time that she had left the community — or even the school, for that matter — since the fateful day that had brought them all together at the Ren. Emily had remained in the safety of the Ren while other members left on missions over the last couple of weeks. Some of them had gone on more than one mission already.

Now it's your time, Em. She'd felt guilty for remaining behind. So here she was, about to risk her neck for the greater good. It filled her with pride.

Well ... She reconsidered. *Fear and pride. Fifty-fifty.* She caught movement out of the corner of her eye as something stumbled out of an alleyway. *Okay. Sixty-forty.*

They moved along the street at a reasonable pace. Nevertheless, to Emily it seemed like they were crawling along. She glanced over her shoulder at the stoic Bill.

Just Elvis and me in this coach. Feels rather exposed ...

She could not disagree with Melissa's tactics, though. Melissa wanted a highly mobile team that could transport an additional forty people.

They also didn't want to leave their home base undefended.

Everybody knew too well that the Rosae Crucis was out there. Emily figured they would be able to handle just about anything with Nat sniping from the roof, Mel on the SAW, and a half a dozen others armed and ready for action.

The bottom line was that the folks at the Ren were at high alert during the operation. Tammy had volunteered to take over the radio, since Jack was going to be part of the home defenses.

Emily had been charged with training the former news anchor on the use of the radio. It all started well enough, but then Emily caught herself looking at Tammy. She was mesmerized by the other woman's near cobalt eyes.

She is seriously fit! Emily remembered thinking. *This woman is gorgeous.*

Emily had spent the next twenty minutes with Tammy, teaching her all about operating the radio while trying not to sound too awkward. She'd felt conflicted about it afterward.

Now Emily drove the bus in silence, thinking back to those moments. All the slang words she'd heard when she was in the British army came back to her.

Maybe they were right. Maybe I am a boydyke ...

The radio broke her train of thought. *"Car one to all. We are approaching the on-ramp now, over."* Emily had to grin, as she could imagine the frustrated look on Abi's face. A signalman was married to her procedure words. But half the radio users were civilians and would not understand prowords.

"Roger car one. Homebus ACK," Bill said into the radio in his sing-song accent.

Emily tried not to smirk. *Sing us a song, country boy!*

"Car two also ACK." Emily grinned, remembering the five-minute lesson in military radio jargon with Abi and Joe. The girl's head barely made it to Joe's chest, so the big man had to stoop down to listen. It had been a funny sight.

"Romeo Echo November to Sierra Two. Message received. We are all clear here. Good luck. Over." Tammy's voice reminded Emily of her earlier dilemma.

She steered the bus around a corner and pushed the thought out of her mind with a small shake of her head.

Can't worry about that now. We've got a job to do.

"Are they here?"

"Who, Mom?"

"The people that live in the lights."

Christine swung to face her mother. She was about to speak when she noticed that her mom's expression was calm, her attention on something in her lap. For a moment Christine covered her face with her hand. Her dad had left about twenty minutes ago.

Christine was scared for her father, and the atmosphere was highly charged. Something that her mother had picked up on.

When are those drugs going to take effect? She's seriously losing it ...

She felt jealous of her brother and father for a moment.

Sure, Dad's on a dangerous mission, and Ethan might have to fight for our safety.

But they didn't have to watch over Mom.

Christine walked over to the window and looked outside. There wasn't much to see. The daughter and mother were the only ones at the Ren who did not have anything to do, and subsequently had locked themselves in their room. They'd begged off any other duties with Melissa, claiming that Rachel was ill.

As if anybody still believes that. She'd seen the looks, growing ever more frequent.

Something is wrong with her, was the unspoken thought.

They would be right.

But so far, nobody had made any accusations. Besides, her dad had brought back all the proper medications. He didn't want to take any chances, so started with the minimal dosage. Even then, it would take days before her old mom would be back.

It was just a waiting game now.

Christine watched as a bird flew by. It was a raven. The large bird was stark black against a sky of light blue and clouds of white. She could almost imagine the sounds its large wings made as it flew.

Whoosh, whoosh, whoosh. As if on cue, she heard the bird caw. It was a sound both harsh and forlorn to Christine. The raven flew out of her field of vision and was gone. The raven did stir another bird from a nearby tree. It took wing and circled the tree fast as a dart.

Haven't seen too many of those lately, she realized. She watched the bird flutter back to rest in the tree and wondered if there would be more birds in the skies again soon.

"That's it. You eat and get strong." Her mother's voice broke Christine out of her musings. She looked over her shoulder at her mom. She was still fiddling with something in her hands.

Curious, Christine stepped closer. "What do you have there, Mom?"

Rachel looked up at Christine with joy in her eyes. "It's Ethan. Come, meet your baby brother!" She held something aloft for Christine to see.

Christine gasped. Rachel's hands were covered in blood. Something brown squirmed in her grip. "Mom!" Cristine reached over without thinking and whacked the creature out of her mother's hands.

Rachel howled in dismay as the mouse hit the ground with a hard smack. It twitched on the hard floor, its back broken. Rachel wailed once more as Christine stamped down on the rodent.

"There he is." Emily could barely hide the relief as John came jogging back.

The Humvees and the bus were parked together in the lot of a strip mall. The off ramp to the highway they had traversed sat just a stone's throw away.

The first thing they'd done was regroup here. Surprisingly, not a single zombie had approached, attracted by the sound of their engines. John had quickly decided to go off and scout the safe zone, which lay about two miles away.

John jogged up to the team. Emily noted the sweat that beaded on his forehead, and the grim look in his eyes.

"What's the news, chief?" BB asked.

"Not good." John shook his head. "There are thousands of them down there."

That made sense. The direct area surrounding them was positively abandoned. She figured that they must have all wandered into the valley, drawn by the living and the noises down there. The safe zone lay in a small valley. She imagined that valley now, filled to the brim with the undead.

And the remnants of a safe-zone population. She shuddered at the thought of being stuck in a tin building surrounded by an ocean of zombies.

"Looks like Mel's plan will be our only chance," John continued.

Emily had figured as much. Melissa had devised a simple plan. It was the Ratcatcher of Hamelin all over again. Except that the catcher was more like bait.

"The roads are clear. Military must have kept them cleared right to the end. That plays in our favor. *If* the plan works." John grimaced. "There are a shit-ton of zombies down there. If the decoy doesn't pull away enough of them ..."

"We're fucked," Keith finished for him. He strode to the Humvee, a familiar ghetto blaster hanging by its handle from one hand and a roll of duct tape in the other. "Don't you worry, John," he called over his shoulder. "We've got this. Right, Joe?"

Joe cleared his throat loudly. "Yeah." He coughed. "Yes. We've got this."

The look on Joe's face belied every word he'd said. Nevertheless, John nodded. "Very well." He addressed all three members of Car Two. "You should have plenty of space to run. Don't get boxed in, though, as they may come out of unexpected places once you've started drawing their attention."

Joe stared. Keith busied himself with attaching the ghetto blaster to the front of their vehicle. Ben simply nodded.

"Everybody else clear? Any questions?" Emily knew her role, as did the rest.

Keith, Ben, and Joe would be the bait. They were going to get back on the highway and take the next exit, which would place them directly east of the safe zone. Ben would open with the SAW and they would draw the zombies at the safe zone toward them. Then they would slowly retreat further to the east, hopefully drawing all the undead with them and signaling the other team to start their approach.

It should work.

In theory, it should work.

Ah, bollocks. It has to work!

"Good. Joe, give us a SITREP every minute or so. Time will be a limited once we've committed." John looked up at the sky. "Speaking of time, it's a-wasting. Let's do this."

The three bait men entered the second Humvee. The roar with which it started reverberated off the concrete ramp and overpass behind them. Emily could almost feel its power.

Bill followed her into the Bus. John and his companions entered the other Humvee.

All they could do now was wait.

"C*ar Two to all. How do you read, over?"*

"Romeo Echo November to Car Two, I read you loud and clear. Over."

"Car One to Car Two. Read you five-by-five. Over."

"Homebus to Car Two. Five-by-five. Over." It felt funny hearing Bill speak just a few feet from her and also hearing him through the radio. It felt even weirder to Emily that she wasn't the one manning the communications device.

Bus drivers in short supply in the apocalypse. Who knew?

"*Car Two about to engage. Over.*" Emily registered the staccato sounds of machinegun fire seconds after Joe's message.

Here we go.

Or don't go, Emily corrected herself as they had to hurry up and wait some more.

Emily and Bill waited tensely for the next message. Roughly sixty seconds later, Joe came back on.

"*Car Two to all. It seems to be working. Ben's taking them down by droves. The nearest ones are about fifty feet away. Over.*"

They waited for the next update. In the far distance, Ben's SAW barked in measured bursts. Emily found herself getting tense.

"*Car Two to all. Ben said that it's working. They're all coming this way. We're still holding ground. Over.*"

They waited again. Both Bill and Emily turned their heads as the measured bursts broke into a prolonged roar.

"*Car Two to all. We are moving. Ben says his first drum is getting low, over.*"

Wow. A thousand rounds.

"*Car One to Car Two. Advise fire discipline to prevent overheating of barrel, over.*"

"*Car Two ACK.*" Emily noticed that the shooting slowed down considerably after that message.

It took well over a minute for Joe to give his next SITREP.

"*Car Two to all. We had to maneuver a bit. Lost sight of the safe zone but continuing to draw the enemy. Over.*"

They listened in for three more SITREPs before John ordered them to start their engines. They crawled toward the safe zone, giving Joe and his team as much time as possible. Several minutes later,

Emily crested the hill with her bus. She could see the glint of sun on metal down in the valley.

That's the place.

"*Car Two to all. You're good to go, John. We're pulling back with ... oh ... tens of thousands of adoring fans. Over.*"

"*Ten four. Good luck, Car One. Out.*" Abi replied.

Emily turned to Bill.

"Okay, mate, time to let them know that we're coming."

Bill nodded. He quickly changed frequencies and contacted the safe zone. "This is Bill from the Ren calling Margot from the safe zone, come in, over."

"*I read you loud and clear. Over,*" a man said. "*This is Dan speaking. I'm a police officer. Margot is with the other women. We've been hearing the shooting and have observed most of the zombies departing the area. We are ready to be extracted. Over.*"

Emily raised an eyebrow and shared a look with Bill. Dan continued to speak.

"*Most of our people and supplies are located at the mess hall. We are prepared for your arrival and the evacuation. We have two men hidden in the parking lot right now. They have commandeered a bus and will follow you in. Just head straight down the main avenue in the zone and you'll see the mess hall on your right about a quarter mile in. You can't miss it — it's a huge building with an open area in front of it. Over.*"

"Understood. We will approach now. See you soon. Over and Out." Bill immediately changed the frequency to share the news with John.

Abi hung up the mouthpiece and turned to look at John. "Do you trust it?"

"Sure. Why not." John thought about it for a second and shrugged. "It is a cop ..."

Abi screwed up her face but didn't argue.

John shrugged and tapped BB on his shoulder. "Okay, BB. Take us in, nice and slow." He reached up for the hatch. Before he opened it, he turned back to Abi.

"If anything goes sideways, we get the fuck out of here. Let Emily know."

She did. A moment later, the relative silence inside their vehicle was shattered when John opened the hatch. They could still clearly hear the noise that Car Two was making. The SAW and to a much lesser extent the ghetto blaster were audible even at this distance.

BB pulled forward. After traveling one block, the two parallel fences of the safe zone came into view. As did the first zombies.

Dozens of undead still wandered inside the fence, apparently unable to find the exit. "Get us nice and close, BB," John instructed. He carefully took aim but did not shoot yet. The first couple of zombies stumbled over the downed fence, just beside the main entrance. They made a beeline for the Humvee.

BB got to within twenty yards of the gate before the first zombie reached them. John shot the thing in the head, the sound of his Bushmaster somewhere between a sharp crack and a pop. He immediately swiveled and started taking out more targets. Emily pulled the bus up behind them, and Bill was ready to jump out and open the gate for the convoy as they had planned.

Within a minute, John had taken out roughly a dozen targets. "Now, Bill!" He waved at the bus.

Bill jumped out of the door and ran toward the gate. John covered him as he worked. The first gate was unlocked and swung open easily. Within a minute, both sets of gates had been opened wide and Bill was on his way back to the bus. John had the soldier well covered, eliminating a couple more zombies before they got within twenty yards of him.

The vehicles started pulling forward and John could see another school bus pull out of the parking lot across the street. It quickly joined the mini convoy as they pulled into the safe zone.

"Abi ..." John reached out for the radio. Abi quickly placed the push-to-talk device in his hand.

"Car One to homebus. Bill, do you see that tower to our right? Over."

"Affirmative, over."

"I want you to climb up there and keep an eye on this area. We need to keep our escape route clear. Over."

"ACK, over," Bill replied. Abi looked behind her to see Bill jump out of the bus and jog over to the guard tower.

E mily watched Bill climb the tower stairs with trepidation.
"Just you and me now, coach." Emily winced at how small and vulnerable her voice sounded.

Luckily, BB pulled ahead, forcing her to focus on driving. The way ahead seemed clear as most zombies had been drawn to the outside of the camp.

More of them trapped inside the fence. You can be sure of that.

The small convoy moved down the main alleyway. Within moments, Emily could see their goal. It was the largest building in this part of the safe zone.

Been there before. In happier times.

They got to the open area just in front of the building. Again, there were no zombies present. Emily watched BB pull a U-turn.

"For a hasty retreat." Emily surmised.

She quickly followed suit, although she required a three-point-turn to complete the maneuver. The school bus behind her followed her lead to park along the width of the mess hall.

Emily put the bus in park but kept it running. She pulled the lever to open the door, grabbed her rifle, and sped to the entrance of the mess hall. She got there at the same time as John, and just as another man came running up from a side street.

The copper. Something about the way he moved made Emily certain of it. Like he was used to wearing a heavy and bulky utility belt.

The man skidded to a halt. He noted the vehicles before settling his gaze on John. He drew himself up. "That's it? This is supposed to be the rescue mission?"

John took a step toward him. Emily caught the dangerous expression on his face.

"Who are you?" the other man challenged.

"I'm a fucking Good Samaritan, is who I am!"

Emily could just about feel the heat emanating from John.

Don't push him now, mate — or you'll regret it, she silently warned the man.

The man eyed the machine gun in John's hands. "Easy there, big man." He holstered his pistol to show that he meant no harm. "I'm officer Daniel Malone," he continued, puffing up his chest a bit as he spoke.

Trying to look imposing. Authoritative. Like he wants to take charge.

She could tell that John was not impressed. "We don't have time to chat. Get your people moving."

The police officer bristled. Abi saw his eyes flare and knew that there was about to be an altercation between the two alpha males.

"The man is right, Dan."

The door to the mess hall had swung open and a man stepped out. Several men streamed out of the building behind him, carrying rifles. The man looked rather plain. Short, with dark hair. Slightly pudgy. Nevertheless, Dan twitched in deference.

"Let's get moving. Gear first," the man said, ignoring Dan.

The others around him moved at his command. They pulled the double doors open wide until they caught on hooks and stayed in position, then jogged into the building. Dan scowled once at John and followed his colleagues into the building.

Emily stared at the man. He was diminutive and of unremarkable looks, yet obviously he had the respect of the people around him. They all jumped to obey his orders, including Dan.

John got to business. "Abi, take over watch. Em, cover our rear. BB, that side." His instructions were accompanied by the all too familiar chopping motions. John moved to cover the front.

"Get your people into the busses asap, mister," he called over his shoulder. "We don't have much time."

Emily scrambled to her spot, past the front end of her bus. She positioned herself so that she could make eye contact with Abi, who had climbed on top of the Humvee. If she craned her neck, she could just make out BB about forty yards away.

"BB, you've got incoming," Abi warned.

"Marty," the safe-zone group's apparent leader called out, "get Raymond and our Mexican friends. Tell them to go help these folks. We need to keep a secure perimeter."

Good. We can use some backup.

The sound of gunfire exploded as BB took several shots. Abi waited until he was done to shout a warning to Emily. A solitary figure had stepped around a building to her left. She needn't have bothered, as Emily was already lining up her shot.

BLAM. Somewhat to her own surprise, the shot was perfect — right between the eyes.

"Get in there!" she yelled, just as two more men took up position beside her. She nodded to them gratefully.

For the next minute, all was silent. The only thing Emily could hear was the rustling of men toward defensive positions and the sound of commands from inside the building as the refugees got mobilized.

"Several bogies incoming." John shouted the warning and knelt. Emily couldn't help but notice the robot-like regularity with which John took his shot.

BLAM. One-one thousand, two-one thousand. BLAM. One-one thousand, two-one thousand. BLAM.

Emily spotted a second target as it listed into view. Its gray skin was nearly the same tone as its hair. An eyeless face swung toward her. She missed her shot and cursed, engendering surprised looks from the men.

That only flustered her more, and it took several rushed follow-up shots to bring the creature down. Emily had no time to be embarrassed, as a bunched-up group of at least a dozen undead stepped into view. The men beside her started shooting.

"Multiple bogies incoming!" Abi yelled out. "Emily needs backup."

Emily kept firing, noting with some pride that her shooting was more accurate than her two companions'. Out of the corner of her eye, she saw an overweight man march over and take position.

Dan, the police officer, ordered some more guys around behind her, but she had no time to look. In between the sounds of gunfire, which appeared to come from every corner now, she could also hear the alarmed sounds of women. The evacuation had started.

It turned into organized chaos after that. The shooting was constant, always from one direction or another as the dead inside the camp approached their position. The defensive lines were shored up, supplemented by gun-toting men from the safe zone.

The remaining refugees moved supplies into the school buses. Emily barely had time to register this, as the battle raged around them.

"I'm out!" BB yelled from his position and jogged back to the Humvee.

Emily knew that they had prepared half a dozen magazines. She had inserted her last mag a minute ago, and she'd need ammo soon.

"Hold the line," she told her companions, not knowing if any of them had heard her over the deafening sounds of gunfire.

She jogged to the Humvee. Abi was ready for her and handed her two magazines. She noted the steady stream of people carrying boxes into the buses as she returned to her position. She also noticed their leader. He stood next to the door, directing traffic.

Why is he not getting into the fight?

"We've got to get a move on," she called out to the man as she passed.

He nodded. "This is the last of it."

The fight continued for another minute, before the stream of zombies decreased. Emily looked ahead and figured they had taken out at least two dozen undead. She guessed that BB and John had taken out just as many from their positions.

We've just shot a hundred of them, she figured, then sobbed sharply.

"Prepare to fall back!" Abi yelled at the top of her lungs.

The end was in sight. Emily's tension rose with every second that passed.

"Fall back!"

The three men beside her moved in unison, turning and entering Emily's bus. Emily followed and pulled the door shut with a sigh of relief.

She cast a quick glance in her rear-view mirror. Her bus was full, although the back half was full of boxes and bags.

"Roll out." The radio speaker blared with John's command. Emily put the bus into gear and they jerked forward.

Two minutes later, Emily stopped the bus to let Bill on. Several more crumpled bodies in the area indicated that he had had his hands full as well. Two men jumped out of the bus and entered a solitary Humvee. Emily wasn't sure if the vehicle would start after sitting idle for weeks, but got a thumbs up from one of the guys around the same time that she heard the sounds of an engine coming to life.

A small cheer went up as they drove through the gate and turned left.

Chapter 46

Brenin

"Man, and war. Three-letter words, both ..."

Brenin had left the high-backed chair on the dais, preferring to sit in one of the benches instead. He eyed the chair from a distance. It almost looked like a throne. The ornate carving at the very peak was a tribute to Summuh.

God... Another three-letter word.

He looked beside him, then over his shoulder at the people sitting behind. His advisors and followers waited, knowing that he would say more.

"My grandfather served in a war, once. I asked him about it often. He told me that no words could describe the horror that was war. Lives were thrown away without regard. Cheap fodder, they were. Sent to the slaughter by their gentlemen superiors. Grandfather described former pastureland, pockmarked by the bombs, and littered with body parts. The ground was mud, even though it hadn't rained." Brenin shuddered for effect. "Yet they persisted in their madness, and sent young men, by the thousands, into a meat grinder."

His face was a mask disgust. Several moments passed in silence. No one dared to speak. Eventually, he continued, his expression softening into one of melancholy.

"They fell, like the petals of the flowering trees in an orchard. Dead uncounted and unending." In silence, he let his head hang. When he finally looked up, a deep frown creased his aged face. "Paladin Kevin has fallen," he said with finality. "My boy is gone ..."

Only two people in the room knew that he wasn't speaking about Kevin just then.

"How many more need to die on my behalf?" He raised his eyes skyward. A sterile, white ceiling greeted him. "I want no more deaths on my conscience." Slowly his eyes dropped. From the ceiling to the throne, down to the raised dais it sat upon, then to the very ground by his feet.

"But we're not done," he whispered, just loudly enough for his audience to hear.

"The vestiges of the old order still cling to power." Brenin stood up and strode toward the dais. He did not climb it but turned to his audience. This time, his expression was one of anger.

"They fester in their bunker like rotting meat. I can smell their stench from here. They must be stamped out. Eradicated. This was Paladin Kevin's desire. We will honor his memory and make it happen. After that, we will avenge him. And after that, I hope that the violence can end ..."

Chapter 47

November 22, 12:15 P.M., Monongahela National Forest

The clearing seemed unnatural. It was nearly a perfect circle, ringed by trees and bushes. It looked pristine. The only visitors to this glade prior to this moment had been forest animals, the trails of deer and various rodents crisscrossing the otherwise unbroken blanket of snow.

Two men approached each other cautiously from nearly opposite directions. The only sound breaking the deathly silence came from the snow crunching beneath their feet. At ten yards distance, the shorter of the two men spoke.

"Captain Donald?"

Donald nodded. "You must be Captain Harry."

The other man quickly closed the distance, and they shook hands. "Yes, sir. Harry Lastra."

"Ellis. Donald Ellis," the taller man said.

The two equals evaluated each other. At this moment, it was unclear who would be the dominant force.

"How was your trip?" Donald asked as they disengaged. He lifted his hand and signaled to his troops. A dozen men melted out of the nearby trees and shrubs and approached.

"Ah. The usual, I'd say," Harry replied, signaling to his own troops. His group was smaller, as only seven men appeared out of the trees behind him. "We've been in a running battle with the undead practically since Baltimore. Barely made it past Washington. We should have traveled straight west. Had a full platoon back in Baltimore." His expression was rueful as he turned back to Donald.

"There were twenty of us by the time we got out of that hell hole. Then we got held up on the I—95…"

Harry spat onto the smooth surface at his feet, the brown-tinged spittle blemishing the brilliant white of the snow.

"We ran into a major roadblock right at an underpass. Those fucking zombies boxed us right in before we could turn around. They leapt down on us from three sides. They just jumped down … All you could hear was bones breaking before we started shooting. It was fucking gross."

He shook his head once more before lifting his head and meeting Donald's eyes. "This is what I've got left. I sure hope this bunker is worth it."

Donald didn't offer up his story just yet, though. "Did your sappers make it? They will be crucial in cracking this nut."

For the first time, Harry cracked a grin. "Four of them, anyway. And plenty of gear. Probably enough to blow the top off a mountain."

The grainy scene showed a snow-filled landscape. At first, nothing happened. Then dark shapes entered the view.

"They're soldiers," Sergeant Ken Laughton said. The scowl on his face prevented any man from disagreeing with him. He sucked on the tobacco tucked up between cheek and gum.

Megan was no man. "What makes you so sure?" she asked.

Ken treated his subordinate to a flat stare. She wasn't supposed to be on his team. But Megan had not been pleased when she was told to report to Sergeant Harris and immediately raised a fuss. She explained that she was experienced as a fighter, not as a secretary.

So she was added to Sergeant Laughton's team instead. The gruff sergeant had accepted Megan with no more than a warning to do as she was told and pull her weight. Megan did not have a problem with that, although she never was the best at respecting a chain of command.

"Hold on."

Ken lifted his hand and looked around. After a moment he gave up and spit a gob of ugly brown saliva into the garbage bin. Nobody complained, so he turned back to the monitor and pointed.

"That's easy, Sally." He'd taken to calling Megan "Sally" for some reason. It annoyed her.

That's probably why.

She thought about saying something, but the sergeant had already continued with his explanation. "The way they move in two lines. The way they step through the snow, and the way they carry their gear. If I was a betting man, I'd say we're looking at grunts."

The shapes moved across the screen. "I counted fifteen men." Winston stated as the last man stepped out of the hidden camera's shot.

Megan had a quick look around the room. Two radiomen converted to infantrymen completed their little team. Ken called them "Hawk" and "Squawk." Meg knew their real names were William and Seth. The strange nicknames made very little sense to her, especially since William had the higher-pitched voice, while Seth possessed the beaklike nose.

"Fifteen, eh." Ken commented. "You can probably add at least two or three more." He turned away from the monitor to face his team. "They will likely have at least a couple of scouts with them. There's only five of us, and that's counting Winston."

He waved dismissively at the young man. All Winston could to in protest was to blush uncomfortably and push the frame of his glasses more firmly up his nose.

Ken continued to speak. "We can get Sergeant Harris and his guys to join us, but that still only gives us eight fighting men. Sorry — and women. I figure they have us outnumbered at least two to one. Squawk, how much time have we got?"

The signalman seemed unperturbed by the new nickname. "This camera is set up one and a half miles from our location. It's pretty much straight to the east. There is another camera set up about a thousand yards out, and we have a couple of cameras overlooking our gate, so we should be able to watch their approach."

"Do we have any more footage?" Winston asked Seth/Squawk.

"Not as of yet. This coverage is only about fifteen minutes old, and it's all bush in that direction. I figure that they haven't reached the next camera yet."

Winston turned back to Ken. "Have you considered that maybe these are friendlies?"

"Nope." The sergeant replied without hesitation. "First of all, nobody knows this location, yet this crew is heading straight toward us. Secondly, they would have tried to contact us if they were friendly. I saw not one but two radios on those men."

Winston nodded. So did Meg. That made sense.

"Speaking of radios," Ken told Hawk, "can you run over to Sergeant Harris and let him know what we've discovered. Tell him to get in touch with General Davies if possible." He turned to Megan as he continued to address the sergeant. "Maybe he can send some help..."

Megan could tell from the look in Ken's face that he expected none.

"We sure as hell could use some." He finished with a scowl.

Chapter 48

Theodore

November 23, 2:00 P.M.

"**D**on't let it happen again." Theodore remembered Dave's expression, guilt, pain and rage all vying for control over the president's features.

What does that even mean? He pondered his dead friend's words.

"Deer."

"Huh?" Theodore snapped out of his daydream.

"Uh. Just a deer, sir," Fred answered, nodding toward the field to their right with his chin.

The deer scrambled away with a combination of bounds and sprints.

Or does a deer gallop? He sighed as he lost sight of the animal.

At least it's not more zombies.

Theodore shuddered as he remembered their first encounter with the undead. Sure, he'd heard about it in Olympus. He'd watched the news and seen the videos on the internet.

Front row seats to the apocalypse. How did we get so seriously fucked?

There were no zombies in the bunker. The powers that be were smart enough to know the game by then. Anybody that fell really sick got taken downstairs. None of those people were seen again.

Ken and his platoon took care of that. Until only Ken remained. That guy must be messed up ...

But they did what they had to do. They didn't want zombies roaming around the bunker. After having experienced them in real life, Theodore couldn't blame them.

Yesterday's travel had been a disaster. They'd left Olympus quickly enough, following the main road out. Unfortunately, the powers that be had blocked the road with massive concrete blocks near the bottom of the mountain. There was no way through. Instead, they had to return practically to their starting point and resort to using roads that were actually little more than dirt paths.

The going was excruciatingly slow. They followed the wrong path and ended up having to backtrack for a while. The mood was far from optimal. They traveled for hours and had to fill up before they had even left the park. On that front they were all right: The back of the Jeep was jam-packed with jerrycans of fuel. No need to take risks and stop at a gas station.

Heck, we wouldn't even have made it to a gas station!

Unsurprisingly, they had not seen a single soul — living or dead — all day. They made it out of the park near sundown, so Theodore started looking for a place to spend the night. He figured the whole setback with the roads did have a silver lining, as they would be camping out in the middle of nowhere. The field they eventually pulled into seemed like the perfect spot, too.

At least they thought so.

They woke up in the middle of the night when something banged against the side of their vehicle. It was pitch-black out. Both men were disoriented as they looked around to spot what it was. The next moment they saw their first zombie. The eyeless monstrosity wore overalls but no shirt, which made Theodore guess it had been a farmer in life.

Farmer John, his subconscious mind dubbed it.

The zombie appeared unsure as it slapped hesitantly at the jeep. Its hesitancy was gone the moment Fred came face to face with it and cried out in alarm. After that, Farmer John grew quite violent. It lunged face first, smacking into the driver's side window. Luckily, it caught the door jamb, as it would have likely shattered the glass. Luckily for Fred and Theodore — not for the zombie, whose face was a mess.

Fred searched his pockets frantically for the key, even as Farmer John slammed both fists into the car. Theodore's training took over. Before Fred realized it, the general had stepped out of the vehicle, wearing nothing but boxers and a t-shirt. And wielding his sidearm.

He circled around the back of the jeep and got the zombie in his sights.

Headshots. Headshots only.

"Hey."

The zombie spun and started toward Theodore.

BLAM—BLAM. Theodore had shot it twice in the head before it took its second step.

The zombie crumpled to the ground. Theodore got closer for a better look. It was hard to make out its features in the dark. He leaned in then grunted in disgust when the smell of decay assaulted his nose.

"More coming!" Fred's muffled warning came through the glass.

The vehicle roared to life a moment later, which in turn spurred Theodore into action. The general stepped back around it, reaching his door just as Fred turned on his headlights.

"Sweet mother of Jesus!" Theodore exclaimed as indistinct shapes turned into dead people.

He wasn't sure if it was a trick of the light, but they appeared almost gray in color. None of them had eyes, and they were mostly bald — even the ones that had been women in life. Their gaping maws seemed to reach for him. Theodore felt a cold flush run down his spine, and he fumbled with the doorhandle.

The door opened when the nearest zombie reached the front of the vehicle. Theodore got in as quickly as he could and pulled it shut just as the zombie slammed a hand down on the hood of the jeep.

"Get us out of here," he grunted through clenched jaws.

The zombie had stepped around the front of the vehicle, so Fred released the brake. They jerked forward — Theodore catching sight of an unimaginably horrible face as they shot past.

"Careful now."

The vehicle rocked and jumped along the uneven ground. Fred slowed down as he drove through the field, avoiding obstacles and zombies alike.

They had laughed with mirthless relief when they hit the tarmac and sped away.

Neither of the men had talked about it since then. They had also decided that they would sleep in full gear from then on.

"Deer."

For the second time, Theodore was snapped out of a daydream — a bad one, this time.

They watched a small herd of deer cross the road and jump the fence to enter the adjacent field. Both nodded, impressed by the leaping power of the creatures.

Five minutes later, Theodore was getting bored again. The view out of his window was repetitive. A bit of countryside followed by some gas stations and mini-marts, followed by more countryside. They were taking the long way to the Yorktown naval station, giving a wide berth to populated areas such as Charlottesville and Richmond. He was glad that they weren't going to Norfolk, which would have been a move obvious rendezvous location. The greater

Norfolk area had about half a million inhabitants. Yorktown, on the other hand, only had a couple hundred. Williamsburg, the nearest town to the north, had fifteen thousand. Not that fifteen thousand wasn't a problem. Or hundreds, for that matter.

Can't avoid 'em all.

Theodore just hoped that the people he was going to meet had kept a low profile.

For now, there was nothing to do but look out the window. Which was not easy, when you only had one eye. It was still pretty damn boring.

Theodore decided to do a self-check. His arm was in a cast. It gave off that dull pain he was familiar with. After all, he'd broken plenty of bones before. The eye didn't hurt at all. His neck was sore from that other shard, though. He put his hand on his chest, where the bullet had entered and Dr. Chopra had subsequently cut into him. He felt a tinge of pain with every deep breath he took, but other than that it didn't hurt much either. The flesh wound on his leg, that one hurt like the Dickens.

Dickens... Does anybody say that, anymore?

Theodore had to admit one thing: He was lucky to be alive.

"Hey, Fred."

"Hmm?" Fred kept his eyes on the road as he drove.

"I never did thank you for saving my life." That did make Fred turn his face. "You know, the firefight back in the bunker. I heard that a guy had me dead to rights. You came out of the control room and took him out."

"Oh, that." Fred looked ahead for a moment. "It really was nothing. I was so scared that I sprayed bullets everywhere. Surprised that I hit him, really."

"Well, you got him. And saved my life. I want to thank you for that, son."

Fred smiled timidly and mumbled, "You're welcome."

They drove in silence for a while before Theodore spoke again. "Was that the first man you'd ever shot?"

Fred's expression turned serious. He nodded.

"I understand, Fred," Theodore said. The young soldier turned to meet the old man's single eye. Theodore hoped that Fred could feel his empathy. "I was a mess after my first mission. Killed not one but two people on that day. Yes, people. One of them was a woman, although I didn't know it at the time ... Anyway, that fucked me up pretty good for a while. My old sergeant got me through it. He told me that I did what I had to do. What I was paid to do. And on top of that, it was either those people or me and my team. That was all true, of course. But what really helped was when he said that it was good for me to be upset about it. *Keeps you human,*' he said to me."

Fred seemed to be near tears. He swallowed hard and got control of his emotions.

"Thank you, sir ... That helps."

They drove some more in silence. After a minute, Theodore turned sharply to face Fred. "Sprayed bullets, you said?"

"Yeah."

"Well, hell, son. I think you might have caught me with one of those strays!"

The vehicle jerked slightly as Fred reacted in shock. Theodore was already laughing.

"Just kidding, Fred." He laughed again. "I don't think you got me. But I do recommend that you take careful aim next time."

They chuckled.

"Yes sir. I will, sir."

"Did you lose anybody?" The question was sudden and felt out of place. Theodore surprised himself by asking it.

Fred's face fell. "My dad," he answered after a moment. "I just hope he didn't turn into one of those..." There was no need to finish that sentence.

"What about a wife? Kids?"

Fred guffawed. "Ah, no, sir. I guess I'm married to the corps. Me, and the other Radioheads."

"Radioheads?"

"Yeah. That's what our unit called ourselves. We've been together for a while. Thought that we'd give ourselves a nickname. Better than Signalman Squad Alpha, second platoon, Charlie company, second battalion of the fourth infantry division." He rolled his head as he went through the various levels of bureaucracy. "And every one of those called themselves something, too."

"Oh yeah?" This wasn't news to Theodore, but he encouraged the young man to expound.

"Sure. Our platoon was called the Warriors. Warriors!" He shook his head. "Couldn't think of anything more original than that, I suppose."

Theodore snickered. "Heck, son. My unit used to be called the Spades!"

Fred's eyes flared wide in surprise.

"Oh, I know what you're thinking — but it wasn't that." Theodore laughed. "We were called the Spades because we were always digging latrine ditches!"

Chapter 49

Chapter

November 22, 2:30 P.M., The Ren

Rosa was curious. Claire had pulled her aside and then beckoned to her. "What is it?" She caught up to the gray-haired woman halfway down the stairs.

Claire smiled shyly. "Just follow me."

They descended the stairs and walked down the hall — toward the room the two women shared with Shelley and Maria.

She showed Rosa in. Near the window, a table had been set up. Several paper-fiber egg flats sat on the table. Rosa immediately knew what Claire had been up to.

"You're growing plants!" she said with an excited clap of her hands.

The women walked up to the table and looked down on the egg cartons. Five 12" by 12" flats sat on the table side by side. Instead of holding twenty-four eggs each, they now held a small amount of dirt. Shoots of various sizes and hues of green poked through the dirt.

"I found a bunch of seeds in one of the closets." Claire waved at the closets that lined the front wall of the classroom. "So I decided to give it a shot."

"You must have been growing these for a little while," Rosa exclaimed in surprise. She looked over at her cot, less than ten fifteen feet away. "How did we not see this before?"

"I've been putting these out every day, after everybody has gotten up." Claire shrugged. "I guess I didn't want anybody fussing about it."

"Fuss about it? This is great." Rosa spontaneously hugged the woman.

Claire smiled as they released each other. "It's been a good distraction."

"Do you know what they are?"

Claire frowned. "I forgot to mark down what I had planted. I know these ones though." She pointed at one group of small seedlings. "They're tomato. I took the innards of one of the last fresh tomatoes we had and planted them. To my surprise, they actually seem to be doing something."

They were doing more than something. In fact, several of the plants appeared to have already outgrown their miniature pots.

Rosa smiled at the older woman. "This is really good. And it makes you feel good — I can tell."

"That one is a pepper plant."

Both ladies turned in surprise at the sound. Q had ventured several steps into the room. The teenager looked hesitant. His eyes traveled from the seedlings to Claire.

"Yes, I think you're right." Claire broke the tension and smiled as she spoke. "Come, see." She invited the youngster over with a wave.

"You probably know what all these are," Rosa suggested as Q walked up.

Q smiled at Rosa and blushed slightly. —

"That's peppers. Not sure what kind, though. These are tomatoes, and these ones here look like herbs. Basil and"—he leaned in and squinted—"cilantro." He held his hand over the plants as he talked. "I think this might be thyme."

"Wow. You really do know your plants." Claire patted the youngster on the back. Q smiled at the praise.

"You've done the right thing, getting these started in the egg cartons." His expression turned more serious as he looked down at them. "But they're going to need to be replanted real soon, or they will become root-bound." Q pointed at one set of plants that seemed to be well ahead of the rest in growth. "Especially that lettuce there. They will need more room so that you can get some good leaves off them." He touched one of the leaves and nodded knowingly. "Yep. they're ready to be transplanted."

"I wonder if they have any plant pots lying around in the school..." Rosa mused.

"I think so. I mean, they had these seeds." Claire looked over at Q. "Do you want to help us find some pots?"

"Yeah, sure." Q's face lit with excitement. He caught himself and added more coolly, "Beats waiting around for Joe and the rest to return."

Rosa nodded in agreement. "I know what you mean. Keeping busy like this ... helps."

"My guess is that the pots will be in the storage room." Claire was already marching to the door.

Two minutes later, they found themselves in the storage. Along the way, they had picked up a fourth person. Maria immediately wanted to help.

The young girl was already walking up to the closets. "I'll check these."

She hit the jackpot on the third closet door she pulled open. They spontaneously high-fived each other.

"You're going to need more dirt." Q suggested. "I can run out and get some."

"Right." Rosa accompanied the teenager to the door. "I know where we can get a couple of buckets."

"Wait!" Maria hustled over. "I'm coming too."

Q stopped at the door. He turned around, his expression thoughtful. "Claire, would you be okay if we set up the plants in another place? You're not getting enough light down here."

"Of course. Where do you suggest?"

The young man thought it over for a second. "The gym. You've got high windows at pretty much every angle — so you should get plenty of light."

"And there's plenty of room in there for us to set up," Rosa agreed. "You know, I think that the rest will also enjoy seeing these plants."

Rosa, Maria and Q turned away, leaving Claire in the supply room. She could hear them travel down the hall, muttering excitedly. A smile crept into her face. Deep down she had known that planting those seeds was going to create something positive.

"Cool," Steve commented as he scanned the indoor garden. "Yeah," Q said.

They had set up an impressive system, of which he was quite proud. Four metal shelves had been attached to each other, back-to-back. The outside ones only had the bottom two shelves, while the inner ones only had their top two shelves, creating somewhat of a pyramid shape. Q had explained that each tier would get maximum sun this way.

Others had noticed their activity and joined in the effort, and when all was done nearly a dozen people had participated. They stood around their construction now, admiring their work and wishing that the freshly transplanted plants would grow in front of their very eyes.

Then the bell rang.

"They're back!" Ethan shouted from down the hall.

The group rushed to the front door with an excited buzz. Ethan was already locking the second door in a wide-open position.

Q followed the group outside with Steve in his wake. He caught sight of the buses as they entered the school grounds. One was already turning into the parking lot, while another vehicle was coming down the street.

"Holy shit. How many people did they rescue?" somebody commented.

"All right, folks!" Joe came jogging up. "We're going to need to do some shuffling."

He pulled out a sheet of paper from his back pocket and studied it for a moment. "Listen, this will just be temporary — so don't freak out."

"Tammy and Breanne. Need you to move your stuff into Rosa's room. Rosa, can you help them get situated please?"

Neither Tammy nor Breanne freaked out. They simply nodded and turned back to the school.

"Melissa. Can you move your and John's stuff in with us? We'll be roomies for a few days. Christine, please help her."

Melissa nodded curtly and turned on her heel.

"Michelle and Romy. Can you move your stuff in with Emily, Abi and Nat? Sarah, I need you to move in with them also."

Michelle and Romy started back. Sarah hesitated, however. "What about Jack?" she asked.

Joe nodded. He had anticipated this. "Jack is to move in with BB and Steve. Steve, maybe you can help Jack out?"

Q looked over at Steve. The boy had nodded mutely, but his eyes were glued to something in the parking lot. The color had drained from his face.

He was about to ask Steve what the problem was when Joe spoke again.

"Q, can you move both your stuff and Keith's into Bill and Ben's room?" Joe folded up the piece of paper and stuck it in his back pocket.

"Sure." Q had looked up at Joe. When he turned back to Steve, the boy was gone.

Curiously, he stared into the parking lot. The final vehicle had pulled into the school grounds and Bill was closing the gate. *What did he see, to get him spooked?* Nothing looked out of the ordinary. Well, for the first time the school parking lot was full as two school buses and three Humvees parked wherever there was space, and dozens of people milled around.

"That frees up five rooms," Joe continued. "We will also convert the media room into a bedroom for the time being, as well as the gym downstairs. Claire, can you take a few volunteers and set up the remaining cots — six to a room? When you run out, we can resort to sleeping bags."

Claire touched Maria and Rosa on the shoulders, and the threesome turned around. "I'll help you guys," Shelley offered, and followed them inside.

Q went in after the women.

"Looks like they rescued a lot of people," Shelley said as he passed.

"That's a lot of mouths to feed." Q couldn't keep the comment from slipping out.

Joe kept himself busy for the next hour, organizing the movement of supplies and people. He roped Christine into assisting him, and wherever he was, his daughter was never far away, clipboard in hand. The operation ran smoothly.

For the most part.

Frank, the self-proclaimed leader of the safe-zone people, complained loudly when "their" supplies were moved into the Ren.

"That's our stuff." He had marched up to Joe.

The police officer who had introduced himself as Dan shadowed the short man.

"Fine." Joe lifted his hands in supplication. "I'll keep a tally of your supplies, so that they don't get mixed up with ours." He waved at the clipboard in Christine's hand.

"Don't get me wrong, Joe." Frank's expression softened. "We might well all join together into one community ... But what if things don't work out? Let's just make sure that we all know who owns what."

That news wouldn't please John. He'd radioed in to Joe as they travelled back to the Ren, gleeful about all the ammunition and weapons these new folks were bringing to the table.

Deal with that later.

"So we'll keep the new supplies separated from the existing supplies. For now, we just need to get everything moved inside," Joe said. "I think that the more important question is how are we going to house everybody. I've asked my people to free up some rooms. It will be crowded for now, but I'm sure we can figure out a workable solution."

His thoughts were already on the houses across the street. They had been cleared a while ago. As a matter of fact, the whole area seemed to be clear. Not a single undead had approached the Ren during the entire operation.

So far. Don't go jinxing yourself, Joe.

"I have forty-one people with me. Do you have enough room for them?" Frank frowned in disapproval before the answer.

"We've got six classrooms and a small gym. I figure we can squeeze five to six into each classroom and the remainder in the gym."

Frank shook his head. "That will never do."

Joe sighed and also shook his head, but in exasperation. "Look, man, we're trying to figure this out."

"I'm not your 'man.' I am the leader of all these people and have an obligation to ensure that they are fed and housed."

Joe's nostrils flared. He could sense that he was about to lose his temper. Frank noticed and took an involuntary step back, bumping into Dan behind him. Nobody said a word.

After a moment, Joe's expression softened. "Of course, Frank. You're right, of course. You've done an admirable job, keeping your people safe. We'll figure out a solution. But for now, why don't we get everybody safely inside the school? We can continue our discussion there."

Frank treated Joe to a deadpan expression. After a moment, his face cracked into a broad grin. "Good. Yes, that sounds reasonable." He signaled to the men behind him. One of them stepped up. "Organize our people to move all the supplies inside." He spoke to the man without breaking eye contact with Joe, overtly flaunting his authority.

"Christine here will show you where they can put your supplies." Joe turned and started walking back to the school. John fell in step with him.

"I saw that," John said as the two men got to the steps. His tone of voice expressed his confusion.

Joe stopped with his foot on the first step and looked at the other man. He grinned, confusing John even more. "I was going to pop that little prick's head off. Then I thought about what Craig would have done. He would have massaged the guy's ego but still gotten his way."

He ascended the steps. John hurried to catch up to him.

"I'm surprised at how well it worked."

They got to the doorway and stopped. John looked at the crowd of people milling near the buses. He frowned. "All those men hang around that Frank character. But the odd thing to me is that they don't seem to be associated with any of the women ..."

John was right. Joe observed the leader of the safe zone as he directed the men. He had not noticed until now that other than the ten or so guys who hung around Frank, the refugees were all women. And they all looked scared.

Chapter 50

Donald

November 22, 4:00 P.M., Outside of Olympus

"They know we're here," Sword Jaheem confirmed, the low boom of his voice seeming to come from deep within his barrel chest.

Captain Donald did not respond immediately. Instead, he continued to observe the tall metal gate set directly into the mountainside. The rusty metal almost fit perfectly into the gray-brown rockface.

"Gut feeling?" he asked his second-in-command.

"Uh-huh," the sword rumbled

Donald lowered the binoculars. "Yeah. I think you're right, Jaheem."

The two men stood just within the treeline, no more than fifty yards from Olympus' front door. There was really nothing to see, other than the gate itself and the road that led directly away from it. They knew that a vast wealth of military intelligence lay within that bunker. It was their mission to get it. More importantly, at least to Paladin Kevin, was the eradication of the last remnant of government. He still remembered the communiqué quite clearly.

Capture the bunker that they so arrogantly named Olympus. Gain access to the military information we seek. But make no mistake, your primary mission is to crush the president's men. Crush the idea of the government, and the United States. Your mission, above all else, is to remove the last modicum of organized opposition, so that none can stand in our way.

"Captain Harry feels that we should wait for Westland. Figures that he will know exactly what to do." Donald continued.

He looked over his shoulder at his sword. Jaheem betrayed no emotion. Donald spat on the ground to show what he thought of that idea.

"I told the dwarf that we don't need to wait. I told him that if there had been a large force inside, they would have sallied out and attacked us on our approach. Hell, they could have sent a couple of drones to wipe us out," Donald said. "But they didn't. Because there's hardly anybody left in there. The last report stated as much. All they've got is their precious bunker. Our diminutive captain had to agree with that."

He was rewarded with an amused grunt. Turning, he had another long look at the gate.

"They probably figure that they are safe in there. Like a turtle in its shell." Donald spat on the ground again. It was a disgusting habit according to his wife.

Ex-wife. Then: *Dead ex-wife.* He spat again, just out of spite.

"Yeah-huh," Jaheem agreed. "Ain't no way of getting them out 'cept the hard way."

Donald grinned at his sword. Jaheem was about as tough and solid as the rock he was standing on. "Just the way you like to do it, eh?"

Jaheem nodded with a confident smile. "My specialty."

"All right. We have Harry's approval to use his precious sappers. They should be getting ready. Go ahead and round them up."

Jaheem saluted, turned and walked away. "We gonna crack that shell wide open," he said as he left.

F ive minutes later, Jaheem had tracked down the squad of sappers. Four men had spread an assortment of materials on a large sheet. It almost looked like they were preparing for a picnic.

Especially the way they crawl over that sheet like ants.

He'd walked up, but the sappers had largely ignored him. He had introduced himself and was met with grunts. Then, just as he was about to get annoyed, one of them introduced himself.

The man had looked up with annoyance, his expression clearly indicating that the massive man did not intimidate them and, in fact, was wasting their precious time.

"Raul."

That was all he'd said. Jaheem looked him up and down and decided he was the most experienced looking of the bunch. Raul was also the grimmest-looking of the four — but not by much.

"Captain Donald wants maximum effect. He figures that the bigger and louder the explosion, the more likely that the opposition will surrender."

The four men still ignored him. They continued to dig though their supplies for items. Raheem noted with annoyance that they all seemed to be chewing something, loudly smacking and slurping as they worked. They wordlessly passed items back and forth, communicating with nothing more than grunts and gestures.

Jaheem waited for a response to his order but got none. He shuffled from foot to foot, then tried again. "What is all this shit, anyways?"

Raul looked up at him with something close to belligerence.

"There is enough 'shit' here to blow your Captain Donald over there, and all of us, to kingdom come. You ought to show it some respect." Raul's regarded the sword coolly, his sunken cheeks working as he chewed.

Jaheem was not a man that quickly angered, which worked out well for Raul. He also thought about what Raul had said. Captain Donald stood about fifty feet away.

Okay. Some respect.

He looked down at the sapper again, but the man had already turned back to his task.

Sappers are weirdos, Jaheem confirmed to himself.

"You'll get your explosion," Raul said as he worked.

This time Jaheem did not bother to respond. He watched them work for a while. Their hands never stopped, and they seemed to communicate without speaking as they handed materials back and forth on unspoken signals. All four chewed furiously, occasionally leaning over to spit a brown gob into the grass.

Bunch of redneck chew-eating bumpkins. Jaheem was disgusted by the habit. It made sense to him that none of the men smoked, though.

Guess they ain't that stupid.

All four sappers stood up abruptly.

"We're ready," Raul announced. He held an array of blocky objects, wires, and shiny metal in his hands, as did the other three.

Jaheem called his own squad over, and they joined their sword as he followed the four sappers toward the edge of their camp.

On Jaheem's signal, nine men cautiously approached the gate. They got there without incident. There was no cover, so the men all knelt and covered the metal portal. If the defenders chose to act now, they could catch the sappers and Jaheem's squad with their pants down.

They needn't have worried. There was no activity whatsoever.

Are there even any defenders?

Jaheem backed his men up several feet to give the sappers some space. They once again knelt and watched the four sappers get to work. Their guns were no longer aimed at the gate, though. There was no point.

For a full minute the sappers worked in silence. They almost moved too quickly for Jaheem to make sense of it all.

Suddenly they all froze.

What the—? He listened closely and could make out a whirring sound. Jaheem turned his head to locate the sound, then raised his rifle along with his men. The whirring sound was coming from somewhere near the door.

Shit and we've got no cover! He was about to order his men back.

"Wha—" one of the sappers exclaimed, but his voice was drowned by the sound of automatic gunfire.

Jaheem hit the dirt. He lifted his rifle and looked for an enemy but saw none. Then, as abruptly as the barrage had started, it stopped. The sound of bullets being fired was replaced by screams.

What the fuck was that?! He looked over at the squad members to his left. They had been cut to pieces. Two of them did not move. The third lay in the dirt, screaming and holding his hip.

"Get away from there!" he ordered the sappers as he got back to his feet.

His last squad member went over to the wounded man, as did two of the sappers. That was another mistake, as the automatic gunfire started up again. One of the sappers went down, the other screamed and limped out of the spray of bullets. His wounded man took several bullets to the midsection and stopped screaming.

His last man jumped forward and half dragged, half carried the sapper back to safety. The other two sappers had already hightailed it back to camp.

Jaheem spotted the culprit this time.

"It's a fucking turret." He helped his man drag the wounded sapper away.

As they retreated, he noticed that the turret didn't seem to be capable of moving. He let another soldier take the wounded man off his hands and walked back toward the gate a few steps. The turret sat in the rock just inside the entryway. It was cleverly hidden but seemed to have a limited angle on the approach. Jaheem stored that info in his mind as he turned back to camp.

Captain Harry was the first man to greet him at the tree line. "Some protection you are, Sword Jaheem." The disapproval was clear on his face.

"There was a turret..." The excuse felt lame under the scrutiny of the angry captain.

"You just lost me one of my sappers, and another one is hurt bad!"

The accusation, along with the sneer of derision made Jaheem snap. In one step he got in the captain's face, which now registered fear. He grabbed the front of the man's jacket, his own face red with rage.

"I just watched three men of my squad get torn to pieces, you dumb shit!" he spat in the captain's face.

His grip was so tight that he nearly lifted the scrawny man. He had a vision of tossing the captain. Luckily for Harry, several men quickly stepped in and separated them.

"What the hell is going on here?" Captain Donald came running up to the altercation.

"Your man assaulted me!" Captain Harry had regained some of his composure and bravery now that a handful of men were holding back Jaheem.

Donald immediately addressed his man. "Jaheem, stand down. Get back to my tent. I'll deal with you there." He turned to Harry. "Sorry, Captain Harry. We've both lost good men just now."

"My sappers are worth many times your grunts," Harry responded.

Jaheem heard this, and it took all his willpower not to turn around and take another run at the man.

"I respectfully disagree with you, Harry." Donald had his men's back. "Now, why don't we forget about the things we just said and did, and work together toward our common goal." It wasn't a question.

Harry drew himself to his full height. "You're asking me to let this insubordination — no, the *assault* of a senior officer — go unpunished?"

He approached the other captain, full of indignation and flanked by several of his men. Unconsciously, Donald's men went to stand beside their leader.

"I will have that man court-martialed. He is done."

Jaheem was ready for a fight. But Captain Donald merely chuckled. That took Harry aback, and he looked up at the other man in surprise.

"You're stuck in the old world, Harry. The dead world. We won't be conducting court-martial procedures any more than we'll be marching in lockstep on July the fourth."

Harry was about to speak, so Donald quickly continued.

"I promise you that I will discipline Sword Jaheem for his transgression. Now I suggest we drop the matter and see to our wounded." The look on his face brooked no argument.

Harry hesitated for a moment, stuck in indecision. Finally, he just shook his head in disgust and took off in the direction of the screams.

Chapter 51

Ben

November 22, 6:00 P.M., The Ren

B en stood back for a moment and checked the time.
Pretty soon.

He had dragged a couple of tables together and laid out multiple items upon them. Ben had a mental list of the items that he would need to take with him — a result of all the training he'd had in his earlier life as a Rosae Crucis optio.

Bedroll. Check.

Thermal wear. Check.

He went over the materials, ticking off the boxes. Then he carefully put each item into his backpack, in the exact order he'd been taught. Items that he wouldn't need until camp was set up were at the bottom. The heavier gear, including the stove and some food, were packed in the center. Things he might need at short notice like his rain gear and his first aid kit, were near the top.

The table contained a myriad of items. Probably not a camper's wet dream — but a pretty good spread for any guy going out for a scramble. He should know. His training had included plenty of scrambles — an ultimate type of camping, usually without a tent and various other comforts.

Except this scramble would likely be a rather dangerous one. He was going to need more than the basic camping gear.

On that note, I'm going to have to borrow a few things.

Ben finished putting the items into the bag and closed the ties. Next, he hefted the bag.

Yep. Still a few items to add. Specifically, weapons and ammunition.

He knew those things would be heavy. But also, very essential.

Ben was confident that he could get into the armory. Security was extremely lax at the Ren. Ben was sure that John was not too happy about it, but the vast majority of people were civilians, so what was the guy to do.

Getting into the armory should be simple.

He just wasn't exactly sure what he would take. Ben figured that at the least he needed a rifle and a pistol. He was hoping for a melee weapon as well. One of the e-tools seemed suitable for that.

Ben couldn't help noticing the new Bushmaster that John had brought with him on his last expedition. It was a sweet weapon, and Ben was quite seduced by it. So much so that he seriously considered stealing it.

Wonder if he's left it in the armory or taken it to his room. Don't think I'd part with it ...

As he changed his mind about taking the Bushmaster, Ben shook his head. He wouldn't need most of the modules that came with it. And leaving those behind would feel like a waste.

Not to mention that John would throttle me when I got back.

If I get back...

But he had no time for those thoughts. He was going on a mission that required all his focus. This was no different than his other missions.

Assess, plan, and execute. Just like you've been taught.

With that lesson in mind, he checked the time once more. It was just about time to go.

His window of opportunity wouldn't be large. However, with all these newcomers around he was confident that he could make it out unnoticed. The best time to strike was when your opponent was preoccupied — and things were pretty hectic at the Ren right now.

Opponent. The word stuck with him for a moment. How many times had he reconsidered? How many times had he had doubts?

I am on the right side now. I know it.

He lifted his bag and swung it over his shoulder, then cast one last glance around the room he'd shared with Bill. He caught his reflection in the window. There was no sign of all the stitches in his head, other than his hair looking somewhat messed up. He gingerly touched the roughened surface of his skull. A small portion of his cast showed past his sleeve.

Ben's eyes moved from his cast to his bearded face.

You look a different man.

It gave Ben a strange feeling of satisfaction. As if he had left the person he'd been behind and donned a new skin. A new persona.

No looking back, Ben.

Time to go.

Chapter 52

Nancy

November 23, 10:00 A.M.

Nuggets stepped out of cover. He raised his nose and circled twice. Nancy thought she could even see the dog perk its ears. She wasn't about to question the animal's abilities. Nuggets had steered them clear of trouble on several occasions already.

It was getting a lot tougher, though.

Nancy was stunned by the sheer number of zombies they had seen so far. What was worse, they all seemed to be heading in the same direction.

Toward the Ren. Toward my friends.

The previous night had been particularly frightening. They were alerted by Nuggets and just managed to sneak into an abandoned house before the zombies appeared. That was at sundown. Next, they had another three hours of nerve-shattering silence, as a horde of zombies passed within a hundred yards of their hiding place. They tried to count the horde but were forced to give up quickly. It was massive.

"Unstoppable," Dean said under his breath.

Nancy heard it and was terribly dismayed. "How are we going to save my friends?" she asked the broad-shouldered man.

It took him a long time to answer that. Even then, his answer was not really an answer at all. "We need to warn them about what's coming." It was almost reason enough for Nancy to give up hope.

Almost.

Instead, they had snuck out before the sun had fully risen and continued their trek toward the Ren, counting on luck and the innate abilities of Nuggets.

Nancy was drawn back to the present as Dean moved out of cover beside her. Apparently, Nuggets was satisfied that the coast was clear. So was Nancy, who followed Dean.

They silently crossed the street and snuck around the side of another house. Nancy sighed in dismay as they entered the back yard.

Another fence.

It was the only way to travel. The undead seemed to stick to the roads. They also managed to move a lot quicker than the hordes this way — traveling as the crow flies, as it were.

Dean scanned the adjoining back yard through the gaps in the fence and quickly decided that it was clear. Nuggets would have warned him if it wasn't, but the young man insisted on checking for himself. Nancy couldn't help but also peek through the gaps.

A small gasp escaped her as she saw something that she'd thought she would never see again.

Dean looked at her, his eyes wide. They had been very good at keeping the noise to a minimum, so he knew this was important.

She signaled for him to come over and peek through the fence. There was a slight downward slope, so Dean could see beyond the next several blocks. A solid-looking red object loomed in the distance.

"It's the wall," she whispered into his ear as he leaned his head to look. "We're almost there."

Chapter 53

Winston

November 23, 11:15 A.M., Olympus security room.

At first the grainy picture showed nothing out of the ordinary. Just what looked to be a large and poorly lit concrete tunnel with a set of metal doors at the end.

Then, in the matter of a heartbeat, it showed a flash, flying debris and dust, and finally nothing.

The blast could be heard all the way in the observation room.

And everywhere else in the compound, I imagine. But only seen by us two. The only people to watch were Megan and Winston.

Winston had been tasked with being the defenders' eyes. His job was to observe the enemy and report any significant events or major movement.

Megan was to be the runner. A task that she felt was way below her station and abilities — something she had made more than clear to Winston on several occasions.

"Not sure if you actually need to warn them that the door is down ..." Winston looked up at the woman uncertainly.

"Do you still have eyes on them?" She ignored the attempt at humor.

They had known that the gate was about to be blasted apart, of course. They had been able to observe exactly what the Rosae Crucis men were doing thanks to an as-of-yet undiscovered camera, mounted surreptitiously in the trunk of a tree.

There was the briefest of moment of hesitation when several men approached the gate. Watching them plant what appeared to be explosives cast all doubts aside for the defenders. These were Rosae Crucis men, and they were here to take the last vestige of government out.

Guess I was wrong, Winston admitted to himself silently. He had hoped that these were good guys. He'd even said so to Ken and the rest as they watched the soldiers approach their position. But none of the others seemed to believe that. Still, he'd secretly held on to the hope that they were the cavalry, riding in to save the day.

Guess they're the cavalry, all right. And we're about to get run down.

Easy, Winston. Ken says we've got some cards to play yet.

Winston glanced at one of the monitors. It now showed the remains of the large metal door, as well as a bunch of rubble. It would be tough going to pick your way through that rubble, and access to the main tunnel would not be easy. Another camera set far back in the tunnel showed some movement as Sergeant Ken set up Hawk and Squawk to cover the tunnel. The approach into Olympus was probably the best place to try and stop the enemy.

Still, the sheer number of soldiers outside made it hard to believe that there was any hope of holding out.

Winston switched to another camera. Ken had disappeared, but he could see the two radio men poke their heads out of cover. Further down, the cloud of dust was already starting to clear.

Hawk and Squawk ... What the heck were their real names? It escaped Winston's mind. A poke from Megan reminded him to switch to yet another camera. This one was outside and gave a clear view of the area directly to the front.

"Nobody is moving. Looks like they're satisfied for the moment." Winston moved the tiny joystick and scanned the area. It did indeed look like the enemy had pulled back.

Ken had figured as much.

"The army is powerful, but slow moving," he'd said, "especially when somebody needs to make a decision."

In fact, Ken had gone on to suggest that they'd blow the gate and wait a while to see if there was any response from the defenders — preferably a big white flag. Failing that, they would cautiously close in and attempt to secure the gate area before any incursions into Olympus itself.

"They probably figured that we've got more turrets around. Learned their lesson."

Seemed that Ken had been pretty much right about everything so far.

They continued to watch for another full minute, but there was no enemy movement. Winston pointed at the screen at one point — they were posting sentries. Satisfied, Megan used her walkie-talkie to share this information with Ken.

Winston released the joystick. The view was locked on the blasted gate and about fifty yards in front of it.

"Good definition on this camera," Winston said.

The fact that most of the mechanical security devices inside Olympus had failed, but the ones outside, exposed to the elements, still worked, filled Winston with indignation and weirdly despondent amusement.

It's like Olympus has a sick sense of humor.

Just then the walkie-talkie chirped. "*I guess they're not stupid. I don't think they will be coming in any time soon. Probably afraid that there are more turrets. Which there are. Or a trap. Which there is. Over.*" Winston could almost picture the disappointment on Ken's face.

Sure, we've got more turrets, Winston agreed. *Won't do any good, though.*

The one at the gate had taken out a couple of enemies before it fried. Unfortunately, when it fried it also fried any others on its circuit, which included the turrets in the tunnel.

"*It's our move,*" Ken proclaimed. Megan looked at her walkie-talkie with wide eyes.

"What are you suggesting?" she asked after a moment. Her tone was full of apprehension. Winston wasn't sure if Ken would pick up on that.

Not sure if he'd care.

There was silence on the other end of the walkie-talkie. Ken must have had the talk button depressed, as Winston could hear a deep sigh.

That's the sound of a man thinking hard. Winston almost broke into a grin as he pictured the sour-faced soldier racking his brain. Another sound, this one sharp, told him that Ken had spat out a wad of that tobacco chew he seemed to love so much.

Still, Winston and Megan waited for him to speak.

"*Sometimes, you have to do what you have to do.*"

The cryptic words were met with confused stares directed at the walkie-talkie.

"*I'm calling back our guys. Sally, go get your dad. It's time for all of us to have a chat with Sykes.*"

Chapter 54

Megan

November 23, 4:55 P.M., Olympus — Presidential suite.

M egan shuffled from one foot to the other.

This place feels ... wrong. Especially for this meeting. "This place" was the president's quarters. The meeting was a negotiation between her dad; Known to everybody else as Senator Williams, and Sykes; Known to everybody in the room as a traitor.

Her dad had argued for this location. "Show him that we respect his position, and he will be more inclined to meet our terms." She disagreed, but here they were: In the former president's meeting area, awaiting the arrival of Sykes.

"Let me do the talking," her father reminded the group.

Ken nodded curtly, a sour expression on his face. The only others present at the meeting were herself and Dr. Chopra. Except she was just to act as security. The weight of the rifle slung over her shoulder also reminded her of this.

Megan started to daydream until Dr. Chopra's heavy dialect pulled her attention back.

"No, Senator Williams, nobody else has come down with the syndrome. Everybody is healthy." The doctor almost appeared to shake his head as he spoke, in contradiction to his words.

Forty-seven. Meg knew that there were forty-seven individuals left alive in Olympus. Her thoughts drifted back to the grainy images of the forces outside. A lot of enemies were at the gate. Less than the number of people at Olympus, but likely more than enough to get the job done.

They are all trained soldiers, and our gate lies in ruins ...

"Fuck." It took her a moment to realize that she had spoken aloud. She looked up, and sure enough everybody in the room was staring at her. "Sorry..."

She felt the color rising to her cheeks at the disapproving look on her dad's face. Ken, on the other hand, seemed to find it highly amusing and flashed a big grin. She almost expected him to give her a double thumbs up for her indiscretion.

She was spared any further embarrassment by the door swinging open.

Sykes stepped through, followed by Hawk and Squawk. Meg had given up remembering their real names.

They guided the former senator to a chair at the table before taking up positions by the door.

Sykes looked awful. A few days in the brig had done him no good. His clothing and hair were a mess, and he stank. On top of that, he was sporting the fading yellow green of bruises on his face.

Ken's handiwork.

Their supposed enemy looked uncomfortable. He fidgeted in his chair and didn't even attempt to compose himself.

"Tony," Senator Williams started, "we called you in here so that we can discuss a peaceful resolution to this situation."

Sykes' eyes flashed wide in obvious surprise, but he kept his mouth shut.

"You might have heard that explosion earlier. The people of your ... Order, are outside."

Sykes let that sink in. He nodded slowly.

Meg watched as her father leaned forward. "Now don't misunderstand me, Tony. You should know that we have more than enough resources to protect ourselves. Your comrades found this out first-hand when they assaulted our gate."

He watched his ex-colleague with an angry frown, only relaxing back into his seat when the other man made no response.

"I want to prevent further bloodshed. On both sides. Hell, you know a bunch of the people here. They're civilians and public servants. Surely you don't want any more people to die?"

"I know, Gene," Sykes finally responded, his eyes on the table-top in front of him. He looked up at the old senator. "I don't." Meg could see emotions play across the man's face. "For my part, I'm sorry."

This time it was Meg's dad who remained silent.

"Our mission ..." Sykes frowned as he thought briefly about his next words. "Our mission was to take over peacefully. We're not a bunch of murderers."

Ken scoffed at that, prompting an angry look from Sykes.

"We're not. Despite what you think, soldier."

"I think you and your *people* are the very definition of murderers."

"You're an animal!" Sykes reached up to his own face and turned back to Senator Williams. "Gene, this guy beat the crap out of me — even after I told him everything I knew!"

"Genocide," came from Ken's corner. Sykes nearly shot out of his chair.

"Okay, hold on," Meg's dad interjected, but his comment fell on deaf ears.

"It's people like you that have carried out the genocide!" Sykes yelled across the table. Ken just grinned.

Fuck, he is good at that. Megan couldn't help but be impressed with the soldier's poise.

"That's enough!" Senator Williams got to his feet and hit the table with the flat of his hand. He stared daggers at the antagonists. "Both of you, reel it in."

"Sorry. I'm done." Ken showed genuine contrition, something that Meg found highly confusing and suspicious.

Sykes looked just as confused at the soldier's statement. He ended up exhaling sharply and sank back in his seat.

"Good." Meg's dad sat down and addressed Sykes again: "We understand that you hold some kind of senior position in your organization?"

"Yes. I am what's called a 'sage' in the Order. Those soldiers outside?" He looked around him at the others. "I can order them to pull back. I can help you."

Meg's father nodded as if confirming his suspicion. "I think a ceasefire would be in the best interest of everybody involved."

Sykes nodded enthusiastically. "Yes. I agree. The time for violence has passed. Now it's time for diplomacy."

"I'm glad you feel that way." Senator Williams looked relieved. "I'm prepared to let you return to your people." He cast a sharp glance at Ken, who obviously disagreed. "In return for some concessions."

"I'm listening." Sykes had regained all his composure by this point. He even went so far as to comb his hair with his fingers and straighten his soiled suit jacket.

"Obviously, we need to cease and desist all hostilities. We ask that you order your men to stand down and retreat beyond the fences — you know, the ones at the bottom of the hill."

"Sounds reasonable."

"I'm sure you are aware of Olympus' security measures. We will be able to tell if you comply."

A little more enthusiastically, Sykes said, "Yes, Gene. You have my word."

Meg watched Ken, awaiting a reaction. The soldier scowled but swallowed his words.

Why doesn't he argue? He obviously doesn't trust Sykes.

Then again, neither do I.

However, Meg's father seemed convinced. "Good. Great." The senator clapped his hands together. "We can start negotiations once your people have pulled back. Starting with some humanitarian aid." He turned to the diminutive doctor at the end of the table. "Dr. Chopra." He inclined his head.

The doctor acknowledged him quickly and turned to Sykes. "We understand that several of your men were shot. We have the expertise and the equipment here to help them."

Sykes leaned forward. "Yes. Of course."

Meg stopped listening as the meeting continued into more mundane matters.

What are we doing? She was inclined to agree with the curmudgeonly sergeant, who she knew disapproved of this course of action wholeheartedly. But when she looked at Ken, his face betrayed no emotion.

That's weird. He should be looking like he is sucking an egg ...

"We'll need some guarantees," her dad stated. "I will get a truce agreement drafted."

"Yes, Gene. That's a good idea. Let's not put too many clauses in there. Just the ceasefire order. It will be easier for me to convince my people to agree to that."

Meg's father checked his watch. "It's after five p.m. I'll get the document written up this evening. Why don't we put you back into your old quarters? Let you get cleaned up? We can send you out tomorrow morning."

"Thank you, Gene. That's very generous of you. I give you my word that no more blood is going to be shed here." He looked at the others around the table. Dr. Chopra seemed convinced and smiled back at the man. Ken just stared at him with dead eyes.

"Okay," Meg's father stood up and extended his hand to Sykes. "Let's not waste any more time here and get on with it." Sykes got to his feet and the two men shook on it.

Good. That went well.

... I think.

Chapter 55

Harry

November 23, 9:00 PM, Rosae Crucis encampment near Olympus.

There was a soft tapping at the entrance.

"Enter."

The vestibule zipped open, and Raul stepped into the tent. Harry's tent was exactly the same as those of his men, except for the fact that he didn't have to share it with any other soldiers, leaving him room enough for a small fold-up desk. The captain sat behind that desk now as he observed Raul.

The sapper's face was dour.

"Stew's gone."

"Ah." Harry screwed up his face. "Damn ... Sorry, Raul."

Raul didn't show much emotion at the best of times. The man moved his jaw, likely chewing the tobacco he and his men seemed to be so fond of.

"Mind if I speak openly, sir?"

Harry scoffed. "I've never stopped you from speaking your mind before, Raul. What is it?"

Raul chewed twice, then looked around for a place to spit. Finding none, he stored the spit into some corner of his mouth instead.

"Tim and I were talking, sir. This is FUBAR."

Harry nodded. He'd been expecting this. "I don't suppose you mean FUBAR in the traditional sense."

"No sir."

Fucked Up by Assholes in the Rear. "You're right. Captain Donald rushed into this. We should have done more surveillance. Hell, there are probably cameras on us right now." Harry shook his head in disgust.

"Well, I'm glad you see it that way." Raul shifted from foot to foot before continuing. "Because we blame Captain Donald for this."

Harry knew what that meant. Raul and his crew of sappers had always enjoyed delivering justice.

"Now, hang on, Raul. We've got a job to do first. It isn't going to do any good getting even with Donald until the job is done."

Raul chewed on that for a moment. He slowly started to nod as Harry continued to speak.

"We're meeting in the morning to plan the main assault. Now, I'd rather wait until Captain Westland shows up with his men — but I'm not going to stop them, if Donald and his troops want to rush into that place." He waited for Raul to acknowledge before continuing. "The bottom line is this, Raul. We've got to take this bunker. What you do after the job is done is up to you. You got me?"

The sapper knew what that meant: plausible deniability. Tim and Raul would get their revenge. Captain Donald would suffer an unfortunate accident. Captain Harry just didn't want to know about it.

A smile slowly crept into the sapper's face. It deepened the lines in his cheeks and made him look ominous.

"I got you, sir."

Chapter 56

Shelley

November 24, 7:00 A.M.

Shelley awoke to the alarm. A quick look out her window showed that it was just getting light outside.

"Maybe that's Nancy," Claire said as she pulled on a sweater. "Maybe she's come back."

Shelley smiled at the older woman encouragingly, although she didn't think that this would be the case.

I doubt it, Claire. I don't think Nancy is ever coming back. But I don't want to say that and hurt your feelings.

They had just made it to their door when they heard gunshots.

Definitely not Nancy.

By the time they got to the stairs, they had counted at least another four gunshots. They knew their role and went straight up to the library, where they were joined in short order by several other residents.

It was of little use, though, as none of the new refugees knew this procedure. Shelley confirmed it when she looked around and only saw original Ren residents around her in the library.

"Should we go get the safe-zone folks?" she suggested. Nobody had a chance to answer as there was a yell outside, followed by another gunshot.

Christine stood up and tilted her head to listen. Shelley and several others followed suit. They could hear sounds of alarm and fear downstairs.

"That's it. I'm going down there," Christine said after several seconds of looking at each other and hearing all the noise coming from below.

Ethan put his hand on her shoulder. "No. You stay with Mom. I'll go look."

Shelley watched as Christine slapped Ethan's hand away. "Fuck you, Ethan. You're not Dad. I said that I'm going to take a look — and I am!" Before anybody could stop her, she was out the door.

Ethan bristled and started to follow his sister but hesitated after a couple of steps. Shelley could see his concern as he looked over his shoulder toward his mother. Shelley followed his gaze. Rachel sat in a chair, her face downcast. The woman's lips were moving.

What's she saying? Sounds like, "Got to keep my babies safe."

Shelley swung her gaze back to Ethan just in time to see him hang his head and sheepishly walk over to sit beside Rachel.

A couple of minutes later, Christine returned. Following in her wake were all the women from the safe zone. The refugees looked scared as they meekly entered the library. Shelley realized that, for the first time, the library felt full of people.

She tried to start a conversation with one particularly nervous woman who kept jerking her head at every gunshot, looking around anxiously as if zombies would burst into the library at any moment.

"Hey. We'll be fine. We've got lots of people to protect us." Shelley frowned as the woman hardly acknowledged her.

Are you really that afraid?

In the end, it didn't matter. The shooting stopped shortly after and the all clear signal rang downstairs. Shelley watched out of the corner of her eye as several Ren folks started explaining what the bell meant to the newcomers.

"I think it's over," Shelley said to her neighbor.

The woman turned her head but barely seemed to comprehend her. All around them, others were getting to their feet. The residents of the Ren were certainly the more boisterous group, joking and laughing amongst themselves — none more than Breanne. The stocky, much-bandaged woman joked and guffawed raucously. The refugees were decidedly more reserved. Especially the woman beside Shelley.

Like she is in shock or something.

"What happened to you guys at the safe zone?" she whispered under her breath. She hadn't meant for the other woman to hear, but the reaction was severe.

"Nothing!" The woman realized that she had spoken out loud and quickly lowered her head. She glanced around and seemed relieved that nobody was paying any attention to her. "Nothing. We—we're not supposed to talk to you." She got up and quickly joined the rest of the refugees.

Shelley watched them; they reminded her of certain animal species that crowded together when predators were nearby — but she couldn't spare it any more thought. She hurried to her feet and was among the first to leave the library.

Downstairs she turned into the hall toward the clinic. She met Joe near the entrance. He had just returned his weapon to the armory.

"No injuries, Shelley," he said, much to her relief.

Before she could respond, another man stepped in front of her and right up to Joe.

"We agreed to come here because we believed that this place was safe!"

It was Frank. He raised a finger, about to continue his reprimand. Joe looked at the finger near his face with a dangerous look, and Shelley noted how quickly Frank lowered his hand.

"You said that we would be safe here..." he continued, slightly less authoritative.

"You *are* safe," Joe responded. "Did you see how much firepower we were able to put together? We'll be practically impenetrable once we get our groups to coordinate with each other."

Frank seemed to consider this. "But I was under the impression that this whole community — this *gated* community was cleared ..."

"We never claimed that. Our guys have been going out every day to clear more houses, and just about all of the roamers have been destroyed."

Frank opened his mouth to speak but Joe continued, waving vaguely in the direction of the front door.

"These ones, they likely were attracted by the noise our vehicles made yesterday. But we were always ready. We had lookouts to spot any danger. And well"—he gestured toward the bell— "you've seen our emergency response. We were out there within minutes. We had practically destroyed all the zombies by the time your first man got outside."

"*My men* were not aware of your emergency response. If they knew, they'd be the first ones to respond."

Shelley watched Joe stiffen.

Here it comes.

Contrary to her expectations, Joe took a deep breath instead. "Very well. I will ask John to instruct your men. I know we were rushed yesterday and didn't have any time for integration. Maybe we can set up an orientation today for your people. There are some other things we need to share. Like the meal schedule."

For once, Frank agreed with the big man. "That sounds reasonable." He glanced over his shoulder at Shelley, then back at Joe. "I guess I just had different expectations. And then, to find out that they can climb ..."

Joe nodded. "Yeah. We only found that out recently ourselves."

One of Frank's men walked past, his rifle slung over his shoulder.

"Say, don't you think your men should store their weapons in the armory, with the rest of the weapons?" Joe asked.

Frank shook head. "My men will not agree to that."

"But they clean the weapons after every use in there. The weapons still belong to y—"

"Sorry, but we're going to have to build up more trust than this before my men will hand in their weapons."

It seemed to Shelley that Frank wasn't sorry at all.

"They know how to clean their own weapons," Frank added. "Besides, I don't think that my people will stay here. It's too crowded, and the sleeping arrangements are not satisfactory at all." He crossed his arms as he spoke, challenging Joe to argue his point.

Joe met Shelley's eyes for a second. "Do you think he has a point?"

Frank turned to Shelley. His arms remained crossed, his expression rather apathetic.

Despite not wanting to, Shelley had to agree. "I don't think we can expect people to sleep in the gym for very long, and I don't think there are enough classrooms to set everybody up."

Sensing victory, Frank flashed a quick smile.

"Maybe there is a way for us to secure the houses across the street?" Shelley asked. "I know that John and his team have cleared those houses."

"That's not a bad idea," Joe agreed. "They'd need some extra security, though. Maybe we should find a way to fence them in. That won't be a problem anymore once we get the whole community cleared."

"Are you asking me to put my people up in those houses?" Frank started to bristle again.

Joe twisted his mouth as he swayed his head. "Maybe not right away. But once we get the place secured..."

Frank looked ready to argue. Just then, a thought must have occurred to him, as his mouth snapped shut. He slowly started to nod as an idea took seed.

"Maybe you're onto something. Yes, the more I think about it, the more I like the idea. Block off the roads on either side, make sure all the backyards have sturdy fences ... Yes." He smiled up at Joe. "I accept your offer. Let's start the planning for this right away."

He'd already spun on his heels and brushed past Shelley before Joe could respond. From his expression, Joe wasn't sure what to say.

Shelley stepped up beside him and watched Frank leave. They turned to each other once the man entered the cafeteria and was lost from sight.

"What a character," Shelley remarked.

Joe harrumphed. "Character. I have a few other words you could use instead."

They grinned at one another.

"Can you believe that he won't share supplies? He has all 'their stuff' piled on one side of the gym. In the meantime, he has no issues eating our food." Joe presented his palm to the cafeteria.

Shelley shook her head, agreeing with Joe. "So, how bad was it out there?" she asked after a moment.

"Half a dozen zombies." Joe shrugged. "One had already climbed the fence when we got out there. The rest were just starting to. We got them all. It wasn't a problem, but the climbing part concerns me. It's like they're learning from each other or something."

"I heard somebody yell," Shelley pressed.

"One of their guys. The fat one. Tripped over his own feet." His expression hardened. "He's got a real mouth on him, too."

"I think there's more going on with these folks than they are letting on. The women, they act all—" She struggled to come up with the right word.

"Scared," Joe finished for her.

"They're scared."

Chapter 57

November 24, 9:00 A.M., Olympus

The door to Sykes' private quarters opened with a slight squeal of protest. Ken walked in without ceremony. He carried a heavy jacket in his hands.

Sykes was already up. He wore a clean suit and was clean shaven, looking every bit the senator he had been. If you could ignore the bruises.

He sat behind his desk and regarded the soldier without commenting. Slowly, languidly, he got to his feet.

"Time to set me free?" he said with a slight smirk on his face.

Ken didn't fall for the bait. His features remained emotionless as the former senator walked up to him. "Your lucky day, I guess."

"Yes." Sykes smiled without mirth. "Not so lucky for you."

"Here." Ken passed a heavy winter coat to the former senator. "Put this on."

Sykes received the coat with a slight look of surprise.

"Temperature's dropped overnight. It's cold out there. Freezing," Ken added.

Shrugging, Sykes reached for the coat. "Small act of kindness?" he suggested as he donned the jacket. It was a military issue, and slightly too large for Sykes. The coat hung down nearly to his knees. "Geez. Couldn't find a medium? This thing feels like its lined with lead!"

"Welcome to the army," Ken replied. "One size fits all. And if you're looking for comfort ... Well, that's never been a word in the army's dictionary."

Sykes barked with laughter and studied Ken with a raised eyebrow. "Huh. A sense of humor."

He stepped back to his desk and picked up the treaty document — then gestured for Ken to lead the way.

They stepped out and walked down the hall, the clicking of their boots reverberating through the abandoned corridor. Less than five minutes later, they found themselves taking a stairwell.

"Almost there," Ken said. "Just one flight of stairs and we'll be at the main entryway."

"Yeah." Sykes continued up the stairs and stopped at the door. "You know, you're actually a decent fellow." He turned around and smiled at Ken.

"Thanks."

"I'd almost forgive you for torturing me. Almost." Sykes' eyes shot daggers.

Ken merely nodded and gestured toward the door. As they stepped through, he looked up at the blackened glass ball that hung in the corner.

The door opened onto a small hallway, no more than ten feet in length. It intersected a much larger tunnel, which in turn led outside. Sykes had taken no more than two steps when he got his feet kicked out from under him. He fell forward with a loud "Oof." Ken immediately knelt on Sykes' back and grabbed a wrist. He expertly stuck it under his knee and fished for Sykes' other hand.

"What ... are you ... doing?" Sykes managed to gasp.

"Just making sure you don't cause any more trouble than you need to," Ken replied calmly as he zip-tied the former senator's wrists together.

He helped Sykes back to his feet. The incident had lasted less than ten seconds. They marched to the large tunnel and turned toward the exit.

"Careful picking your way through that rubble," Ken cautioned.

"Why the fuck did you tie me up?" Sykes demanded as indignation took the place of shock.

Ken spun his captive around, his face dangerously close to the other man's. "You better get the fuck out of here, and fast." Everything on his face promised violence.

"You—You'll just shoot me in the back!" Sykes accused.

"No, man. You've got it all wrong. I promise that I won't shoot you."

Sykes frowned. He clearly distrusted Ken. He turned his head and looked at the exit.

"I won't forget this." With that, he made his way toward freedom.

"I know that *I* won't," Ken whispered softly after the retreating man.

"There they are."

Megan and Winston sighed with relief as the two men stepped into the hall and into the view of the closed-circuit camera.

She had gasped in alarm when she saw Ken's face in the CCTV shot from the stairwell. He had smiled maliciously. She knew right away that he was up to something and told Winston as much.

But here they were after a slightly longer than expected pause. In the tunnel, leading to the exit.

Something still didn't look quite right to Megan, though. She got her face closer to the small monitor, willing the grainy picture to clear up for her.

Ken and Sykes exchanged a few words. For a moment it looked like Ken was going to hurt the traitor.

Do it. Megan hated Sykes and everything he stood for. The man had made a mockery of her own father's position. *Just take one swing. For me.*

However, Ken turned the man loose. Megan leaned back in disappointment.

A second later, it was Winston's turn to lean closer to the monitor. "What the hell?"

"What is it?" Megan couldn't figure out what had riled up the young man.

Winston did not respond right away. They both stared at the grainy picture intently. Then it became clear.

"His hands are tied."

Megan felt a sudden dryness in her mouth as she saw Ken step out of view. It only took a second for the sergeant to step back into camera. He was carrying a scoped rifle.

"Holy shit..."

They stayed rooted to the spot, mesmerized by what the monitor showed. In near disbelief, they watched as Ken set himself up in a shooting position.

"What the fuck is he doing?" Winston slowly turned from the small screen in front of him. Megan had already pulled away from the desk.

"I don't know, but there's going to be trouble," she said as she reached for her rifle.

C aptain Harry walked up the slight incline to Captain Donald's position. He was flanked by his two swords.

"Remember what I said, Raul. I don't want any funny business," he told the man walking on his right. He cast a quick glance to see if Raul would acknowledge his command.

An ugly look passed over the sapper's face. He'd lost his second man last night and blamed Captain Donald along with his goon, Jaheem. He wanted revenge. Harry knew that sappers were a close bunch. He also knew they were dangerous as hell.

And insane ...

Raul caught his captain's eye. "Yes. Of course, Captain."

I should have left him at camp. But they had come too far. Besides, Harry needed his swords for this. They were planning their assault on the bunker.

They entered Captain Donald's camp and headed straight for the largest tent.

Not only is the man a fool, but he's a pompous, arrogant fool.

They were met by two soldiers at the entrance to the tent.

"Guards? Really?" Raul scowled at the men.

Harry was about to scold Raul when a commotion at the bunker caught everybody's attention.

"What's happening?" Captain Donald demanded as he and Jaheem stepped through the tent flap. Neither men acknowledged Captain Harry or his man.

"We have movement at the bunker." A runner breathlessly announced. had arrived from the perimeter. Donald and Jaheem immediately took off in the direction of the bunker, leaving Harry to follow in his wake.

They got to the perimeter just in time to see a figure stumbling through the rubble of the gate. "Don't shoot!" he yelled from the edge of the wreckage.

"Put your hands up!" one of the soldiers yelled back.

Harry glanced around and found that they had the bunker entrance well-covered. This didn't seem to be a sally by the defending forces.

"Don't shoot! It's me, Senator Sykes; Sage Anthony," the man said as he stumbled forward.

"Hands up!" the soldier repeated.

The man continued to rush toward their line.

"Hold your fire," Jaheem called out.

Just then a shot rang out. Harry ducked behind a tree and looked around. *That shot came from the bunker!*

One of the soldiers to the right of their position collapsed onto the ground with a groan.

Before anybody could call out, a return volley of fire pumped into the approaching man. He shuddered several times as bullets impacted into his mid-section and chest. The man lost his footing and fell backwards.

Another shot rang out. Harry could hear the thud of the impact and the accompanying cry of pain. It was so close to him that he quickly ducked behind a tree.

Donald's men continued to fire into the bunker. Sparks flew everywhere as bullets ricocheted off metal and rock.

"Cease fire!" Captain Donald yelled.

Still, it took two more commands before the last man stopped shooting. Everybody stayed in cover. Harry watched Donald poke his head out from behind his tree and squint as he tried to get a better look.

"Fuck ...That *is* Sage Anthony." Donald turned to Jaheem. "We need to go get him. He might still be alive." Neither man held out much hope for that, from the looks on their faces.

Several nervous minutes followed. The tunnel was shrouded in darkness, making it impossible to see if the shooter was down, had retreated, or still lay in wait. Putting on ENVGs made no sense, as it was still way too bright outside to make the night-vision goggles useful. Finally, one of the soldiers had the idea of using smoke.

Donald approved the maneuver, and three canisters arced through the air to land around the tunnel entrance moments later. They waited for the thick smoke to completely envelop the tunnel then sent in two men to collect Sage Anthony's body. The men ran in a low crouch, grabbed an armpit each, and had the corpse back to safety moments later.

Captain Donald and Jaheem made a beeline for the dead senator. Harry and his swords followed.

"It's Sage Anthony," the soldier confirmed. "He's gone, sir." He had checked for vitals. One look at the corpse could have confirmed death, though, as it was riddled with bullets.

"What a fucking mess," Harry said. *What a fucking mess you've made, Donald,* was what he thought.

"Flip him over. Untie him," Donald urged.

Jaheem stepped over to comply. Harry's eyes narrowed as Jaheem worked on the dead man's bonds.

Why does his jacket look so bulky?

"Get down!" Raul yelled and pulled the captain to the ground. Less than a second later an explosion ripped through shrubbery, trees and men alike.

The sound of an explosion reverberated down the tunnel, reaching the dogleg in the tunnel where Ken stood.

"Music to my ears," Ken muttered, allowing himself a satisfied smirk as he dropped the trigger onto the ground. He looked up as he heard the footsteps of people approaching.

Several seconds later, Megan burst through the stairwell door, followed by Hawk and Squawk.

For a moment they all stared at each other in silence. Megan spotted the trigger at his feet and looked up from the device into the sergeant's face.

"What did you do?" Her expression clearly betrayed her distaste.

"Get off your high horse, Sally," Ken replied. "Sykes was never going to help us, and I was never going to give up this place without a fight."

"Now we'll never know the answer to that." She gestured toward the trigger. "Did you strap a bomb on him?"

"Yup. I guess that's accurate." Ken nodded solemnly. "He was giving me some lip, so I roughed him up a bit. For all he knew, I was zip-tying his hands, but in reality I was turning on the receiver on the bomb he had on him."

"Of course." Hawk jumped into the conversation excitedly. "That's why you wanted Sykes to wear that heavy jacket. You'd already planted an IED on him."

"Nothing improvised about it, Hawk. Just a good old brick of C4 coating the inner lining of that jacket. And a detonator, of course." He winked.

"So, getting my dad to meet with Sykes was all just a ploy?" Meg wasn't ready to let it go.

Ken's demeanor turned sour, as his scowl clearly expressed. "Maybe you don't get it, Sally. But I do." He stepped up to her so that their faces were mere inches apart. To Meg's credit, she didn't back down. "There is no negotiating with them. Those fuckers killed the world! Sykes was going to say anything to save his own skin, but I tell you this, Sally: There is no way that they would have spared us."

Meg still refused to back down. "So you made the executive decision to attack them. Without anybody else's consent or knowledge."

"Hell, yeah, I did!" Ken raised his voice. He clamped his mouth shut, then backed up a step. "When I first got here my platoon counted fifty soldiers. Those bastards killed forty-nine of my brothers and sisters." For the first time, Ken showed his pain; he glanced away. By the time he turned back to Megan, he looked resolute. "I'm not asking them for mercy, and they will receive none from me."

Megan softened after hearing that. Ken backed further out of her personal space, obviously not comfortable with what he saw.

"They killed my parents, and my little sister," Hawk said.

Megan nodded. "They killed my mom..." She shuddered as emotion threatened to overtake her.

"My parents died a few years ago, and I've got no brothers or sisters," Squawk started. He shook his head slowly, and his hand shot up to rub his beaklike nose. "But *they* killed my dog. I loved that dog."

At each admission, Ken assented. "Now it's their time to die. They might have had us outnumbered. They might do it again." He elbowed Squawk playfully. "But I'm pretty sure that the odds have evened up somewhat."

Meg had turned serious once more. "There's no way they are going to leave."

"True. And it was always true — you're just realizing it now." Ken scanned all three faces. "We're in a war. Whether we like it or not. That includes all those people." He waved behind him, indicating the residents of Olympus.

Squawk snickered. "We're in a war with an army of four." The faces around him sobered him up immediately.

"Squawk is right," Ken said after a moment. He locked eyes with Meg. "We're going to need a bigger army."

Chapter 58

Theodore

November 24, 10:00 A.M.

Theodore flipped down the visor to shield his eyes from the sun.

Eye. His hand immediately shot up to the bandaged portion of his face. *Funny. Can't feel any pain. Just a bit of a headache.*

He stared outside and tried to focus on objects. His depth perception was not what it used to be, but other than that he could almost swear that his eyesight had improved.

"Huh. How about that?" he murmured to himself.

"What's that, sir?" Fred asked.

Theodore looked over at the young man. His first thought was to shrug it off. Ignore the question and let things drift back to the long spell of silence they had surely both enjoyed. Then he thought about Winston. Those puppy-dog eyes pleading for recognition and attention.

Don't be a crotchety old ass: Talk to the boy. It's not his fault that we broke down and lost a full day.

"Uhm. I was just noticing how my one eye seems to be working pretty well despite the other eye being—" Theodore frowned at the memory of seeing a shard of metal flying toward his face. "Gone."

"Super sensory," Fred blurted out.

Theodore looked at him blankly.

"I think that's what it was called. Super sensory. Or something like that. Anyway, my ex-girlfriend was really interested in that kind of stuff. She even made us go out for dinner once at a restaurant, where we ate in darkness. 'Heightened senses,' she called it. I just ended up spilling a bunch of food on my crotch."

Fred laughed then. It was a pure, good-natured laugh. Theodore had regretted engaging the man in conversation right up to that point. Now he liked the sound.

"Anyway," Fred continued after an embarrassed glance toward the general. "There is a bunch of research that proves that when one sense is lost, the others are enhanced. Like how blind people have better hearing and sense of smell or taste. Not that you're blind, sir," he added hastily.

Theodore thought about it for a moment and nodded. "Yeah. I think I've heard of that too. What did you call it? Super senses?"

"Super sensory, sir."

"Right." Theodore looked up at the interchange they were approaching. "My super sensory is telling me that our turn-off is up ahead."

"Yes, sir. We're supposed to follow the freeway as it veers south."

Their conversation stopped as Fred slowed down to navigate through some parked vehicles. A city gradually appeared to their left once passed the interchange. Objects of a world lost loomed ahead and to their left. One massive structure in particular grew as they approached. It had been a sports stadium in the recent past. Now it was a ruin. Theodore could only guess at what had occurred to destroy the structure.

Fire. But by natural or manmade causes? Theodore imagined a lightning strike and fire raging unchecked, followed by the vision of scared people lashing out at everything around them in their despair.

Or was it us? Theodore recalled only too well the authorized bombing runs. *Weren't those all out west, though?*

Fred had unconsciously slowed their vehicle as they neared the destroyed colossus. He jumped slightly when Theodore spoke next.

"'When falls the Coliseum, Rome shall fall; And when Rome falls ... the world.'"

Fred looked at the general with genuine awe. Theodore noticed and smiled. "I didn't make that up. That was a quote from Lord Byron."

They had passed the stadium. The road continued to be clear, so Fred picked up speed again.

"That's what us generals do," Theodore continued. "We look up quotes and try to sound smarter than we really are." He laughed at his own joke. Then he realized that this was the first time he had laughed for a long time.

It does feel good. So Theodore continued to laugh.

After a moment, Fred joined him.

Chapter 59

Joe

November 24, 10:30 A.M., 98 Aspen Ridge Road.

"This is it," BB announced as they arrived at the two-story house.

He parked the Humvee and waited as Bill flipped the top hatch and surveyed the area.

"We're all clear," he announced after a minute.

"Okay. Let's get going." Joe opened his door and stepped out.

Keith and Emily also opened their doors. They quickly busied themselves with gathering up radio gear and cable.

BB and Bill continued to provide security as the other three moved the gear into the house. There was a moment of trepidation as Joe opened the front door, but the inside was silent. He stepped into the house with a small sigh of relief and an embarrassed smile.

They had the radio set up in the upstairs bedroom less than fifteen minutes later. And soon after that, Keith pulled in the cable that he had run out to the neighboring radio tower. Emily connected everything and turned on the radio with anticipation.

Joe got to do the honors. "CQ, CQ, CQ. Hotel Oscar Hotel One. Read, over."

The answer was immediate. "Hotel Oscar Hotel, this is Romeo Echo November. Read you loud and clear, over."

A small cheer went up in the room. "Booyah!" Keith punched the air.

"We read you five by five, Jack." Joe grinned.

The thought of moving their main radio had been a good one. The reception up here would be several times better than in the school. Especially hooked up to that antenna.

"Proceeding with the scan. Will contact you again when we're done here. Over and out," Joe concluded.

Their plan all along had been to scan the frequencies to see if anybody else was broadcasting. Joe secretly hoped that they would get several hits — especially now that their area of reception was so much larger.

Twenty minutes on, he was forced to admit defeat. Not a single peep. Nobody else was out there. At least, nobody else was broadcasting.

By that time BB and Bill had come upstairs. They had finished securing the main floor of the house. No one was getting into this place unless they had crowbars and sledgehammers and knew how to use them.

Or there are too many of them. Joe shuddered to think about being stuck in this place, surrounded by a vast horde of the undead.

Cut it out, Joe. He shook his head and forced a grin onto his face.

"Guys, I think we've done about as much as we set out to do. Em, let Jack know we're on our way home, would you?"

Joe left the bedroom and entered the bathroom just down the hall. He turned the tap, but the water pressure seemed to be too low.

Guess we can't have it all. He caught sight of his face in the mirror and the melancholy smile slipped from his face.

Damn, Joe. You've lost weight. He stroked his chin. *And you need to shave that beard off!*

He wasn't displeased by what he saw overall, though. He'd needed to lose weight. If anything, he looked younger. More vibrant.

But that beard's got to go.

Keith poked his head into the bathroom. "We're all done here, Joe. Water running?" he asked, shrugging when Joe shook his head. "Oh well. Guess we'll have to bring some supplies on our next run."

Joe followed Keith down the stairs and to the front door. Joe closed the door and locked the improvised padlock they had installed.

"We'll be back."

"Geez, Keith," Joe scoffed. "That's not even the actual quote."

Keith shrugged. "I know. I was thinking of doing 'Hasta la vista, baby.' Or maybe "You shall not pass!" He shrugged. "Can't nail it every time."

Joe smiled and patted Keith on the shoulder. "No. Guess you can't."

They got in the Humvee and Joe cast one last glance toward the house. The plan was to set up the place so that the radio would be manned all the time. For now, they'd stick to daily excursions.

He just hoped that all the effort would prove to be worth it.

Chapter 60

Megan

November 24, 4:00 P.M., Olympus

Megan inched forward, keenly feeling the rough edges of the rubble as it dug into her torso. The cold air from outside seemed to seep in from the jagged hole ahead, bathing her in its chill. Out of the corner of her eye she could see Ken. The sergeant was hardly discernible, even to her at less than ten feet away. He was faster than her and was now crawling a full body-length ahead.

That annoyed her.

She touched a piece of concrete with her foot. It rocked slightly, knocking into other rubble pieces. The sound was muffled and there was no way anybody else could hear it. Nevertheless, Ken fixed her with a stare that could kill.

She mouthed a "sorry" and felt small. That feeling was quickly replaced by anger. She suddenly wanted to mouth two other words toward Ken, starting with "fuck" and ending with "you."

They started moving forward again, and Megan's anger slowly faded. She really should be pleased with the sergeant. He'd asked her to accompany him on this little mission. It showed that he trusted her. Maybe even respected her.

Not that he'd say those words.

Maybe that was also in part due to her success in drafting volunteers for the defense of Olympus. Twenty out of the remaining twenty-seven people had stepped up. Of those, half had weapons experience — although most of that ranged from avid hunting to that one trip to the shooting range. To Megan's surprise, her own dad also volunteered. He had been a pacifist for as long as Megan could remember — she could recall the terrible disappointment he'd expressed when Megan signed up for military service. She could also remember the rebelliousness that caused her to sign up in the first place, and the regrets that followed for the next year or so.

At any rate, their small crew had been bolstered in numbers. With the right strategy they might hold back the enemy, until ...

Until what? Until General Davies shows up with the cavalry?

She certainly didn't hold out much hope that they would win this on their own.

Ken held up a hand, signaling that they had gone as far as they could. They had made it to a spot within three feet of where the gate to Olympus used to be. Megan had a brief look around and could only be impressed with the damage that had been wrought.

A bit of overkill, she surmised after observing the sheer damage. It looked like half the cliff face was blown away along with the gate itself as twisted metal and chunks of concrete mixed with the very rock of the mountainside.

A slight movement to her side called her attention. Ken had lifted binoculars to his face.

Right. Megan reached into her pocket and fished out her own spyglass.

It took her several long moments before she spotted somebody. The lookout was well hidden, and the only reason she'd spotted him was because he reached up to scratch his face.

Shortly after, she saw a two-man team, apparently on guard duty.

Funny. They're still wearing US Army gear, complete with the flag. You'd almost believe that we were the bad guys.

"Sniper." Ken whispered so softly that it could have been the wind. "Eyes down. Don't move."

Megan froze. She hadn't seen a thing, but her gut seized up in a knot, nonetheless. She knew with absolute certainty that Ken wasn't joking around.

For what seemed like an eternity, Megan remained frozen. A muscle low in her back started to complain.

"Okay. Move back. Now." Ken too started squirming backwards.

They crawled with extreme care, Megan feeling like every tiny movement painted a huge target on her back. Finally, they got into a crouch upon Ken's signal and executed a low jog through the deepening darkness and back to safety.

"That was close. Good thing we put on our makeup!" he said with a grin.

By makeup, he meant gunk. Thick black gunk that smelled of petroleum. Megan had been as hesitant to apply the tarry substance as she was thankful for it now. Ken's grin felt out of place, though.

Seems like the only time he's in a good mood is when he delivers death or narrowly avoids it.

Megan swallowed hard. That *was* close. She shook her head. "I didn't see much. A lookout. A couple of guards ..."

Ken nodded. "Yeah, I didn't see much either. They don't have night-vision goggles — or they weren't wearing them. That's something. They don't seem to be set up to charge our location. More like they want to starve us out."

"Why?" Megan frowned. "Why aren't they attacking? Surely they must know that we're ripe for the picking."

"Might be that they're afraid of our defenses. That turret ripped them apart." He thought about that, then shook his head. "No. I don't think that's it."

Megan could see the tiniest glint as his eyes met hers.

"They're waiting for something," he said.

"Waiting for what?"

Ken was silent for a moment. She could see his body shift and imagined that he was staring at the gaping maw where the gate used to be. "Wish I knew, Sally. Whatever it is, it can't be good."

"So, what else did we learn?" Megan asked.

"They're cautious. That doesn't help our cause." Ken started heading back down the tunnel, and Megan quickly followed him. "We know that they've got at least dozen men out there. More than enough to take us by force. But they might suspect more traps. Maybe that's why they haven't struck yet."

He walked for a moment in silence. They reached the corner and the sergeant abruptly stopped.

"They're waiting for something. I feel it in my bones. Maybe they're bringing in some heavy guns. Or more explosives."

Shaking his head in disgust, he faced Megan again.

"I don't like our odds here, Sally."

Chapter 61

Ben

November 24, 5:30 P.M.

Ben loved the silence.

He knew how some people would be bothered by it. The lack of any human noise would hang like an oppressive blanket over those who were used to planes and helicopters in the sky, the constant hum of traffic along highways, and the buzz of people themselves.

Not Ben. He loved the peacefulness of it. Maybe even more than that, he loved that the only sounds he heard were natural sounds. He had even heard and sighted the occasional bird. One afternoon, he watched a large bird of prey aloft on the winds high above him. The bird seemed to follow him for half an hour, always circling overhead.

He heard the calls of deer and realized that for once they wouldn't be hunted during their mating season. Grunting, clicking, and mewling sounds seemed to be all around him during certain portions of his trek. He knew these to be mule deer, having hunted the proud bucks of the species in the past.

His favorite sounds were those of nature itself. They were subtle. But now, with the silence, they could be heard and enjoyed. He reveled as he listened to the wind blowing over a ridge or through the trees, and to water running down creeks and streams. At one point he crossed a river, deciding to swim rather than find a bridge. When he got to the other side, his body ached with a combination of fatigue and cold. He wrapped himself in his thermal blanket and

465

popped into his sleeping bag to warm up and rest. What he had not counted on was falling asleep within minutes, the sounds of the river easing him into unconsciousness.

The last couple of days had flown by.

Ben had snuck out of the Ren unnoticed that night, just as he planned it. He'd hightailed it to the nearest garage, where he'd managed to bring a vehicle back to life. The next several hours had been all about making distance.

He ditched the vehicle once he crossed the state line and continued on foot. Ben trekked through the countryside, traveling as the crow flies. He avoided all populated areas, which was a challenge sometimes, as towns and villages seemed to be everywhere.

This way he was able to minimize his run-ins with zombies. There were only a few occasions when he was left with no option but to destroy the undead. He had become adept at it, truth be told. A single zombie posed little threat to him, and even in pairs they were easy to put down. The problem was that they tended to herd together.

Yesterday he had been traveling down a gravel road in a densely wooded area. He'd turned a corner to be confronted with the sight of several dozen zombies. They were moving in the same direction but turned as one when Ben pulled to a stop and his foot skidded on some gravel. He had to admit that the sight of dozens of faces swinging his way, many without one or both eyes, was unnerving to say the least. Three of them were runners, and he had no option but to take them out. Ben knew fire discipline and shot each zombie in the head before they got to within six feet of him.

He knew that the noise would attract more zombies, so he was forced to move quickly. He jogged back fifty feet before ducking into the woods. What followed was reminiscent of a fox hunt, as Ben sought to penetrate a net of zombies which were closing in on his location.

That was as near as he had gotten to getting caught. He reminisced about the event as he walked across a farmer's field. Ben was so caught up in the memory that he almost missed the noise. At first, he stopped and put his nose in the air as an animal would. Within a few seconds, he had identified the sound.

That's a vehicle. And it's coming this way!

It didn't take Ben long to decide what to do. He backtracked to a small gulch he had crossed minutes ago and dove into it.

No more than five seconds passed before he spotted a pickup truck barreling down the road. He spotted two passengers as they passed his position. The truck turned right at the next crossroads. He watched it disappear into the woods.

Ben got to his feet and moved forward, listening intently. It sounded like the truck had pulled to a stop somewhere up the road.

Curious, Ben decided to follow. He heard the vehicle move again and imagined they had stopped to open a gate.

They're not far. And it's on my way.

Ben got to the road that the truck had turned down. The first thing he noticed was that there were bodies along the side of the road. By the looks of them, they had been destroyed a while ago. He followed the road, spotting more bodies here and there. All was silent again as went into the woods.

Several minutes later, he stood before a gate. Fresh tire marks indicated that this was the property the truck had entered. Ben hesitated for a moment, considering his options. Curiosity won, and he climbed the gate.

The sun was starting to set, which meant that this place in the woods was already nearly shrouded in darkness. He followed the dirt path for fifty yards, then he spotted the ranch house another hundred yards ahead. Ben considered if he should make his presence known.

Stake out the place first.

The men had taken seats in a covered deck just off the side of the house. They'd started drinking by the sounds of it. They started talking. A few minutes later, Ben had approached close enough to make out what they were saying.

"You ever seen *Gone with the Wind*?" a man asked.

"Nope, can's say as I have," another man replied.

"Ah, too bad. It's a classic." The first man paused for a moment. "I always meant to watch it, but the thing is fucking four hours long. Four hours! Anyway, I finally did watch it. Just recently, too. It was on my day off. Sunday. Lazy day, I calls it. Anyway, where was I ..."

"*Gone with the Wind*," the second man reminded him helpfully.

"Oh yeah, right. *Gone with the Wind*. What an epic movie." First man paused again as he poured himself another drink. "It's about the Civil War. Naw, actually it's about a lot more than the Civil War — but it takes place during it. It's kind of about how some people coped with it all."

"Kind of like this?"

"Like what?"

"Like this! The zombie fucking apocalypse this!"

"Whoa take it easy feller!" First man considered what his friend had said. "Yeah, maybe kind of like this. You got desperate people out there, and you don't know who you can trust. That happens in *Gone with the Wind* also."

This was followed by silence. The pregnant pause lasted for long moments. "You goin' to finish your story, Al?" second man prompted impatiently.

"Right. Sorry. I was reminiscin' an' all ..."

Ben could hear the first man, Al, take his drink and place the glass back on the table.

"There is this one scene in the movie where Scarlett — that's the main character — shoots a soldier right in the face. Fucking kills the guy, dead."

"She have a good reason?" second man asked.

"Yeah. He was going to rape her or something. I don't remember, exactly. But yeah, the guy had it coming."

"Okay. So, what's so interesting about that?"

"Well, the interesting part is this. She goes and says: 'Well I guess I've done murder.'"

Al had mimicked a female with a high southern accent. It was almost comical.

"Then she starts to drag the body off," Al went on. "But before she gets too far, she says, 'I'll think about that tomorrow.'"

There was a thoughtful pause, and the men refilled their drinks before Al continued, "I've been livin' like that for the last couple of weeks. Committin' sins. Then thinking about them tomorrow. Always tomorrow."

"All right," second man concluded. "What you're sayin' is that we worry about answerin' for our sins tomorrow."

Ben could hear a clack as Al put his glass down forcefully.

"Oh, no. That wasn't what I was thinking at all." There was the sound of him refilling his cup. What I was thinking, BJ, was that we've done some bad things. We've killed some people that didn't deserve no killin'. We killed that couple and had our way with that daughter of theirs."

"Hoowee!" second man interrupted. "She was a little spitfire. I still got scabs on my back from those sharp fingernails of hers."

"Shut up, BJ. Just for one fucking minute — will you shut up and listen to what I'm saying?"

"Aw, take it easy Al."

"It's just so annoyin' when I'm trying to be serious and you think this is one big party."

"Well, it has been. A party. But I can see that you're achin' to tell me how it ain't."

"All I'm sayin' is that we done bad. We done evil, even. That ain't who we were before all this syndrome crap happened, BJ. We ain't evil. But we gone and done some. I figure that one day that's gonna catch up to us."

A chair scraped. One of the men had leapt to his feet.

"What are you doing?"

"I got no patience for your bellyachin', Al. You're ruining my buzz."

Another scrape, followed by the blast of a sidearm. One of the men screamed. This was followed by two more blasts of the sidearm. Ben listened intently to the silence that fell.

"Ah, damn it, Al. Now you gone and made me shoot you." The tone was accusatory rather than apologetic.

BJ must have pulled the chair back in place and sat down. "You made me spill my drink." Again, a glass was being refilled.

Ben sat quietly as BJ continued to drink for the next twenty minutes. He was surprised that no zombie approached in that time-frame.

They must have cleared the area. Or have a sturdy fence.

BJ had started muttering to himself. He kept calling out to Al as if the other man were still alive. At one point, BJ stepped into the house and Ben tensed. A moment later he came back out, apparently with a fresh bottle of booze.

"I wanna die. I wannadie, Iwannadie," the drunk man muttered.

Ben waited. He knew what he would have to do. And from the sounds of it, BJ wanted the same thing.

Chapter 62

Dermott

Dermott walked out of his apartment building. His body had sustained some damage. His foot was broken, causing him to limp, and he'd lost a handful of perfect, whitened teeth. His mouth was now the dark color of blood. From the corner of his mouth hung a small piece of cloth, the small portion of a purple t-shirt snagged in the jagged leftovers of his teeth. He had no feelings of remorse for killing the old man. He had no thoughts at all.

The person who used to be Dermott only knew the call of the others. The horde called him. The horde called all. So he moved out of the smashed doorway and onto the landing. He navigated down the concrete steps and lurched to the pavement of the street.

There were others there. A stream of them. Dermott joined the flow as they, too, answered the call. He was aware of another stream marching in the same direction, one block over. Individually, they were not aware of the others. Yet as a collective they knew in which direction they had to walk. Eventually, he would see the glow himself. The glow of the others — that which he was meant to snuff out.

They marched. By the hundreds. By the thousands. Knowing that they would become part of a vast lake, its waves preparing to wash over any obstacle.

A flood of the dead was coming, to stamp out the flames of the living.

Chapter 63

Nancy

November 24, 7:15 P.M., Nearing the wall.

Nancy stabbed downward with the shovel, neatly severing the zombie's head from the rest of its body. She thought she was getting used to it, but still shuddered as the head rolled away.

At least she wasn't personalizing them anymore. In fact, she hardly even noticed whether the zombies she was dispatching had been male or female, young or old.

She looked up in time to see Dean ground another zombie. He cast a brief glance at Nancy before moving on.

My turn. She strode up to the fallen zombie. Half of the head had been smashed in, but she did not want to take any chances. She placed the shovel against the unresponsive zombie's neck and thrust downward sharply. Separating head from body had become easy. It was the one positive, if one could call it that, of the degenerating condition of the zombies.

They worked in silence, quickly dispatching one more zombie before following Nuggets and slipping away down an alley. Nancy caught up to Dean, and the unlikely pair shared a nod.

That had gone well. Better than expected.

Better than the last time. Nancy fleetingly thought back to the day before. There was no use in dwelling on the past.

They traveled another two blocks before starting to look for a hideout. The sun would be down soon, and night presented a significant advantage to the undead.

They were in luck. Their preference was a bungalow-style building with an open door and no fencing around the yard, which happened to be just about every house on this particular block. Bungalow so that there was no chance of getting trapped upstairs. Door ajar meant that whatever had been inside had gotten out. No fencing meant that it would be easier to get away.

Wow, how my thinking has changed. Nancy almost chuckled out loud at the thought.

They quickly entered one of the houses, did a check of the building to find that it was indeed abandoned, and closed the door. Only then did they allow themselves to relax.

The kitchen was their first stop. Not to look for food — although that would follow soon. No, they went straight to the sink. Dean pulled the lever on the tap and was rewarded with a short gurgle followed by a stream of clear water. The former shortstop and the old lady spontaneously high-fived. Running water was a gift.

First, they filled up their water bottles. After that they immediately started taking off their gear. They washed themselves as efficiently as possible. That had been Nancy's influence. She could not and would not abide bad personal hygiene. Especially with rotting corpses everywhere — whether they attacked you or not.

However, they didn't go for actual showers in the bathroom. Locking yourself into a room and turning on a noisy shower was just too risky.

They finished washing up but did not turn the water off. They still needed to wash the gore off their weapons and clothes.

The whole process had become a regular routine over the last few days. Enter the house. Clear the house. Secure the house. Check for running water and wash up.

Do not get separated.

Then followed the search for food, the quiet preparation and shared meal, and the evening of sharing stories, plans and grief. It was good and needed. For both.

Nancy and Dean searched the kitchen. The hamster mentality of people meant there was no shortage of durable foods. In fact, every house they had stayed in so far had far more food than expected.

"Mmmm." Dean held up two large cans. "Ravioli!"

His grin was infectious. That seemed to spur him on. If he got a smile, he wanted a laugh. If he got a laugh, he wanted a bigger one.

He put on his most cheesy Italian accent. "Ay! Oh! Imma want to eat da spaghetti!"

"Ravioli," Nancy corrected.

"Ravioli!" Dean parroted in the accent.

Nancy gave him what he wanted. She laughed.

She watched him beam at her as he put the cans down on the counter, then turn back to the cupboards looking for more treasure.

What a character. Ern, you would have loved this kid.

They ate supper in the small eating nook off the kitchen as daylight faded outside. The living room provided ample space and comfortable seating, but also featured large bay windows. Caution trumped convenience.

Heating the meal without electricity had only proven to be a minor inconvenience. Just about every house in the city featured a barbecue in the back yard. It was a simple matter of Dean dragging it into the back door without attracting attention.

They took the first few bites in silence.

"You know, I honestly think this used to taste better," Dean said between bites. It didn't stop him from spooning the meal into his mouth with vigor.

"Don't eat so fast. You'll give yourself a gut ache," Nancy replied. To his credit, Dean slowed down a little.

Nancy took a bite and carefully tasted the food before swallowing it down. "This does taste a bit bland. Not like it has gone off — but like it's gone stale or something."

Nuggets certainly didn't seem to mind. The dog had happily devoured its bowl of human food already.

Dean nodded in agreement. "Actually, I've been noticing that about most of the food since this all started."

Nancy screwed up her face. "I'm sure it's all related. All those crops going bad and the cattle dying. That had to do with those nanobot things."

She held the spoon in front of her and observed the food. The red of a tomato sauce and the off-white of the pasta steamed slightly with the remnants of heat. "I bet the same stuff existed in these canned foods. But there was no energy to fuel those bots, so they died." She turned from her food to her companion. "Leaving the food tasting stale but still edible."

She hesitated for a moment, picturing a myriad of crawling things inside the food. Finally, as if to prove her point, she took the bite. She chewed it carefully and shrugged.

Dean mirrored her shrug and continued to eat with enthusiasm.

It was dark outside, but the nearly full moon and an incredible array of stars provided just enough light for Dean and Nancy to see what they were doing. Dean had dragged a loveseat from the living room into the kitchen, and the companions sank into the small couch with contented sighs.

But Dean jumped straight up again a moment later.

"What is it?" she asked in fear and alarm. Nuggets had reacted similarly to its owner's sudden movement. The dog was instantly on alert.

"Sorry. It's okay. Nothing to be alarmed about."

"You almost gave me a heart attack."

"Sorry," Dean repeated with a fitting look of contrition. "It's just that I have a hunch about this place." The remorse was replaced by excitement. "First, we have all of these canned pastas and food."

Dean waved toward the cupboards and their backpacks, which now had a couple cans added to the collection of food.

"Next," Dean continued, "we have all the bags of chips."

One large bag sat on the counter. They were planning to devour the contents of that bag as an evening snack. Dean got into his role now. He paced toward the living room, stopping well away from the windows.

"Then we have all of this."

He pointed to the far wall. Nancy took in the view: large flat-screen TV and sports memorabilia on the wall. It started making sense to Nancy.

"It's elementary, my dear Nancy." Dean pretended to hold a pipe.

"All right, Sherlock — I'll bite. What's your point?"

"There is beer in this place." His grin was infectious once again. "I'll bet there are several lukewarm cans of goodness in that fridge over there."

They had avoided opening refrigerators and freezers, knowing that they would be met by the terrible stench of rotting foodstuffs. This was one of those high-risk, high-reward types of situations, though.

"What do you say?" Dean asked as he approached the stainless-steel appliance. "Should I go for it?"

The love for beer was yet another thing that Nancy and Dean had in common. "Yes. You'd better be right, Mr. Holmes," she warned him, sternly waving a finger.

Dean took an exaggerated deep breath and opened the fridge door. He bent so that he could quickly scan the shelves and suddenly reached in with the speed of a striking snake.

"Ta—daa!" He flourished a bottle of beer.

"Hurry!" Nancy prompted him. "Get them out before the smell kills us."

Dean busied himself, and several moments later he'd slammed the fridge door shut. Four bottles of beer stood on the counter beside the fridge. He winked at Nancy. Success. The smell was terrible but would fade quickly — especially considering the prize. He pretended to check his watch, then looked up at his companion. "It's beer o'clock."

Nancy cackled despite the lame humor.

Ten minutes later they were both on their second beer, along with their second bowl of chips. They enjoyed the drink and food in relative silence, knowing they would get to talking later. They always did.

We've done well. Nancy thought. First of all, they had managed to get ahead of the leading elements of the massive horde. There was also no doubt about it now — the zombies were traveling in a straight line toward the Ren. They had observed the horde from a distance for a while and still could only guess at the numbers.

Thousands. They could agree on that. And the horde was growing all the time. Nancy observed first-hand how individuals and small groups gravitated toward the horde. At least it meant that all the undead were relatively in the same location.

Tomorrow it would be a straight run to the Ren to warn her people. After that, it was anybody's guess. She was sure that John and several others would want to make a stand and fight. Nancy didn't think it a good idea.

Hopefully, cooler heads will prevail, and we can make a run for it. She took a sip of her beer as she thought about that.

What if this horde just keeps on following? Is any place safe? She took another long draught of her beer.

"What's on your mind?" Dean had spotted her involuntary headshake.

She glanced at her companion. "Ah, just wondering what's going to happen when we get back to my friends. That horde ... I'm not sure if there is any stopping them."

Dean pushed out his lips as he considered. "Yeah, there are a lot of them. But they're no match for us. Not the way we're handling ourselves."

Nancy appreciated the compliment. They *had* handled themselves well these last couple of days. To start with, they had learned to travel light and fast. Their senses seemed to have improved — or maybe it was just their street smarts — as they were able to avoid most conflicts by watching and listening. When they did run into the undead ...

"You've really got this zombie-smashing thing down," she told Dean, who beamed.

They had quickly devised a tactic that worked. Unless there were too many zombies. In those cases, they ran like hell. But they no longer feared going into an altercation with groups of half a dozen or less.

Listen to this. She paused at her last thought. No less than a week ago she would have quaked at fighting a single zombie. Now, and thanks to her new companion, all that had changed.

Nancy the zombie slayer. She didn't really like the ring of that, so she quickly stowed the thought away.

Movement and agility. Those had been the key to their success in fighting zombies. Dean had taught her that you had to keep moving to prevent the zombies from cornering you and swarming you. He had also instructed that they keep moving at angles. It seemed difficult for the undead to process this: They couldn't cut you off if they didn't know where you were going. Also, they were so awkward that they often fell over or tripped each other up, which only made the disposal part easier.

Disposal. Yeah, I like that.

She reached into the bowl and came out with several chips.

Feels like old times. On the couch with the old man. Except her old man was gone.

She felt a slight pressure on her knee and looked down to see that Nuggets had rested his head on her leg. His eyes were on the prize in her hand. Nancy snorted good-naturedly and held out a chip to the dog, who took it from her fingers with infinite care.

The dog deserved a chip. Nuggets had been their savior on several occasions already. The dog just seemed to know when it needed to act. He made for the perfect distraction, often running circles around the undead, who inevitably ended up on the ground. The dog was there to draw attention when things got hairy. And he seemed to know where Achilles' tendons were, too.

Glad you're on our side, pup. She fed the dog another chip and petted its head as it ate.

"Sophie didn't like beer," Dean said to start the nightly conversation. "She wasn't really into drinking in the first place." He took a sip of beer and studied the label for a moment. "Me, on the other hand, I enjoyed it a little too much. The days before we met, I had what you could call *a little drinking problem.*"

He continued to look at the beer bottle in his hand.

"We were all young and invincible once," Nancy said.

"Stupid. Young and stupid," Dean corrected.

Nancy chuckled. "Pretty much the same thing."

Dean thought about it for a moment. "Yeah. Guess you've got a point there."

"Did Sophie get you to quit drinking?"

"No. She got me to hang out less with bad influences." He turned so he could face the older woman. "And you know what? After a while I realized that she was right."

"Sounds like a smart woman." Nancy smiled kindly.

"Yes. Smart. But above all else, loving. She was so good to me ... Probably better than I deserved." Dean's face fell. "I really miss her."

Nancy touched his arm and he met her eyes. "It's okay, dear. I miss Ern terribly too. I missed him so much that I ran away from everything that I still cared about. But you — you did not give up. You found Nuggets." The dog perked up at hearing his name and inched closer to the odd couple. "You took care of him."

She patted the dog on the head while Dean scratched his side. Nuggets contorted himself to maneuver Dean's scratches to exactly the right spot, his hind paw kicking in response.

They chuckled.

"I'd say Nuggets took care of me as much as I took care of him."

"Good. I may be old, but I can still learn things. What you've taught me is that we shouldn't give up. There are lots of people — some of whom we know and some of whom we haven't met yet — that will need us."

Dean held out his bottle to Nancy. "I like that. I think Sophie would have liked that, too."

They clinked bottles and took a swig. The beer was almost done.

Again, Nancy started to laugh softly. "Ern would have told us to quit our bellyaching and get over it. But he would have wanted me to help the others. He was a proud man. Always ready to lend a hand and always refusing to ask for help himself."

"I think that I would have liked Ern."

"And I know Ern and I would have loved Sophie." Her eyes slipped toward the window. Dean followed her gaze.

"We'll get there," he said softly. "We'll get there in time to warn them."

"Yes. We will." She took a sip of her beer and sloshed the remaining liquid in front of her. "We'll rest up tonight. But tomorrow it will be time for our final push. To the wall and over." She put the bottle down and watched the froth slowly dissipate.

"I just hope that ladder is still there."

Chapter 64

Ben

November 25, 6:45 A.M., Rosae Crucis Primary Domicile

"Nope. Nothing." The guard craned his neck for one more look before turning back to his companion.

"Probably that cat," the other guard said as his colleague made it through the underbrush. "Somebody must be feeding the damn thing. It keeps returning."

The first guard was back on the small path. "Yeah, but can you blame them? The thing is so cute."

The guards started down the path, which appeared to be little more than a game trail.

"Go on, say it. I can tell you're itching to say it."

"Homo."

The guards laughed at the private joke as they moved further through the trees and out of sight.

Ben waited another full minute before stirring. He got into a crouch so that only his head and shoulders penetrated the under-brush.

That was close. The guard had stopped a couple of yards away. Close enough for Ben to make out the brand of his boots.

He thought he had timed it well. He'd observed the movement of the guards around the wall and fence that enclosed the com-pound. Five minutes. There was supposed to be a five-minute gap between the roaming pairs of guards. He'd waited until the last set passed by, then gave them another minute and a half. He was up and over the fence in a matter of seconds, landing on the soft lichen-covered ground. Quickly he left the fence and the fake game trail, stepping into the thick brush.

Then he heard the approaching guards. He rushed further into the underbrush and sank down. He thought he had not made a sound.

Guess I was wrong. Going to have to be more careful.

Ben worked his way deeper into the wood. Eventually, the underbrush gave way to trees. He knew which direction to travel — he'd circled the compound and thoroughly scouted out the area.

It was completely off-grid and extremely well-hidden. Ben imagined that any aerial photography yielded little to no clues as to what lay hidden here. One portion of the compound had a wall around it — wide enough to hold a walkway. But even that manmade feature had been camouflaged. The fence did not run in straight lines, which was a great way to hide it in plain sight.

Ben had forced himself not to rush into this. He had retreated to a nearby hill and climbed a tree so that he could scout the area from another angle. Ben was able to pick out portions of the wall and fence because he knew what to look for, and only with the help of his binoculars. Of real interest to him, however, was what lay beyond those boundaries.

He spotted about a dozen structures inside the compound. They were all so carefully crafted that it took him long minutes to differentiate between the structures and the surrounding woods. Not only were they camouflaged but irregularly shaped. They stood no taller than two stories, meaning none of them reached as high as the trees around them. The biggest structure seemed to have a huge gap in the roof.

Maybe a courtyard? Ben wasn't sure. What he knew was that this was the place.

And this is the time. There was no going back now.

Ben's plan wasn't very complicated. Honestly, he didn't have a clue as to what he was getting himself in to. Would there be hundreds of Rosae Crucis people in those strange structures? Or would it just be the leadership, surrounded by a few guards? Ben guessed that it was somewhere in the middle. Those structures didn't seem large enough to house hundreds.

What he needed to do now was get as far as possible without being spotted. Getting over the fence and closer to the compound was the first step. Getting to the structures was the next one. He figured that the largest structure would be his goal.

What happened after that? He would have to roll with it.

Some plan. Yet it didn't stop him from creeping further through the wood toward his destination. He had one, single mission: Kill Brenin.

He figured that the Rosae Crucis would fall apart with Brenin gone. Brenin was the glue that kept the organization together. At least, that's what he kept telling himself. He'd had plenty of doubts. Plenty of times when he'd almost turned around and hurried back to his new friends.

But the crux of it all was that Ben needed to blame somebody for the apocalypse. And Brenin fit the bill for that. Brenin needed to pay.

Besides, he wasn't so sure the people at the Ren would accept him back, seeing as he'd disappeared on them.

I could be found guilty of desertion by both sides. That thought amused him.

Ben spotted the first structure up ahead — about two hundred yards away. It wasn't the biggest structure, and therefore not his final destination — but he'd have to sneak past it to get to his goal.

He approached the building and saw that it was made entirely of wood and camouflaged just like everything else.

The wood probably keeps this place from showing up. He imagined satellites flying overhead. Big Brother always watching, but not noticing the clandestine activities carried out here. He wondered, not for the first time, whether the government had been even partially aware of the Order.

Ben stepped around a tree and froze. There was movement up ahead.

The person had not seen him. In fact, he or she had not even glanced in his direction. *He,* Ben corrected as he watched the cloaked person travel down another cleverly disguised path. Whoever it was, he seemed oblivious to his surroundings and only had eyes for the path ahead. Which made Ben's decision easier.

You're going my way. Ben slipped away from the tree and followed.

Chapter 65

Johnny

The early morning sun stood low in the sky. It cast elongated shadows that reached down the pavement like dark talons.

Some of the shadows moved.

Johnny had been watching them for a couple of minutes now. The shapes that cast these shadows were human. The way they moved told Johnny right away they were a threat.

They were alive. *Two of them. And a dog.*

Before reaching for his rifle, Johnny watched through his binoculars for another moment. He set up with ingrained efficiency. Within moments, he had them in his sights.

The big guy seemed to be the easiest target. He seemed to be dressed in bulky armor. Johnny grinned when he saw the weapon — a club or mace — that dangled from his hip. Johnny would have loved to see the guy in action.

He sighted the trailing person.

An old woman.

He hesitated for a moment. Not out of concern of a fellow human being. A few weeks ago, you were either in the Order or you were an enemy of the Order. Now Johnny figured he had no friends at all. The Rosae Crucis had no doubt labeled him as a rogue. It was Johnny versus the world.

No, he hesitated to check the sun's location and the strength and direction of the wind. Wouldn't want his shot to miss the mark. He was going to eliminate these potential threats. Here and now.

First the woman. Then the man. Not shooting the pooch, though. There was a limit to Johnny's cruelty.

He prepared, ensuring that the rifle was well-supported and steady. He tucked his face back in and got his eye behind the scope.

Breathe in. Breathe out and squeeze the trigger. Re-sight. Breathe in. Breathe out and squeeze the trigger.

That's what would have happened. Yet Johnny had hesitated.

What are they doing? He spotted the dog circling back. In the next instant, both of his targets ducked into the gap between two houses.

Did they spot me? Johnny quickly covered the scope, although he was sure that there was no glare. He carefully placed his rifle on the ground and pulled out his binoculars.

The answer became apparent thirty seconds later, when a handful of zombies appeared up the street.

How did they know?

The dog. Of course.

The zombies seemed unaware of the couple and their dog. They seemed more intent on something else as they all moved in unison.

Joining up with the horde. Johnny couldn't be sure, but he had a hunch. He watched them with a mix of fascination and disgust.

Wonder why they don't have flies all over them? His binoculars weren't powerful enough to show the bugs, but he knew they weren't there. They had been conspicuously absent on every zombie he'd gotten close to.

Johnny stayed rooted in place, long after the zombies stepped out of sight. He never did catch sight again of the barbarian and the old woman.

"Your lucky day ..." he whispered out into space. The barbarian and the old woman. That odd couple never knew how close they'd come to their demise.

Chapter 66

Ben

Ben watched as his prisoner slowly came to. First his body jerked slightly, followed by a fluttering of his eyelids. The eyes opened, blinked. The shoulders twisted slightly but met resistance because the wrists were tied together. Finally, his captive's eyes opened wide as realization set in.

"Don't struggle," Ben said.

The young man struggled.

"Don't," Ben ordered. For emphasis, he showed his knife.

The young man froze.

"Good." Ben kept the knife out for the moment. "Listen. I'm going to remove your gag. Do not try to yell." He placed two fingers on the throat of the prisoner, who nearly seemed to faint at his touch. "This is where your vocal cord is. I will cut it before you can make a noise."

He brought his Ka-Bar closer to his prisoner. "Besides, we're far enough away. I don't think anybody is going to hear you." Ben had no idea if they were far enough but figured it wouldn't hurt to say it.

"I'm going to remove your gag. I promise you that I will not hurt you as long as you answer my questions. Do you understand?"

The man's eyes had become as big as saucers at the sight of the knife. They traveled back and forth between the knife and Ben's face twice before he nodded.

Ben removed the gag. He held his knife in his left hand, resting it on the man's shoulder. The tip of the knife hung suspended a mere inch from the man's neck.

"Please—" the man began, but a stern look from Ben stopped him in his tracks.

"I will ask questions. You answer," Ben instructed.

The man swallowed and remained silent.

"What's your name?"

"D—David."

"David," Ben repeated. "What is this place?"

David's eyes flared for a moment. He moved his head ever so slightly, trying to look down to the knife. Slowly his eyes drifted back up to meet Ben's. "This is the Primary Domicile."

Ben nodded. "Good. You didn't lie. This is the PD of the Order. Of the Rosae Crucis. Very good, Adept David."

Again David swallowed. His eyes betrayed his shock.

Yes. Now you understand that I know about this place, and the Order.

"Now, this part is important. Don't leave anything out. I'll know if you do."

David nodded.

"Brenin. I need you to tell me, step by step, how to get to him."

Ben peeked around the corner.

Good. He didn't see me. Or if he did, he didn't care. I'm just another adept heading to the chapel.

Thank you, David.

His prisoner had been helpful. Extremely helpful, even. He'd detailed the layout of the bunker perfectly, right down to how many guards were present. It appeared that Ben was in luck, as a large portion of Brenin's personal guard was somewhere else.

The disguise seemed to be holding up as well. The cloak was a bit tight on him, but the two people on his way had not given him a second glance. The glaring overhead lights and whitewashed walls helped, as people tended to keep their eyes down.

They must think they are completely secure here. It wasn't a crazy thought, considering the remoteness of this place and how most of it was underground. Never mind the fact that just about everybody else in the world was dead.

Ben waited for the guard to look the other way before quickly darting across the hallway. This was the direction of Brenin's audience chamber.

Just one more turn. Ben got to the corner and stole a glance down the hallway.

Shit. There was a guard. There wasn't supposed to be. The guard was supposed to be inside the room.

Does that mean there is another guard inside?

Ben considered turning around for the briefest of moments. Then he thought about Garcia and Collins. About Peters, Durant, and all the other brave people who had died.

You owe them this. Time to pay up.

He took one last deep breath to settle his nerves, unsheathed his knife and concealed it in the folds of his cloak, and stepped around the corner. Ben approached with as casual an air as he could muster. When he got ten feet away, the guard turned to face him.

"Brenin is not seeing visitors," the man said curtly, the multiple scars on his face giving him an intimidating look and making the sentence sound like a threat.

Ben continued to step forward, trying to get into range for a quiet takedown. He was dismayed, as the guard became instantly alert and started to raise his rifle. Then the man hesitated as he saw Ben's face, and a small glint of surprise shone in his eyes.

It was the opening Ben needed. Like a flash, he had closed the distance. The man tried to say something, but it was already too late. Ben stabbed the man in the belly and, using the heel of his hand, stunned his opponent with a strike to the chin. He stepped around the guard smoothly and his Ka-Bar flashed in the light before it plunged into the base of the other man's skull. The guard was instantly dead; the only sound in the hallway was made by his body collapsing to the floor with Ben's assistance. Ben tried to extract his knife, but it was stuck fast. His eyes were on the door to Brenin's chamber. Ben reached into his pocket and produced the cardkey he'd need to get in.

Did they hear me?

He had no time to waste. He took off the cloak, checked his M4 and prepared to barge through the door.

B en rushed through the door, weapon raised and ready to dive if somebody shot at him. What he saw, however, surprised him. There was only one person in the room. Sitting in an oversized chair on a raised dais, reminiscent of a throne.

It was an old man, bent over, with his face down and hands on his knees. All that Ben could make out was the bald and spotted top of his head.

Ben quickly scanned the corners, his aim never leaving the old man. Once he was satisfied that they were alone, he closed the door behind him and stepped forward into the middle of the room.

For a moment, Ben thought that the old man was dead, for he had not moved at all since Ben burst in. But as he got closer, he could see the body rise and fall with breath. Slowly, the old man raised his head and faced his would-be executioner.

A flash of recognition crossed the gnarled face, to be quickly replaced by a slightly amused look.

"It's you," he said simply.

Ben lifted an eyebrow in confusion. Did he know this man? He'd heard about Brenin, of course. But he was absolutely certain that he had never met the leader of the Rosae Crucis, the sentinel himself.

Brenin chuckled at the young soldier's perturbed reaction. "Ha. We did our job well ... You don't know who I am, do you?" It wasn't a question.

"You're Brenin. The cause of all this." Ben kept his rifle pointed at the old man, even though he was convinced that Brenin would not be making any funny moves. He might be sitting on a throne, but he was a beaten man, nonetheless.

Brenin considered Ben's words for a moment. The pregnant pause seemed to drag on a lot longer than it should, but Ben could see the old man thinking. Deciding.

"Yes," Brenin said, his voice low yet clear. "I am the cause. I am a monster." He looked angry at his own admittance. The anger only lasted a moment, and the old man now regarded Ben with clear eyes. "I know you. Does that surprise you?"

Something *was* familiar about him. Surely, Ben had seen him at some event. He subtly shook his head.

Brenin's face remained neutral, but his pale blue eyes bored into the young soldier. "I've been keeping an eye on you for a while. I was concerned when Paladin Kevin reported to me that we had lost touch with you, Brenin."

"My name is Ben. Not Brenin." Ben suspected that the old man was up to something and raised his rifle alarmingly.

"You would be committing patricide, if you shot me." The corner of his mouth rose in a slight smirk. "I'm your grandfather, Brenin."

That stunned Ben, and the tip of his rifle dipped a moment. "I told you. My name is Ben ..."

Brenin smirked and shook his head. "No. Your real name is Brenin. Doesn't that make this an interesting situation?" he said with an amused smile.

Ben frowned. "You're trying to confuse me."

"On the contrary, grandson. I'm trying to enlighten you." Brenin raised both hands in a gesture of acquiescence. "Look ... can I get up? I assure you that I am no threat to you."

Ben took a step closer to the dais, his weapon still at the ready. "Just don't try any funny stuff."

The old man slowly got to his feet. He gave Ben a grateful smile. "Thank you. I sit in this chair for many hours every day." He patted the top of the chair and regarded it with affection. "It's over a hundred years old, this chair. Older even than me." He looked back at Ben. "It's not an easy burden, grandson."

Ben fought to keep his expression calm.

Grandson? Can it be true?

"How do I know that you are really my grandfather?" Ben asked.

"A fair question." Brenin thought about it for a second, then with a soft sigh he began to speak.

"Your father, whose name was Cornelius, was my youngest child. Your mother and he—" Brenin's face turned wistful. "They were a wonderful couple. Totally devoted to the Order. I was very proud of them, and they loved me. So much so, that they named you after me when you were born.

"Now, don't misunderstand; my first name is actually not Brenin. It's Lester. But my middle name is Brenin."

Ben had lowered his weapon. It was now pointed to the ground in front of the dais. He did not fear that Brenin would try anything. He knew the old man had a lot more to say, and although he figured that he had limited time, he needed to hear this.

"They were killed when you were just a boy. You probably don't know exactly what happened to them. That's another story unto itself. One that I hope to be able to tell you."

Brenin's eyes drifted to the rifle before settling back on Ben.

"Your uncle — my other son, Martin — took you in after that. Well, you know Martin as well as anybody. He practically raised you by himself."

This was true. Ben did remember Uncle Martin quite clearly. Funny, he was barely five years old when his uncle took him in, but Martin had always insisted that Ben call him uncle and not dad or father. He had stayed with his uncle until Martin, too, perished. Ben was fifteen.

Good and bad memories there, so Ben pushed them away.

"Martin was a good boy. He wasn't the best father figure, but he stepped up when they took Cornelius away from us. He did the best he could with you. I tried to help out whenever I could. But I was already a high-ranking individual within the Order at that time and didn't want to risk Martin's life. Or yours." He smiled sadly.

"Okay," Ben stated. His rifle had risen slightly. "Say I believe you. You're my grandfather. But that doesn't change what you did. You've killed ... everybody!" Ben lifted the muzzle some more. It was now pointed at Brenin's feet.

"Don't go through with it, grandson."

Ben raised the muzzle so that it was now pointed at Brenin's belly. On his turn, Brenin raised both hands again in surrender.

"Will you at least let me explain what happened? This was all a b—"

SLAM

The door burst open behind Ben.

BANG

Ben turned and dove behind a bench, narrowly avoiding a bullet. The wooden bench bucked as it took the impact of another shot. Ben timed it right and popped up. He shot blindly, hoping that his assailant would duck down. He did.

Out of the corner of his eye, he saw Brenin circle around the back of the dais. He couldn't give it any thought as his assailant popped up, rifle out and ready to take a shot.

Ben was faster and more accurate. He shot the man twice, once in the chest and once in the head. His opponent's shot went well wide. Ben immediately covered the door, but no other adversaries showed themselves.

Brenin! Ben felt a moment of anxiety as he thought that he'd let his quarry escape. He leapt to his feet and ran around the dais, prepared to end it once and for all.

Gone!

There was no sign of the old man. He could hear the yells of alarm coming from down the hall and knew that he only had a few moments left. He scanned the wall furiously, looking for a secret door. After several tense seconds, he found it. It was a small latch, stuck in an indentation of the wall and painted the same color so it would be difficult to spot. He lifted the latch and pulled. Sure enough, a slender door opened.

Ben stepped into a tiny hallway. There was only one direction to go, from which light emanated. Ben stepped forward, intent on catching the leader of the Rosae Crucis. Intent upon murder.

The secret hallway intersected another hallway, this one of regular size. Ben didn't know which way to turn, but he heard Brenin gasp. The sound came from Ben's right and sounded like it was just around the next corner. Ben ran. He had to catch the old man.

He rounded the corner at a run. So intent was he on finding Brenin that he ran headlong into a trap. He barely had time to look up as the butt end of a rifle smashed into his forehead. Ben crashed to the ground, hard. He lifted his rifle, but it was kicked out of his hands. He heard a crack as something in his hand broke. Another blow from the stock of a rifle knocked him unconscious.

I failed, was the last thought he had.

It did not stop there, though, as another buttstroke slammed into his skull. A geyser of blood sprayed the floor and wall behind Ben.

Chapter 67

Nancy

November 25, 8:00 A.M., The Ren

The Renaissance School for Gifted Children loomed ahead.

Just a block away now. Nancy subconsciously picked up her pace. The fence, the fields — they all looked exactly the same. She wondered if the people inside were the same as well.

Not for the first time, she wondered what type of reception awaited her.

"Whoa. Slow down, Nancy."

She came to an abrupt halt. Dean took several more steps to catch up to her. "Sorry, Dean. Guess I'm just anxious to see everybody again."

Dean smiled softly and placed his oversized hand on her shoulder. "It will be fine. They're going to be happy to see you."

Nancy nodded but was not convinced.

They started walking again. The parking lot started to become visible through the fence.

"Hmm? There are some new vehicles here. I think they've got visitors." She glanced over her shoulder at Dean. "Last time they had visitors, it ended in a shootout."

Concern was etched on his face. He put a hand to his mace. Nancy reached out and put her hand on his. "They would have seen us by now. Nothing we can do but walk up to the gate."

"All right." Dean reluctantly let go of his mace as they continued to walk.

The school door swung open when they were still several yards from their goal. "Nancy?" a youthful voice called out.

Maria ran out before she could reply.

"Oh my God, Nancy. It's you!" Maria came running up to the gate. She skidded to a halt when she cast her eyes on Dean.

"It's okay, Maria. This is Dean. He's helped me get back here. We're here to warn everybody ..." Nancy decided against alarming the girl any more than she already had.

Maria still hesitated, a wary eye on Dean. Nancy chuckled. "Yeah, I know. He looks like some character from *Mad Max* ... But he's one of the good guys."

"*Mad Max*?" Maria asked, prompting both Dean and Nancy to laugh.

"Before your time, I guess," Nancy explained. "Anyway, Dean's with me. He's harmless."

That seemed to be good enough for Maria, and she busied herself with the gate. The next moment she squealed with joy as Nuggets trotted up and licked her hand through the fence.

"You've got a dog," Maria exclaimed excitedly, splitting her efforts between removing the chain and petting Nuggets through the fence. Dean had to pull the dog away so the girl could focus on getting the gate open.

"Where is everybody?" Nancy asked as the girl continued her struggle with the heavy chain. Maria gave Nancy a guilty look. "They're all in this big meeting. I forgot to ring the bell. Just saw you and, well, ran over." She shrugged.

"John's not going to be happy with that. You know he's got rules." Nancy smiled kindly at Maria. "He'll just have to forgive you for this once."

Maria got the chain off the gate and the new arrivals squeezed through. Dean helped put the chain back in place, speeding up the process.

"Do we have some new guests?" Nancy asked, flicking her chin toward the now crowded parking lot.

Maria looked uncomfortable. "Yeah."

That made Nancy frown. "Is everything all right?"

The girl did not answer immediately as they started back for the school. "There's a lot of arguing, but I *think* so."

Nancy did not get the chance to ask any more questions as they entered the Ren. The noise coming from the cafeteria suggested that many people were gathered in there, and that a fight was brewing.

Although Nancy stepped down the hall resolutely, Dean hesitated.

"Maria? Can you stay here with Nuggets? I don't think he'll do well with that crowd."

"Sure!" Maria happily dropped to the ground and stroked Nuggets.

"Nuggets. Stay," Dean instructed. The dog didn't look like it was going anywhere. Dean quickly jogged after Nancy just as she entered the cafeteria.

The sheer volume of sound and people was tangible. It left Nancy momentarily stunned. When she finally did gather her wits, she noted that all the people clustered near the entrance to the cafeteria were women, but none were familiar to her. Somewhat dismayed, she pushed past them. They meekly moved aside as she progressed with Dean in her wake.

"You've offered us nothing but lies so far. Is it any wonder that we don't trust you?" a stranger accused.

There was a buzz of sounds — both of agreement and of dissent. The situation seemed so tense that nobody noticed Nancy's presence.

"Hang on, that's not true," Joe said.

"You said this place was safe. And yet we had a zombie *inside* the fence!"

Nancy got a better look at the speaker. He was a short, dark-haired man. He wore a suit.

A lawyer. Or a politician. She instantly conceived a dislike for the middle-aged man.

"You *are* safe," John argued. "That was one single zombie — and it never got within touching distance of the school."

He drew himself up to his full height, which wasn't as impressive as his sheer bulk. A man beside the lawyer did likewise, and although he was taller, he lacked the muscle mass. John seemed to note the challenger. Even from the distance, Nancy could detect the dangerous glint in his eyes.

"John. Please." Joe had gotten to his feet. He put a hand on John's shoulder.

John didn't budge until Melissa tugged him back.

"And here's the kicker," the lawyer continued. He looked around him at his supporters. The men all looked back at him hungrily. "The school might be safe. But you're already talking about kicking us out."

His supporters grumbled angrily.

"You've told me yourself that there isn't enough space in he—"

Joe was cut off as the stranger barreled on, "You want us to move to the houses across the street. Where there isn't even a fence to protect us."

He tut-tutted and shook his head.

"Even your own people can see the folly in that plan," the stranger added.

Nancy saw the hesitation in some of the Ren residents.

He's actually winning them over! Well, we've got bigger fish to fry.

Nancy cleared her throat loudly. Several people saw her and gasped in surprise. Others immediately rushed toward her.

"Nancy!" Claire, Sarah and Rosa yelled as one. They threw their arms around her, and all started speaking at the same time.

"Excuse me!" the lawyer yelled.

People froze in place. He scowled at Nancy, obviously upset at the interruption.

"*I* was talking here. You can wait your turn." He deftly turned his back to her to continue the argument with Joe.

"I don't think so."

Nancy wormed out of the hugs. She reached over and pulled Dean's mace from his belt. Gripping the handle with both hands, she slammed the head of the mace into the floor with a loud bang. She slammed the mace four more times and felt slightly out of breath when she stopped, but all eyes had turned to her.

"Everybody shut up!" Nancy commanded.

"Who the hell are you?" the lawyer demanded. He opened his mouth to say more, but Nancy slammed the mace once more to cut him off.

"Shush!" Nancy pointed the head of the flanged mace at the man, who blanched. She lowered the heavy weapon immediately, her arms starting to shake at the effort. "Whatever your problems are, they are nothing compared to what I came back to tell you."

That got everybody's attention.

"There is a horde of zombies coming this way. Thousands of them. As near as we can tell, the main body of this horde is less than a day away."

She let that sink in for a moment.

"We either need to get the hell out of here"—she eyed John and Melissa—"or you guys need to come up with a plan."

The decision to stay and fight was reached almost immediately.

Frank grumblingly agreed to park his grievances after Joe asked him flat-out if he wanted to take his people and supplies and run. The small man made a show of considering it but quickly agreed to stay. As a matter of fact, he insisted on being involved in the defense of their community.

The first order of business was to ask all noncombatants to leave the cafeteria. There was plenty to do, and plenty of catching up with Nancy for the Ren residents. Joe pulled aside Emily and Tammy before they left. The three of them had a quick conversation, and the women nodded, walking away purposefully.

That still left over twenty men and women in the room. John was quietly impressed when he added them up. It was a sizeable force. He did note that they were two unique groups. The fighters from the safe zone were all men. They bunched together, leaving Dan, the police officer, and Frank to stand front and center. In sharp contrast, the men *and women* from the Ren all pushed in closer to hear and see what was being planned. Most of them had opinions too, should they be asked.

"We should take the fight to them," Michelle said confidently.

Or not asked, John amended.

There was a third group — albeit a group of one. Nancy's companion stood out like a sore thumb.

Looks like Conan meets Mad Max! Hope he's as dangerous as he seems ... The guy hadn't said a word yet, but it spoke volumes that he remained in the cafeteria. He was willing to fight.

"Okay." Melissa had finished listing the number of fighters. She stepped into the middle of the room and introduced herself to the newcomers. Next, she suggested that the fighters should go and prep — which was code for, "Get out of here and let the thinkers plan the action."

"Not you." John pointed at the Conan/Mad Max character, just as the large man got to the cafeteria exit. "We're going to need some info."

The fighter returned to the middle of the room, looking self-conscious. Melissa had to gently usher several Ren residents out the door, finally leaving a group of six people.

John pulled out his map of the city and laid it on the large table that had been brought in. Everybody stepped closer to see. He used a marker to trace the border of their walled-in community. Then he turned to Dean.

"Big man. What's your name?"

"Dean."

"All right, Dean. I'm John." He turned to the map. "Dean, about this horde: Do you have any idea how many zombies we're talking about?"

Dean shuffled from one foot to the other. "Hard to say."

John looked frustrated with that answer. "Give me an educated guess. Nancy said thousands. Are we talking one or two thousand, or tens of thousands?

"A couple of thousand?" He seemed unsure, then added, "Yeah. Two, maybe three thousand would be my guess. They fill the street entirely for about four blocks. There are smaller groups on the parallel streets too, but those ones are constantly shoving their way into the main horde at every crossroad." He looked up. "Sorry. To answer your question: Anywhere from two to five thousand. It's like some big march. March of the dead." He caught himself rambling again and stopped talking.

"Now," John said, after snorting at the estimate, "can you show me where and when you saw this march of the dead last?"

Dean walked up to the map, studied it a moment, and put his finger on a spot. "Here. Yesterday, around mid-afternoon."

John marked the spot. He tapped the map with his prosthetic finger, noticing the look of distaste on Frank's face with a quick sideways glance.

"Good. Did you see them prior to this? Give me their locations and the times you saw them. That way I can figure out their direction and how fast they're moving."

Several minutes later, he had three more locations and times marked. There was no doubt to anybody standing around the table that the horde was heading straight for them. John traced a line from the location of the horde to their community.

"Damn." He grimaced as he tapped the spot where the zombie march and the wall would intersect. "Just our fucking luck, too. From the looks of this, they are going toward the busted gate."

"Why are they coming here?" Frank asked. He hid his fear poorly. "I mean, how do they keep finding us?"

"I've seen it before," Dean said. "They definitely communicate, but they also seem to have some kind of internal radar system. They seem to go after groups of people more often than individuals. I'm just guessing here, but maybe all you living folks together in this place stand out to them."

Melissa had completed some calculations while they talked. She put her finger on the location where the horde would strike. "I figure that we've got three to four hours. Six, tops."

Everybody let that thought stew for a minute.

"Seems like we got lots of firepower here." Dan looked at the other planners in turn. "Maybe that big broad was right. Maybe we should go out there and wipe them out, instead of waiting for them to get here."

"That would make sense. But how do we know that this is the only zombie horde bearing down on us?" Melissa replied.

Apparently, Dan could not think of an answer to that question and wisely held his tongue.

"We've got some time. I think that we should send out a couple of scouts to check the perimeter." Mel turned to John. "Barricading the front door isn't going to help us if the enemy is at the rear."

"You're right." John nodded at his wife. "We should use a couple of the Humvees. They can get around the perimeter quickly. Spot-check over the wall at certain places." He frowned as he thought about the logistics. "That will take hours, though."

Frank guffawed. "What? You think they're coordinating their attacks?" He laughed dismissively.

John's irritation visibly rose at this. The ex-soldier stared hard at the civil administrator and Joe jumped in to diffuse the situation. "We don't know that for sure. But I do think it would be wise not to take chances. Tell us what you're thinking, John. We're all on the same side here."

A mini staring contest continued between John and Frank. Joe shuffled awkwardly from foot to foot as the two alpha males faced off. Frank finally dropped his gaze, pretending to look at the map.

John maintained his gaze on the diminutive man for a moment longer before turning to Joe. Then he turned to Melissa.

"I wouldn't want to commit all of our fighters right away. Not until we know where the threat is coming from." Mel pointed at the map. "We can set up one hell of a welcome at the gate. I'm thinking one or two SAWs and a few snipers on the wall. If they stick to the road, it will be a turkey shoot." She looked over at Frank and Joe in turn. "If the other teams don't spot any trouble, then they can join our main defensive line at the gate. That should make about a dozen defenders. We'll keep a group of fighters here at the Ren. Whoever is left. They can provide reinforcements where and when we need it. Maybe we keep a couple of guys here, to run ammunition."

Or pick up our wounded. John was familiar with the tactic.

He watched Frank as his wife spoke. His expression had changed from dubious to thoughtful to amenable. "We will help, of course."

"Great. That's very reasonable of you," Joe said before John could speak.

"As a matter of fact, why don't we use our Humvee as one of the scout vehicles?" Frank addressed Joe, pointedly ignoring John.

John didn't care. He had endured much greater slights in his career. "We can squeeze five guys into our Humvee. We'll take a SAW and set that up at the gate. Joe, get teams together for the scout vehicles. Three-man teams should be good enough. The rest of the fighters stay behind at the school. We can use the minivan to run reinforcements, etcetera."

"Will that be enough?" Joe showed his concern. "Five guys, to hold back thousands?"

"I'll take the most experienced shooters with me." John left no doubt that he would be defending the gate.

Frank spoke up before anybody could say a word. "Take my best man, Dan. Also take Carlos, Hector and Doug."

"Any of your guys experienced in shooting a SAW?" John asked.

At Frank's blank stare, Dan shifted around uncomfortably.

That was enough of an answer for John. He turned to Dan, ignoring Frank. "I'll take you and your guys, but we'll squeeze one of my guys, Bill, in with us."

Out of the corner of his eyes he could see Frank bristle at the slight. *Good. Have a taste of your own medicine, little man.*

"Okay," Dan said. "Are we done here? I'll go collect my guys." John looked at Melissa, who nodded.

"Yep. I want to be set up at least an hour before they get to us. Let's get everybody loaded for bear and pull out ASAP." He looked at the clock. "It's just after ten a.m. now. Let's gear up and be prepared to pull out by eleven." John folded up the map.

I've got to check on the SAW. Make sure it's in working order. John was already itemizing his actions, even as he put the map in his back pocket. *Collect Bill. We'll need extra ammo. I've still got one claymore left. Got to bring that. Oh, and organize our reserves …*

He barely noticed that Frank stepped forward. "This is all fine, but I'd like some time to speak to my people first."

John shot him a curious glance.

"Just the men — just the fighters," Frank quickly corrected. "I just want to explain the situation to them and make sure they are all bought in to the plan." He put on a disarming smile.

Although John's intuition told him that something else was going on, Joe agreed before he could say anything.

"Sure thing, Frank. We'll let you have the cafeteria."

He put his hand on John's shoulder and gently guided him toward the exit. Melissa followed. Dean was already long gone.

All his men were present. Frank strode around them in one lazy circle. He waited until they stopped talking. All eyes followed him as he returned to his spot in front of them. Just how he liked it. His eyes traveled over their heads to the doors.

"Mouse, get over there. Make sure nobody is eavesdropping," Frank instructed.

Marty hustled to obey. He quickly opened the door and poked his head out. Satisfied, he shut the portal and gave a thumbs up.

"Dan." Frank acknowledged his right-hand man before turning to his men. "Come beside me."

The police officer stood next to Frank, the brawn to his brains.

"These people, they panic too quickly." Frank gestured dismissively toward the door, his face a mask of contempt. He turned as if addressing the door and the people beyond it. "You guys saw what happened the other day — when they came to 'rescue' us. All they had to do was make a bunch of noise and lead the zombies away. That probably would have worked here. But their plan for today should work as well. Just mow them down as they smash themselves against the gate. Then I realized something."

Frank slowly turned back toward his audience, and this time his expression was sinister. "That old bag that barged in here. She presented us with a golden opportunity."

"What's the golden opportunity, Frank?" Hector, who considered himself the spokesman of the Hispanic members, asked.

Annoyance at the interruption flashed across Frank's face. *I'll deal with you later, Hector.*

"Think about it: This place is perfect. A walled community that is practically cleared of zombies. A headquarter building that's like a fortress."

"I thought you said—"

"I'm talking, Hector. And I know what I said." Frank couldn't hold back his annoyance this time. "Just shut up and let me do the talking. The talking and the thinking."

Hector looked angry but kept his mouth shut.

"I want these fools on their toes. Of course I am not going to say that they've got the perfect setup. What do you reckon our women would think? Do you want them to start to feel safe? Want them to start talking to them? What do you think this John character would do if he heard the truth?"

Hector's face fell. He nodded quickly. "Yes. You're right."

Frank watched Hector intently for a moment. Satisfied, he looked up at the rest of the group and continued. "This is our chance, guys. John and all his fighters are going to be out there. We need them split up." He turned to Dan. "That's why I volunteered you. You need to make sure that we mix our guys up with some of theirs."

He couldn't keep the smirk off his face.

"Then, when the threat is gone, you make sure there are some accidents. They talked about sending out a couple other teams to check the walls. Get our men embedded with them as well and take those guys out quickly. Nobody is going to look up if they hear a gunshot."

It was all coming together. Not everybody was convinced, though.

"But what about the zombies? Shouldn't we be concerned about them?" one of the men asked.

"No." Frank waved him off. "My guess is that this Dean character was exaggerating. Besides, you all saw the walls. There's no way in hell that zombies are going to make it over. Back when I was running the safe zone," Frank said, never missing an opportunity to flaunt his power and influence. "I had a short meeting with the military administrator. I had asked her about the dwindling resources. She told me that she could keep the camp safe from thousands of zombies with ease. All she needed was about twenty soldiers. '*Shooting those things is like shooting fish in a barrel,*' she told me.

"But by the end, we only had ten soldiers left at the camp. Even that might have been enough. Then some idiot panicked and crashed through the fence — and that was it."

He looked rueful for a second, but then continued.

"Anyway, we've got plenty of fighters here and a solid wall for protection. There's no way that any zombies are going to take this place."

Pleased with himself but annoyed at how stupid his audience was, he let that sink in.

Idiots. It's just like city hall. Just make sure you're the smartest guy in the room.

He put on a winning smile. "Are you with me?" He received nods in return.

Hector wasn't completely convinced by the plan, however.

"Aren't the remaining people going to be up in arms when we come back without their men? I saw at least one female soldier, and a couple of those women look ready for a fight."

"Are you afraid of women now, Hector?" Frank asked pointedly. He lifted his hand before the Mexican man could complain. "Relax. I will take care of the home front. What we need is some kind of signal..." He thought about it for a second and had an eureka moment. "I got it. Dan." He turned to his right-hand man. "You give the signal by throwing a couple of grenades."

They had wisely kept their stash of grenades and other special toys from John and Joe.

"It's perfect," Frank said. "We'll be able to hear the explosions. They'll think that it's a problem, so I'll convince Joe to send the reinforcements then. You just make sure that you've taken care of John and that other soldier, and set up an ambush for the rest."

"Raymond," he told the obese man. "Make sure that you're part of the reinforcements. Make sure you stick to the back. They try to run and you take them down." He grinned at the fat man. "They won't know what hit them."

Raymond cackled maliciously in agreement.

Frank's expression grew stern. "Whatever happens, I want John dead by the end of this."

"We'll make sure of it, Frank."

"Good. There's nothing to stop us from taking over once most of the men are gone." He saw predatory smiles on a couple of faces and guessed what they were after. "It will be just like back at the camp."

"No," Hector also wore a malicious smile. "Better."

"I want first go at that Tammy," one of the men said.

"Hey, *I* want Tammy. She's a real looker, that one," another man added.

Frank snorted. "Don't worry, boys. Maybe the two of you can take her together." That elicited a couple of grunts which could have been laughter.

"I've got a better idea." Raymond said, his eyes full of lust. "You know that loudmouth Joe? Well, I'm going to fuck both his wife and his daughter. Right in front of him." He elbowed another man in the ribs as several men chuckled.

"All right, all right." Frank raised his hand for silence. "Yes, we will be taking over today. Yes, you will get your reward. But you've got a job to do first."

Pausing dramatically, he looked at the men in front of him. They were thugs, gangsters, and corrupt cops. All of them simpletons and bullies. His kind of people.

"Kill their men."

Epilogue

Theodore

"We're getting close." Theodore looked back down at his map. "Take the next exit and go north. There should be a sign."

"Yes, sir!" Fred replied eagerly.

Theodore couldn't blame him. He was excited to see some actual living people too. He looked out his window and saw a town.

Williamsburg, he recalled as he watched the town flow by to his right. *Wonder how many Williamsburgs there are in the US.*

The exit that they had passed moments ago proudly announced the Colonial Williamsburg Visitor Center. For some reason, it saddened Theodore. Maybe it was because nobody would be going to that visitor center, or maybe even the town of Williamsburg, ever again.

The landscape had definitely become more urban over the last hour of travel. This was despite their route, which circumvented all cities. Richmond was the last city they had skirted.

Richmond. Seems to be one of those in just about every state as well.

It looked pretty messed up. A fire must have blown through the city or was still raging, as they observed thick, dark smoke billowing from what they guessed was downtown. It left both him and Fred wondering as to the cause of the fire.

"Maybe there are some survivors left down there?" Fred had ventured.

It was just as likely that some industrial building or power plant, left unmonitored, had gone up in flames. Or a lightning strike. Or a million other possibilities.

Yet their first thought was always to consider that there might be living people.

Wishful thinking, I suppose.

Theodore continued to look out his window. The remnants of Williamsburg faded out of sight as they crossed an overpass. Theodore caught an ornamental street sign below him saying Colonial Parkway.

"Maybe we will be the new pilgrims," Theodore mused.

"Huh?"

"Ah, nothing, Fred. Just lost in my thoughts."

Theodore looked ahead and noticed a plethora of green signs. "Heads up. I think our turnoff is coming."

Sure enough, they entered a butterfly interchange and exited, heading north. Theodore observed two things instantly. The first was that the roads weren't clear as they had been on the interchange. The second was the massive, big-box stores to his right, including a movie theater.

That had been one of their things. *Oh, Agatha ...* They hardly ever went out for dinner or anywhere, really. But at least once a month, they would catch a movie together. They would have an early supper and take the time to dress up for the occasion. Then they would drive down to the local movie theater. They would go back and forth about what movie to watch, although both already knew Agatha had figured it out days ago.

That was their date night.

I miss you so much, my dear.

"What the heck is that?"

Fred's comment was perfectly timed to interrupt Theodore's reverie and pull the general away from his misery. He followed the radioman's gaze and frowned in confusion for a moment.

"No idea — oh, wait. It's a waterpark," he said as the large, blue snakes of water slides became more recognizable.

"'Home of America's steepest water slide,'" Fred read in the caption underneath the park name. "I was never one for those things. Don't like getting wet," he added as the waterpark disappeared behind them.

"What about eating after midnight?" Theodore asked, a sly grin on his face.

The question was lost on the radioman, who just looked confused.

"Gremlins?" Theodore ventured.

He was rewarded with the same blank stare.

Theodore chuckled. "Before your time, I guess."

The amusing moment turned sour a moment later.

"Heads up."

Ahead, half a dozen shambling forms walked down the street. They turned as one when they heard the approaching vehicle.

"Can you weave through them?"

"I'll try."

Fred clenched his jaw and slowed the vehicle. They weaved from one side of the street to the other over the course of the next minute, managing to stay out of range of all but one zombie. That one lunged at the jeep as it passed, slamming its upper body into the passenger door before falling to the pavement. The jeep bucked as it ran over something. Neither of the men looked back to see.

The road cleared up, and Fred was able to increase speed. "They were heading in the same direction as us."

Theodore nodded. "Yeah. I guess those reports were correct. They seem to home in on the living." He pointed; several more zombies were up ahead.

These ones were sparse and spaced out far enough for Fred to easily get around them.

"Almost there," Theodore said as they passed a sign.

They were about arrive at their destination. The road took a slight bend up ahead. They spotted several forms in the ditch as they took the bend.

"Looks like we're not the first visitors."

Fred's attempt at humor fell flat, as Theodore was all business.

"Slow down. Come to a stop about ten yard back of that gate."

Theodore was already undoing his seatbelt. They could see movement on the other side of the gate as several men moved around beyond the barrier.

"Stay in the car," Theodore ordered as he opened his door and stepped out. He held his hands over his head and waited beside the car while a flurry of activity took place on the other side of the gate.

A man called out after a few seconds: "Please identify yourself."

"General Davies. Here to meet Commander Graves."

"Please come forward and show identification."

Theodore bristled slightly, annoyed at the formality as much as at the delay. "Mind if we do this on the other side of the gate? There are some unwelcome visitors around the bend behind us."

The guardsmen weren't sure how to proceed. Theodore could see them exchange uncertain looks.

"Come on, son. Who the hell else do you think I could be?"

The guards nodded at each other, their decision made. "Okay, sir. Sorry. Please proceed through the gate and pull over at the guard shack."

One of them immediately started to slide the gate open.

They were on the safe side of the fence two minutes later. Theodore had walked in on foot while Fred maneuvered the jeep into a parking space beside the small guard shack. The guardsman had checked Theodore's credentials as they walked to the vehicle together.

"Apologies for the delay, sir. We're trying to follow procedures..." The guard trailed off.

"That's all right," Theodore scanned the man's name tag and insignia. "Petty Officer Brooks." Theodore swung open his door and prepared to enter the vehicle.

"You can proceed up to HQ. Just follow this avenue for about half a mile." Brooks indicated the road with a wave of his hand. "You'll see a department store and a low-rise office building on your right, just before the road bends. That's where you will find the commander."

"Thanks."

Theodore was about to tell Fred to drive when Brooks spoke up again. "Sir? You mentioned that there were some more zombies approaching. Just how many did you see?"

"About four or five. Then there's another half dozen or so, about a mile further back."

The Petty Officer seemed relieved at the news. "Thank you, sir." He saluted the general as Fred moved the vehicle forward.

Fred drove along the avenue, leaving Theodore lost in thought. He was excited and anxious to see more living people. As if on cue, he spotted a rabbit fleeing into the nearby trees. He rolled down his window for the first time since leaving Olympus and was rewarded with the screeching of seagulls in the distance. Sure enough, they watched a couple of the marine birds take to the air as they approached another bend in the road. The birds rose with the flapping of wings and high-pitched cries. Theodore watched them wheel before flying off in another direction. They certainly weren't as numerous as they had been, but Theodore was thankful.

Not all is dead in the world.

Word of their arrival must have preceded them, as a sailor flagged them down and directed them into the parking lot. They parked the jeep and got out. The sight of several men and women moving between buildings on some business or another felt surreal.

"It almost feels ... normal." Fred gave voice to their thoughts. Theodore could only nod in agreement.

They watched as another sailor came jogging out of the office building. He saluted sharply once he got close enough. "General Davies, sir. Welcome to the Chestham Naval Supply Depot. Commander Graves and Captain Tanner are just this way — if you'll follow me."

Theodore was pleased that they could get right to business, but nevertheless had a moment of hesitation. "Wait here, Fred," he ordered the radioman before turning back to the newcomer. "Lead the way."

He walked with the seaman toward the entrance. The sun felt warm on his back despite the humid chill in the air.

"Can you make sure my man gets a hot meal and a comfortable bed?" he asked the seaman as they approached the door.

"Of course, sir." The seaman opened the door and gestured ahead. "Right this way, sir."

The seaman led Theodore through an open area positively abuzz with activity. Theodore couldn't keep the smile off his face after seeing so many young, healthy individuals.

"Everything all right, sir?" The seaman had noticed his expression.

"Of course. Just happy to see you guys. Lead on."

The seaman led Theodore to an office. The door was already open. "Right in here, sir. I will go take care of your driver."

"Thank you, son. Oh, and he's a radio operator," he said with a wink before entering the office.

Two men and one woman stood at attention inside the bright office. The sun poured in through the window and blanketed the desk in a warm light.

"At ease." Theodore walked straight up to the commander. "Commander Graves?" He extended his hand to the man.

"Yes, General Davies, sir."

"Glad to meet you, Commander. You can call me Theodore." The men shook hands.

Theodore noticed a slight look of concern cross the commander's face, although he wasn't sure if it was due to his appearance or the breach in protocol.

"This is Commander Tanner, and this is Lieutenant Commander Checker." Graves indicated the other officers in the room.

Theodore shook Tanner's hand. "James," the man said as they shook.

"Lisa," the lieutenant commander said in her turn.

"General Davies," Commander Graves said, drawing Theodore's attention. "There is something we need to discuss immediately."

Theodore assented. "Yes. We have a lot to talk about."

"What I mean is that there has been radio contact not more than thirty minutes ago. An SOS, as it were."

The buzz in the office made sense to Theodore now. "All right. Go on."

"Well, sir," the commander seemed uncomfortable. "The call — it was for you."

END

About the Author

Marco de Hoogh was born in The Netherlands, youngest son of Gerard de Hoogh; published author of 17 books, and Truus Sierat; artist and most wonderful person in the world. Yes, Marco is a mama's boy. Marco moved to Canada when he was twelve, and calls Calgary his home.